ALSO AVAILABLE FROM
CATHERINE COWLES

The Tattered & Torn Series
Tattered Stars
Falling Embers
Hidden Waters
Shattered Sea
Fractured Sky

Sparrow Falls
Fragile Sanctuary
Delicate Escape
Broken Harbor
Beautiful Exile
Chasing Shelter
Secret Haven

The Lost & Found Series
Whispers of You
Echoes of You
Glimmers of You
Shadows of You
Ashes of You

The Wrecked Series
Reckless Memories
Perfect Wreckage
Wrecked Palace
Reckless Refuge
Beneath the Wreckage

The Sutter Lake Series
Beautifully Broken Pieces
Beautifully Broken Life
Beautifully Broken Spirit
Beautifully Broken Control
Beautifully Broken Redemption

Standalone Novels
Further to Fall
All the Missing Pieces

D1569934

For a full list of up-to-date Catherine Cowles titles,
please visit catherinecowles.com.

Broken
HARBOR

CATHERINE
COWLES

Broken
HARBOR

CATHERINE COWLES

sourcebooks
casablanca

Published by Sourcebooks Casablanca, an imprint of Sourcebooks
P.O. Box 4410, Naperville, Illinois 60567-4410
(630) 961-3900
sourcebooks.com

Originally published in 2024 by Catherine Cowles.

Cataloging-in-Publication data is on file with the Library of Congress.

Printed and bound in the United States of America.
LSC 10 9 8 7 6 5 4 3 2 1

FOR ALL THOSE WHO FEEL LIKE
THEY AREN'T DESERVING OF LOVE.
SPOILER ALERT, YOU ARE.
LET THAT SHIT IN.

PROLOGUE

Sutton

TWO YEARS EARLIER

"IF I EAT ALL MY VEGSTABLES, WILL I BE BIG ENOUGH TO PLAY hockey?" Luca asked, his words slurring as sleep tried to pull him under.

My lips twitched, as I tucked the blankets around him. "I think it's a good start."

The last thing I wanted to think about was my sensitive five-year-old trying to play a sport as violent as hockey. Or any contact sport, for that matter. Because I knew all too well what the outcome could be.

"Can we go...to the rink...tomorrow?" Luca asked, yawning his way through the question.

"We'll see," I hedged. Inwardly, I cringed, doing the mental math to figure out if I could swing the rink fee, skate rental charges, and snack Luca would inevitably want. The restaurant I worked at afforded me good tips, but living in Baltimore was expensive, and I could never work the dinner crowd. It wasn't as if I could trust Roman to be home to watch Luca consistently.

On my breaks between the breakfast and lunch shifts, I'd walk around the nearby park and dream of living somewhere the air was always fresh, and Luca had a yard to run around in. Somewhere safe.

We'd had that once before everything changed. Now, I was running myself ragged, just trying to keep my head above water.

"Mommy?" Luca asked, his voice barely audible now.

"Yes, baby."

"Love you."

My chest gave a painful squeeze. "Love you more than bees love honey."

Luca didn't answer this time. Sleep had finally won out. We followed the same pattern every night: one book and then endless questions until they grew slower and farther apart.

But even when I was exhausted beyond measure, I relished every second of it. Because I knew those moments would be fleeting.

I leaned over Luca and brushed his light-brown hair out of his face—hair that was all Roman. But Luca's eyes were me. A unique blue that was more like turquoise. Roman said it was the thing that had stopped him in his tracks.

Part of me wished I had boring eyes so Roman would've skipped right over me. But then I wouldn't have Luca, and he was the gift of a lifetime.

Slowly, I pushed to my feet, waiting to see if Luca stirred. Nothing. His tiny chest rose and fell in a steady rhythm until he finally let out a little snore. A grin tugged at my lips.

I knew I was good to do my fairy cleaning now. The only time I could successfully dust and mop in here was when Luca was comatose. Otherwise, there was a Tasmanian devil on my heels. One that left toys, books, and puzzles in his wake. Or thought he could use my freshly mopped floors as a skating rink.

Grabbing my duster from the spot by the door, I moved around the tiny room. Back when life was golden, Luca's nursery had been four times this size. Before everything fell apart.

But it wasn't the size of the room I missed. It was the family we'd been. The dad Roman had been. A man who'd playfully teased and told epic bedtime stories. Before an endless spiral of opiates forever changed who he was.

I looked down at my left hand where the ring used to be. There was still a faint line. Maybe it would always be there, marking what was lost—or maybe what had never been to begin with.

Even with Roman working his program now, too much had been fractured to repair, at least for me. But I had hope that he could still be the father Luca deserved.

My duster skimmed over some action figures and a robot. A football his dad had given him that still made me cringe because it had been a sports injury that had taken Roman down the dark path to begin with. I moved over an array of photos—happy moments of us all together from years ago and more recent ones of just Luca and me.

I walked to the set of cube drawers that held all Luca's toys, tossing a few stray ones in, then frowned when I saw a charging cord hanging free. It must've come loose when Luca grabbed something today. He would riot if he didn't have his tablet for the bus ride we took to get him to school.

Sliding open the drawer, I stilled. No tablet. *Crud.*

I set the duster down and quickly pulled out each drawer. No tablet. It wasn't like it was a super fancy one, but it had taken weeks of saving to get it for Luca. I hurried over to his nightstand. It wasn't there either.

A feeling of unease slid through me, and my eyes closed. The sensation was too familiar. Missing items of value. Roman's accusations of me being careless and losing things. But it was never that. It was him hocking them to feed his addiction.

I straightened my spine, sending myself a silent assurance that the tablet was simply under a couch cushion or forgotten in my tote bag I carried all our most important things in to get through a day. Crossing the room, I slipped out and closed the door softly behind me.

I'd given Luca the bedroom in our small apartment while I took a Murphy Bed in the living area. It was the most practical solution and the safest. But that also meant my clothes and our few remaining valuables were scattered in unlikely places. The hall closet. A sideboard I'd gotten at a garage sale and refinished. Even one of the kitchen cabinets.

Doing a quick scan of the tiny space, I still didn't see the tablet. I lifted couch cushions but didn't find it there either. My heart rate picked up as I saw one of the tiny drawers on the sideboard ajar. It wasn't unease that slid through me this time. It was sickness. A nausea that had bile churning.

I hurried over and slid the drawer open. I didn't have expensive jewelry. Anything Roman had ever given me had been sold long ago, either by him in a quest to ease his pain, or by me, trying to get back on my feet. Everything was costume now. Things I wore to look nice at my job.

The only thing of value I had left was a necklace that had been my grandmother's. It wasn't littered with precious stones, but it *was* gold. A locket adorned with a bumble bee, a marker of the phrase she'd always said to my grandfather and me. *"Love you more than a bee loves honey."* Inside it was a photo of her and my grandfather right before he left to serve in World War II. That photo was the real jewel. Because you could see the love they shared. The love I'd always dreamed of but never had.

My fingers stretched to the back of the drawer where the box lay. The second I felt it, I breathed deeper. Pulling it out, I quickly opened it, and the world fell away. There was no gold locket inside, no promise of a forever love. It was empty.

Pain sliced through me. Roman had been here for thirty minutes today. That was all. But apparently, that was enough time for him to do this. I didn't let him have unsupervised visits with Luca. Not after everything. And I always checked his pupils when he arrived, a practice I'd never have thought to do before.

But he wasn't high today, at least not as far as I could tell. He'd been happy to see Luca. Was cordial with me.

I ran over the visit in my mind. The snack I'd served them both as Luca chattered about school and showed Roman a hockey video on his tablet. But then my manager at the restaurant called, and I'd stepped into Luca's room for five minutes to take it.

Five minutes, where Roman had free rein in my apartment.

I was so stupid. If the last few years had taught me anything, it was that I didn't have the luxury of trusting anyone. Hot tears stung my eyes as my fingers tightened around the empty box. Apparently, it was a lesson I still needed to learn.

A knock sounded on my door, and I swiped at my face. Marilee was coming over to watch one of those teen dramas with a love triangle between a vampire, a werewolf, and a clueless human girl. But I was the real clueless one.

I hurried toward my door, trying to paint a mask of cheeriness because Marilee would lose it if she knew Roman had screwed me in yet another way. I unlocked the door without checking the peephole and quickly opened it. "Sorry, I—"

My words cut off as I took in the two hulking men in the doorway. Living in…not the best part of town, I had a radar for who to avoid. If I'd seen these two on the street, I would've crossed to the other side. They were both stocky with thick necks, the muscles bulging off the sides and bleeding into their shoulders. They were also covered in tattoos that were an array of images and text in a language I couldn't read.

"Is Roman home?" the slightly taller one asked, his accent Eastern European of some sort. Russian, maybe?

My stomach pitched at the question. "He doesn't live here. He's never lived here."

The man's mouth kicked up on one side. "Don't lie. I hear it causes wrinkles, and you're so pretty."

Bile surged up my throat, but I squared my shoulders, refusing to show fear. "Check with the Baltimore County Court records. We've been divorced for over a year. He lives in Pulaski."

The slightly shorter man's eyes flared in surprise before he hid it. "He was evicted from that spot over three months ago. Said he was staying here now."

Evicted? My mind raced at all the lies Roman had spun over the last month.

"As far as I knew, that's where he was living. I don't have any money to pay off whatever debt he probably owes you. If he was here, I'd shove him right out the door. He's been lying to me for the last three years—"

"We have a source who said he was here today," the taller man said.

I stilled. *Hell.* Whoever these guys were, they weren't messing around if they had eyes on my apartment. I prayed for a neighbor to open their door. Ideally, the twenty-something down the hall who was into mixed martial arts.

"He was. For about thirty minutes. And then he left," I said, my hands beginning to tremble. "He's not here, and I don't know where he went."

The larger one's eyes narrowed on me. "Well, it's a good thing we don't need him here for this. You're going to be a warning for your husband. And if he doesn't hear this, we'll go for the boy next."

I moved faster than I ever had in my life, rushing to slam the door. But I wasn't fast enough. The man's booted foot stopped it from closing, and he gave me a hard shove into the apartment. I opened my mouth to scream, but it was cut off by a blow to my temple that had me seeing stars.

Before I could get my bearings, a punch landed in my ribs and stole my breath. But I didn't even think about the pain. All I could think about was Luca sleeping twenty feet away. No one would fight for him but me. I was his only protector.

My palm came up in a strike, and the man cursed as his nose began to bleed. The second man laughed as he said something in a foreign language but quickly moved in with a hook that landed on my cheekbone.

White-hot pain flared in my face, but I still tried to land a blow on him, too. I wasn't strong enough. The first man spat out blood in my hallway and then kicked me so hard that I crumpled to the floor.

They didn't stop. Blow after blow landed until I knew I was fading, and all the while, there was only one name on my lips.

"Luca."

CHAPTER ONE

Sutton

TWO YEARS LATER

DO YOU HAVE IT ALL? DO YOU PROMISE? MY STICK AND MY PADS and my helmet and my skates and my—"

"Little dude," Thea said, humor in her voice. "I saw your mom check the list *three* times. She's got you."

I sent her a grateful smile but knew it was also tired. I'd been up since three this morning baking The Mix Up's usual fare and three dozen cupcakes for a sweet sixteen. My eyes burned, and I was running on the strongest coffee we had.

But it was worth it. Because I was living my dream. A bakery of my own, with an apartment above the shop that meant I could do those early hours with nothing more than a baby monitor that alerted me when Luca woke up. I wasn't exactly grateful for what had happened to me, but the civil settlement I'd received after my attack had given me just enough to make the trip cross-country and get The Mix Up off the ground.

Luca cocked his head to the side in that adorable way he had as he took in my coworker and best friend. "You're *sure*, Thee Thee?"

She pinned him with a mock stare. "Would I steer you wrong?"

He grinned at her. "Did you sneak a Cookie Monster cupcake into my lunch?"

Thea held out her hand for a fist bump.

Luca smiled wider and tapped his knuckles to hers. "You're the best!"

I slung the massive gear bag over my shoulder—equipment that had taken me months to save up for, even though I'd gotten most of it used. "What am I? Chopped liver?"

Luca's nose wrinkled. "Gross, Mom."

He'd lost the penchant for calling me *Mommy* more than a year ago, and I still missed it. "Come on, future ice-rink superstar. We need to get going or we'll be late."

He bolted for the back hallway.

Thea gave my arm a squeeze. "You okay?"

"Shouldn't I be asking you that?" I challenged. She'd been through an ordeal weeks ago that had almost cost her everything. But I wasn't surprised that she was already back at work despite my—and her boyfriend, Shep's—protests.

Thea rolled her eyes. "The doctors cleared me for work two weeks ago. I gave Shep an extra week as a courtesy, but you know I was going stir-crazy."

I pulled her into a quick hug. "I get it. But just know, we're all going to be worried about you for a while."

She squeezed me back hard. "So lucky to have you."

"Damn straight," I said, releasing her.

"*Moooooom,*" Luca called from the back door.

Thea laughed. "Better go before Wayne Gretzky over there steals your keys and drives himself to the rink."

I shook my head but knew she was probably right. "Call if you or Walter run into any issues."

"We've got you covered, boss," she called as I headed down the hall.

Luca was bouncing on his toes, practically vibrating with

excitement, but he didn't break the rule of heading into the back parking area without me.

"Okay," I said, and Luca shoved the door open, letting some early morning sunlight stream in.

As we stepped outside, I took a deep breath and let the fresh pine air fill my lungs. I'd given myself another dream by settling in Sparrow Falls. The small town nestled in the Central Oregon mountains had an endless supply of fresh air. People stopped to help their neighbors. And I felt...safe.

My phone buzzed as if challenging that.

I squeezed my eyes shut, praying it wasn't Roman as I slid the device from my pocket. Relief rushed through me at the sight of a friend's name.

Rhodes: Family dinner Sunday. You in? Say you're in. I need some hang time with my best guy.

I grinned down at the screen. Shep's sister, Rhodes, had done her best to pull me into the Colson crew, a family whose ties were a mix of blood, adoption, and foster care, but whose bonds of love were stronger than any I'd ever witnessed.

Me: We'd love to. Ask Nora if I can bring dessert.

Rhodes: I know we'd all love that. Plus, it'll save us from Lolli volunteering her "brownies."

I chuckled as I beeped the locks on my small SUV. Rhodes' grandmother was notorious for trying to sneak special ingredients of the marijuana variety into her baked goods.

Me: I promise to save everyone from the munchies.

I headed toward the SUV's back hatch as Luca climbed into his booster seat, but my gaze couldn't help but zero in on Roman's name. I didn't know how he kept finding my new numbers, no matter how often I changed them. I kept telling myself we were safe as long as he didn't know where we were. But that didn't stop the dread I felt from pooling in my stomach at each new message.

> **Unknown Number**: Come on, Blue Eyes, help me out. For old times' sake. Once this debt is settled, we'll both be free. xx Roman

The only problem was that Roman's *debt* was tens of thousands of dollars, and that was with the Petrovs alone. Who knew who else he'd borrowed and begged from or promised to repay? All I knew was that even if I had that sort of money, the payoffs would never end.

I shoved the phone into my pocket and lifted the back hatch. Out of sight, out of mind. I grunted as I hoisted the massive duffel bag inside. If a seven-year-old's gear was this heavy, I could only imagine the weight of an adult's.

Shutting the hatch with an *oomph*, I headed for Luca's open door. He knew the routine. While he was allowed to buckle himself in, I always had to check. I gave the seat belt a quick tug as I scanned the booster seat and latches. "You're good to go."

"Duh, Mom."

My lips twitched. Seven going on seventeen. "All right, Superstar. Off we go."

I climbed behind the wheel as the sun beat down on us. It felt all sorts of wrong to be heading to a hockey camp in the middle of July, but I was grateful for the childcare. Summer meant camps for Luca because I still needed to work. Thankfully, he was always excited about them, and none more so than the one focused on his obsession.

I turned right on Cascade Avenue, the main street through town that housed a total of three stoplights. The buildings were mostly made of aged brick with an Old West vibe that gave them a different sort of character than Baltimore had. The fact that the town made it a point to have flower beds at each corner, and businesses decorated with window boxes and pots, meant Sparrow Falls had a charm you couldn't beat.

Pair that with the natural beauty that surrounded it, and I knew I'd never leave if I had a choice. The Monarch Mountains were to the east, four peaks still coated with snow in the middle of summer. To the west was Castle Rock, a series of golden rock faces that were a climber's dream. The area called to outdoor enthusiasts of all kinds. But that wasn't what it gave me. For me, it was one thing and one thing only...

Peace.

After everything that had happened in Baltimore: the attack, the months of recovery where Marilee slept on my floor to help care for Luca while I recovered from what we'd told him was a car accident while I was in a taxi, the fear that clogged my throat every time there was a knock at the door... I'd needed that peace more than air.

"Mom, did you know The Reaper started playing when he was *six*?" Luca asked, cutting into my spiraling thoughts.

"You might've mentioned that," I said, trying to swallow my laugh. Thanks to Luca, I had memorized just about every fact about his favorite hockey player on our closest team, the Seattle Sparks.

"He had the third most goals of any player in the whole league, Mom. I'm gonna be just as good as him. Watch. And I'm gonna be fierce, too. He slammed one guy into the boards so hard he broke his arm."

I winced. "Hurting people isn't a good goal, Luca. And I don't like hearing you talk like that."

My son let out a huff of air. "He wasn't *trying* to break the guy's arm. But the guy did a dirty hit on The Reaper's teammate on purpose. Teddy got hurt pretty bad. And Reaper was just trying to protect his bro."

His bro?

I shuddered at the facts Luca had laid out. "This doesn't sound like the best sport for you to take up. What about soccer?"

"Soccer's dumb, Mom."

"To some people, it's not," I argued.

Luca just stared at me through the rearview mirror as I made the turn toward Roxbury, a nearby town with the ice rink and the bigger stores we needed every so often.

"What about golf?" I asked hopefully. Golf seemed contact-free.

"*Mooooom*, have you seen what they have to wear?"

My kid had a point there. I slumped against my seat. Maybe he'd do this camp and realize he hated hockey. Wearing all that gear had to be a total pain. And ice rinks were cold.

Luca chattered on and on about hockey, The Reaper, the Seattle Sparks, and anything else even remotely having to do with ice-related things. And, just like always, I couldn't find it in me to keep him from something that lit him up. So, I gave in. I'd scrounged for the gear, scrimped for the exorbitant cost of the camp, and drove him the twenty-plus minutes to the rink so he could have his dream.

We pulled into the rink's parking lot, and I grabbed a spot at the end of one row. I cringed when I saw Evelyn Engel helping her son, Daniel, out of her SUV. Everything about the woman was…perfect. Down to her name. Not in a flashy way, but in an I-have-everything-together way.

Her mid-range SUV didn't have a speck of dirt on it, and I was sure there wasn't a Goldfish crumb to be found in the back seat. She wore flawlessly pressed khaki shorts that hit mid-thigh and a cap-sleeved, pale-pink blouse. And, of course, her jewelry matched perfectly.

I hated myself for the envy that flared. No matter how hard I tried, I just couldn't seem to juggle all the balls. As I looked down at myself, I took in the flour smeared across my jeans and the dab of blue frosting on my shirt that I knew would leave a stain. My blond hair was piled in a bun that I was pretty sure I'd put in place with a butter knife this morning.

Sighing, I turned off the engine. "Ready?"

Luca was quiet for a moment, nibbling his bottom lip.

Concern swept through me, and I twisted in my seat to face my kid. "What's wrong?"

He didn't answer right away, but I waited patiently, knowing he would in good time. His gaze dropped to his lap. "What if I'm not any good?"

My heart gave a painful squeeze. "Well, it's always hard when we try new things, right?"

Luca's turquoise gaze lifted.

"Remember when I was trying to learn how to make a soufflé?" I asked.

A smile tugged at Luca's lips. "You said a lot of bad words."

I winced but laughed. "Words we're not supposed to say, right?"

"Right," Luca agreed quickly.

"But I just kept practicing and finally got it. No one expects you to know everything going into this. That's why you're at camp. It would be no fun at all if you already knew everything."

Luca's shoulders slumped. "If I knew everything, I could be playing for the Sparks already. That would be the *best*."

I grinned at him. Already wishing his life away while I desperately tried to hold on to these vanishing moments of childhood. "You know, I bet getting to the Sparks will be a lot sweeter if you remember how hard you worked to get there."

Luca mulled that over for a moment. "The Reaper did say playing peewee was his favorite."

"See?" I had no idea what peewee even meant, but if it kept my kid in the moment, I'd take it.

"Okay, I'm ready," Luca declared, his confidence surging back to life as he unbuckled himself.

"That's what I like to hear." I reached back and gave his knee a squeeze. "Love you more than bees love honey."

He rolled his eyes but still gave me what I wanted to hear. "Love you, too, Mom."

Releasing Luca, I slid out of my seat, only to be greeted by Evelyn's warm smile.

"Hi, Sutton. How are you?"

"Good, thanks. You?"

"Wonderful. Excited to see them start camp today. Will you be able to stick around and watch?"

It was an innocent question, but it was also a dagger to the chest because I couldn't stick around for more than a handful of minutes. I had to meet a supplier at the bakery. It felt like I was always missing things. Moments. Ones I'd never get back.

"Not today, but later this week," I informed Evelyn.

She pressed her lips together but nodded.

I felt the disapproval. I didn't need another reason to feel like one of the items I was currently juggling had fallen to the ground. So, I turned and moved toward the back hatch where Luca was bouncing up and down.

I couldn't help the small laugh that left my lips. I loved seeing that excitement, the life coursing through him. Lifting the hatch, I grabbed his bag. "Ready, Superstar?"

"I'm gonna smash 'em into the boards just like The Reaper!" he cheered.

A wave of nausea slid through me, but I forced a smile. "Or you could just practice skating *really* fast."

Luca shrugged. "That, too."

"Sutton," Evelyn called from around the side of my SUV.

I tried not to cringe and forced a smile as I hoisted the bag over my shoulder. "Yes?"

She sent me a pitying look. "Your tire." She pointed at the rear wheel. "Looks like it's going flat."

My gaze snapped to the tire. It was almost completely deflated. A burn lit behind my eyes as I stared at the vehicle. It wouldn't be just one I'd have to replace; it would be all four. I'd worked so hard to get an all-wheel-drive SUV since Sparrow Falls saw its share of snow, but that meant when one tire went, you had to replace them all.

I closed my eyes for the briefest moment, trying to do the mental math on what this would cost me. I'd emptied out most of my savings to get Luca set up for this camp. This would completely wipe out my emergency fund.

"Mom?"

Luca's voice cut into my swirling thoughts, and I forced my smile wider as I turned my gaze to my kid. "Everything's okay. I just need to change this tire real quick."

"I have AAA," Evelyn offered.

"That's okay," I said, my cheeks burning. "I've got it."

"Here," she said. "Give me Luca's gear bag. I can get them all checked in while you handle this."

My chest tightened, but I nodded and handed her the bag. "Thank you." I turned to Luca. "You gonna be okay?"

He just grinned and nodded. "Daniel and I are going to dominate!"

I wanted to laugh but couldn't quite get myself there. "I'll be inside in just a minute. Have fun dominating until then."

Evelyn gave me a little wave as she guided the boys toward the rink. Everything hurt. It felt like I was holding my life together with duct tape and a prayer and had just run out of both. But I couldn't stop now. I had to keep pushing on.

Heading to the rear of the SUV, I pulled open the panel that revealed the emergency tire. One that stated it was good for only sixty miles. I sighed. I'd have to go to the mechanic's on my way home. I tugged my lip between my teeth, doing a silent equation for how long that would take and praying I'd make it back in time for the supplier meeting.

I heaved out the tire and jack, along with the instruction manual. After a thorough read, I got the jack in place and began cranking. As if I needed one more failure reminder today, I was panting within seconds. Workouts had been another thing that had fallen by the wayside. At least my arm muscles were strong from everything I did at the bakery.

My hands slipped from the jack crank. "Mother frickin' son of a biscuit-eating grandma."

A low chuckle sounded behind me, and I froze. There was something about the tenor of it. The way it spread like smoke and coated my skin in a pleasant shiver.

Crap on a cracker.

I tried to hold on to my mad as I sought out the source, but that failed the moment I took the man in. He stood in athletic joggers and a tee that pulled taut over a broad chest. It took my eyes a few seconds to reach his face because he was so damn tall. Everything about him was finely honed muscle. Like a work of art or a weapon.

Thick scruff covered an angular jaw, and his nose had the slightest crook that made me wonder if it had been broken before. A ballcap shielded part of his face from view, but I could just make out his eyes—a blue so dark it was the sort of color only found at the bottom of the ocean.

"Gotta say, that's some creative language," the man said.

Hell, his voice was just as bad as his chuckle. The sort of tone that had all the tiny hairs on my arms standing at attention. "I didn't realize someone was lurking around like a creeper," I snapped.

The man held up his hands in surrender. Hands that looked strong. Long, thick fingers and callused palms. The kind of hands that could lift you up and throw you on the bed—*hell.* I needed to quit that line of thinking and fast.

"Was just heading over to see if you needed some help," he said. "Looked like you were doing battle with that tire."

"I'm good." My voice was tight, my back molars clamping shut.

The man arched a brow. "You sure about that? I'd hate for any harm to come to a biscuit-eating grandma."

I scowled at him. *Seriously?* Was he making fun of me when I was obviously on my last thread of sanity? "I'm fixing it. And I don't need some overgrown sportsball person getting in my way."

The man's lips twitched. "Sportsball?"

I gestured at him. "You're obviously some sort of athlete. The gear. The muscles—"

"The muscles, huh?" he asked, amusement lacing his tone.

My scowl turned to a glare. "Not interested."

The man just chuckled again. "Understood. Good luck to you and Grandma. Don't steal any of her biscuits."

"Whatever," I muttered.

"Oh, Warrior?"

I glanced up, still glaring, only harder now that the man had given me a nickname.

He grinned at me, the action hitting me somewhere low I didn't want to look too closely at. He gestured to his cheek. "You've got a little something right here."

I stilled as the man turned to walk away. Even his walk was hot. Probably because his ass looked muscular enough to bounce a quarter off, even in those damn joggers.

I needed to get laid.

Scrambling to my feet, I hurried to the driver's side door and flipped down the visor. Grease was smeared all over the side of my face.

Great. Just great.

CHAPTER TWO

Cope

I WALKED AWAY FROM THE WOMAN WITH WHAT FELT LIKE THE first genuine smile I'd had in months, those hypnotizing turquoise eyes flashing in my mind. She was fierce, that was for damn sure. Fiery and more than a little determined. I respected the hell out of it. Even if I wished she'd let me help.

I couldn't help glancing over my shoulder for one more look and nearly tripped over my feet. She was leaning into the front seat of her SUV, examining her face in the mirror, but her positioning made the denim of her jeans pull taut across her heart-shaped ass and curvy hips. Hips I'd love to sink my fingers into as I—*hell*. I was going to hell.

Jerking my gaze away, I forced myself to focus on the facility in front of me. Even from the outside, it looked a hell of a lot nicer than where I'd grown up skating around here. Not as nice as our professional facility in Seattle, but few places were. And the community was lucky that Arnie had decided to build a new spot like this one.

Just as I was about to reach the door, my phone dinged. I adjusted the gear bag on my shoulder and pulled the device from my pocket, seeing my teammate and friend's name on the screen.

Teddy: Don't shoot the messenger but someone got ahold of a video of the fight.

I cursed. It wasn't as creative as Warrior's biscuit-eating grandma, but it had a hell of a lot more Fs involved.

I switched out of the text thread and went to a hockey blog. The video was the first thing on the home page. I tapped on it. Marcus and I circled each other as a voiceover sounded. "We're used to seeing brawls on the ice, but not usually between teammates."

The video showed me ripping off my gloves and decking Marcus. The footage had obviously been taken from security cameras at the rink. It was slightly grainy and had no sound, which meant you couldn't hear the foul shit coming out of the asshole's mouth before I decked him.

The voiceover went on to ask what had been wrong with me lately. And wasn't that the million-dollar question? I'd love to have given them an answer, but I didn't have one. All I knew was that the tips the press was getting weren't helping.

Every possible slip-up seemed to be under a microscope. But worse than that was the made-up shit. Everything from me supposedly being rude to a server to accusations of me sleeping with anyone and everyone. And that crap wasn't me. I wasn't a saint, but I wasn't a dog either. And being raised by two incredible women for the majority of my life meant I had a healthy respect for them.

Plus, if my mom or Grandma Lolli ever heard about me mistreating a woman, they would kick my ass.

I wasn't sure who had it out for me in the media, but they'd combed through my trash, broken into my ex's private social media accounts to steal photos, and now this.

My phone dinged again as a new text came in.

Linc: Ignore the video, and don't fuck this up. If all goes right, this will give you a little of the good press you need.

I pulled my ballcap lower on my forehead as if that would shield me from all the attention headed my way. I was lucky as hell the owner of the Seattle Sparks had my back. He was more than a good boss; he was also a friend. Maybe because we read in each other that we'd both been through our share of hardships. Perhaps because we both had a love for the ice and the pure game without the bullshit. Either way, I was grateful to have him at my back.

Me: You got it, boss.

Linc: Fuck off.

My lips twitched but that hint of a grin quickly slid away at the reminder of the video. It was the last thing I needed when I was already on thin ice. I cracked my neck, trying to alleviate some of the pressure that always gathered there after a shoulder injury, and opened the door to the rink.

The moment the air hit me, a million memories came with it: my dad helping me lace up my skates, him and Mom and the rest of the Colson crew in the stands, yelling their heads off at my peewee games. I missed that. Missed what it felt like before I went pro, and all the bullshit entered the picture.

I moved through the facility, admiring what Arnie had created. There were two rinks, a restaurant and snack stand, multiple locker rooms, and even a gym. I wandered deeper into the space until I reached the skate rentals. A young girl who looked to be around fifteen stood behind the counter.

"Can you point me toward Arnie's office?" I asked.

"Sure—" Her words cut off as her gaze locked with mine. Her eyes widened. "Copeland Colson?" she squeaked.

I winced. "Call me Cope, and let's just keep my presence here between you and me."

I knew it was a fleeting wish. Before long, word would get around that I was back. That I was volunteering with the kids' camp here.

But Arnie had promised he'd kick the lookie-loos to the curb. I just wanted to hold on to my anonymity a little longer.

The girl's eyes only widened further. "O-of course. I won't put you on blast. I just—I—" She closed her eyes for a brief moment, trying to center herself. "I play center like you. I've watched your footwork about a million times, trying to learn it. And your wrist shot? It's killer."

My brows lifted in surprise. By the look of her, I would've thought she was a figure skater. Possibly working the counter to pay for ice time. "Hockey player?"

She nodded. "Arnie's trying to pull together a girls' team for next year."

"That's sick. I'm coaching the kids this summer, so if you hang around after camp one day, I can give you thirty minutes of my time."

The girl's eyes lit up like I'd just promised her a pony. "Seriously?"

I nodded. "It's no big thing. All I ask for in return is you telling me where Arnie's office is."

She blushed. "Sorry. Staircase is down that hall." She pointed. "Head up, and he's the first door on the right."

"Thanks."

The girl nodded, resembling one of those bobblehead dolls, and I couldn't help but chuckle as I walked away.

I made the trek to Arnie's office in under two minutes. The plaque on the door read *Owner & Head Asshole*. It fit the cantankerous man.

I rapped three times on the door, and he bellowed from within. "Come in and stop trying to knock my damn door down."

I grinned as I stepped inside. "Hasn't anyone taught you to watch your mouth yet? There are children around."

Arnie scowled at me. "Hasn't anyone taught you to respect your elders? Being a hotshot doesn't give you the right to be a dick."

My grin only widened as I crossed to one of the chairs opposite his desk and lowered myself into it, dropping my bag onto the floor. "How the hell are you?"

"Better than you by the looks of things." He arched a brow as if challenging me to argue.

"The press are assholes," I muttered.

Arnie leaned back in his chair. I was pretty sure it was the same one he'd had when I was six and started at his first rink. "They can only do so much if you don't give them the raw material."

A muscle in my jaw began to flutter. "I'm doing the best I can."

Arnie scoffed. "Don't wanna hear a laundry list of excuses, boy. Just do your job and do it well."

"Not sure it qualifies as a job if I'm doing it for free."

The man sitting opposite me scowled, the grooves in his face deepening. "Don't give me a buncha lip. I might be old, but I can still kick your ass."

One corner of my mouth kicked up. "I have no doubt. Now, wanna fill me in on this camp?"

Arnie jerked his head in a nod. "We got kids ten and under for this group. You'll have to split 'em up when you start scrimmaging, but I got our usual coach to help you out. Figure you two can tag team."

"Sounds pretty straightforward."

"Even you should be able to pull it off."

I chuckled. "Aw, Arnie. I missed you, too."

"Piss off," he muttered.

"Hey. The girl working the skate counter. What's her story? Said she's a hockey player."

A shadow passed over Arnie's face. "Hayden. Good kid. Mom's a piece of work. Hayden works here summers and after school. Brings her two younger sisters a lot. Get the sense she's more mom than older sister to them."

Shit.

"You know you can always call Fallon if you need help in that arena." My younger sister was a social worker, and her bleeding heart meant that she would fight to the death for any kid who came across her desk.

"Sometimes, the system does more harm than good. Not everyone gets lucky enough to land with the Colsons."

My parents had been involved with the foster system for as long as I could remember. I had one adoptive brother, Shep, and four foster siblings, Trace, Kyler, Rhodes, and Arden. Fallon was my only blood sibling. Other than the brother we'd lost. I shoved thoughts of Jacob down. I couldn't deal with that today.

"I get it," I told Arnie. "But if you sense it's bad, *call* her." Or I would.

Arnie waved me off. "You know I will. Now, get your ass on the ice."

I grinned as I pushed to my feet and grabbed my bag. It was good to be back. Arnie's familiar, thorny care was a hell of a lot better than the politics I dealt with on the Sparks. At least with him, I knew he gave a damn. In Seattle, everyone was just watching their own backs.

Heading down the stairs, I heard the din of excited voices. The camp was set to have twenty-four kids. Not a ton, but more than enough. And wrangling them for almost a full day would be a lot.

As I moved in the direction of the chaotic noise, I stopped in my tracks. There was the woman from the parking lot. She was crouched in front of a little boy who had the same turquoise eyes. Her head was bent toward him as she seemed to gently encourage, a faint smear of grease still on her cheek.

The boy beamed up at her like she hung the moon, and I didn't blame him. But then I put the pieces together. She had a kid in my camp. Which meant she was likely married or had a partner.

A flare of disappointment speared me. It shocked the shit out of me because my last attempt at a relationship had ended in disaster. It wasn't my thing. People getting too close, wanting to know the secrets I did everything I could to keep buried. It was better this way—Warrior being taken.

Because there was one truth I couldn't deny: I'd always be better off alone.

CHAPTER THREE

Sutton

L UCA BOUNCED UP AND DOWN ON THE BENCH AS THE COACH I recognized from the times I'd been here with Luca during free skates stepped in front of the bleachers.

"Welcome, everyone," Coach Kenner called.

The kids all cheered in response.

Kenner grinned. "I'm glad to hear you're all excited." His gaze skimmed over the crowd, pausing on me. His smile turned warm. He was likely a decade or so older than my twenty-nine but was attractive and fit.

I searched for a flicker of something, anything, but there was nothing. He was exactly the kind of man I needed to feel a flutter for: kind, responsible, good with kids, and with a steady job. Still, nothing. It was like I was dead inside.

But then I remembered the flush I'd felt at the sound of parking lot man's voice. The way my skin heated and prickled with awareness. *Crud.* That sort of charmer was not in the cards.

"All right, if you're excited now, just wait," Kenner went on. "I have a pretty epic surprise for you… I'd like to introduce our second coach for the entirety of camp. Please welcome Copeland Colson. Also known as—"

"The Reaper!" countless kids yelled, including mine.

Luca was on his feet, shouting and cheering, but I could only stare as I looked up, up, up into dark-blue eyes. The pieces came together in jerky snaps. I'd known one of the Colson brothers played hockey but had thought he lived in Seattle and only came home for a week or so at a time. But here he was. And not only was he a hockey player, he was also my son's obsession—and the man I'd called a creeper in the parking lot.

I wanted to crawl under the bleachers and die.

"Hey, everyone," he greeted. "You can call me Coach Cope or Coach Reaper if you want. I've always wanted to be called Coach."

Everyone laughed, and I was pretty sure the mom next to me let out a longing sigh.

"I can't wait to hang out with you for the next month. We're going to have a blast and play the heck out of some hockey!"

More cheers erupted.

"All right, kids," Coach Kenner called. "Hit the ice for a light warm-up."

Everyone around me started moving, but I caught Luca's arm. "Are you sure about this?"

He had that wild-eyed look he got when he'd had too much sugar. "Are you kidding, Mom? This is the *dream!*" He pulled his arm free and waddled to the rink in his gear that made him look like an Oompa Loompa. I just had to watch him go.

A throat cleared. My gaze snapped to the source, but I already knew what I'd find. Cope stood there, a smile playing on his lips—lips that looked made for kissing and... I shook myself out of my stupor.

Not going down that road.

I straightened, meeting his gaze dead-on. Well, as much as I could, being at least a foot shorter than him. "Coach," I greeted.

That smile widened. "Like the sound of that."

"Power hungry?" I muttered under my breath.

Cope just chuckled, and damn if my skin didn't react the same way it had earlier. Every nerve ending stood at attention like they were crying out for Cope's touch. I curved my arms around my waist, hugging myself as I tried to ignore the shiver running through me.

Cope frowned. "Cold?"

"I'm fine."

"Might want to bring layers tomorrow. Can get pretty chilly rink-side."

"I'll keep that in mind."

"Sutton," Coach Kenner greeted. "Good to see you. I see you met Cope."

I forced a warmer smile for Kenner. "Nice to see you, too. I need to get back to the bakery, but my cell is on the admission form if you run into any issues."

Kenner's expression gentled. "Luca will be fine. Don't you worry. No one is going to play full contact."

Relief swept through me. "You might not want to tell Luca that. He has his heart set on smashing someone into the boards." I sent Cope a scathing look. "Apparently, he learned that from his favorite player, The Reaper."

Cope winced, looking a little guilty. But I just headed for the parking lot and away from the man with the haunting blue eyes. Because if there was one rule I lived by, it was this.

No athletes. Never again.

It was one of *those* days. One of the no-good, very-bad ones. I tried to remind myself that none of it was catastrophic. Luca and I were safe and healthy. We had a roof over our heads and food on the table. But even after chanting that over and over in my head, I was still about to lose it.

"That bad?" Thea asked as I dropped my head to the fridge in the bakery's kitchen.

I'd just finished meeting with my new supplier because my previous one retired. The new guy seemed on top of it, professional and polite, but his prices were nearly double.

"It'll be fine," I lied. I'd gotten good at lying. Because if I didn't, Thea and Walter would try to help. And they didn't need the weight of my problems.

Walter patted me on the shoulder in a grandfatherly gesture. "You've had a day."

"And it's not even noon," I muttered, forcing myself to straighten. I turned and leaned my back against the fridge, letting the metal surface cool my skin. At least this time, it was overheated due to panic instead of hypnotic blue eyes and all the muscles. "Why didn't you tell me Shep's brother was coaching the hockey camp?" I asked Thea.

Her brow furrowed. "Trace or Kye? I didn't even know they played hockey."

I shook my head. "Cope." Even saying his name made my skin heat. *Damn him.*

Thea's green eyes widened. "Cope is coaching Luca's camp?"

I bobbed my head in a nod.

"Shep said he was heading back to Seattle."

"Apparently not. Because he was there in all his glory, and Luca nearly lost his little mind because Cope is also his favorite player."

This time, Thea's eyes nearly bugged out. "Cope is The Reaper?"

"Shouldn't you know that?" I accused. "He is your boyfriend's brother."

Thea shrugged. "I'm not really a sports fan. Shep talks about Cope, but not really his career. And I don't think he knows Cope is coaching." She pulled out her phone and began tapping on the screen. "I'll ask him what's up."

The bell rang, signaling a new customer. I forced a smile to my face and stepped out from behind the counter. I struggled to keep that smile in place as I took note of the newcomer. Rick Anderson looked completely out of place in my bakery, even though he owned the building. He looked out of place in the small town altogether.

He wore a dark suit that had to make him sweat buckets in the almost ninety-degree heat outside, his dark hair was slicked back with far too much gel, and his eyes were beady like a rat's.

"Sutton, it is so wonderful to see you. How are you and little Luca doing?"

The muscle in my cheek began to twitch. "Good. We're doing really good. You?"

"Oh, I can't complain. Just purchased two more buildings, so business is good."

"Congratulations. That's wonderful. What can I get for you today?" I asked, hoping like hell I could move things along.

Rick sent a look of disappointment that read faker than his veneers. "I'm actually here on business. In all my expansion, I'm afraid I realized that I've cut my tenants too much of a deal. I need to raise your rent for the bakery and the apartment upstairs. All the details are here." He tugged a folded paper from his pocket and set it on the counter. "This will take effect at the start of the month for the bakery, and next week for the apartment since that's week to week."

"But can't you only raise my rent once a year?" Rick had increased my rent three months ago. That had hurt, but I'd managed. Renting the apartment upstairs week to week had helped, but nothing would save me from another increase.

Those beady eyes narrowed on me. "Our lease agreement doesn't guarantee you that, Sutton. And prices are going up around Sparrow Falls. I have to keep up with the times. I'm sure you understand."

I didn't understand. But I also couldn't speak. All I could think about was the fact that even if Rick *was* doing something shady, I didn't have the funds to hire a lawyer to fight it. And it wasn't like someone would magically show up and have my back.

Some part of my brain was aware of Rick's too-fancy shoes clicking on the floor as he headed out after completely exploding my world. My hands trembled as I picked up the piece of paper. When I opened it, there was nothing I could do to keep the tears from springing to my eyes.

The figures on the sheet were insurmountable. I could keep the bakery or my apartment but not both. There was no way. And if I let go of either, I'd lose everything.

CHAPTER FOUR

Cope

MAYHEM REIGNED AS THE KIDS CHARGED ACROSS THE ICE, letting out screams and battle cries. Some raced, others crashed into each other, enjoying the protection their pads afforded. It was fucking adorable.

Kenner skated to a stop next to me. "How's it feel being on the other side of things?"

I watched as Luca darted around another kid named Daniel. His skating was damn good for someone with no hockey experience. "Kinda nice," I admitted. "Reminds me of when the game was pure."

Kenner raised a brow at that.

I quickly changed tack, the feeling of showing too many cards churning in my gut. "And it feels damn good to be the one holding the whistle." I picked it up from around my neck and gave two short blasts. "That's it for today, you monsters. We'll see you tomorrow."

There was a mixture of cheers and protests, but all the kids started toward the boards and their waiting parents. I couldn't help scanning the crowd in search of blond hair and turquoise eyes. The moment I caught sight of her, I couldn't look away.

It was more than just how beautiful she was. It was how she curved around her son in a move equal parts protection and attunement as if what he was saying was the most important thing in the world. Growing up with the siblings I had and knowing the things that had brought most of them into foster care, I knew that it was far too rare to see that sort of attention.

And I knew what a gift it was. I'd felt that. As if nothing was more important than the absolute nonsense coming out of my mouth. An invisible blow hit me in the solar plexus, but it might as well have been a stone fist. It didn't matter that it had been seventeen years since I'd lost Jacob and my dad; grief still lashed out like a sucker punch. Grief *and* guilt.

"I wouldn't go there."

Kenner's voice cut into my spiraling thoughts, and I blinked, trying to pull myself from the darkness and the memory of screeching tires and shattering glass. So much pain. Slowly, the rink came back into focus.

Sutton was almost done helping Luca out of his gear. *How long had I been staring? Shit.* I forced my gaze toward my fellow coach. "Sorry, what?"

Kenner inclined his head in her direction. "Sutton Holland. I wouldn't go there. I sense she's been through a lot."

I stiffened, the reaction fueled by too many things. First, Kenner clearly had his sights set on Sutton. My annoyance at that was beyond ridiculous when all I'd shared with the woman was a few bantered barbs. Second, the woman who kept stealing my attention was apparently single—not a temptation I needed. But more than everything else was the knowledge that something in Sutton's past may have harmed her.

Kenner likely meant she had a dickhead ex. But I couldn't help worrying that it was something more. My gaze cut back to Sutton as if my eyes had a mind of their own. Luca's hand was firmly in hers as they headed for the facility doors, and she carried the massive gear bag as if it were nothing.

It was more than clear that she was used to shouldering the weight of the world. I had the most bizarre urge to go after her, take the bag from her hold, and carry it to her damn SUV. A vehicle I hoped had a new tire by now.

"Cope?" Kenner pushed.

I shook my head. "Sorry, it's not that. She just reminds me of someone."

What a stupid lie. I'd spent maybe ten minutes with the woman and already knew she was one of a kind.

"Oh, sorry," Kenner mumbled. "Didn't mean to overstep."

The hell he didn't. He wanted to piss a circle around Sutton. I knew guys like him. They played the long game. Pretending to be an unassuming friend but always with the goal of getting in her pants.

My back teeth ground together as I forced a smile. "No worries, man."

A flash of movement caught my attention as a figure pushed onto the ice. Her ease of motion told me she was at home there. Her skates told me she was a figure skater.

She crossed the rink in six long strides. "I heard we had a legend in the house."

Her gaze slid over me in a look that had me fighting not to take a step back. *Jesus.* The girl looked barely over eighteen. And that was *not* my thing. Not since I'd been eighteen. And that was twelve years ago.

"Raven," Kenner greeted coolly.

The girl smiled sweetly at him, curling the end of her inky black ponytail around her fingers. "Coach. Aren't you going to introduce me to your friend?"

Hell, I didn't want to be introduced.

Kenner's lips twitched. "Looks to me like you already know him."

Her cheeks flushed. "You know what I mean."

"Nice to meet you, Raven. I gotta jam. See you tomorrow, Coach." I shoved off the edge of my skate, darting around the girl and toward the boards, but the moment I saw the two figures waiting there, I almost went back to the piranha in spandex.

Of all my siblings, *of course*, Trace and Shep were here. Every sibling seemed to have a role in my family. Trace always kept us in line, which was fitting since he was the eldest and had also become sheriff of Mercer County.

Shep was the caretaker, the one who always made sure we were okay. In the past, the well-being of others had come at the expense of his at times. But since meeting Thea, I'd sensed a shift in him. He was more balanced. But that didn't change the number of times he checked in on us all.

I forced an easy smile as I skated over to the exit—the kind of grin my brothers expected of me. Because I had my own role to play. Easygoing. Daredevil. A touch reckless. It was easier to stay there than to let anyone in on the truth.

"Who narced on me?" I asked as I stepped off the ice and onto the mat.

"Chill," Shep said. "No one narced. Thea has a friend with a kid in this camp. She wanted to know why Thea hadn't told her you were one of the coaches."

I winced as I sat on the bench and unlaced my skates. The accusation was clear in Shep's words. He wanted to know why the hell I hadn't told *him*. And Trace's silent stare was enough to punctuate the point.

Sliding off one skate, I grabbed my carry bag. "New development. Linc and Coach Fielder thought it might be a good move for me."

Shep and Trace were silent for a long moment as I took my second skate off. It was Trace who finally spoke. "Because of the media coverage lately."

There wasn't judgment in his tone, but I felt it anyway. In the sheer knowledge that he'd been checking up on me. Sometimes, Trace felt more like a parole officer than a brother.

I shoved my skates into my bag and slid on my sneakers. "You know the media are vultures."

More silence. This time, Shep did the talking. It was like they were playing out some sort of good-cop, bad-cop routine. "What's going on? There's a video of you punching Marcus Warner without any provocation. That's not you."

My fingers fisted around the strap of my gear bag. No, it wasn't me. And that should've been the first clue there was more to the story. But Shep wasn't even giving me that.

And in some ways, I understood it. There was a reason I'd been named The Reaper. Because I was known for being brutal on the ice. If you came for one of my teammates, I'd come for you.

Which was exactly what had happened during that game against Dallas. It had been a bloody battle from the moment we stepped on the ice. But I'd felt it even before. A warning that crackled in the air.

My left wing, Louie, had gotten a stick to the ribs, and I wouldn't let that fly. I'd gone for the Dallas player responsible, but it had left Teddy open. Two opposing players had taken him out, and he ended up with a brutal slice to his forearm that meant sitting out a few games.

I could still hear Marcus's words from practice the next day. *"Our team captain just had to play the hero. Didn't you, Colson? But we all know the truth. The only person you give a damn about is yourself. And it could get the rest of us killed."*

"Cope," Shep pressed. "Tell us what's going on."

I shoved to my feet. "Nothing. I'm good. Just the press biting at my heels, and it'd be nice if my brothers had my back instead of thinking I was a loose cannon about to explode."

It was a dick thing to say, but I didn't stop to apologize. I just headed for the doors and out into the summer heat. But the temperature did nothing to take the bite off the chill that had settled in my bones. One that said I was a hell of a lot worse than a loose cannon. And bashing people into the boards wasn't keeping my temper in check the way it once had.

CHAPTER FIVE

Sutton

MY EYES BURNED AS I PULLED INTO THE RINK'S PARKING LOT. These super early mornings were trying to kill me. Today's extra cupcake order had been for an engagement party. Thankfully, the bride-to-be had wanted whimsical over tried and true bridal white. She'd asked for cupcakes representing significant moments in her and her fiancé's lives.

It had been a fun project, where I'd gotten to hear all about their journey together. We'd opted for the mascot of the college they went to, which was an adorable beaver, a frisbee for their competitive frisbee golf hobby, a sunset over the mountains for where he'd asked her to be his wife, and my favorite, a likeness of their beloved schnauzer, Samson.

But the intricate artwork always took me three times as long as my more straightforward fare. I was exhausted, my back ached, and I was pretty sure my vision still hadn't recovered from all the squinting. It was worth it, though. Because I was getting more and more referrals from within the community. And maybe if that kept going, I could find a way to keep the bakery and my apartment.

"Coach Reaper says we get to pick our nicknames at the end of this week," Luca said as I pulled into a parking spot.

I still couldn't help but wince at the awful name. *Reaper?* Who picked that as what they would be called throughout their career?

"I'm pretty partial to Superstar," I said as I turned off the engine.

Luca rolled his eyes, looking so much older than his seven years. "*Moooom*, that's dorky."

I clutched my chest. "Knife to the heart, kid. You don't like my nickname?"

Luca giggled, looking more his age. "It sounds like I'm bragging."

He had a point. I twisted in my seat. "You know, I like that you're thinking about how your nickname might make other people feel. Shows me how kind you are."

Luca's cheeks pinked. "I don't like it when people make me feel bad about something. Like I'm not as good as them."

A wave of fierce protectiveness surged, and I had to bite back the urge to demand to know who had ever made him feel bad about himself so I could hunt down a bunch of soon-to-be second-graders. Instead, I calmly said, "It's great that you can remember that and try not to do the same."

Luca's little mouth fought a smile. "But I still want something *really* cool."

I grinned. "Of course, you do. I think we need some time to brainstorm. How about we watch *Mighty Ducks* tonight, eat our weight in cupcakes, and make a list?"

He beamed, and, God, that smile was a gift. It was the kind of grin that said my kid had no worries beyond picking the coolest hockey nickname imaginable. And that was what I'd been working so hard for. What I'd fought for when I packed my apartment up in the dead of night and drove across the country for days. What I'd worked countless double shifts and sold plasma for. What I bore scars for.

My fingers itched to trace the faint line from the split lip or the raised flesh on my side where I'd been sliced by that enforcer's steel-toed boot. But I resisted. It was a miracle I'd hidden the worst of the damage from Luca as it was. I wasn't about to be the one to remind him.

"Mom, you are the *AWESOMEST*!" Luca cheered.

I laughed, releasing the painful memories and holding on to the good. "I love being the awesomest. Are you ready to go kick some hockey booty?"

"Duh!" Luca unlatched his seat belt. "Can I get out?"

I quickly looked around the parking lot. "Sure. But stay right by the car."

Luca nodded, slid out of his booster seat, and shoved the door open. I hurried to extricate myself because I didn't trust my kid's willpower to keep himself in place. Crossing to the rear of my SUV, I lifted the back hatch.

Luca bounced up and down, telling me all about what they'd done yesterday for the tenth time. Whatever this hockey bug was, he had it bad. And I couldn't help the nerves that settled in deep. Ones that set me on edge.

It felt wrong to hope that Luca didn't have what it took to go the distance with this sport. But was it really bad to wish he was just good enough to play through high school and then call it a day? I wanted him to do something perfectly boring for a career. An accountant or dermatologist sounded nice.

But as I slung the massive duffel over my shoulder and closed the hatch, I couldn't help taking in the sheer joy on Luca's face. *That* was what I wanted most of all. His happiness.

And if hockey gave him that, so be it. I'd be the most diehard hockey mom around. I should probably watch some YouTube videos. Or maybe there was a how-to guide somewhere.

I reached out a hand, and Luca took it, swinging our arms back and forth as he talked a mile a minute, throwing out terms that might as well have been a foreign language. When we reached the sidewalk, he dropped my hand and ran ahead to open the door.

I dipped my head in a mock bow. "Thank you, kind sir."

Luca just giggled again. The moment we were inside, he took

off running toward his fellow campers. So much for being the awe-somest. I placed the bag in a row of others and moved toward the trophy case on the far wall.

My vision blurred slightly as I took in the rows of awards and team photos. I blinked a few times, clearing the burning sensation as I rubbed at the knots in my lower back. My gaze stopped on one photo in particular. The boys looked a year or two older than Luca was now. They were caught mid-celebration, holding up a large cup. Some were laughing, others cheering, but my eyes were stuck on one in the middle.

He was helping one of the coaches hold the cup, but his focus was on the coach himself. There was so much reverence and respect in his stare. The hair was blonder in this photo than the light brown it was now. But I would've recognized those dark-blue eyes anywhere.

That fact should've scared the hell out of me, but I couldn't pull away. The man Cope gazed up at looked so much like him that I figured it had to be his father or another relative. I knew from Thea that the Colsons had lost their eldest brother and father in a car ac-cident many years ago. And staring at the photo now, I could see the loss had been a great one.

"What's with the sad eyes?"

I whirled at that now-familiar tone, the one that had me want-ing to roll around in it like a dog in its beloved mud. *What the heck was wrong with me?*

"Cope," I greeted.

He grinned, but there was a heaviness beneath it. Something that told me his existence wasn't all sunshine and roses, even with his hockey-star status. Or maybe it was just the knowledge of what he had lost.

The grin slipped a little. "You okay, Warrior?"

"What's with the nickname?" I asked, trying to change the subject and not wanting to know if he could see all the ways I was fracturing.

One corner of his mouth picked back up again. When it did, I saw that he had his own faint scar there. "Can't tell me you're not determined to fight all your own battles," Cope said, the smile falling again. "But you look exhausted."

That stung my pride. Apparently, my expertly applied concealer wasn't doing its job today. "Is that a nice way of saying I look like shit?"

I expected Cope to panic, get flustered, apologize. Any of those responses. But he just stared at me, one eyebrow slightly cocked. "Do I look like an idiot?"

"Not sure you want me to answer that, Hotshot."

"Definitely a warrior. She's not afraid to level the death blow," Cope muttered, amusement lacing his tone. "I may miss a lot of things, but one of those will never be how fucking gorgeous you are. Doesn't matter if you're covered in grease or flour or have dark circles you're drowning in. None of it will take away an ounce of your beauty."

My jaw went slack as I gaped at Cope. I didn't have much dating experience. I'd gotten together with Roman my first year of college and had been on a total of three dates since we'd split. But even with my minimal experience, I'd gotten used to one thing. Game playing.

The tactics and strategies differed from guy to guy, but the arena was the same. And it was exhausting. But here Cope was, shooting straight and to the point.

"I, uh—"

"Mom!" Luca called, waddling toward me in his gear and skates, his face scrunched. "My skates feel too tight."

Panic shot through me as I felt the blood drain from my face. If Luca had outgrown his skates overnight, I didn't have a solution. My emergency fund was gone, and my rent on both properties had increased. I was running on fumes.

Cope's gaze moved from Luca to me and stayed on my face for a bit. "Hey, Speedy. Can I take a look?"

Luca looked up at his idol and beamed, then nodded. "Sure, Coach Reaper."

Cope grinned and instantly crouched, dropping his bag onto

the floor. His fingers moved deftly around Luca's skates and laces before he glanced up at me. "You using waxed laces for his skates?"

My brow furrowed. "Um, I'm not sure. They came with a fresh set, and I put those on." I'd watched three YouTube videos first to make sure I was doing it right. I just hoped the secondhand store hadn't given me the wrong laces.

Cope quickly untied the skate and rubbed the lace between his fingers. "Waxed."

"Is that bad?" I asked, worrying my bottom lip.

"Not at all," Cope assured me. "But it gives the skate a tighter feel, more rigid." He looked at Luca. "Are you used to skating in the rentals from here?"

Luca nodded. "Mom got me these right before camp."

"Bingo," Cope said with a grin. "They use cloth laces for the rentals. It gives the skate a little more flexibility. I grew up skating with cloth and switched to waxed in high school."

Luca tugged his lip between his teeth, a move I knew he'd learned from me. "You use waxed now?"

Cope nodded. "I don't want my skates having too much give on the ice."

"I can keep the wax ones," Luca said quickly.

Cope chuckled and moved to unzip his bag. "There's plenty of time for that. Let's switch you to cloth for now. You don't want blisters to keep you from skating."

"No," Luca agreed begrudgingly.

Cope pulled a set of white laces from his bag.

"You don't have to do that," I started.

Cope's dark-blue gaze cut to me. "It's no problem. I brought some extras in case anyone had issues."

"Thank you," I whispered. "Just let me know how much I owe you—"

"Warrior," Cope chided softly. "Just let me do something nice. It's good for my ego."

My lips twitched. "I'm not sure your ego needs any help."

Cope grinned as he went back to work. "Fair point."

"Sutton," Evelyn called as she headed in my direction. "Do you need me to give Luca a ride back to the bakery today?"

"Bakery?" Cope asked as he slipped one of Luca's skates off his foot with ease.

Evelyn sent him one of her perfectly poised smiles as she smoothed auburn hair that was already expertly pulled back into a chignon. "Yes, our Sutton here is quite busy at The Mix Up. It can be hard for her to manage drop-off and pickup."

Annoyance flared at the reminder of all the ways I was failing to juggle the countless things I was responsible for.

Cope's gaze shot to me. "You work at The Mix Up?"

I gave him a small nod. "I own it."

A huge smile broke out over his face, one that had me sucking in a sharp breath at its potency. It was real, I realized. No forced fakeness. And Cope truly smiling? It was lethal.

"Thea brought some cupcakes from there to a family dinner the other week. They were incredible. Cute as shit, too. With little bumblebees on them," Cope said, grinning wider.

Evelyn gasped. "Coach Colson. Watch your language, please."

Cope's brows lifted. "What'd I say?"

"The s-word," she hissed.

Luca giggled. "If I say a bad word, I gotta do extra chores."

Cope's lips twitched as he turned back to me. "Want me to come over and mop the bakery floors? I can give Speedy here a ride home."

Evelyn let out an exasperated huff. "I am guessing you do not have a booster seat in your vehicle, Mr. Colson. Children under the height of fifty-seven inches and the age of eight are required by *law* to ride in one. Thankfully, *I* have an extra in my SUV so I can safely transport Daniel's friends."

Cope stared at her for a long moment. "Have you ever thought of getting a job with my brother Trace? I think you two would get along."

"Excuse me?" she spluttered.

"That attention to detail and letter-of-the-law stuff? Two peas in a pod."

I struggled to hold in my laugh and eventually had to cover it with a cough.

Evelyn straightened and turned to me. "Do you want me to give Luca a ride?"

That heat in my chest was back, the flush of guilt at being unable to manage it all. "I'd really appreciate it. Thank you."

"Of course." Evelyn shot Cope a dirty look and headed off in Daniel's direction.

Cope clapped the sides of Luca's skate. "You're good to go. Meet you on the ice?"

Luca nodded enthusiastically. "Thanks, Coach Reaper." He waddled off before we could get in another word.

Cope pushed to standing, and the height difference had my head spinning. His tee pulled against the planes of muscle in his chest as he shoved his hands into his pockets. "That lady's a piece of work."

I shook my head. "She just has it all together. Isn't used to people who aren't perfect, I think."

Cope was quiet for a moment as he studied me. "That's cool if micromanaging rules and regs is her thing, but it sure as shit isn't cool if she's using backhanded compliments to make you feel bad about having a job. One you should be fucking proud of because I heard you turned that bakery around. And those cupcakes are some of the best I've ever had in my life. And I'm not a stranger to sweets."

An odd sensation swept over me. Discomfort. As if my skin was too tight for my body. "It's not like that—"

"It is," Cope cut in. "And you shouldn't let anyone talk to you that way. I'm sure as hell not."

"Cope—"

"Warrior, remember? That means not letting idiots put you down."

A burn lit somewhere deep—the pain of remembering how long

it had been since someone had reminded me of my worth. I wasn't sure it had happened since my grandmother passed.

It wasn't that I didn't have good friends. I did. But with them, I tried to make it seem like I had it together. Like nothing fazed me.

So why was it that the bad boy of hockey was the one to see through it all? Why was he the one who saw…me?

CHAPTER SIX

Cope

COACH KENNER PLACED THE WHISTLE BETWEEN HIS LIPS AND blew. "Okay, team. Let's finish today out strong. One last skating drill."

Two days in, and we were already seeing who had a gift for the ice and who would likely stay in the hobby lane. That sort of thing could change somewhat, *if* a kid really got a taste for the sport and worked their ass off to get better. But there were certain things you couldn't teach.

Instinct. A feel for the ice. The uninhibited lack of fear.

I'd spotted a few already. A twelve-year-old named Eddie was already playing at a seriously competitive level. Jayden, a nine-year-old, had a gift for puck handling. And one of the few girls in the camp, Shannon, was kicking some serious ass.

But it was Luca who had me awestruck. The kid could *fly*. It was like he'd been born on the ice. No fear. Only sheer joy every time he got to skate full-out. And after a couple of demonstrations, he could stop on a dime. The puck handling would come as he got more and more comfortable skating with the stick in his hand.

"Reaper, you want to walk them through it?" Kenner asked.

I nodded. "Think of it like an obstacle course on ice." I gestured to the squat orange cones on the rink set apart at different intervals. "We're focusing on adjusting footwork at greater speeds. Go as fast as you feel comfortable with while trying not to disrupt any cones."

"Let's go," Kenner yelled and blew his whistle again.

The kids formed a line and began working their way through the setup with varying degrees of success. One boy was so determined to make it at record speed that he tripped and took out the whole line of cones. I braced for tears, but when he sat up, he shot both arms up in triumph, sending everyone into fits of laughter.

Luca was the second to last kid to go. I hadn't missed how he'd intently watched everyone else, seeing where they struggled and how they succeeded. Smart little dude.

Kenner blew his whistle again, and Luca was off. He took the course in half the time the last kid had. Absolutely flying. He rounded the ice, taking the second leg even faster. The campers went silent as they watched, but just before he reached the end of the course, his stick hit one of the cones, sending it flying.

Luca skidded to a stop, his shoulders slumping in defeat. His face scrunched in a mixture of frustration and the effort it took to force back tears. God, the kid was going to kill me.

I pushed off, skating toward him as Coach Kenner reset the cone for the final kid to skate. I reached Luca in five long strides. My hand landed on his shoulder with a couple of pats, the same way my dad and coach had always done with me. I crouched lower so we were at eye level. "Don't let one cone wreck a stellar run."

Luca stared down at the ice. "I almost had it."

"Want to know the most beautiful thing about that run?" I asked.

Luca's eyes lifted to mine, so similar to his mom's. They were older than his years, too. Wisdom lived there. "What?" he whispered.

"You went for it. You didn't play it safe. And you absolutely *flew*. You have a gift, Speedy."

Those turquoise eyes widened, shock and pure pleasure filling them. "I do?"

"Damn straight, you do."

Luca fought a giggle. "Mrs. Engel will be real mad if she hears you say the d-word."

I didn't hold back my chuckle. "Good thing she's too far away to hear me." But I hadn't missed her watching me like a hawk during camp. As if suggesting I give Luca a ride without having a booster seat made me dangerous to every child at the practice.

"Good thing," Luca echoed. He nibbled on his bottom lip for a moment before asking the question that was clearly stewing. "How do I go for it but not mess up?"

God, he was adorable. "We learn from our mistakes. What did you feel when you hit the cone?"

Luca's little brow furrowed for a moment, and I could see him replaying the skate in his mind. "Before I hit it, I kept switching what I was looking at. Going back and forth between the cones and where I was going. But I was almost at the end and forgot to look at the cone. Forgot I had to think about my stick."

"Bingo. Now you'll know for next time. But you're also still getting used to the stick. The more you skate with it, the easier it'll be," I assured him. "You're doing amazing."

Luca's cheeks reddened, but he grinned hugely. "Thanks, Coach Reaper."

Kenner blew his whistle. "We are done for the day. See you tomorrow, everyone."

Some kids charged toward the rink exit and their waiting parents while others still raced around the ice in whatever game they'd made up. My phone buzzed as I started to head for the bench. I slowed and pulled it from my pocket.

Angie: How's it going down there?

I winced at the text. It was hard to tell whether she was reaching out as head of PR for the Sparks or as my ex, which meant I had to thread the needle carefully. The last thing I wanted was to make her think there was an opening there.

Me: Good. Hope all is well.

Kind but to the point and ending the conversation. But my phone quickly dinged again.

Angie: Need me down there for anything?

Hell. That was the last thing I needed. But I'd brought this on myself.

Me: All good.

I shoved my phone back into my pocket just as two kids whizzed past me, Luca being one of them. As I followed their progress, I caught sight of a familiar figure at the edge of the rink. Before I could wave or head in that direction, Luca was moving.

"Rhodes!" he yelled, skating toward my sister.

Her smile was instant, her hazel eyes lighting at the greeting. Damn, it was good to see that. She'd been through so much over the past few months, and we'd all been worried. But apparently, recovery from nearly being killed by a psychopath came easier when you were head over heels in love. And while her ex-FBI-profiler boyfriend, Anson, might be a broody son of a bitch, he would do anything to keep Rhodes safe and happy.

"Luca!" she called over the noise of the excited kids. "You were incredible. I can't believe you didn't tell me you were a hockey superstar."

The smile that split his face was so massive it had to hurt his cheeks. "I'm gonna play for the Sparks, just like Coach Reaper."

The light in Rho's eyes danced as she looked up at me. "Coach Reaper, huh?"

I flipped her off behind Luca's back, which only made her laugh.

"Luca," Evelyn called. "Come on. We need to go." The scathing look she sent me told me she'd seen the middle finger I'd offered my sister.

"Aw, man," Luca muttered.

I patted him on the back. "I'll see you tomorrow, Speedy."

He nodded and then looked at Rhodes. "Can I come help on the Victorian soon?"

With the help of Shep's construction company, my sister was renovating her family home that had nearly been destroyed by a fire years ago.

"You bet. I know Anson would love your help."

That had me choking on a laugh. Because I couldn't picture the cantankerous ex-profiler-turned-contractor taking on a tiny assistant. Even if he *was* gone for my sister.

Rhodes sent me a glare and mouthed *rude* as Luca headed for the rink's exit. I moved closer to the boards and my sister. She hadn't come to live with us until she was thirteen, when her parents and sister were killed in a house fire. But her close friendship with Fallon from years before meant I'd always thought of her as a little sister.

"This coaching gig looks good on you," Rhodes said, leaning against the boards.

"Careful, the power of this whistle has already gone to my head."

She laughed. "I'm not shocked."

"So," I began, "who asked you to come check up on me?" All these sibling visits had a war of emotions playing out inside me. Gratitude that they gave a damn, mixed with annoyance at their lack of confidence in me holding it together.

Rhodes just rolled her eyes. "No one, Copeland."

"Shit. She's formal-naming me. I'm in trouble."

"Damn straight. But don't act like I'm here to put you in cuffs and drag you away for questioning."

"You'd never," I shot back. "You're not Trace."

Rhodes pinned me with a stare that had me snapping my mouth closed. "Don't be a dick. Trace loves your cranky ass just as much as I do."

A fresh wave of guilt washed over me at the memory of blowing him and Shep off yesterday. As oppressive as their check-ins could feel, I knew the reason behind them was love. "Sorry," I muttered. "You're right."

"Hold on a sec." Rho pulled out her phone. "I just want to get this on video for the sibling group chat. Say that one more time."

"Oh, piss off," I groused.

She laughed and shoved her phone back into her pocket. "So, how's it feel to be coaching instead of playing?"

"You know, I like it more than I thought. Reminds me of when Dad used to coach my eight-and-under team."

Rhodes stilled, and I instantly knew I'd made a misstep. I never brought up Dad or Jacob. Not because I didn't think about them every fucking day, but because it was too hard to talk about them. But being back in Sparrow Falls for longer than I had been in years, and working with hockey kids like this, had the memories slamming back with full force.

And I didn't have access to my typical tools to keep them at bay. No games, no training, no practices. I'd spent four hours working out last night, never more glad that I'd installed an over-the-top gym at my place here, even if it only got used a few weeks out of the year.

"Sometimes, remembering them feels more painful," Rhodes whispered. "But I promise it's good."

Fuck. Rhodes knew this sort of pain better than anyone. But she didn't know what it felt like to know that at the heart of it, their deaths were your fault.

A burning agony lit in my gut. Like a brushfire sweeping through muscle and sinew, burning everything in its sights. "Yeah," I choked out. "Listen, I gotta go." I waved to the young skate counter clerk. "Told someone I'd help them with a wrist shot."

It wasn't a total lie, just a stretch of the truth. Which was better than me biting her head off like I'd done to Trace and Shep the other day.

Rhodes studied me for a long moment before nodding. "Don't forget, family dinner Saturday night."

I groaned. That was the last thing I wanted to do. But maybe if I showed my face, played the easygoing shit-stirrer, these family visits to the rink would cease.

Rhodes reached out and flicked my ear. "What torture, getting fed amazing food and being forced to spend a couple of hours with your family."

"Did you just flick me?"

She arched a brow. "What're you gonna do about it, ice boy?"

I shot forward, grabbing her in a headlock over the boards and giving her a noogie.

Rhodes squealed, batting at me. "I'm going to get you for this, Copeland Colson."

I just laughed as I released her, skating backward toward the exit. "I'll be watching my back, Rho Rho. And I've got panther-like reflexes."

"Reflexes won't save you when I put laxatives in your coffee!" she yelled.

Hayden laughed as she headed to the ice, looking between Rho and me. "Sister?"

I chuckled. "That obvious, huh?"

"One of my sisters would've said the same thing."

"Good to know I'm not alone." I pushed back from the boards, skating in reverse. "So, want to show me what you've got? We can work on that wrist shot."

Hayden's golden eyes widened. "Now?" she squeaked.

"I've got exactly fifteen minutes. I think that's long enough to give you some things to work on."

She didn't wait. She ran for the skate counter, grabbed a pair from a shelf along with her stick, and sprinted back.

I laughed as she laced up. "I'm not gonna disappear on you, kid."

She shook her head. "Not wasting a minute of your fifteen."

Hell. I admired that sort of dedication. "Okay, do a couple of loops to warm up and then hit it." I skated into the center of the rink, watching Hayden move across the ice. She had the same grace as the figure skater but there was more power behind it.

Hayden rounded the ice three times before picking up a puck with her stick and heading for the goal. She hit the three positions needed for the shot and the puck hit the net, but it lacked the force she could've gotten.

I skated toward her. "You're thinking about the positions, aren't you?"

She winced but nodded. "They aren't second nature yet."

"They will be with time," I assured her. "Right now, I actually want you to think about hand placement on the stick. Your thumb is supposed to be pointing down, but it's shifting to the side. You're going to lose power and accuracy when that happens."

Not everyone took critique well. Some argued they weren't doing that at all or told me I was wrong, but not Hayden. She simply nodded and rounded to make another approach. This time, the shot hit the net with a hell of a lot more force and in the top left corner.

"Hell yeah!" I called.

Hayden beamed. "Thanks, Mr. Colson."

I winced. "That makes me feel eighty. Just call me Coach."

"I'll call you Coach," a sultry voice purred.

My face screwed up before I stopped myself, and Hayden choked on a laugh. I blanked my expression as I turned around. "Raven."

"Want to help me with my skating technique?" she cooed.

"Actually, I'm late for a meeting I totally forgot about. Hayden, keep working on it. It'll be second nature before you know it."

She gave me a mock salute and turned back to the net.

Raven huffed out a breath of annoyance, but I ignored her and skated straight for the exit. That girl scared the hell out of me.

I hopped off the ice, walking on the mats to take a seat on a bench. I chatted with a few lingering parents and kids. The moms batted their eyelashes in what I hoped were harmless searches for a thrill because all three wore wedding rings.

Lacing up my sneakers, I stood just as my phone buzzed in my pocket. Sliding it out, my sibling text chain flashed. We were in a constant battle, trying to one-up each other with names for the chat. The current moniker was *The Den of Dysfunction*.

A photo had been shared of me racing two kids from one end of the ice to the other.

> **Rhodes:** Our brother dearest has a real gift for wrangling the rug rats.

It only took a matter of seconds for Kyler to reply. He always gave me the most shit, probably because we'd been the ones to get in the most trouble. Kye hadn't come to live with us until he was sixteen, and even then, it was clear he lived with demons. Even though we were close, he never opened up to me about what he'd been through.

The truth was, I didn't think he truly talked to anyone but Fallon. It shouldn't have been a surprise. She was the empath of our family, the bleeding heart who took the world's pain on as hers.

> **Kye:** Probably good. Because who knows when the baby mamas are going to start coming out of the woodwork.

I tapped the camera icon, snapped a picture of me flipping him off, and sent it.

> **Kye:** Touchy, touchy, hockey boy.

> **Fallon:** Be nice. I think it's sweet that you're volunteering, Cope.

Kye: Hear that? You're just a sweetie pie, cutie patootie, Copey pants.

Fallon sent him a series of emojis I was pretty sure meant she was threatening his life. I shook my head, bending to grab my bag and slide it over my shoulder. When I stood, it was to find Arnie standing there, a grimace on his face.

"What's wrong?"

He shook his head. "Got a problem." He held out his cell phone.

There was a text from a familiar name on the screen. The owner of the Sparks. My friend. But he hadn't come to me, likely because his back was against the wall.

Lincoln Pierce: Got an anonymous tip about Cope using steroids. Need you to drug test him today. I can't give him a heads-up or it could call the results into question.

Fucking hell. Tips to the press were one thing. But accusing me of drug use? That was something else entirely. And it meant one thing. Someone was trying to ruin my career.

CHAPTER SEVEN

Sutton

"Y OU NEED TO STAND RIGHT HERE, REMEMBER?" I ASKED LUCA.
He nodded, his beekeeping hat sliding around on his head comically. "I'm not scared. They won't sting me."

I grinned at my kid. He was the coolest. And way braver than I had been when I first started this endeavor.

So many of the recipes I had called for honey, and I'd had the bright idea that I could make my own by putting hives on the roof of the building. I'd read countless articles and watched endless YouTube videos on urban beekeeping, trying to learn how to do it. While we didn't live in a city, we didn't have acres of land to install hives on the ground either.

But this worked. I had three hives and plenty of potted flowers that Thea helped me keep alive since I did not have a green thumb. So, the bees had plenty to feed on up here. Luca and I had built our hives together over a series of weekends last year. Now, it was time to harvest the honey.

There was something about the meditative place I had to go to when tending the bees. Not letting tiny displays of aggression or the fear of being stung stop me. Because at the end of the day, I knew we were helping each other.

I sprayed the mix of essential oils that sent the bees deeper into the hive so I could remove the honeycomb on the highest level. This was the overflow, so they'd still have enough to sustain them in winter—and winters in Sparrow Falls could be brutal.

My fingers tightened around the hive tray as a couple of bees slid out and over my gloved hand. I just kept breathing, reminding myself I was safe. It had given me an exercise of sorts. A way to practice calming my mind when the fear hit.

That happened sometimes. A memory of the men in my apartment. The feel of the boot cracking my ribs. My lip splitting. The pain. The terror that they'd get to Luca.

Keep breathing.

I lifted the first tray and laid it on the cart. The bees on my fingers lifted, taking flight and heading back into the hive. I admired their bravery. Their intelligence. They knew how to get themselves out of bad situations and find someplace safe. We were similar that way.

"They're pretty," Luca said from behind me. "And I like their sounds. It's like one of those big concerts. You know, with all the instruments?"

"A symphony?" I asked.

Luca nodded as I pulled out another tray. "Buzzing together and making music."

I liked thinking of it that way. And they were working together to create. Honey, a home, safety.

"Do you think Coach Reaper will be at dinner tonight?" Luca asked, moving on from the bees.

My grip on the third tray tightened. "Maybe. I'm not sure." But I couldn't help hoping he wouldn't be, even though I knew Luca would be disappointed. His hero worship had reached level eleven on a chart of ten, especially after *The Reaper* had been the one to give Luca his nickname.

I understood the urge. I'd caught sight of Cope on the ice this week. It was breathtaking how he moved across the surface, a combination of beauty and power all wrapped up in one potent package. But the fact that he'd seen the cracks in my façade of strength had me twitchy, worried that he'd be the one to figure out all my secrets, my shame—things I didn't want anyone to know.

"I *really* hope so," Luca went on, oblivious to my inner turmoil. "I've been practicing all the puck-control things he taught me this week, and I wanna show him."

My lips pressed together to hide my grin. "You'll be able to show him on Monday."

"I know, but sooner's better. Then he can give me more tips. You'll tell him how much I've been practicing, right, Mom?"

I couldn't keep the grin from my face as I placed the final tray on the cart. "No kid is as dedicated as you. And I will be sure Coach Colson knows that." Last night, I'd had to pry the hockey stick from a sleeping Luca's hands.

"Okay, good." Luca worried his bottom lip as I replaced the lid on the hive. "You know, maybe we could put a mini ice rink up here so I could *really* practice."

I burst out laughing. "Luca. You don't think having your own ice rink is a little extreme?"

He grinned at me, his missing incisor making him look extra adorable. "It's worth asking, right?"

My kid. I might not have been the perfect mom, but I'd taught him to dream big.

Luca hopped from one foot to the other as I knocked on Nora and Lolli Colson's front door. The multi-generational duo kept the working ranch in immaculate condition. I knew they had plenty of ranch-hand help, but they guided that ship.

Even though I'd been here countless times, I couldn't help but look around in awe. The property itself was absolutely majestic, looking out at both the Monarch Mountains and Castle Rock. It was the kind of view I longed for but knew I'd have to sell a hell of a lot more cupcakes to get.

Still, I'd keep holding on to that dream. Just like I'd hold an image of this farmhouse in my mind, with its perfect white siding and picturesque wraparound porch, complete with rockers and swings.

I ached to give Luca a home like this. It was more than the sheer size and beauty of it, it was the knowledge that he could be safe running through the fields. It was the warmth that lay inside. The family that filled the structure.

I longed for that. For Luca *and* for me.

The door swung open, and I was met by Nora's smiling face. Her light-brown hair was swept back in a loose bun, and she was clad in an apron. As she looked down at Luca, her green eyes twinkled. "Oh, goody, two of my favorite people."

Luca threw his arms around her in a big hug. "Mom brought pav—pav—what is it called again?"

"Pavlova," I said, laughter in my voice.

Nora pulled me in for a quick hug. "Ooooh, sounds fancy."

"It's basically meringue and whipped cream with berries. The berries are so we can make believe it's remotely healthy."

Nora chuckled as she released me and then motioned us in. "I like kidding myself about sugar."

She led us into the open-plan living, dining, and kitchen area that had floor-to-ceiling windows on the back wall, allowing us to take in the glory of the view. The space was already packed with the Colson crew.

Rhodes and Anson were in the kitchen, working on what looked like a salad. Kye was kicked back in an overstuffed chair, a beer in hand. Fallon was bent over a puzzle with Trace's six-year-old daughter, Keely, as the Colson sister I knew the least looked on.

Arden was stunningly beautiful with dark hair and eyes a mix of gray and violet, but she held things close to the vest and didn't venture out too often. If I created the incredible sculptures that she did, I might not leave my workshop either.

Thea and Shep were cuddled together on the couch, looking as happy as could be, while Trace sat bent over his phone, fingers flying. The eldest Colson was likely neck-deep in a case of one sort or another. Over the past few months, I'd learned that no one was as dedicated to justice as he was.

I breathed a sigh of relief at the lack of Cope's presence. He'd probably gone back to Seattle for the weekend or something. The only other person I didn't see was—

"Lolli!" Fallon squeaked. "What are you wearing?"

I braced as the woman in her mid-eighties appeared from the hallway doing some sort of twirl. She wore cowboy boots, a sequined miniskirt, and a T-shirt with a bedazzled pot leaf on it that read *Mary Jane Queen*. "What do you think? I made the shirt myself. I thought us girls could hit the town after dinner. Get us some action."

"Supergran, you are *so* sparkly," Keely whispered in awe. "Can I have a shirt just like yours?"

Lolli crossed to her great-granddaughter. "Of course, you—"

"Don't even think about it," Trace warned. "It's bad enough her camp counselor pulled me aside and told me she was talking all about this new game she heard her supergran talking about called *knocking boots*."

Kye choked on a sip of beer and then raised his bottle to Lolli. "Get it, Lolls."

She sent him a wink. "You know I will."

Shep groaned. "Not information I need…ever."

"Quit being such prudes. Live a little. What d'you say, girls? Cowboy bar after dinner?" Lolli asked, doing a shimmy shake.

"I can't," Fallon said, placing a piece in the puzzle. "I have to make a home visit after this."

That had Kye narrowing his eyes on her. "Where?"

She let out a little huff. "Doesn't matter."

"Fallon…" he growled.

Over the past few months of getting to know the Colson crew better, I'd noticed that Kye was especially protective of Fallon. I understood it in a way. It was clear she had a tender heart and the two had a special bond. But there were times I swore they were communicating without words, as if they had their own silent language only they could understand.

"The Pines," Fallon muttered, pushing to her feet.

"I'm going with you," Kye demanded.

Fallon squared her shoulders and pinned Kye with a look that would've had me taking a step back. "This is my job, Kyler. I can't have you tagging along, glaring at everyone who looks at me sideways."

A muscle began fluttering wildly in his cheek, and his grip on the beer bottle tightened. "I'll stay in my truck, but you're not going alone. You know that area is rough at best."

Her dark-blue eyes, so similar to Cope's, flashed. "Yes. And I also know there are good people in hard situations there."

"It's not the good people I'm worried about," Kye muttered.

"Take Fletcher," Trace cut in. "He's on duty tonight."

"I don't need—"

"Fallon," Trace cut her off. "There's determined, and then there's stupid. Going alone, at night, to an area that's known for drug activity and plenty of violence borders on the latter. You know the sheriff's department will provide backup to any social worker who requests it."

Fallon let out a huff of breath that sent the hair around her face fluttering. "Fine."

Kye's grip on his beer bottle loosened, making the ink covering his hands shift sort of like an animated film. But the tension in his shoulders stayed, along with the look of worry deep in his eyes.

"*Thank you,*" Trace stressed, dipping his head to meet his sister's gaze.

She nodded, then sent Luca a grin. "Want to come help us with this puzzle?"

He pushed in closer to me, suddenly seeming shy.

As if reading the emotion, Keely sent him a megawatt smile. "Come on, Luc. It's really hard. We need you."

His cheeks flushed slightly, and I swore his eyes went a little unfocused. *Oh, shit.* This was crush city, and I wasn't sure how Trace would feel about that. Before I could say anything, Luca darted over to the table to join Fallon and Keely, leaving me in the dust.

"What can I get you to drink?" Thea called as she crossed to the kitchen.

I loved seeing her so at home here, so comfortable. For a woman who'd been so determined not to let anyone close, she'd ended up with a mountain of support behind her.

"I'd love some iced tea. Thank—" My words cut off as my phone rang. I pulled it from my pocket as *Unknown Number* flashed on the screen.

My stomach sank. I'd changed my number the day I got the flat. If this was Roman, he was getting faster at finding my new contact info. And there were only so many times I could change it before people started to notice, and I ran out of excuses.

"You okay?" The voice wasn't one I'd expected. I hadn't even heard Arden move, but she was by my side now, those gray-violet eyes asking a million questions. It wasn't that she was quiet per se, she certainly spoke her mind when she had opinions about things, it was just that she didn't feel the need to fill the quiet. She only spoke with purpose.

I forced a wide smile. "All good. Just a supplier. I need to take this. Be right back."

With Luca happily working on the puzzle with Keely and Fallon, I headed for the back door. I didn't stop at the deck, knowing everyone inside would watch me. I headed down the steps toward the fields of cattle and horses.

It was the horses that drew me, the way they exuded peace and power all at once. I leaned against the fence, staring down at the phone's screen as it rang and rang. I didn't dare answer it. I couldn't.

After my attack, I'd hoped the silver lining would be that I could serve as Roman's wake-up call. Instead, it drove him deeper into his dark spiral. A detective on my case told me that he'd moved on from opiates and cocaine to heroin and fentanyl.

A burn lit behind my eyes. He'd had the world at his feet once. A round-two draft pick for the Baltimore Blackbirds. One of the best wide receivers in the league. And I'd given up every dream I'd had to go with him.

Hadn't finished college or even gotten a job once we moved to Baltimore. I hadn't thought it would matter. We were going to build a family. That was all I focused on, so willing to let Roman take care of me that I'd forgotten all about my dreams of opening a bakery one day.

And all it took was one bad hit to change everything. One knee surgery after another. And I hadn't realized the pills had a hold of Roman until it was too late. Until he was being booted from the team for a positive drug test and had us in an endless amount of debt.

I'd tried to help. Attempted to support Roman however I could. I got him into Narcotics Anonymous, therapy, made sure there was no alcohol in the house, and never drank in his presence. But nothing had been enough. And *I* was the one who paid the price. Luca and me. Because after our divorce, when I filed for full legal and physical custody, Roman couldn't even be bothered to show up for court.

My phone flashed with a new text, and only then did I realize it had stopped ringing.

> **Unknown Number:** Listen, you little slut. I gave you EVERYTHING. All I'm asking is for you to do me a solid and pay a little of that back. Is that too much to ask? You took everything from me.

The pressure built behind my eyes as the burning intensified.

> **Unknown Number:** You owe me. And if I don't get it, I'm sending Petrov's goons after you. You know what he's capable of.

A shudder ran through me. I was ice-cold, even though it was still in the mid-eighties. Petrov. I'd learned after my attack that Roman had gotten mixed up with Russian organized crime. And those monsters didn't play when it came to getting their money back. But there was also no way to cut off the head of the snake.

The two men who'd attacked me were sentenced to fifteen years in prison, thanks to a shop's security camera catching them outside my apartment building, but they'd likely get out in five. They hadn't said a single word during their interrogations or during their trials. They'd simply accepted their sentences as their boss looked on. Someone whose eyes I felt on me in the courtroom. A boss I *never* wanted to see again.

A hand landed on my shoulder, and I whirled, my knee coming up on instinct, ready to fight.

"Easy, Warrior."

CHAPTER EIGHT

Cope

SHE'D LOOKED SO DAMN SAD. AND WORSE, SHE'D LOOKED *scared.* That potent mix of emotions had pulled me in, the urge to try to help flaring from somewhere deep. But I didn't have the sort of fix-it skills Shep and Trace had. Only I couldn't stop myself from trying.

My hand moved down automatically to block as Sutton tried to take out my balls. The move shouldn't have surprised me. She was a warrior, through and through.

"Hasn't anyone ever told you it's rude to sneak up on someone?" Those turquoise eyes flashed with a welcome heat.

I liked the anger a hell of a lot better than the sadness and fear. "I don't think it can be called sneaking when I said your name." Surprise flashed across her expression. "You were just too engrossed in whatever was on your phone to hear me."

Sutton's gaze darted to the device. She quickly locked it and shoved it into her pocket, but I didn't miss the look of panic on her face as she'd taken in whatever was on the screen. An unsettled feeling swept over me, but I struggled to keep my expression and tone relaxed.

"Want to tell me about it?"

Those stunning eyes lifted to mine. "Why? So you can swoop in and fix it?"

That wasn't me. That was Shep. The ultimate fixer. But something about Sutton made me want to be that for her. "Maybe. Or so you can let it out and stop it from eating you up inside."

Sutton let out a shuddered breath as she leaned back against the fence. "Is that what you do? Talk your problems through?"

I couldn't help but chuckle. "Fair point. One for one."

Sutton frowned, a hint of confusion playing on her features.

So, I ripped off the Band-Aid. "I decked a teammate, and the press got ahold of the footage. Some of the higher-ups want to trade me."

Sutton's jaw went slack as she gaped at me. "Why'd you punch him?"

I stilled, my body tensing as I cocked my head to the side, studying her. Those who found out about the fight never asked that question. They wanted to know if it would affect my playing, the games I was eligible for. If I'd be fined. At some point, I'd become more hockey player than human being.

But not to Sutton. Maybe it was because she didn't know anything about hockey. But I sensed that wasn't the case. She was the kind of person who wanted to get to the heart of the matter. The *real* stuff.

I stared at her for a moment longer before I spoke. "He said it was my fault that one of our teammates got injured in the playoffs."

Sutton didn't look away, searching my eyes for something. "Was it?"

There it was again, that brutal honesty carving to the heart with expert scalpel skills. And in a world of pretty lies, it was refreshing. "Yes, and no."

She pinned me with a stare that threatened to pull the truth out of me.

"Part of hockey is letting your opponent know you won't let them get away with hurting your teammates."

Sutton's nose scrunched in an adorably disgusted look. "Is this where the *smashing them into the boards* comes in?"

A chuckle slipped past my lips. It was the last sound I would've expected, given what we were discussing. "See, learning all the hockey lingo already."

She shook her head, sending her blond waves cascading around her shoulders. I had the sudden bizarre urge to reach out and touch the strands to see if they were as soft as they looked. I wanted to tangle my fingers in that hair as I took her mouth, as I took *her.*

Fuck.

I shoved the image from my head and ordered my dick to obey. I tried thinking about something else. Like the smell of the locker room after a game when we all ditched our reeking gear.

"Slamming someone into something doesn't seem like a good solution to a problem," Sutton muttered.

"Most of the time, you'd be right. But not on the ice. Think of it as setting a boundary or giving a consequence."

She sent me a droll look. "So, body-slamming someone into a solid surface is the same thing as me taking away Luca's toys for two days if he doesn't pick them up when I ask?"

My lips twitched. "Exactly."

"I find that a little hard to believe."

I shrugged. "You gotta play the game to fully understand, I think. If the other team knows they can hurt our players without any ramifications, they'll just do it more."

"Isn't that what the refs are for? To stop that sort of thing?" she asked, a hint of worry settling in those beautiful turquoise eyes.

"In some cases, yes. In others, no."

"Then they need to do a better job," Sutton snapped.

I grinned at her; I couldn't help it. "Need you at my next game to lecture the refs into doing better."

She rolled her eyes. "Fine. They aren't up to the job. So, you have to do it?"

"Exactly." A feeling of dread settled into my stomach as I

remembered the game. The second to last one we'd played that season. "Player on the other team pulled a dirty move with my left wing. I went after him, but when I did, it left another teammate, a friend, open to attack."

Sutton instantly read my shift in mood. "Who?" she whispered.

"My friend, Teddy. My right wing. He's a little smaller than most players but makes up for it with how fucking fast he is. But two guys on the other team got to him, one tripped him while the other took him out with a dirty hit. He went down hard. Skate caught him on the arm. Bad. Severed some important vessels. There was extensive bleeding."

Memories flashed in my mind of all that blood spilling over the ice, the medics rushing out. The smell of it. It mixed with memories of long ago. The metallic tang in the air. The pained sounds from the front seat.

"Cope."

A hand landed lightly on my forearm, gently tugging me from the knot of torturous memories. The ones that haunted my dreams and made it impossible for me to even share a room with anyone, let alone a bed. I blinked a few times, the world around me coming back into focus. "Sorry," I croaked.

"Don't be," Sutton said, her voice pitched low. "I know what it's like to get lost in memories."

Her hand dropped away as she stepped back, and I felt the loss instantly. Her heat was gone, but the place she'd touched still tingled. Pins and needles, like a hand waking up after losing all feeling. It was almost painful, but I wouldn't have traded it for anything.

"Your friend, Teddy, is he okay?"

I nodded. "Had minor surgery to repair things. Should be back to full contact by next season."

I'd reminded myself of that over and over every time the guilt set in. Every time it nearly swallowed me whole.

Sutton was quiet for a moment. "And how are you and the other player? Is everything okay?"

I shook my head and made a tsking noise. "You already got more than your share. It's your turn. Tell me what gave you those sad eyes."

Sutton didn't look away, but shadows swirled in those turquoise depths now. I watched the battle, hoping like hell she wouldn't give me a brush-off and give me something real. Her gaze shifted away from me and toward the mountains before she finally spoke.

"A ghost."

Before I could ask anything else, she was moving—away from me and toward the house. In a matter of seconds, *she'd* turned into the same thing, and I was left wondering if the exchange had ever happened.

CHAPTER NINE

Sutton

SUNDAYS WERE GOLDEN DAYS. A MIX OF HECTICNESS AND happiness. Even though the bakery would be a crush in the morning, the afternoons always slipped into a lazy haze with only the occasional customer coming in, even during the summer.

Luca stood on his specialty step stool that allowed him to cook or bake with Walter or me. Today, Walter was giving him a lesson on how to make his famous chicken and white bean chili.

"We want to get those onions cooked down nice and thorough so they're almost caramelized," Walter instructed.

Luca nodded, then cast a quick glance over at his teacher. "What's caramelized? Like the candy?"

Walter chuckled and turned to me. "Smart cookie you're raising over here."

"Too smart for me to keep up with," I called back as I spooned cake batter into muffin tins. It was true, too. Whatever sort of math they'd started teaching kids was over my head, and Luca was only through first grade, about to start second.

Luca's nose scrunched the way mine did. "Candy onions do *not* sound good."

Walter laughed harder. "Salty-sweet, my boy. Salty-sweet. Not to the point of sugar but it balances the dish. And when you top it with a sharp cheddar—" Walter kissed his fingers like an exaggerated Italian chef. "Perfection!"

Luca still looked skeptical.

"You'll see when we do our taste test," Walter promised.

Luca grinned at him, the gap from his missing tooth showing. "The taste tests are my favorite part."

"Told you he was a genius," Walter called as I put the cupcakes into the oven.

God, we were lucky to have found him. Walter had been born and raised in Sparrow Falls, only leaving to join the Army at twenty-two. But he'd opted to be a culinary specialist instead of walking out onto the front lines, saying, *"I'm a lover, not a fighter."*

After coming home to Sparrow Falls, he'd worked in insurance for most of his days. But after retiring, he'd gotten bored quickly. And when I put a *Help Wanted* sign in the window of The Mix Up, he'd answered the call and had been with us ever since.

"Are you two mad geniuses going to keep it in line if I do a little paperwork?" I asked, wiping my hands on a towel.

"Duh, Mom," Luca called.

I pinned Walter with a stare. "No more cupcakes until *after* chili."

"*Mooooom*," Luca protested.

"You've had two already today. Do you want me to go to mom jail for giving you too much sugar?"

Luca giggled. "Mr. Trace would never lock you up."

I grinned, moving in to tickle his side. "I don't know, Trace seems like a rule follower to me." In every way. I'd noticed that he was a stickler for keeping things neat and tidy and always following through on his word. And while he expected a lot from others, he was hardest on himself.

Luca squealed, shifting out of my grasp. "Don't worry, I'll come visit and bring you cupcakes."

"Best kid around," I called as I headed for the main area of the café.

"Duh!" Luca yelled back.

"Love you more than bees love honey!"

"Double duh!"

I laughed as I grabbed a ham and cheddar croissant and my pile of paperwork, heading to a table in the corner. I stopped to check on our only patron at the moment, a woman who seemed caught up in what looked like an amazing book. She waved me off with a grin, and I headed for my destination.

Lowering myself into the chair, I let out a long breath. My muscles ached, and my head felt heavy. I knew I'd been pushing things a bit too hard lately, but I wasn't sure what other choice I had.

The papers on the table glared up as if reminding me exactly why I'd been pushing so hard. I nibbled on my croissant as I looked over bank accounts and supply order forms. I crunched and re-crunched numbers. Even with paying the apartment rent week to week, managing it all would be impossible. I'd looked up the fees to consult a lawyer about the rent increase, but their hourly rates were worse than what I paid the landlord.

Tears pressed against the backs of my eyes, the pressure of them taunting me, trying to get me to break. But I wouldn't. I couldn't. Not with Luca in the kitchen, and me needing to get through the rest of the day.

The bell on the door sounded, and my head jerked up to see Shep and Thea headed my way, shopping bags in tow. I forced a smile but knew instantly that Thea saw through it.

"What happened?" she demanded. "Is Luca okay?"

"He's fine," I assured her. "Making chili in the kitchen with Walter."

Thea's shoulders slumped in relief, and my heart squeezed

at how deeply my friend loved my kid. Her gaze roamed my face. "What's going on?"

I opened my mouth to lie and then realized it was no use. I'd have to move out of the apartment before long, and Thea wouldn't miss that. I plucked up the letter from Rick and handed it to her.

She took it, her face reddening as she scanned the sheet. "That prickish asshole. He already raised your rent a few months ago."

Shep moved in closer, his amber gaze moving between the two of us as he set the bags down. "May I?"

My face flamed with embarrassment, but there was no sense in hiding it from him either. "Sure."

He took the paper from Thea and read it quickly, a muscle in his jaw beginning to tick wildly. Finally, his gaze lifted to mine. "This is illegal, Sutton. I know because I have a few rental properties myself. In Oregon, you can only raise the rent once in a calendar year. And you have to give your tenants thirty days' notice when you do."

I nibbled on my bottom lip. "I'm month to month with the bakery now since it's been over a year, but I'm week to week with the apartment. That's always given me more flexibility—"

"You don't have to explain," Shep said gently. "If you're week to week, the same rules apply. After a year, he could raise your rent again, but he has to give you at least a week's notice."

My stomach cramped. I shouldn't have been surprised that Rick was pulling something shady. He'd always seemed smarmy and pompous. "I still don't think I can do anything about it. I can't exactly afford a lawyer to take this to court."

"How about I call that douche baguette and tell him where he can shove his rent money?" Thea offered.

Shep's lips twitched. "Let's not give Trace any reasons to arrest you, Thorn."

She sent him an annoyed look. "I'd do the time. That guy's a prick, and he always stares at Sutton's ass when he's in here."

That had Shep stiffening and his gaze moving to me. "Does

he make you uncomfortable? I'd be happy to call him on your behalf—"

I shook my head quickly. "He gives me the ick, but it's nothing I can't handle."

Shep didn't look all that appeased. "Reach out to him via email or text so there's a record. If he gives you a hard time, I have a contact with the county who handles this sort of thing."

God, Shep was a good one and exactly who my best friend deserved. Taking a deep breath, I picked up my phone and typed out a text.

> **Me:** Hi, Rick. I think you must've made a calendar error in raising my rent. Mine was already raised in April, so it can't be raised again until April of next year, according to the state of Oregon's tenant rights. Let me know if you need anything else or a copy of that notice. Thank you!

My teeth tugged at my lip as I set my phone down. "See? All done."

At least I had a few more months to figure out my next steps. But come next spring, I had a feeling Rick would raise my rent as much as was legally possible.

Thea pinned me with a stare. "You haven't been sleeping enough."

"I'm fine, *Mom*."

Her hands went to her hips. "Don't you take that tone with me, young lady."

I chuckled. "Thanks for having my back. Both of you."

Shep's arm went around Thea's shoulders, pulling her against him. The action was so effortless and comfortable it made my chest clench. I wanted that. The knowledge that I had someone to lean on, to count on. A true partner.

He sent me a kind smile. "If you need anything, just say the word. Rick isn't exactly known for having a stellar reputation."

Of course, that was who I'd ended up with for a landlord. It couldn't be any other way. It was just how my luck ran. But I'd put far too much energy and money into this bakery and couldn't just move buildings. I'd go under if I did.

My phone dinged, and I looked down. The second I read the text message, all the blood drained from my head.

> **Rick:** This was me looking out for you, Sutton. I didn't want to have to play hardball, but you've left me no choice. I need you to be out of the apartment above the business within the stipulated notice period in accordance with the state of Oregon. You have ten days.

CHAPTER TEN

Cope

MY SUV'S ENGINE STILL HUMMED AS I SAT IN THE RINK parking lot, staring down at my phone. Teddy had sent me the article with the words: *What the hell is going on, Reap?* But I didn't have an answer. All I could do was stare at the headline.

Seattle Sparks' Superstar, Copeland Colson, Tested for Drugs.

My back molars ground together as my grip on the phone tightened. Of course, these asshole gossipmongers didn't tell everyone that my test had come back negative. They just let it hang that I'd been suspected of juicing.

When Linc called me that morning to let me know the test was negative, I'd finally started breathing again. I knew I hadn't taken any banned substances—of any sort. But given my luck lately, I didn't put it past whoever was messing with me to fake the results. That thought had my gut twisting as my phone dinged in my hand.

> **Teddy:** Don't let the assholes get you down. The team will put out a statement, and everything will be all good. Now, tell me how it is wrangling a bunch of tiny monsters.

I wanted to believe Teddy, but the thought had been planted in people's heads. I could lose sponsorships—or worse. And I knew Linc would face even more pressure to trade me. He already felt like crap for having to test me in the first place, but if he hadn't played things by the book, the pressure would've been even worse.

Me: They're so fucking cute. A few show real promise, too.

Teddy: They're kicking your ass, aren't they?

A chuckle left my lips, and...damn, I needed that.

Me: They sure as hell have more energy than I do. Makes me feel old as fuck.

Teddy sent a GIF of an old man in a walker.

Teddy: Think they'll let you on the ice with one of these?

I sent him a middle finger emoji followed by a GIF of two grandpas in a wrestling match.

Me: Can still kick your ass any day of the week.

Teddy: In your dreams. I skate laps around you.

That much was true. He was faster than anyone I'd ever played with. Luca had the potential to be like that.

Me: There's a kid here who could beat you one day. He flies across the ice. It's like his skates barely make contact.

Teddy: Dude. I need to see that in action. Maybe I'll come down one week. I can help coach.

I grinned at my phone. It would be good to see him and make sure he really was healing and okay.

Me: The kids would lose their tiny minds. Let's do it.

Teddy: Done. I'll text you dates.

I was about to respond when the text screen disappeared, replaced by an incoming call. I couldn't help the groan that left my lips at seeing Angie's name on my phone. I'd been a fucking idiot to ever get involved with her. Not because she wasn't a good woman but because mixing business and relationships was always a bad idea. Now, we were left dancing around each other awkwardly.

I turned off my engine and sank back in my seat. Normally, I loved the feeling of the buttery soft leather; just another perk of the ridiculously expensive Bentley SUV. But today, none of it was comfortable. The leather was too hot, and the seat suddenly felt rigid.

As I stared down at the phone, I thought about letting it go to voicemail. God, I was a dick.

I hit accept on the screen. "Hey, Ang."

"Debating whether or not to answer?" There was a hint of amusement in her voice. That was a good sign.

"Possibly," I admitted.

She let out a sigh that sounded like it carried the weight of the world. "Cope, I'm not the bad guy here."

I stiffened, my grip on the phone tightening. "I know you're not."

At least she wasn't the one pulling the strings. But Angie also knew I hated the press game. Sure, I could turn on the charm, but that was just to keep them all at bay. Give them what they wanted and not the truth.

"You don't act like it," she muttered.

I was quiet for a long moment, unsure of what to say. Because there wasn't anything *to* say. And everything between us was simply awkward silence.

It made sense. Angie and I had never fit. There was an attraction there, sure, but there wasn't more. And at the end of the day, being with her had only made me feel emptier.

Angie finally spoke. "I emailed you a statement. Let me know if you're good with it or want anything changed. The gist is this: The Seattle Sparks regularly drug test their players. This ensures a healthy team year-round. Copeland Colson was one of the players recently tested. His results came back clear, just as they always have. And then all the team mumbo jumbo."

"That's fine, Angie. I don't need to read the rest. I trust you." I was suddenly so damn tired. It was the kind of exhaustion that lived in your bones and no amount of sleep could get out. I loved hockey but was so sick of the games that went on outside the rink.

Angie paused for a moment as if summoning her courage. "What's going on, Cope? You've been distant from everyone. You punch Marcus out of nowhere—"

"That prick deserved it," I snapped.

"I have no doubt he did, but Marcus has always been an asshole who likes to push people's buttons. You never punched him before."

Fuck.

Angie was right. I'd been playing with most of the guys on the team for years, including Marcus. Competitive youth hockey was a small world, and we'd all sort of grown up together. Even though it was surprising that the son of one of the most well-thought-of players to ever play the game was such a jerk, I'd gotten used to his barbs and prickish ways.

I'd never snapped. I'd simply dealt with it how I always had, by taking my frustrations out on the ice, the opposing team, and by working harder and longer than anyone. It made me a hell of a hockey player. But none of that seemed to be working now. And the nightmares had gotten worse, coming a few times a week instead of once a month.

I was cracking, and I didn't have a clue how to stop it.

"Cope." Angie's voice was soft now. "Talk to me."

Hell.

She was the last person I wanted to talk to. Because opening up to her could signal we were something we weren't. And that wasn't fair to her.

"I'm good, Ang. Pulling my shit together. You know this random tip for a drug test wasn't on me."

She was quiet again, and then there was the familiar anger. "Why did I think you'd tell me a damned thing? It's not like you ever let me in. No matter how hard I try."

The line went dead, and I dropped my head back against the seat. Just one more failure to add to the bunch. But it wasn't like Angie's accusations were wrong. I *hadn't* let her in. Not the tiniest bit.

Sure, I played the part: dinners and functions. The sex was good and frequent. But I never stayed the night. Couldn't. Because I had no idea what I'd do to someone if they happened to be in bed with me when I woke up from one of those nightmares—the ones where I was fighting to get out of that damn car and get to my dad and brother.

I squeezed my eyes shut, trying to fight off the oncoming headache. Alone was better. Necessary. And I'd make peace with that in time.

Pulling my keys from the engine, I slid out of my SUV and grabbed my bag from the back. Just as I was about to reach the doors to the rink, I heard a familiar voice.

"Coach Reaper! Coach Reaper!" Luca yelled.

I steeled myself, bracing for the sight of Sutton. The way her blond hair caught the sun or how her turquoise eyes flashed when she was giving me shit. Dinner on Saturday had been pure torture because all I'd wanted to do was look at her. But I'd known I couldn't. Wasn't about to give away my interest around my nosy family. That didn't mean I didn't steal glances—as many as I could get away with.

I turned, a jab of disappointment hitting me as I took in Luca and Thea walking toward me. That disappointment was quickly followed by concern. "Is Sutton okay?"

The words were out of my mouth before I could stop them, and I didn't give a damn what they betrayed. I just needed to know she was all right.

Thea nodded quickly, but shadows darkened her features. "She's fine. Just had a couple of appointments this morning. So, I got some quality time with my best guy here."

I tried to force one of those carefree smiles I was known for. "Shep know he'll never be number one in your heart?"

"He's been informed," Thea said with a soft laugh.

"Thee Thee will always love me best," Luca said, swinging their hands between them.

"That's because she's smart," I stage-whispered as I held open the door.

Luca giggled, dropping Thea's hand and running inside toward his friends. I held the door for Thea and quickly moved in behind her as she passed.

"What's really going on?"

Thea jolted, her gaze jerking to me. "What do you mean?"

"Something's wrong. You're worried about Sutton."

Thea muttered a curse. "She wouldn't want me telling you."

My gut tightened, a sick feeling sliding through me like an oil spill infecting ocean waters. "But you're going to tell me anyway because maybe I can help."

Thea shook her head, brown hair cascading around her face. "Not this time."

"Thea," I growled.

She looked at me for a long moment, her gaze sinking past the layers people normally stopped at. Finally, she sighed. "Sutton's landlord is being a real dick. He tried raising the rent for the bakery and the apartment above twice in one year."

"That's illegal," I ground out.

"Shep told Sutton as much, and when she pointed that out to the landlord, he told her she had to be out of the apartment in ten days."

Anger coursed through me. Who the hell did that to someone?

Especially a woman trying to raise a kid on her own. "Wait, they have to give thirty days' notice."

Thea shook her head again. "Sutton was renting week to week, so there aren't the same protections."

Week to week. Because she likely couldn't afford more. A slew of curses flew through my head, but fast on their heels was worry. The number of tenancy options you'd find mid-month were slim and likely the worst of the worst. I didn't want her and Luca dealing with that.

"What's the landlord's name?" I demanded.

Thea arched a brow. "There's nothing you can do to stop it. He's within his legal rights."

"Thea," I gritted out. "Tell me the bastard's name."

Her eyes flared in surprise. "Rick Anderson."

I was going to find that piece of shit and ruin him.

CHAPTER ELEVEN

Sutton

I F I THOUGHT I WAS EXHAUSTED BEFORE, IT HAD NOTHING ON
today. Every part of me felt as if it had taken a beating. And maybe
it had.

I'd gotten up at three this morning to make sure I got all the
baking in before I had to leave to look at apartments for Luca and me.
Thank God I had Walter and Thea to fill in and get Luca to hockey
practice. Having to ask Evelyn for one more favor likely would've
crushed me.

Rolling my shoulders back, I tried to alleviate some of the tension
there. No dice. Whether it was from all the baking or stress because
I was about to uproot Luca's life again, I wasn't sure. But it certainly
hadn't helped that every apartment I'd seen so far was an absolute
dump. Nothing I would feel comfortable moving Luca into.

I stared up at the small apartment building in an area of town
I wasn't all that familiar with. Frowning, I took in the chipped paint
on the siding, the grass growing through cracks in the pavement, and
the door propped open in a way that meant anyone could get in. My
stomach hollowed out. I didn't have a great feeling about this one

either, but it was my last stop before heading to pick up Luca from camp. Maybe it was better on the inside.

Turning off my engine, I climbed out of my small SUV. I shut the door and beeped the locks before glancing down at my phone. The building manager had texted, telling me to meet him in 4F, saying he'd be showing the unit all day.

Taking a deep, steadying breath, I started for the building. With the door propped open the way it was, I didn't have to buzz to be let up. Maybe that was because the apartment was being shown. I hoped so.

There was no elevator, even though the building was four floors. And, of course, this apartment was on the top. At least that meant no overhead noise.

As if the Universe had sensed that thought, shouts sounded from down the second-floor hallway, and they didn't sound all that friendly. My chest tightened as I forced myself to keep climbing. I paused when I reached the fourth floor, listening for more noise. I heard music and the sounds of TV shows, but nothing overtly loud.

Good. That was good. I said it over and over as I walked down the hallway to a door propped open with a crumbling cement block.

"Hello?" I called, peeking my head inside.

A guy in his mid-forties pushed up from a lawn chair, stubbing out a cigarette in an ashtray. The scent of cigarette smoke clogged the air, and I couldn't help wrinkling my nose.

"Sutton Holland?" he asked, his gaze roaming over me in a way that made my skin crawl.

I nodded, the motion jerky. "Ben?"

He grinned. "That's me. Manager extraordinaire." His gaze dipped to my cleavage and stayed there. "Ready for the tour?"

I cleared my throat, and Ben's gaze moved to my face, but he showed no shame in being caught ogling me. *Great.*

Squaring my shoulders, I stepped inside. "I think I'll just show myself around." It wasn't as if the space was large.

Ben stared at me for a moment longer. "Gotta do my job. Plus, I'm a gentleman."

I fought the urge to snort. I'd just bet he was.

Ben began talking about rent prices and utilities, but I already had that information from the management company. So, I moved around the space, trying to survey as much as possible. It did have decent light, but that only exposed everything wrong with it.

The linoleum flooring everywhere was peeling and torn in places, and the floorboards beneath didn't look in good shape. A small peek at the carpet in the smaller bedroom, which was closer to closet-sized, was stained with...I didn't know what. The bathtub had a brown stain around the drain rim that had me fighting not to heave. And when I stepped into the primary bedroom, the stench of smoke, sweat, and something I couldn't identify was almost too much for me to take.

"It's a steal," Ben said, stepping into the bedroom behind me. "Won't find another two-bedroom apartment in Sparrow Falls this cheap." His gaze roamed over me again. "But we might be able to work out an arrangement that gets it even cheaper."

My jaw went slack. Was he suggesting what I thought he was?

He crossed the space as I moved backward, and my heart hammered against my ribs. *Shit, shit, shit.* I fumbled for my purse. I had the mini pepper spray Thea had gotten me in there. If I could just—

"Ben." The single word cracked like a whip, and I nearly wept with relief at the familiar face in the doorway.

The manager whirled, redness creeping up his neck at the sight of Trace in his sheriff's uniform. "What d'you want?" Ben griped.

"First, I want to know why you were backing a woman into a corner," Trace growled, fury streaking across his expression.

An indignant look took root on Ben's face. "I was doing my job. Giving a tour. You gonna try to arrest me for that now, too?"

Trace's eyes narrowed on the manager. "You missed your meeting with your parole officer."

Ben's eyes shifted to the side. "I had to work. Can't lose my job, or I lose my parole."

"You've been giving tours for five days straight?" Trace challenged.

Ben's feet shifted this time. "Had to get the apartment ready."

Trace scoffed. "Sure, you did. Good thing we're here to escort you to your meeting now."

Panic streaked across Ben's face, and then he was hauling ass toward the door. He wasn't a small man, but he moved like a ballerina now, dodging Trace and booking it through the exterior door.

My jaw dropped, my attention moving back and forth between the door and Trace. "Don't you need to chase him?"

Trace just shook his head. "Got officers waiting on either end of the hall."

A shout sounded, and then some scuffling, before another voice called, "Tried to deck me, boss. Want me to arrest him for assaulting an officer?"

"Do it," Trace called through the open door. Then he turned back to me. "What the hell are you doing here, Sutton?"

I bit my lower lip, my cheeks flaming. "I need to, um, find a new apartment."

Trace's brows snapped together. "Why? You've got a great setup now."

I worried my lip between my teeth. "Rick is kicking me out. He wants to raise the rent and—"

"That goddamned prick," Trace swore.

"It's okay."

"It's not," Trace said, looking even more furious. "And you sure as hell aren't staying here. There are more shady people in this building than in all of Sparrow Falls. It's not safe. You can stay with Nora and Lolli—"

"No," I cut him off. "I'm not imposing on them. I'll just keep looking. I've got nine more days. I'll find something."

And if I didn't? What the hell would I do then?

I gripped my keys so tightly I wouldn't have been surprised if the metal teeth cut into my skin. The pain would've been welcome compared to the feeling of being completely helpless and out of options.

I struggled to keep my breathing even as I pulled open the door to the rink. I tried to paste on a happy smile, one Luca wouldn't question, as I reminded myself that I'd find a way. I might have to move one town over where things were a bit cheaper, but I could do that. I'd lose money on gas, but I'd win on rent.

Pain and disappointment burned brightly. One town over meant Luca would have to switch schools to one that wasn't as good. We wouldn't be as close to the second family we'd begun to build with the Colsons. And it meant losing our sense of home.

But we'd be safe. I reminded myself of that over and over as I walked deeper into the skating facility. We weren't back in Baltimore within Roman's reach, or worse, that of the people he owed money to. I could figure out the rest.

"Warrior?"

I turned, startled at the sound of Cope's voice.

He scowled the instant he saw my face. "What's wrong?"

I opened my mouth to lie but simply couldn't do it. I was too tired. My shoulders slumped, and it was a miracle I didn't just slide to the ground. "Not my best day."

Cope moved into my space, hesitating for a moment, his jaw working. "I'm going to hug you."

My eyes widened in surprise, both at the gesture and him demandingly asking for permission. "O-okay."

He didn't wait, just pulled me into his hold. The scent of mint and sage swirled around me. *Clean*, was all I could think. As if the scent could wash away the events of the day. But it was more, because as gently as Cope held me, I could feel his strength. And it was far too great a temptation.

I let myself fall. It was reckless, but I didn't think I could stand for a moment longer, not on my own two feet. Cope came right up to meet me, taking more of my weight.

The urge to let my tears fall was so strong. The pressure built, the burn intensifying. But I did everything I could to hold back. Instead, I simply *breathed*.

I let the mint and sage course through me, washing away the fear and panic, wiping clean the worry and obsession. The feeling of Cope's heart beating against my cheek grounded me in a way I hadn't felt in almost a decade. Steady, strong. I knew I shouldn't let his presence, his *touch*, do these things for me. Depending on someone in that way was the sort of risk I couldn't afford to take. But I couldn't rip myself away.

One more minute.

I'd give myself just a handful of seconds to restrengthen my walls. Then I'd be ready to face whatever battle lay ahead.

Cope's hand slipped under my hair, and his fingers dug into the muscles of my neck and shoulder.

I couldn't help the tiny sound that slipped from my lips. I told myself it wasn't a moan, but I knew I was a dirty liar.

Cope's voice came out in a low, rumbling growl. Like a bear who'd just awoken from hibernation. "Your shoulders are like cement."

"Thank you?" I mumbled in a hazy stupor.

"You need a massage. And maybe a muscle relaxer," he grumbled.

"What I'd really kill for is a bath. An hour of steaming-hot, no-one-bugging-me-with-a-single-problem bath time."

Cope's fingers stilled their ministrations. "You don't have a tub in your apartment?"

Just the word *apartment* had reality sweeping in again. I forced myself to push back, out of Cope's hold and away from his strong warmth. The act was pure torture, but I'd been through worse.

I shook my head. "No tub, but it's all good. I'll use a heating pad tonight."

I shifted from foot to foot, feeling eyes on us. A handful of moms looked on with curiosity, a couple with disdain, and a few with outright jealousy. A figure skater who didn't look old enough to drink glared in my direction. And Coach Kenner had hurt in his eyes.

Hell.

These were all reminders of why I needed to stay far away from Cope Colson.

He frowned down at me, clearly displeased by the distance I'd put between us, and maybe my lack of bathtub, as if both were a personal affront. "Heard your landlord's being a dick."

I stiffened. Had Trace texted him? Or had Thea let something slip? I guessed it didn't matter in the long run. Word would get around eventually. "He's not my favorite person at the moment."

"You can stay at my place." Cope said it so easily, as if it was no big thing to offer refuge to someone who was practically a stranger *and* her son.

"You don't know me," I blurted out.

He lifted one shoulder and then dropped it carelessly. "Know what I need to. You do everything you can to give that kid the best life imaginable. You work harder than anyone I know. And you cut to the heart of things. Don't waste time with bullshit and pretty lies. You're a good woman, Sutton, and you deserve someone to cut you a break."

My eyes were burning again. "Thank you," I whispered.

A grin played at Cope's beautiful mouth. "No big thing. My house is so big I probably wouldn't even see you."

I barked out a laugh. "Why am I not surprised?"

Cope was silent for a moment, waiting for my answer.

"I can't. It doesn't mean I don't appreciate it. I just—I can't." How could I explain the need to stand on my own two feet without telling him everything? How I'd nearly lost it all the last time I let someone *take care of me*? I needed to make it on my own.

Annoyance flickered in Cope's dark-blue eyes, but he quickly shoved it down. "All right. Then at least let me be Speedy's ride. There's no need for you to waste time shuttling him back and forth from the bakery when I drive right by there."

"You don't need to do that."

"I *want* to," he argued.

"You'd need a booster seat and—"

"I got one."

I blinked up at Cope, my jaw going slack. "You got a booster seat?" I said the words slowly as if trying to master a foreign language.

He nodded. "The Clek Oobr one. Those mommy blogs said it was the best. And I had one of the experts come and install it. Blogs said it was important to get it in right."

I gaped at the man opposite me. The hockey star known for his brutality on the ice had been reading mom blogs? I swallowed, trying to find the words I wanted. Instead, a ridiculous question popped out. "You've been driving around with a car seat in the back of your fancy SUV?"

I'd seen that vehicle a few times now and hadn't missed the Bentley emblem on the front. I didn't even want to know how much it cost. Or how quickly my kid could ruin the back seat with Goldfish crumbs and sticky fingers.

Cope grinned at me full-out. The effect was devastating. "A booster seat doesn't make it any less badass."

I arched a brow at him. "Might hurt your game, Hotshot."

Cope's eyes hooded, his gaze dropping to my mouth. "Warrior, with my skills, nothing hurts my game."

Heat flared low in my belly. That confidence that bordered on cockiness shouldn't have been a turn-on. But it was. I wanted to know what it would be like to let go and have Cope take control. To know what it was like to have that big body pinning me to the mattress or taking me from behind. Powering into me and—I slammed my eyes shut.

I couldn't think about that. Because it wasn't going to happen. And that meant Cope was free to find someone else to share those moments with.

The thought had a sick feeling sliding through me, way worse than when I'd smelled the stale air in that awful apartment. But I'd just have to deal with the disappointment. It was a feeling I was familiar with by now.

CHAPTER TWELVE

Sutton

I STARED AT THE MAN HUNCHED OVER THE WATER HEATER IN ONE of the back storage rooms. This one was filled to the brim with cleaning supplies. Various mops, rags, bottles, and buckets. Between that, the massive water heater, and the plumber's size, the space felt stifling.

I should've held on to that heat, pulled it into my bones to carry it with me for the freezing shower I'd likely be faced with when I finished my day. Just like I had for the past five days. The only saving grace was that Luca could take his showers after camp at the ice rink.

Five days.

The accusation hung in the air, proving both the fact that my landlord was a dick of epic proportions and that I was a total failure. It had taken me days to force Rick into getting a plumber out here. And I still hadn't found an apartment for Luca and me.

Pressure built behind my eyes. Everything was either in an unsafe area or building, or far too small. Right now, my best option was a one-room guesthouse with a kitchenette. I might not be able to cook a full meal, but at least Luca and I would be safe.

As if the thought had conjured it, a text flashed on my phone.

> **Unknown Number:** Come on, Blue Eyes. Help me out this once. I'd hate to have to go to the courts about custody of Luca.

Anger washed away the overwhelm in a flash. That was all Luca was to Roman—a pawn to be used in some disgusting game. He didn't see my boy for what he was: kind, hilarious, and the best thing that had ever happened to either of us.

My stomach churned as I stared at the message. It didn't matter that Roman would never get custody, he could still put Luca and me through hell trying. And given everything going on right now, I didn't exactly have the funds for a top-notch lawyer.

I tapped on the screen and quickly blocked the number. I was done changing mine, I'd run out of excuses for why I was doing it, and Roman always seemed to find them anyway.

Taking a deep breath, I reminded myself that he had no idea where we were. And even if he did, he was too caught up in the throes of his addiction to make his way across the country or file any paperwork for custody.

"Ms. Holland, when did the heat go out?" the plumber asked, cutting into my mental spiral.

I tried to shake myself out of it the best I could. "Call me Sutton, Bernie. And it was sometime on Monday. I noticed it as we were cleaning up for the day." It also meant we were forced to do dishes by hand, making sure to use bleach to sanitize. But more importantly, every time my patrons washed their hands, it was with ice-cold water.

He frowned at the large machine. "This should've been replaced years ago. You're gonna need a new one."

My head dropped, the pressure behind my eyes returning. This was Rick's responsibility, not mine. But what were the chances of me getting him to pay for one quickly? "How much do they usually cost?"

Bernie scrubbed a hand over his red beard. "Anywhere from a thousand to two."

My eyes fell closed. I told myself to keep breathing. Everything would be okay if I just kept up with the ins and outs. "Let me call Rick."

Bernie made a humming noise in the back of his throat, and I knew he thought I was screwed. I didn't disagree. So, I simply moved out into the hallway, noticing the strains of one of my favorite country artists coming over the speakers in the main café. I pulled out my phone and hit Rick's contact number.

He answered on the fourth ring. "What now?" he clipped.

I stiffened but kept breathing, struggling to keep my tone calm. "Bernie's here looking at the water heater."

"You're welcome, by the way. That's going to cost me two hundred bucks."

I bit the inside of my cheek. "He said the water heater needs to be replaced. That it should've been done years ago."

Silence reigned on the other end of the line, then came a slew of curses. "He's just trying to upcharge me. I'm not paying for a new unit. That's ridiculous. You probably just messed something up."

My back teeth ground together. "Rick, I have never touched that water heater. I have no reason to. It's your job to keep this building in working order, not mine. So—"

"Put Bernie on the phone," Rick snapped.

I gripped the device tighter but stepped back into the tiny storage room. "He'd like to talk to you," I told Bernie with a sympathetic look as I extended the phone to him.

Bernie groaned but took it. "Stop being such a dipshit and let me fix the nice lady's water heater."

My brows flew up. Apparently, Bernie was used to Rick's runaround. I could only hear one side of the conversation, but it was clear Bernie was giving as good as he got. At least I hadn't thrown him to the wolves unprepared.

"Yeah, yeah," Bernie said and then handed the phone back to me.

I took it, pressed the device to my ear, and stepped outside again. "Rick?"

He grunted across the line. "I'll get the water heater, but it's going to take me a few days. I don't have that kind of cash just lying around."

The hell he didn't. I'd driven by the massive house Rick lived in, had seen the car he drove. Everything about his existence was over the top. You didn't run two dozen rental properties without having an emergency fund for them.

"Please, Rick." Shame washed over me at having to beg. But it was the last day of camp for the week. Luca would need to shower this weekend, and I wouldn't put him under freezing water.

"That's the best I can do." Rick hung up without another word.

I gripped my cell so tightly it was a miracle the screen didn't crack. Slowly, I pulled it away from my face and stared down at it. What the hell was I going to do?

The pressure behind my eyes pulsed in angry beats. A burn lit with each flare, tears demanding to break free. But I couldn't let them. Because if I broke now, I might never get back up again.

The back door swung open, sending light and noise cascading into the hallway.

"Mom!" Luca yelled. "You won't believe it! We had our first scrimmage, and I scored! It was the awesomest!"

I forced a smile to my face but felt my cheeks twitch with the effort. "That's amazing, baby. I can't wait to hear every detail."

Cope moved in behind him, a grin tugging at his lips. "I definitely think we've earned some cupcakes. What's the special today?"

Cope had driven Luca to and from camp every single day since he offered, but the only payment he'd agreed to take was cupcakes. And he had a thing for my more creative ones.

"How do you feel about orange Creamsicle?" There was a slight tremor to my voice I hoped like hell Cope couldn't hear.

His gaze narrowed, scanning my face. As he did, I saw a flutter in his jaw muscle. "Speedy, why don't you go tell Walter about your goal? I'll come meet you for cupcakes and milk in just a second."

I opened my mouth to argue. Luca was my buffer, my safety blanket. I knew Cope wouldn't push to know what had happened with Luca present. But my kid was off like a rocket at the promise of telling someone else about his day's triumphs.

Cope moved closer to me, making the hallway feel as small as the storage closet. "What happened, Warrior?"

The nickname was a knife to the heart, slicing through with vicious pain. The pressure behind my eyes threatened to break me wide open. "I'm not a warrior. Not even close. I'm barely holding it together."

Cope moved in even closer, his hand slipping under my hair and kneading my neck. "Talk to me."

He was the last person I should've been sharing any of this with. The last person I needed to lay my burdens on. But I found everything tumbling out of my mouth: the string of bad apartments, the run-in with Trace, him telling me a building wasn't safe, Rick's assholery...

The only thing I left out was Roman. Because that piece carried too much shame.

"And then the water heater broke on Monday. Bernie said we need a new one, but Rick is dragging his feet."

Cope's hand flexed around the back of my neck, and his expression went thunderous. The urge to take a giant step back was strong. This was the kind of fury I knew Cope played with, the rage his opponents faced.

"Are you telling me you've been taking ice-fucking-cold showers all week?" he snarled.

I swallowed hard. "Luca can shower at the rink, so it's just me. It's not that bad. I—"

"Get your shit. Now. Luca's, too," Cope growled.

My jaw went slack. "Excuse me?"

Cope's eyes narrowed. "You're not staying in a place with no warm water. Not for one minute more. So, get your stuff. You're moving in with me."

CHAPTER THIRTEEN

Cope

FURY PULSED THROUGH ME LIKE WAVES OF FIRE. IT TOOK
everything in me to keep my hold on Sutton gentle and not haul
her over my shoulder to get her and Luca into my SUV and safely
home. But it was more than anger at what that asshole, Rick, was
putting her through.

It was that she was out of options. Sutton planned to move her
and Luca into a tiny one-room guesthouse because it was the only
safe option she thought she had. But it wasn't.

When I had Shep design my house, he'd rolled his eyes at how
over the top it was. But the truth was, I didn't spend my money on
much. I had a ridiculous vehicle, sure, but I invested in my homes—
my penthouse in Seattle and my place here in Sparrow Falls.

Here, I got wide-open spaces. A place to breathe. And I wanted
the house to have that same comfort. That meant a gym and a screening room. Massive living, dining, and cooking spaces. A library and
an office. Ten bedrooms, thirteen baths, a pool, and a hot tub.

Plus, the space I'd created for Arden, giving her the job of property manager. She had a small guesthouse and a large workshop big

enough to house her monster sculptures and other over-the-top art pieces. And finally, a small barn and paddock to care for her two horses. It all came together to create a place where she hopefully felt safe.

I wanted to give that to Sutton and Luca, too. I just didn't want to look too closely at the *why* of it all.

Sutton gaped at me, those beautiful turquoise eyes widening with shock. "Cope, I can't—"

"You can, and you are. I get that you're used to going things alone. But you've got people around you who care. Let us help."

She worried her bottom lip. "I can sign the lease for that guest-house tomorrow and—"

"Warrior," I growled. "Five hundred square feet for two people isn't enough space. I've got a whole wing that you and Luca can have to yourselves. There's tons of property for Luca to explore. A pool and a pond. He'll love it."

Sutton tugged harder on that lip, and I sensed her wavering.

"If you don't feel comfortable staying with me, then stay with Mom and Lolli. You know they'd love to have you."

Her eyes glistened. "Why are you all so nice?"

Those unshed tears broke something in me, and I pulled Sutton against my chest. "You deserve more than nice, Warrior."

She shuddered against me. "You don't know that."

My hands stilled on the back of her neck, and then I picked up my kneading again. "I may not know what you've been through, but I know it's something." Every instinct I had told me that. And the idea of hardship hurting her, or worse, that pain coming at the hands of a human being, slayed me. "You deserve a break. Let me help you."

Sutton's hands fisted in my tee as if she were holding on for dear life. "I've worked so hard to stand on my own two feet. I can't give that up."

"You're not." My fingers sifted through her silky blond strands. "Just because you let someone give you a place to rest for a while doesn't mean you aren't standing on your own two feet."

Sutton's head tipped back, those hypnotic eyes clashing with mine. She was searching, looking for something I couldn't identify. I just hoped like hell she found it.

Her throat worked as she swallowed. "You're sure? It wouldn't be for long. Just until I can save a little more and—"

"Stay for as long as you want. My house is empty most of the year anyway. It'd be nice if it got some use." If it got some life injected back into it. Just admitting that out loud was a reminder of how empty I'd let my existence become. Hockey, training, appearances. Rinse and repeat. There wasn't fun anymore. There wasn't even connection beyond the ridiculous siblings' text thread.

Something shifted in my chest, the uncomfortable grind of bone against bone because it felt like nothing else was filling the cavity. And for the first time in a long while, I wanted there to be.

Sutton stared at me for a long moment. "I have to get up before the sun, and Luca needs someone to watch him—"

"Warrior," I cut her off, giving her neck a squeeze. "I can wake him up and get us both breakfast. I do it for myself every morning. And I'm already up early to get in a workout before camp."

She let out a long breath. "He's cute, but he's a lot," Sutton warned. "He'll talk your head off and try to convince you all he needs to exist is sugar for breakfast, lunch, and dinner."

I chuckled at that. "Little man after my own heart. But I'll remind him we need protein to build those hockey muscles."

Sutton's perfect lips twitched, and I wanted to trace the pillowy softness with my tongue, to know what they felt like wrapped around my—*nope*. Not going there.

"I pay some sort of rent," Sutton began.

"Hell, no."

"Cope—"

"No. You wanna pay me? You let me be your taste tester for whatever cupcakes you're working on next."

A flicker of a smile rose to Sutton's lips. "That's Luca's job, and he's pretty partial to it."

"Two sets of taste buds are better than one," I countered.

She was quiet for one beat, then two. "Okay."

The sensation of victory swept through me, better than when we'd made it to the Cup two years ago, and I couldn't help the absolutely ridiculous grin that spread across my face. "Really?"

Sutton lifted one shoulder and then dropped it. "Just remember you asked for this when Luca's trying to wake you up at five in the morning to practice sports puck moves."

I barked out a laugh. "Sports puck?"

She grinned up at me, and the action hit me right in the solar plexus, stealing the air from my lungs.

"I'm up on all the lingo. Clearly."

I shook my head. "Come on. Let's get you two packed."

Flipping on my blinker, I turned onto Cascade Avenue. I glanced in my rearview mirror to make sure Sutton and Luca were behind me. She had the address plugged into her navigation system, but I didn't want her to feel like she was making any part of this journey alone.

Once we were on the main drag out of town, I hit a button on the steering wheel. "Call Anson."

It wasn't a move I made often. I had his number in my phone, but it certainly wasn't on my Favorites list. The truth was, I'd been skeptical of my sister's boyfriend at first. But the ex-profiler had been there for her in the worst moments of her life, so I was slowly coming around.

"Cope," Anson greeted. The broody bastard might've shown more signs of life lately, but it still didn't make him warm and fuzzy.

There was no point in beating around the bush, so I just cut to the heart of it. "Need a favor."

"What kind of favor?"

Anson was right to be suspicious. I could've been asking him to dissolve a body in lye for all he knew. My grip on the wheel tight-ened. "You have a friend who's a hacker, right? Someone who can dig up dirt on people?"

His friend had been instrumental in bringing Thea's ex down and getting justice for countless women the guy had tormented.

"I don't have friends," Anson muttered.

I choked on a laugh. "Whatever makes you feel better, dude. An associate?"

He was silent for a moment. "What do you need?"

That familiar rage pushed at the box I'd tried to force it back into. "As much dirt on Rick Anderson as you can find. Something that will make him sell all his properties to me—and on the cheap because that fucker deserves to lose some money."

The sounds of a construction site faded, and I knew Anson had walked away. "Who is he, and what did he do?"

"Does it matter?"

"If you want Dex's help, it does. He's a crusader these days. Only gets motivated for a cause he thinks is just."

My jaw worked back and forth. "He's a local asshole who's mess-ing with Sutton. Trying to raise her rent over and over. When she pushed back about her legal rights, he kicked her and Luca out of the apartment above the bakery. She can't afford somewhere decent to stay right now."

A low growl sounded across the line. "You're not serious."

"I am." But I wished like hell I wasn't.

"Her cupcakes are fuckin' heaven," Anson muttered.

I choked back a laugh. Of course, Sutton's cupcakes were the thing to win the cantankerous prick over. "That mean you're helping?"

"I'll get Dex on it ASAP." Anson paused. "Where is she going to stay for now?"

I shifted in my seat. "Takin' her and Luca to my place."

There was a beat of silence. "You like her."

I could hear the smile in Anson's words, which only pissed me off. "That's what you got from all of that?"

"Pretty much."

"Fuck off and help me fix this."

"Done," Anson clipped and hung up before I could even say thank you. Typical.

I pulled up to the massive gate Shep had installed at the mouth of my property. It might've seemed like overkill, but I got the occasional overzealous fan trying to sneak in. And I liked the extra protection—for Arden more than me.

I waited until Sutton's small, navy SUV pulled up behind me. I'd already given her the code to the gate, but it would be easier if she could just pull in after me. I hit the opener on my visor and wished I could see the property through her eyes.

In my mind, it was the perfect patch of land. Removed from town and with epic views of the Monarch Mountains and Castle Rock. The quiet stillness out here helped put my restless mind at ease. I hoped she felt the same.

The moment the gate was open, I stepped on the gas, and Sutton followed right behind me. You couldn't see the majestic views yet. The only thing in front of us was a winding lane flanked by aspen trees. It wound through the landscape for several minutes, leading us across a bridge over a creek until it finally opened to the vast spaces.

I took a moment to really take it in. The golden stone faces of Castle Rock, and the staggering peaks of the Monarch Mountains that were still capped with snow. It was the perfect reminder of how small we were compared to the rest of the world.

The house itself stood as a complement to the surrounding scenery. A blend of deep reddish wood, stone, and glass, it was massive for sure, but when the backdrop was endless nature, it didn't look overly ostentatious.

I rounded the curved driveway and came to a stop by the front doors. I'd get Sutton a remote for the garage so she could bring her SUV in out of the elements, but for now, here was good. I cut my engine and slid out of the vehicle, only to find Luca already jumping out of Sutton's.

"Coach Reaper! This is your house?" he called.

The awe in his voice was clear, and it sent a feeling of pride coursing through me. "It is, Speedy."

"This is freaking AWESOME!" Luca jumped and then proceeded to do some sort of dance that had very little rhythm involved but was fucking adorable.

Sutton shut the door to her SUV, her gaze moving from the house to me as she swallowed. "It's certainly beautiful. And big."

"Is big bad?" I asked her, my brow furrowing.

"Depends," she said, dropping her voice.

"On what?"

Those turquoise eyes flashed. "If you can remember what's most important."

CHAPTER FOURTEEN

Sutton

SHOULDN'T HAVE LET THE LITTLE TRUTH SLIP FREE. BECAUSE AS Cope studied me, I knew he was putting together too many pieces. Ones that created a picture I didn't want him to see.

I'd learned the lessons at far too high a cost. It wasn't the things you surrounded yourself with that were important; it was the people. And if you got too caught up in chasing the next high, whatever the form, you could lose what mattered most.

As if reading that, Cope moved into my space, not crowding me but creating intimacy. "This house is family."

My brows rose, questioning how that could be.

"Ten bedrooms. One for each of my siblings, Mom, and Lolli. Plus, a loft with bunks for Keely. So, if we all want to stay here on Christmas Eve, we can."

My heart lurched at that. Just enough for the whole Colson crew to fit. Because they were important to him.

"The design itself was Shep's first big custom project for Colson Construction. It put him on the map in the architectural space."

I swallowed hard. "You gave him his big break." And I knew he'd gone on to build a massively successful business.

Cope shrugged. "As you can see, it wasn't exactly a sacrifice."

One corner of my mouth kicked up as I took in the house with new eyes. "No, it wasn't. It's beautiful."

Cope inclined his head to the left. "Arden lives down that road. Has a guesthouse and workshop for her art. We put in a barn so she could keep her horses, and Keely can come ride with her."

A burn lit in my chest. So much thought for everyone else. "What about you? What did you put in for you?"

He grinned. "Come on. I'll show you." He climbed the front steps as Luca danced around us. Plugging a code into the lock on the door, he twisted the handle and stepped inside.

"Holy crackers, Mom! This is like a mansion. Coach Reaper, is this a mansion?"

I couldn't even answer Luca because I was struck dumb by the view. The entire back of the house was windows. All three sides were practically pure glass. But the picture they created tugged me forward as if my feet had a mind of their own.

I heard Luca's and Cope's voices in the background but kept moving until I reached the captivating view. I felt Cope at my side more than I saw him. His heat, the strength that seemed to vibrate off him in waves.

"It's one-way glass. We can see out, but no one can see in," Cope explained as he reached for the handle of a slider. "But this is what I did for me."

He slid the door open with ease, and I saw it was one where you could open the whole wall. But I was already stepping out, unable to resist. The back deck was an outdoor lover's dream. The expansive patio was tiered into different sections. On the top tier to the left was a large outdoor dining space, complete with an overhead covering to protect from the sun. On the right was an outdoor sectional with a firepit in the center that would be perfect for chilly mountain nights. The second tier had countless benches and planters, creating a maze of places to sit. And finally, a stunning pool seemed to disappear into the pond beyond it, like you were floating on water. Cope had created the perfect harbor.

"You have a *pool*?" Luca shrieked.

There was a flash of panic in Cope's expression. "Does he know how to swim?"

"Like a fish," I said, amusement lacing my tone. "We'll be lucky if we ever get him out of the water."

Relief swept through Cope. "A fish, I can handle."

"Cope," I whispered. "This is magical."

He grinned down at me. "My favorite part of the whole house."

"I can see why. You could live out here."

"I do. Well, other than the hours I log in the gym."

I arched a brow.

He shrugged. "Professional hockey player. Makes sense for me to have somewhere I can stay in shape. It's in the basement. There's a screening room down there, too. Shep's a sucker for movies, so I let him have his way there."

"Of course, there's a screening room," I muttered.

Cope chuckled. "Can I show you your rooms?"

"Yes! I wanna see my room!" Luca yelled, overhearing us.

It was hard to pull myself away from the beauty, the quiet peace. I could hear the creek as it babbled and fed the pond. I could've sat out here for hours, taking in every detail, but I forced my feet to follow my son and Cope inside.

Cope led us up a giant staircase. I immediately began decorating it for Christmas in my mind. Acres of pine garland punctuated with antique red bows. It would be a sight to see.

"My room's right at the end of that hall," Cope said, pointing to the left.

My cheeks flamed, thinking of running into Cope in my pajamas while getting a glass of water in the middle of the night.

"What about me?" Luca demanded, bouncing on the balls of his feet.

"Manners, Luca," I warned.

He sent me an exasperated look. "What about me, please?"

One corner of Cope's mouth kicked up. "This way."

I dropped my voice. "He already thinks he's the coolest kid known to man because you're his chauffeur. This is going to send him over the edge."

"I live to serve," Cope said, a mischievous smile playing on his lips as he led us down the opposite hall and into an absolutely stunning room. The walls were a calming gray except for an accent wall that made you feel like you were living in a breathtaking black-and-white photo. It was a blurred forestscape with tall trees and a foggy, atmospheric feel.

"This is *sick*!" Luca hollered, full-on jumping now.

"I thought you might like this one," Cope said with a grin. "You've got your own bathroom through there. And this TV has a game console. Kye's partial to gaming, so I had to set him up."

Of course, he had.

Cope winced. "We should make sure those games are age appropriate."

"I can tackle that," I assured him.

Luca made a running leap onto the bed. "I'm never leaving this spot."

Cope grinned at me, one of those devastating, truly happy smiles. I was starting to see that his most joyful moments were when he made someone else happy. That knowledge made me want to give that right back to him.

Cope turned to me, that grin still playing at his lips and making my insides do some sort of acrobatics move. "What about you, Warrior? Ready to see your room?"

More spiraling spins and dizzying flips. No, I wasn't ready. Because as amazing as all this was, it wasn't something I could get used to. Luca either. "Sure," I said, forcing my smile brighter. "Luca, you want to come?"

"Naw, I wanna chill in my room," he said, tucking his hands behind his head.

God, was he seven or seventeen? My rib cage tightened, making it harder to take a full breath. These moments with him would be so fleeting. Before long, he wouldn't want cupcake movie night with me; he'd opt to go out with his friends instead. Then he'd be driving, at college, and gone out into the world.

Cope's arm pressed against mine as he ducked his head. "Hey, you okay?"

I swallowed, trying to clear the ball of emotions gathering in my throat. "Sometimes I blink, and he's had a growth spurt."

Cope wrapped an arm around my shoulders. "Pretty sure he's still your little boy."

"For today, maybe," I mumbled.

"Come on, Mama. Let's show you your spot." He gently guided me out of Luca's room and across the hall.

I didn't try to escape the gentle hold he had on me. I should've, but I couldn't find the strength. Cope's warmth was like the world's most comfortable blanket. I wanted to pull it around my shoulders and hold it close.

Cope pushed open the door, his hand sliding to my lower back as he urged me inside. My feet felt like lead. Some part of me didn't want to see what beauty lay beyond the threshold.

As I stepped inside, I sucked in a breath. I'd been right. It was beautiful. Too beautiful. The walls were the palest turquoise—the kind of color that made you wonder if it was there at all. But at the same time, the tone had a sense of calm washing over me.

There was a large king bed against the wall closest to the hallway, one that looked like an overstuffed cloud with its white duvet and endless array of pillows. But it was the view from the bed that had me gobsmacked.

It was the same breathtaking picture as downstairs, but because we were on the second floor, it felt as though we were hovering. Floating on a sea of water, forest, and mountains.

My eyes burned, and my nose stung. I'd never stayed in a room this nice before. No place that felt this *me*.

"What do you think?" Cope asked, his voice barely above a rough whisper.

"It's beautiful," I told him honestly.

"The color reminds me of your eyes. It felt like it was meant to be."

My gaze jerked to him. "My eyes?"

"Turquoise. Like the Caribbean Sea. Could find a world of peace in those eyes."

It wasn't just my eyes burning now. It was everything. People had remarked on my eyes for most of my life. Roman had certainly been taken in by them. But had anyone really taken the time to see beyond the standard blue? *Blue Eyes.* Just thinking the nickname had pain coursing through me.

But not Cope. He saw tone and quality. And more than that, he saw feeling.

"Come on," Cope said, that smile back on the corners of his mouth. "You haven't seen the best part."

He strode toward an open door I knew had to lead to a bathroom. But I wasn't sure how much more beauty—more *seeing*—I could take. Still, I followed. And when I stepped into the en suite, I couldn't help my audible gasp.

The antique tub sat in front of another massive window, looking out on that same incredible view. You could soak in the warmth of the water and the peace of the view all at the same time. "Cope…"

"Not too shabby. There's a shower, too." He gestured to the large, marble-tiled space in the far corner. "Should be stocked as far as toiletries go, but let me know if you're missing anything, and I'll have my housekeeper grab it."

I was still gaping at the tub, unable to get any other words out.

Cope's hand slipped beneath my hair, kneading my neck. "Set this water as hot as it will go and have a nice long soak. I'll bring your bags up and have dinner ready when you're done."

I goggled up at him. I was struggling to process so much. The fact that, for the first time in years, someone was taking care of me was at the top of that list. But I focused on a tiny detail. "You cook?"

One corner of Cope's mouth kicked up. "I'm full of surprises, Warrior."

CHAPTER FIFTEEN

Sutton

MY TOES PEEKED OUT OF THE BUBBLES, THE DUSKY MAUVE POLISH I'd painted on them the other day standing out against the white ceramic. I could just make out the soft strains of Luca playing a video game across the hall, but it was the kind of noise that faded into a meditative background, assuring me that my son was safe and happy.

I, on the other hand, was a prune. A happy one. I'd added hot water to the bath twice, soaking up every ounce of heat. I wasn't sure what the bubble bath was made of since the label was in French, but it smelled heavenly.

I knew I shouldn't get used to any of this, but that didn't mean I would stop myself from enjoying it. I let my eyes fall closed for a moment, taking it all in. Maybe if I cemented the memory, it would be enough to sustain me when we had to leave.

After a few more moments of warmth, I forced myself to pull the plug. It would be rude to stay in the bath all night, and I could see the sun sinking lower into the horizon, painting Cope's property in a cascade of pinky reds. An artist could paint this landscape a hundred times over and still not capture it all.

Maybe Arden did, I thought as I stood from the bath and grabbed a fluffy white towel from a perfectly folded stack. I knew Arden often worked with metal as her medium, but I had to imagine the landscape inspired her regardless.

Quickly drying off, I wrapped the towel around my body and poked my head into the bedroom. The door was closed now, and my three duffel bags sat on the bench at the end of the massive bed. I pulled out a pair of sweats and a matching top covered in abstract bumblebees. I probably should've gone for something more appropriate—jeans and a T-shirt, maybe—but after the day's events, I couldn't force myself into hard pants.

I pulled on the soft, fleecy cotton and refixed the bun on top of my head. Grabbing my slippers from another bag, I slid my feet into the worn shoes and headed across the hall.

Luca's fingers flew over a controller, his eyes locked on the screen.

"I'm heading downstairs. Cope is making us dinner," I told him.

"Mm-hmm," he said with a nod.

"Think you could come with me so you don't starve to death by video game addiction?" I pressed.

The corners of his mouth pulled up into a grin. "Just let me finish this level, and I'll pause it."

"Promise?"

"Swear," Luca vowed.

His swear meant he'd try for three more levels but would eventually make it downstairs. I'd take it.

"All right. Yell if you get lost. This place is huge."

"This place is *awesome,*" Luca corrected.

A weight settled in my belly. I wanted to be the one to give my kid all these amazing things. A house he could be proud of. The room of his dreams. Space to run and play.

One day.

One day, I'd give us all that and more. But for now, I'd have to settle for one foot in front of the other. I made my way down the hallway to the stairs, taking in every detail as I descended them. The house was a mix of old and new. Rustic, aged beams and modern metals. Black-and-white photos mixed with textured paintings that brought in pops of color. But everything about it was beautiful.

Strains of soft, bluesy music wafted toward me, along with the scent of garlic. My stomach rumbled as I followed the call of both. When I reached the kitchen, I stopped dead.

It should've been the gourmet cooking space that had me frozen to the spot, but it wasn't. It was the man dominating it. He stood at the stove, focused on a saucepan. His hair looked as if it was still damp from a shower, making the strands appear a few shades darker than their normal light brown.

Cope had changed into gray sweats that hung low on his hips and a worn T-shirt with some sports team emblem. The cotton looked the kind of soft that only came from washing it too many times to count. As the music ebbed and flowed in the background, Cope tapped a foot in time. A bare foot.

There was something about that, his toes peeking out from beneath baggy sweats. The movement. It felt like a sight I didn't have any right to see.

I forced my gaze up to Cope's face as if that would help. Not a chance when his devastating beauty was a sucker punch that stole all the air from my lungs. My eyes couldn't help but narrow in on the scar bisecting his lip—one so similar to mine.

Clearing my throat, I forced myself past the threshold. "When you said you were full of surprises, you weren't kidding."

Cope didn't look up right away. He stirred whatever was in the pan before taking it off the heat. "I don't mess around when eating's involved." Once he'd set the pan on a cool burner, he turned, leaning a hip against the counter. The scar deepened as one corner of his mouth kicked up. "I like the pj's."

My cheeks heated, but I lifted my chin. "They are very serious sweats, I'll have you know."

"Fucking cute," he muttered.

The words landed somewhere deep in my chest, making a home there. "I like bees."

He arched a brow at that. "The kind that sting you?"

"The kind that make honey. They only sting when you go on the offensive. If you let them be, they'll give you the sweetest gifts."

Cope stared at me for a long moment as if reading too much truth beneath my words.

"Plus, I couldn't bear to put on real clothes after that bath," I added, trying to shift his knowing stare.

It worked, and Cope's devastating smile stretched across his face again. "How was it?"

I moved in closer, playing with fire. "Heaven. But you should know that, given it took me two hours to get down here."

Cope chuckled, the sound teasing my skin and causing a pleasant shiver. "How's Luca?" he asked.

God, I loved that, too—his care when it came to my kid. I never would've thought standing in a kitchen would be reckless, but with Cope, it was danger personified.

"He's currently playing some video game with dragons and archers, at least from what I could tell."

"One of Kye's favorites," Cope said with a smirk. "Those two probably have a similar maturity level."

A laugh bubbled out of me. "I'm gonna tell him you said that."

"He'll know it's the cold, hard truth," Cope shot back.

We were both quiet for a moment, the music swirling around us.

"So, what smells so amazing?" I asked, needing to cut the tension in the air and have something other than Cope to focus on.

"Pasta pomodoro. I wasn't sure if there were things you and Luca don't eat, so I thought this was safest. I've got a salad and some garlic bread ready to go, too."

I inhaled the scents of tomatoes and garlic and couldn't help the sigh that left my lips. "Italian is my favorite."

When my eyes opened, it was to find Cope's blue gaze locked on me. "Happy coincidence. Because it's my favorite cuisine to cook."

My heart picked up its pace, skipping, jumping, and diving into a roll. "When did this love of cooking arise?"

Something passed over his dark-blue depths, some shadowy emotion I couldn't quite pin down. Cope shifted in place, turning back to the stove as if to check something. "After my dad died, it felt like the one thing I could do to help. I discovered I had a knack for it."

An ache rooted itself in my chest. I didn't know what it meant to lose a parent. Not really. My father had never been in my life, and my mom dropped me on my grandmother's doorstep when I was three. It took me a while to realize what a kindness that had been.

My mom wasn't cut out for consistent care and nurturing. She was too busy chasing one adventure after another. But my grandmother had given me more love than I could've ever hoped for. And I knew what losing her had cost me.

I searched Cope's face, wanting to know more but not wanting to cause him pain. "Car accident, right?"

Cope's knuckles bleached white as he gripped the pan's handle. "Yeah," he rasped.

It had been the wrong thing to ask, and guilt swept through me fast and hard. "What's your favorite dish to make?" I asked, trying to change the subject as quickly as possible.

His grip loosened. "I make a mean pork ragu over polenta."

My eyes flared at that knowledge. "You don't mess around."

One corner of Cope's mouth kicked up. "I don't have time to do it all that much. That's what makes the off-season nice."

"I volunteer as taste-test tribute because I'm hopeless when it comes to cooking."

Cope stared at me for a long moment. "Sutton, your baked goods are some of the best things I've ever tasted."

"I'm good at *baking*," I corrected him. "That is like night and day from cooking. Figuring out the right measurements and flavors in baking just makes sense to me. Cooking? I'm all thumbs."

Cope shifted closer—so close we were almost touching. Close enough that I could just catch flickers of mint and sage. "Sounds like we make a pretty good team," he rasped. "Dinner and dessert. Salty and sweet."

Oh, hell.

Suddenly, I couldn't stop the images that rose of Cope licking chocolate frosting off the column of my neck and then dipping lower. His heat swirled around me as his eyes dropped to my mouth. My lips parted, and my breath hitched.

"Mom! I'm *starving*!" Luca yelled from the staircase.

I startled, moving backward and pressing a hand to my chest over my hammering heart as if that could get my heart rate to slow. But Cope didn't look fazed in the slightest; he simply glanced over my shoulder and called, "Come and get it, Speedy."

Shit. Shit. Shit.

My first night here, and I'd already almost kissed Cope in his damn kitchen. Who knew where that would've ended? I needed to get a grip on my hormones and find some self-control. But as Luca came running into the kitchen, and Cope sent him the most devastating smile—one that had my ovaries crying out to make mini Copes here and now—I knew one thing.

I was so totally screwed.

CHAPTER SIXTEEN

Cope

LUCA SAT BLEARY-EYED AT THE BOOTH IN THE CORNER OF THE kitchen. Over the past almost two weeks, I'd learned that he was not a morning person. It was the one time of day when he was quiet. But he was also hilariously adorable, with his hair all askew as I made us breakfast.

My phone dinged on the counter, and I reached for it as I stirred the ham and veggie scramble. I slid my thumb across the screen, and my sibling group chat opened.

Kye has changed the group name to Only Fams.

Kye: How's diaper duty treating you, Copey?

I glared down at my phone. I knew he was just giving me shit, especially when he'd been the one to help Trace out the most with Keely during his divorce. He'd played chauffeur, babysitter, and bedtime story reader, complete with all the voices.

Me: Need I remind you of this gem?

I quickly scrolled through my favorites album on my phone until I found the picture I wanted of Kye. He was sitting at a tiny table in Keely's room, having a tea party. His massive size, complete with tattoos covering his arms and snaking up his neck, would've been enough for a chuckle, but the fact that he was wearing a pink tutu, a tiara, and a feather boa really took it over the top.

Rhodes: 😂 🖼️ I forgot about this photo. We need to get it framed.

Kye: You told me you deleted this, you asshole.

Me: I lied.

I never would've gotten rid of blackmail material as good as this.

Fallon: Don't you dare ever erase this! Arden, can you make us an oil painting version? I'm going to hang it in Kye's tattoo studio.

Fallon tagged Arden's name to force an alert to her phone. She and Trace were the most silent on these chains. Trace popped in occasionally, attempting to keep us in line, but Arden wasn't exactly one for technology.

Kye: Arden, don't you dare.

Arden: Do you assholes know what time it is?

Fallon: Sorry, A. Didn't realize.

Shep: Some of us work normal hours, you vampire.

Arden sent a doodle of a fanged face, and I couldn't help but chuckle. Arden was a night owl who got so caught up in her work she could forget to eat, sleep, or step outside for some fresh air.

Trace: How are Sutton and Luca doing?

A bite of jealousy grabbed hold at my brother asking about them. I shoved it down as I slid the scramble onto two plates that already held wheat toast. Sutton and Luca deserved all the people in their corner they could get.

Me: Good. Speedy and I are just about to have breakfast and hit the ice. Sutton's already at the bakery.

She was used to those early morning hours, but I hated the idea of her driving the winding country roads in the dark. Some deranged part of me wanted to hire her a driver. Or, even better, a night nanny to stay with Luca while *I* drove Sutton to the bakery.

Rhodes: I'm so glad she's staying with you. Spoil them a little, would you? They deserve it.

Shep: Don't think that'll be an issue. A little birdie told me Cope already got a trampoline for the backyard and all the pastry accessories someone would need to turn his kitchen into a bakery.

My back teeth ground together as my fingers flew across the screen.

Me: Tell Thea she's a traitor.

I could see my siblings laughing at me in my mind. Flipping the chat to *Do Not Disturb*, I shoved my phone into my pocket and carried the plates to the table. "Heading out of zombie land yet?" I asked.

Luca's gaze lifted from his place mat, and he muttered something I couldn't quite understand. But the second I set the plate down, he started shoveling bites into his mouth.

"Easy there, killer. Your mom is gonna be really peeved if you choke on my watch."

Luca grinned, showing bites of a half-eaten scramble. "It's so good. Don't tell her, but you're a way better cook."

I laughed. "Your secret is safe with me."

The truth was, I loved cooking for Luca and Sutton. I got the occasional chance to do it for my family, but most of the time I cooked just for me. And something about that felt a bit empty.

The sound of my doorbell cut through the early morning silence, and Luca's head popped up. "Who's here? It's barely morning."

I chuckled as I pushed to my feet. "It's a surprise."

Luca's eyes lit. "Like a puppy?"

I froze. "You want a puppy?"

"I've been asking Mom *forever*, but in our last apartment, we weren't allowed." He frowned. "Probably our next one we won't be allowed either. But you could get one. Look at all the places he would have to play."

Fuck. This kid deserved a dog. A pet was a rite of passage. I hated the idea that Luca wouldn't get one.

But I shoved those thoughts down for now. "No dogs today, but you might like this surprise better."

Luca followed me out of the kitchen and toward the entryway. I punched in the alarm code and flipped the lock, opening the front door.

Teddy's lean form filled the doorway as he grinned at me. "Damn good to see you, brother."

He hauled me into a back-slapping hug, and I could already tell he was moving better than when I'd seen him last. Relief swept through me at that. He was okay. And that meant he'd be back on the competitive ice where he belonged in no time.

Teddy released me and turned to the tiny human staring up at him slack-jawed. "You must be Luca. I've heard you're amazing on the ice."

Luca's mouth closed, then opened, then closed again. "You're Teddy Jackson. The Lightning. Am I dreaming right now?" He rubbed at his eyes as if to check.

Teddy chuckled, giving me a slap to the stomach. "Why can't *you* give me this kind of greeting?"

I grinned at Luca. "Good surprise?"

"The best!" He whirled to Teddy. "Cope told you about me?"

"Won't shut up about you, kid. Says you're a star in the making."

Luca's head jerked back in my direction, but his voice went quiet. "You said that? Really?"

God, this kid was going to kill me. "I did, and I only speak the truth."

Luca stayed silent for a moment and then hurled himself at me, arms wrapping around my waist in a fierce hug. My arms went around him in answer, holding him close.

My gaze met Teddy's over Luca's head, and he mouthed, *"You are so fucked."*

I already knew it because, less than two weeks in my house, and I already couldn't remember what the place had been like without them. And that was seriously messed up. Because after that first night in the kitchen, Sutton hadn't shown me any signs of interest. It was as if she'd built up her walls again and reinforced them with the world's strongest steel.

But she'd made one fatal error. She hadn't taken into account that I knew what it took to break down barriers. No matter how bruised and bloodied the battle made me, I never gave up. Especially when the light at the end of the tunnel was her.

Coach Kenner's whistle blew, and four kids raced across the ice. Luca was second from the left and paired with three others who had two to four years on him. It didn't matter. Halfway to the other end of the rink, he was already pulling ahead.

"Damn, man. You weren't kidding. That little dude has a gift," Teddy muttered, not taking his eyes off Luca.

"I know. If he sticks with it, he'll go all the way for sure."

"How's his mom feel about that?"

I chuckled, remembering how Sutton had called the old hockey game we'd watched the other night a *brutal bloodbath*. "Hockey's a little violent for her taste. She would've preferred Luca picked something like golf."

Teddy's nose wrinkled as if he'd smelled something bad. "*Golf*? That would be cruel and unusual punishment."

"You're preaching to the choir. Just don't tell Marcus that." That douche canoe *loved* golf.

Teddy barked out a laugh. "That's what happens when you grow up with a hockey god for a dad. You get into all those ritzy hobbies. I'm gonna get him one of those hats with a pom-pom on it as a preseason gift."

I shook my head, my lips twitching. "I'd pay good money to see that."

The four campers raced back toward us, but Luca was already at least ten yards ahead. He sailed past us, abruptly stopping on the edges of his skates. He still took a tumble occasionally, but he was getting better and better at staying on his feet.

"Little dude!" Teddy yelled. "That was freaking sick."

At least he hadn't dropped an F-bomb. Coach Kenner had already needed to give Teddy more than a few warnings about his language, and I saw Evelyn Engel glaring at us from the sidelines. *Hell.*

I high-fived the other skaters before making it over to Luca. Teddy was hunched down, talking shop with him, giving him a few pointers on his turns and stops. Luca came alive under the lesson, his eyes alight as he moved in a turn to check that he was understanding.

I loved that Teddy had given him this because, while I was fast, Teddy was the speed master. If anyone could make Luca the best of the best, it was him.

Luca grinned up at me, revealing a tooth just starting to grow into the hole from his missing incisor. "Can we stay after and practice a little more?"

"You've been skating for hours. Aren't you tired?" I asked, amusement lacing my tone as we skated to the boards.

Luca shook his head. "I could skate forever!"

Teddy chuckled. "Maybe you could, but I'm starved, and I heard your mom has the best bakery around. Think you could give me a tour and tell me the best things to get?"

Luca beamed. "Totally, Coach Jackson. I know all the best cupcakes. My mom always lets me have one after school or practice."

A scoff had my attention lifting from Luca to Evelyn standing rink-side, her arms crossed over her chest. Annoyance flickered down deep as I raised a brow in her direction. "Something you want to say?"

Evelyn let out a huff of air. "I just hardly think it's appropriate to give a child sugar every single day."

Luca glared at her. "You're just mad because Daniel hates your cupcakes. He says you make 'em with carrots instead of real sugar. He always asks me to sneak him one of my mom's."

Evelyn gaped at Luca as Teddy tried to cover a laugh with a cough. Evelyn's spine snapped straight. "It's *carob,* not carrots, and it's perfectly delicious."

"Keep telling yourself that, lady," Teddy muttered.

"Daniel, we need to go. You have your cello lesson," Evelyn yelled, her voice going shrill.

Teddy shook his head. "Poor kid. She probably has him scheduled to within an inch of his life."

Daniel rolled his eyes at Luca in commiseration as he skated past, and I clapped him on the shoulder pad. "Killer shooting today. Keep up the hard work."

The kid grinned up at me. "Thanks, Coach Reaper. I'll practice tonight."

"After cello," Evelyn snapped.

Daniel ducked his head. "After cello."

Jesus. That mom needed one of Lolli's pot brownies. Stat.

CHAPTER SEVENTEEN

Sutton

THE STRAINS OF COUNTRY MUSIC SWIRLED AROUND ME AS I maneuvered between tables, balancing coffees, teas, and an array of baked goods. It was a dance I'd perfected over the years, having waitressed long before I scrounged up the money to buy the bakery and transform it into The Mix Up. The tray felt like an extension of my body at this point.

I stopped to chat with some tourists and regulars along the way. I'd even put together a little pamphlet of local recommendations to give to those who were new in town. It felt like a nice way to repay the community that'd welcomed me when I needed it the most.

I slid an iced tea and sandwich onto a table for one and grinned at the woman sitting there. "One chicken pesto panini with extra sun-dried tomatoes."

Fallon grinned up at me. "Thanks, Sutton. This is my favorite midday treat."

As I glimpsed a hint of shadows under her eyes, I knew she more than deserved it. "I'm glad you're taking some time for yourself." I inclined my head toward the stack of files. "Or at least feeding yourself while you work."

She chuckled. "Life's a balance."

"I know that well."

Fallon studied me for a moment. "Are you hanging in there okay?"

I nodded quickly. "Cope's been a lifesaver." I tried not to flush at the fact that his entire family, and a large portion of the community, knew he was doing me this favor. "Hopefully, I won't have to impose for that much longer."

Fallon's hand snaked out to squeeze my arm. "Don't rush it. Everyone needs a safe place to land once in a while. It doesn't make you any less of a badass."

I swallowed, trying to clear the burn lighting along my throat. I didn't need to be a badass, but I also didn't want to get used to someone being there to help when they wouldn't always be. And Cope's time in Sparrow Falls was limited.

"And it's good for my brother," Fallon went on. "He's lighter. And not just in his fake, jokey way. Coaching this team, helping with Luca…it's given him a purpose I think he really needed."

Something shifted in my chest. It wasn't painful, but it wasn't comfortable either. "He's a good man. Luca thinks he hung the moon."

Fallon's mouth curved slightly. "And what do you think?"

My stomach hollowed out. I wasn't completely sure how to answer that question without lying straight to Fallon's face. Thankfully, Rick saved me by stomping down the back staircase and leading a couple who'd been viewing my old apartment toward the door.

All my and Luca's belongings had been moved out and put into storage on Cope's property. Just another thing I owed him and the Colsons for. But from what I could tell, Rick was having trouble renting the space that had been my home for so long. Maybe it was the fact that there was a noisy restaurant below it. Or it could have been the astronomical rent Rick wanted. Regardless, he was striking out so far.

Rick glared at me, seething so hard he was practically spitting. A lead weight settled in my stomach. I had a feeling I might be out of a bakery space when the year was up.

The bell over the door jingled before Rick could reach it, and Lolli stepped in. She was a vision in a billowy skirt with too many colors to count. She jingled as much as the bell with her countless bracelets and necklaces. And she wore a T-shirt knotted at the waist that read *Photosynthesis is FUN* with a big pot leaf.

"Careful, Ricky Boy, you keep scowling like that, and your face will freeze that way. Then how will you convince innocent people you're a kind landlord instead of a snake in the grass?" Lolli said, keeping her tone light.

The couple's eyes went wide as they looked between Rick and Lolli. Rick's beady eyes flashed. "Clearly, the drugs have gotten to your head."

Lolli flipped her silver hair over her shoulder. "I think you could use a little Mary Jane in your life. Might chill you out enough to get your priorities in order instead of trying to take advantage of everyone in your orbit. Honestly, maybe we should go for a pot enema. Might clear out your bullshit."

"Lolli," I whisper-hissed.

"What?" she asked with mock innocence. "I speak the truth."

"Listen to your little friend over there," Rick growled. "I'd hate if things got *more* uncomfortable for her here."

My stomach bottomed out as if the floor had simply disappeared from under me, and I was in free fall. I wouldn't put it past Rick to sabotage the entire building just to stick it to me.

He stormed out of the bakery as all the customers looked on. *Great, just great.*

Lolli hurried over to me. "That pompous, prick-nosed piece of garbage. Next time I see him, I'm not using my words. I'm going to hit him with some of those jiu-jitsu moves Arden's been showing me."

"Oh, Jesus," Fallon muttered, dropping her head into her hands. "Please, don't make Trace arrest you on assault charges."

"It'd be worth it," Lolli muttered, then moved closer, giving my arm a rub. "You okay, honey pie?"

I nodded, still not able to speak. Because while I'd guessed it before, I *knew* Rick had it out for me now. I was so caught in the web of my panicked thoughts that I didn't hear the bell ring this time. I wasn't aware of any newcomers until a tiny whirling dervish hit me in the side, his arms going around me in a tight hug.

"Mom! You won't believe it. Teddy *Lightning* Jackson came to help coach today. And he taught me all sorts of speed tricks. He wants to try your cupcakes, too. I told him I'd pick out the best ones."

My gaze moved from the nothingness I'd been staring at to Luca's entourage. There was a leanly muscled, boyishly handsome man standing next to Cope. He sent me a grin. "Heard you're the best of the best. I think I need to take at least a dozen back to Seattle with me this afternoon."

Heat hit my cheeks. "I do my best. Why don't I pull together a sampler for you? On the house."

Teddy's grin pulled wider. "Are you trying to get my ass, er, butt kicked? Reaper will flatten me the next time we're on the ice if I let his girl cover my cupcakes."

His girl?

The words sliced through me with a mix of craving and pain. Because somewhere along the line, I'd started to want that. It didn't matter how reckless or dangerous it was. I wanted to know what it felt like to belong to Cope, not as a possession but as the person he wanted with every fiber of his being.

"Warrior," Cope said, his voice low and throaty, making my gaze jump to his. "Something happened. Your face when we came in…"

That jolted me out of those stupid, stupid thoughts. I gave Luca's shoulder a squeeze. "Want to go help Walter pick out a dozen cupcakes for Teddy?"

Luca's light-blue eyes flared even brighter. "Yeah! I'm gonna get the Cookie Monster ones, and the bumblebees, and the triple-chocolate mudslides. I'm gonna put some cookies in the bag, too."

"Thanks, little dude," Teddy called, but there was concern on his face now, too.

Crap.

The moment Luca was gone, Cope moved even closer. He slid his hand under my hair and squeezed the back of my neck. "What happened?"

His voice was gentle, but a demand radiated through the words—one that sent a shiver coursing through me. Not one of dread but one of promise.

"That prick stick Rick was in here glaring at her, that's what," Lolli said with a huff. "I told him to watch it, and he threatened Sutton."

Cope's fingers flexed on my neck. "He. Did. What?"

Fallon groaned. "Don't use the word *threaten* around Cope. Are you trying to make him lose it?"

"It's true," Lolli huffed. "I still think a pot enema would clear Ricky right out."

Teddy's brows flew up. "A pot enema?"

"Cleanses the bullshit," Lolli said with a grin.

"Someone save me," Fallon muttered.

I hoped the exchange would lighten Cope's mood, but when I looked up into those dark-blue eyes, I saw no sign of that. Instead, there were sparks of fury. "What. Did. He. Say?"

I pressed a hand to Cope's stomach, the move one of pure instinct, an attempt to soothe. But the moment my hand pressed against the hard muscle, I knew I'd made a mistake. I could feel ridge after ridge of his abdominals—the kind of washboard that wasn't supposed to exist in real life. "He was just an ass. That's all. Nothing new."

It was a miracle I got the words out, given my tongue felt like I was in anaphylactic shock.

"Someone tell me what happened," Cope growled.

Teddy thumped him on the back. "Breathe, Caveman. No need to break things. Your girl's right here, and she's just fine."

I tried to ignore the *his girl* thing.

Fallon looked from Cope to me before finally speaking. "Lolli's right. He's a dick of epic proportions. He made some veiled comment about how he'd hate if things got more uncomfortable for Sutton here."

A muscle in Cope's jaw fluttered so wildly it looked like a butterfly about to take flight. "I'm going to kill him."

This time, Teddy grabbed both of Cope's shoulders and squeezed, giving him a little shake. "Let's take it easy on the k-word, all right? You don't need the press getting wind of that sort of thing right now. And you sure as hell don't need an assault charge."

"Don't worry," Lolli cut in. "I'm going to use my jiu-jitsu on him." She pulled some sort of punch-kick combo that didn't look like it was part of any sanctioned martial art.

"That's my girl!" Walter shouted from behind the counter. "You show 'em, tiger!"

"I'm not your anything, you old coot!" she shouted back.

"You will be once you break down and marry me," Walter called.

The patrons began laughing. At least this was a better distraction than Rick and his scene.

Teddy grinned and released Cope. "I think I might need to move to Sparrow Falls, man. I love your family."

"They're easier to love with a little distance. Trust me," Cope muttered.

"Hey," Fallon snapped, smacking her brother. "We are awesome."

"Keep telling yourself that, Fal." Cope bent his head so we were at eye level, our foreheads almost touching. "You okay, Warrior?"

My breath caught in my throat. I shouldn't have inhaled as he got close because all I could smell now was mint, sage, and a hint of sweat. And holy hell, the combination was potent. "I'm good," I squeaked.

"Promise?"

I nodded. "Swear."

It was the biggest lie I'd told in years, which was saying something given all the secrets I was keeping. But nothing could compare to the lies I was telling myself. Like that I wasn't falling head over heels for Copeland Colson.

Luca's little face scrunched as he leaned back in his chair. "I didn't want to like broccoli."

I tried to hide my smile behind my napkin but knew my eyes danced as I met Cope's gaze across the table. He didn't do anything to hide his chuckle.

"It's broccoli rabe, not broccoli, so you're safe."

That only made Luca's face scrunch harder. "So, it's part of broccoli?"

Cope shook his head. "It's actually a different plant altogether."

Luca threw up his hands. "Then why would they call it broccoli? Broccoli's gross. This poor rabe stuff is probably getting passed over because of its name."

Cope's lips twitched as he reached for his wineglass. "I'm taking that to mean you liked dinner."

When Luca sat down at the table and saw the green stuff mixed with his pasta, he'd nearly thrown a fit. It wouldn't have been our first battle over vegetables, but Cope had intervened with a miracle.

He'd told Luca he needed help with the recipe and an expert taste tester. Luca's note before trying a bite had been to get rid of the green stuff. But when he actually tasted it, his only note had been, "More cheese." And what *wasn't* better with more cheese?

"It's hard to admit you might actually like a veggie," I said with a smile.

Luca rolled his eyes. "Don't think this is gonna happen a lot."

I held up both hands in mock surrender. "I'd never."

"Since I ate it all, can I go play video games?" Luca asked hopefully.

I waved him off. "Thirty minutes, then it's bath and bed."

"Nice! I can scorch the Earth at least twice."

I tipped my head back as Luca took off, letting a groan slip free. "Am I going to turn my kid into a bloodthirsty criminal mastermind by letting him incinerate the planet every night?"

Cope chuckled. "I think you're safe since it's dragons and evil sorcerers."

I twisted my neck, sending a series of pops through it. "I hope you're right."

Cope leaned over, reaching out so his fingers could dig into my flesh. "Neck bugging you again?"

My gaze found his and held. "How do you always know?"

He shrugged and kept kneading with delicious pressure. "My neck can bug me from a shoulder injury. I know the signs. You twist your head a certain way when it hurts."

My tongue darted out to wet my suddenly dry lips. I didn't want to think about how he knew that. How closely he watched me and seemed to understand without me saying a word. And more than anything, I didn't want to get used to the gift of his knowing. But I couldn't find it in me to pull away.

Cope's eyes darkened, the blue turning stormy. His gaze dropped to my lips, and my heart sped up. He was close. So close I swore I could feel his breath teasing my mouth, a tempting promise of what was to come.

"Warrior." It was more rasp than word.

I opened my mouth, unsure if it was to push him away or kiss him, but I didn't get a chance to find out. The doorbell rang, jerking us out of the moment.

Cope cursed softly. "I'm changing the gate code."

I bit my bottom lip, a chuckle slipping free.

Those dark blues flashed. "Not fucking funny," he grumbled. "My siblings need to learn the definition of boundaries."

"Hey, whoever it is, used the bell. They probably have the code to get in through the front door if they wanted."

Cope muttered something unintelligible as he pushed his chair back and stood. I followed, gathering a few plates as I went. I started cleaning up the kitchen as Cope's voice wafted through the air.

"You have impeccably shitty timing, Sheriff."

I bit my bottom lip again, this time to keep from laughing as the sound of footsteps moved toward the kitchen. "Hey, Trace."

As I turned, I caught sight of his face. Trace was the most serious of the Colson siblings, though even with that, he normally would've laughed or given Cope a hard time about his comment. But his expression was completely blank. Something about it set me on edge. I slowly put the bowl in the sink. "What happened?"

Cope's gaze snapped to me and then to his brother. He'd missed the signs, too caught up in his annoyance and used to his siblings making surprise visits to realize something was wrong. "Trace?"

His brother's throat worked as he swallowed. "Teddy was in an accident on his way back to Seattle."

It was as if Cope had been struck by lightning; his entire form snapped straight. "Where is he? What hospital?"

Pain streaked across Trace's features. "I'm sorry, Cope. He didn't make it. He's gone."

CHAPTER EIGHTEEN

Cope

I'M SORRY, COPE. HE DIDN'T MAKE IT. HE'S GONE."

Trace's words echoed on repeat in my head as I stared out the window. The view that normally brought me such peace gave me nothing now. All that existed was an endless slideshow that flipped me back and forth between pain and numbness.

I knew I should be doing something, anything, but I couldn't get myself there. My house had been an endless revolving door of family members, but that only made it worse. Because it wasn't just losing Teddy that hurt. It was the memory of losing Dad and Jacob all those years ago.

Trace hadn't realized how eerily similar his words were to Mom's from back then. How I'd come to in the hospital, and she'd been right there, her face so pale that I thought she was a ghost for a second.

"Dad?" I croaked, my throat so dry I thought it might crack.

Pain shattered my mom's expression, her face crumbling. "I'm so sorry, Cope. Your dad and Jacob...they didn't make it. They're gone."

The agony of that knowledge had sent me spiraling. The stitches in my lip, broken ribs, and concussion were nothing compared to the pain of knowing that I had caused their deaths. It was all on me in every way imaginable.

And now, there was another black mark on my soul. Another life cut short that I'd have to atone for. No price would be great enough.

Fingers curled around mine. "Cope?"

I jolted, some part of me recognizing it wasn't the first time Sutton had said my name. I blinked a few times, clearing my vision and bringing her into focus. "Sorry, what?"

"Can I bring you some soup and a sandwich?" she asked, hope bleeding into her question. "I didn't make the soup. Promise. Your mom brought it."

I knew she was trying to make me smile, and I wanted to give her that. Sutton had been taking care of me for the past forty-eight hours, making sure I ate and trying to get me to sleep. But I couldn't get my mouth to curve the way I knew it should. "I'm good right now."

"Cope," she said softly. "You haven't eaten anything today."

My stomach did feel hollow, but that wasn't any different than the rest of me. "I can't. I just—I don't think my gut can take it."

Sutton's fingers convulsed around mine, tightening in a grip that told me she wasn't letting go anytime soon. "What can I do? What do you need?"

"You're doing it," I rasped. "This. It's good."

I didn't deserve the kindness or comfort, but I took it anyway. I was a greedy bastard like that. But still, some part of me needed Sutton to know who I really was. "This would never have happened if he hadn't been worried about me."

Because that was Teddy. The best friend, through and through. Always looking out for his teammates, friends, and family. And now, because he'd come to check on me, they'd lose out on that gift for the rest of their days.

Sutton gripped my hand harder, shaking it. "Don't you dare."

My eyes flared as the shock of her words settled in.

"Don't you *dare* put this on yourself. It's no one's fault. It's a horrible tragedy, but no one thing or person is responsible."

But she was wrong. It was Teddy's fault for driving too fast around the curve on a mountain road. It was the sky's fault for starting to rain just enough the oils on the road made the pavement as slick as ice. But most of all, it was my fault for giving Teddy a reason to be here. Just like I'd given my family one to be in that SUV that night.

"He wouldn't have been here if it wasn't for me." My words were barely audible and like a cannon all at once.

Sutton moved then, sinking to the floor, her knees digging into the plush rug beneath the sofa. She pushed herself between my legs, her hands rising to frame my face. "Cope. He was here because he loved you. Because you meant something to him. And from everything I've heard these past few days, you weren't alone in that. He showed up for the people he loved. *That's* Teddy's legacy. It's the most beautiful kind you can have. Don't steal that from him."

Everything burned. My eyes. My throat. My fucking guts. But I knew Sutton was right. I couldn't erase Teddy's legacy. I'd just have to find a way to live with the guilt. I'd done it before. I could do it again.

Sutton dropped her forehead to mine, our breaths mingling. "I'm so sorry. I'd do anything to take this away. To fix it. The way you did for me."

My arms went around her; I couldn't stop myself. Her warmth and heat were too alluring. I wanted to lose myself in everything that was Sutton. To forget all the darkness that swirled in me.

"Warrior," I rasped.

"I'm right here," she whispered. "I'm not going anywhere."

So damn close. I swore I could taste her already. Cinnamon, sugar, and something else. The promise of pureness, of cleansing. I wanted it all. My fingers twisted in Sutton's shirt, bringing her even closer. Then my fucking phone rang.

We didn't jerk apart like when Trace had rung the bell. We stayed just as we were for a long moment until the ringing began anew.

I forced myself to release Sutton and reached for the device on the arm of the sofa. Linc's name flashed on the screen. That stew of nasty emotions was back, but I forced my finger to slide across the screen.

"Linc," I said in greeting.

He was quiet for a moment. "I'd ask how you're holding up, but I don't make a habit of asking stupid questions."

I felt a flutter in the muscles of my mouth like my lips knew they should smile but couldn't quite do it. "Glad you don't do that."

And I knew he wouldn't start with the placating, "*I'm so sorry for your loss*" bullshit. Because Linc knew what it was like. He'd lost someone close to him in one of the worst ways imaginable. But that meant this was likely stirring up shit for him, too. "You hanging in?" I asked.

He knew what I meant. We'd only talked about that time in his life once when we were both nearly blackout drunk after an especially vicious loss that knocked us out of the playoffs. We'd smoked cigars and drank whiskey into the early morning hours. And we never talked about it again.

"I'm fine," he clipped.

I wanted to scoff. We were both terrible liars these days. "Did you need something, or are you just playing Mr. Sensitive and checking in?"

Linc sighed. "Sorry, man. I just got out of a meeting with Teddy's parents."

That was a knife to the gut and also explained Linc's lack of control. "Are you in Iowa?"

"They're here. In Seattle."

"Oh." It made sense. They'd have to claim the body. Clean out his house. The burn was back, thinking about every piece of Teddy they'd erase.

"They're going to do a small service here on Sunday. I told them I'd arrange it, but they asked for you to give the eulogy."

"What?" The question was out before I could stop it, and there was a bite to the word.

Sutton's hands tightened on my thighs, reassuring me that she was still there, just like she'd promised.

"You were his closest friend. They want you to do it," Linc said softly.

I tried to swallow a few times before my throat finally obeyed. "Of course." I said the words even though I didn't mean them at all. "I'll head up tonight."

"Don't drive," Linc cut in. "I'm sending my jet to your local airstrip. It'll be there sometime after three."

That would make it easier. I wouldn't have to take the same path Teddy had or drive an hour to the main airport in Central Oregon to catch a commercial flight. "Thanks."

"I'm here. Whatever you need."

"You, too." But I knew Linc would never take me up on it.

I ended the call and stared down at Sutton. She looked up at me, a crease in her beautiful brow. "What did he say?"

"Funeral on Sunday. They want me to give the eulogy."

Sympathy washed over her features. "An honor. But so incredibly hard."

It was an honor I didn't deserve. One I wasn't sure I'd get through. Not alone. "Will you go with me?"

It wasn't sympathy that flashed then, it was sheer panic—an emotion that didn't make any sense. "I—um, I have Luca."

"Mom can stay with him. She loves that kid."

Sutton's throat worked as she struggled to swallow. "I'm not sure it's a good idea."

"Warrior," I whispered, shock settling in.

"I-I can't. I'm so sorry, Cope."

"You can't go to my best friend's funeral?" There was accusation in my words, a flicker of anger. I held on to that because it was so much better than the pain.

"I'm so sorry, I—"

"It doesn't matter." I shoved to my feet, sending Sutton jerking back on her haunches. None of it mattered. It wasn't like I hadn't been alone in my grief and guilt before.

CHAPTER NINETEEN

Sutton

THE SILENCE ECHOED OFF THE LIVING ROOM WALLS AND SENT vibrations through my ears. Something about the absence of sound was absolutely deafening. I couldn't move. Even as my brain told me to get up and go after Cope, my body wouldn't obey.

And maybe that was for the best. Because what would I do once I got there? Spin some lie? Tell him I couldn't be there for him when he needed me the most? After everything he'd done for me?

Pain radiated through my chest in vicious waves as I lost all feeling in my knees. That pins-and-needles sensation traveled through my legs as the agony spread along my sternum. It would be so easy to say yes, go with Cope, and be the shoulder he needed. But I knew what would be waiting at a funeral of that magnitude.

The press.

The same vultures that were waiting outside the hospital when I was released. It wasn't as if I'd been major headline material, but it was enough to garner national attention. The ex-wife of a disgraced football player beaten by his seedy connections. Photos of my swollen and bandaged face as a friend wheeled me to their car. The coverage of the trial that followed.

I couldn't risk that sort of attention now—the kind that would tell Roman where I was. And the risk it would bring if he decided to drop the information on Petrov.

It wasn't a lie that Luca needed me. He'd bawled his eyes out when he found out his new best friend wasn't here anymore. He was bouncing back the way kids did, off to play with Keely for the afternoon, but that didn't mean he wouldn't have his moments. Ones where he needed me. The problem was, Cope needed me, too.

A beep sounded from the front door lock. I knew I should move. Stand. I shouldn't be here when whoever was at the door walked in. It looked ridiculous, me on my knees, just staring at the place where Cope had been.

Footsteps pounded down the stairs as the door swung open.

"Cope—" Arden's sentence was cut short as he stormed past her, a duffel slung over his shoulder. "Where are you going?" she yelled out the open door.

But he didn't answer. I heard a door slam in the distance and knew he'd gotten behind the wheel of that fancy SUV. I just prayed he'd be careful. Safe. The miniscule local airstrip designed mainly for hobbyists was only a few minutes away. I'd heard enough of Linc's offer to know that a plane would be meeting Cope there. That was good. He'd be okay.

The moment I thought that last sentence, I knew it was a lie. Cope might be physically safe, but he was as far from *okay* as you could get.

"Sutton." Arden's voice was soft, not delicate in any way but gentle, nonetheless.

The sound jerked me from the haze of guilt currently holding me hostage. She was close. Standing right beside me. I'd somehow missed her crossing the threshold and coming through the living room. I knew I needed to say something but couldn't get my body to do that either.

I expected Arden to pull me up and get me sitting on the couch, but instead, she sank to the floor with me. She didn't make a move to touch me, simply sat beside me, those cool, gray-violet eyes searching. And she didn't ask even a single question.

That was the thing about Arden. She wasn't afraid of stillness. She moved and spoke only with purpose, though not because the world around her told her she needed to.

Finally, my knees gave way, and I fell fully to the carpet. My ass hit the floor in a way that jarred my spine and rattled my teeth. "I hurt him," I whispered.

Arden's gaze shifted, but there was neither condemnation nor empathy in it, simply understanding. "It's a messy business being human. We hurt, and we get hurt."

I pulled my knees to my chest as if I could hug myself and bring some of the comfort I so desperately needed. "It was the last thing I wanted to do. Not when he was already in so much pain."

I caught a flicker in Arden's gaze this time, an echo of Cope's pain in her because she loved her brother so deeply. "Something tells me you didn't do that for shits and giggles."

"He wanted me to go to the funeral with him."

The words were barely audible, but Arden's focus still jerked to the door as she realized where her brother had gone. "Hell," she muttered, then turned back to me. "And you're not ready for all that attention."

No, I wasn't. That sort of focus had never been my thing. But I would've paid the price again and again if it meant being there for Cope. Unfortunately, it was way more complicated than that. "It's not about being ready. I *can't*."

I bled every ounce of feeling into that last word, hoping Arden would somehow understand without me telling her the story.

She tensed, her hands squeezing nothing as I watched the mental pieces come together. "There's someone you don't want to find you."

I nodded in answer.

"Are they a risk to your safety?" Arden asked instantly, and I understood why. Thea had just been through an ordeal with her ex, which made the Colsons incredibly aware of what people from our pasts were capable of.

But when I thought about whether Roman was an actual danger to me, I wasn't sure. He might try what he could to bleed me dry. Could give my location to Petrov. But would either of them get on a plane and cross the country? For what? To make an example out of me? It wasn't like I had money to spare.

"I don't know." It was the first time I'd said the words out loud. The first time I'd admitted, even to myself, that I might be running from shadows.

Arden moved slowly, her hand covering mine. "I know what that's like," she whispered. "Is there a reason to fear, or have we simply stopped living?"

Something in those words told me she understood better than most, and I couldn't help but wonder why. I didn't know the circumstances around Arden coming to live with the Colsons, just that she had come into foster care at the age of twelve and was the youngest of them.

But she didn't seem young as I looked into those swirling eyes. She had an old soul, one I knew had been through more than its fair share.

"I feel like I can't trust my perception of things anymore," I admitted. I remembered a psychiatrist who had come to see me in the hospital. A kind man with graying hair and smile lines around his eyes. He'd told me I may have PTSD from the incident and said I'd need to be kind to my brain as it tried to protect me.

Arden's mouth pulled into a half-smile. "Sometimes, those monsters seem worse simply because we haven't turned on the lights."

God, was that ever true. "I'm tired of living in the dark." Tired of feeling like I was running when I'd done nothing wrong.

That half smile on Arden's face grew into a full one. "Then maybe it's time to step into the light."

CHAPTER TWENTY

Cope

THIS SUIT WAS GOING TO STRANGLE ME. NO MATTER HOW MANY times I adjusted the damn tie, I still felt like I couldn't breathe. And it didn't matter how expensive the material was; it felt like itchy burlap.

"Cope." The voice was soft and full of empathy. And, God, it made me a bastard, but it wasn't the one I wanted to hear right now.

I turned to face the owner. "Hey, Ang."

She instantly moved into my space, wrapping her arms around my waist and pressing her face to my chest. It was a move she'd made countless times, but it felt empty now. I didn't feel the comfort I did with Sutton's mere presence. I didn't feel the understanding I got without Sutton saying a word. I felt...nothing.

Still, I returned the hug and patted her back gently. She held on for a beat too long before finally releasing me. When she tipped her head back, red hair cascading down her back, her green eyes sparkled with unshed tears. "Are you okay?"

That was the last fucking question I wanted to answer, but I did my best to force a smile I knew likely looked more like a grimace. "Hanging in there. You?"

Her arms fell from mine, and she took my hands in hers. "I just can't believe this is happening."

I was a prick. A callous asshole because Angie needed comfort, and all I could think about was how to get her to let go of my goddamned hands.

"Angie." Linc's voice cut through the air like a knife. There was power behind it, something likely trained from birth. That's what happened when you were raised in one of the wealthiest families in the world. I just happened to know that he hated his family with the passion of a thousand blazing suns—his dad, at least.

Angie released my hands and took a huge step back. "Lincoln."

He gave her a brusque nod. "Would you mind checking in with security? I want to make sure no media makes it into the church."

Angie's lips pursed in a move I knew meant she was annoyed, but she didn't voice it. "Of course."

My gaze moved to the owner of the Sparks as Angie walked away. "We both know you have this place locked down tight." Linc wasn't the kind of guy who left things to chance. He was aware of all possibilities and had multiple contingency plans for each of them.

He lifted a single brow. "You didn't need rescuing?"

"I'm not a fucking damsel in distress."

Linc let out a low chuckle. "Tell that to the look on your face. It was sort of a cross between panic and nausea."

I scrubbed a hand over my stubbled cheek. "I never should've gotten involved with someone associated with the team."

"Not to say I told you so, but…"

"Fuck off," I muttered.

"You ready?" he asked, all traces of humor gone from his voice.

No. The last thing I wanted to do was get up in front of a crowd and tell them why I never deserved a friend as good as Teddy. Just picturing the pews jammed full of people had my chest tightening.

"Ready," I forced out.

"You're a shit liar," Linc muttered.

"I'll do what I need to do," I clipped.

Linc searched my face. "I can tell the Jacksons you aren't up to—"

"No. I've got this."

Linc didn't look convinced, but he nodded. "All right. I'm going to make the rounds. Let me know if you need anything."

"Will do." My palms were already sweaty, my breathing shallow. *Fuck.* I needed air.

I moved through the crowd of players, taking up all the space in a small side room at the back of the church, and forced myself to nod and give chin lifts to teammates as I passed. My lungs tightened with each passing second. I quickly slipped into the hallway and nearly collided with someone.

"Sorry," I muttered.

The other figure simply grunted as he glared at me. "Surprised you even bothered showing up. But I guess you have to play the role of golden boy," Marcus snapped.

"Not today, all right? Pick any other day to be an ass of epic proportions. I'll even give you a free shot to make up for me embarrassing you in front of our entire team. Just not today."

The fist came out of nowhere. One second, I was standing there. The next, Marcus's knuckles were connecting with my jaw. My head snapped back with a vicious crack.

But fuck, that bite of pain and the flare of anger that followed were a hell of a lot better than the grief, guilt, and panic I'd been feeling seconds ago. The moment my head righted itself, I threw a hook shot to Marcus's ribs, and he grunted in pain.

It wasn't long before he retaliated, attempting to tackle me to the ground. We hit a wall instead, sending a framed photo crashing to the floor. The sound must've alerted people to the altercation because my teammates spilled into the hall a few moments later.

Two guys grabbed me—one on each arm—and yanked me back as another two caught Marcus. He spat a slew of curses in their direction and tried to break free, but the two enforcers didn't show any signs of letting go.

Linc stalked in, moving between us, fury washing over his face. "What the fuck is wrong with you two? This is a goddamned funeral. A church."

"Might not want to say 'goddamned' in a church, boss," Frankie muttered, not letting go of my arm. Linc sent him a withering stare. "Got it. Shutting up, boss."

Linc looked between Marcus and me. "I don't know what the hell is going on between the two of you, but you need to fix it. We're a team. And Teddy would be ashamed of both of you right now."

The words were worse than any blow Marcus could've leveled. Because they were the cold, hard truth. Teddy would've kicked my ass for pulling this shit, even if Marcus *had* been the one to start it.

The pain was back, fiery agony searing through muscle and sinew. "Need a minute," I croaked. The desperation in my words had Frankie and my other teammate releasing me.

I didn't wait for another condemnation from Linc, just spun on my heel and stalked down the hall. Angie stood there, a look of shock on her face. "Cope—"

She reached out, but I dodged her grasp. "Don't," I clipped. "Just don't."

I stalked down the hall, hitting the door with *Exit* emblazoned on it, the force enough to rattle my bones. The moment I stepped outside, I sucked in air. It wasn't the kind of fresh I could find in Sparrow Falls, but it was better than the thick, too-hot air of the church.

Clouds had gathered, threatening rain the way they often did in Seattle. But it fit today. Part of me hoped the sky would open, and a lightning bolt would take me out. It would be so much easier.

My breaths came faster and faster, each one shallower than the one before. The burn lit in my chest, and each breath felt like inhaling acid. It was too much. Images of Teddy blurred with ones of my brother and dad. Pictures of twisted metal and the sounds of pain.

Black spots danced in front of my vision as my world tunneled. And then someone was there. A tiny body propped me up as a hand pressed against my chest. And then I heard *her* voice.

"Breathe, Cope. Breathe with me."

CHAPTER TWENTY-ONE

Sutton

THE MOMENT I SAW HIM AROUND THE SIDE OF THE CHURCH, bent over and gasping for breath, my heart stopped. Everything in that moment was so opposite of the strong, vital man I knew. Everything about it was *wrong*.

I'd moved on instinct, trying to shoulder some of the weight Cope had been carrying alone for too long, attempting to give him back a little of what he'd given me. I pressed my hand harder against his chest. "Breathe with me."

I recognized the signs of a panic attack from the handful I had after my assault. The only thing that helped me was stuff that brought me back to the present, items that jolted me into the here and now. I just hoped the feel of my hand over his heart could be that for him.

"Warrior?" he croaked.

It was more sound than a word, a garbled collection of syllables that cracked my damn heart. "I'm right here. Look at me."

I watched as those dark-blue orbs seemed to try their damnedest to focus. His breaths sounded like wheezing, pained inhales. I pressed my hand harder against his chest. "I'm here. I'm with you."

Some of the glassiness cleared from Cope's eyes, and his breathing slowed a fraction.

"That's it. Nice and easy. With me." Everything hurt, not because of anything I was going through but because I could feel Cope's pain. It bled into the air around us, seeping into my pores and taking root.

"My warrior," he rasped, his forehead dropping to mine, his breaths easing even more.

We stayed like that for...I didn't know how long, just breathing together. Because sometimes that was all you could do. No words could soothe the ravaged wounds of grief. All you could do was be present in the pain with the person experiencing it. That was a precious gift because people often couldn't withstand the discomfort of someone else's sorrow.

But I could shoulder it for Cope. Because he deserved all that and more.

"You came," he whispered.

"Sorry it took me a minute to find my way."

Cope pulled back a fraction, his eyes searching mine. Then he closed the distance again, pressing his lips to my forehead and branding me forevermore. "It doesn't matter. You're here now."

My heart jerked in my chest, rioting at the danger this man was to me in so many ways. But I'd been living in the dark for far too long. And Arden was right; it was time to step into the light.

When Cope pulled back, I lifted my hands to his face, letting the scruff there prickle my palms. "Tell me what you need."

Cope's throat worked as he swallowed. "I don't know if I can do it."

"The eulogy?"

He nodded roughly. "Hell, I don't know if I can even go back inside the damn church." He paused for a moment, his gaze moving to the trees beyond the side alley. "I haven't been in a sanctuary since my dad and brother's funeral."

My fingers tightened on his face. "Not even for a wedding?"

Broken HARBOR 147

Cope shook his head. "Always made excuses for why I couldn't make the ceremonies. It just—it's like I'm back there."

An ache took root in my bones as if my body was pulling his pain into me. "What would Teddy say?"

Cope's mouth twisted. "He wouldn't give a damn about any of this."

"What about you? Do *you* give a damn about it?" Because Cope was the one who had to live with his choices today.

He let out a shuddering breath. "I want to honor him. I want to tell his parents what a privilege it was to be his friend."

My hands dropped from Cope's face, and I threaded my fingers through his. "Then let's do that. I'll be with you every step of the way."

Cope squeezed my hand in a death grip. "Promise?"

"I'm with you."

He swallowed again, then nodded his head slowly.

"Let's do this." I led him toward the side entrance, and Cope opened the door.

At least a dozen eyes shot to us the moment we stepped inside. Sweat beaded and ran down my spine, but I didn't run. I kept hold of Cope's hand and didn't let go, just like I promised. A redhead in a sleek black dress stared at us in shock, her mouth falling open as her gaze dropped to our joined hands. Apparently, this sort of thing wasn't the norm for Cope.

Another man in an expertly tailored suit strode forward. I knew the suit had to be custom-made because he was so tall I had to crane my head back to meet his hazel eyes. He looked at me with perplexed curiosity before turning to Cope. "Got it together?"

Cope nodded. "Sorry, Linc."

"Don't apologize. Just tell me if you need an X-ray and promise there won't be a brawl in the chapel."

My eyes widened and jerked to Cope. "You were in a fight?"

"It was nothing," he said quickly.

"Tell that to the smashed photo and Marcus's bruised ribs," Linc shot back.

Crud. None of that was good. I squeezed Cope's hand and met the team owner's stare dead-on. It took some doing because he had the height and a leanly muscled fighter's build, but I didn't cower. "Cope's got it handled."

One corner of his mouth quirked up. "Looks like you're the one to keep him in line." He extended a hand, a glimpse of ink peeking from his sleeve. "Lincoln Pierce."

I accepted the shake, trying not to let my hand tremble. "Sutton Holland."

"Pleasure to meet you, Ms. Holland."

"Sutton, please."

He nodded. "Call me Linc. All my friends do." Cope made a noise that almost sounded like a growl, and Lincoln's face split into an outright grin. "Going to be fun as hell watching this one go down."

I stared as Linc turned and strode back down the hall. *What the hell did that mean?*

Teddy's service was what all memorials should be. A mix of humor and heart, laughter and tears. It only took me a matter of minutes to peg which of Cope's teammates he'd gotten into a fight with. The blond-haired, green-eyed man glared in our direction for the first fifteen minutes of the service until someone next to him elbowed him hard in the ribs, making him wince and avert his gaze. I knew he had to be Marcus.

Thankfully, the man kept his focus on the front of the church after that. Teammates, friends, and coaches took turns going to the podium and sharing readings or stories. Each one made my heart ache for everything the world had lost with Teddy's death. He was a bright light snuffed out far too soon.

As the head coach finished his story, he turned in Cope's

direction. "There's one more person who needs to speak today. Teddy's partner in crime and punishment, Copeland Colson."

There was a scattering of light laughter at Coach Fielder's remarks, but Cope didn't move right away. I leaned into him, squeezing his hand that I hadn't let go of. "Just talk to me. Tell me who Teddy is. I'll be right here."

Cope still didn't move for a beat, then two. When he rose, he released my fingers at the last possible moment. He climbed the steps to the podium, pausing to clasp hands with the coach. When he finally reached the lectern, Cope's eyes instantly found me, and he didn't look away. He also didn't speak.

I'm right here. I mouthed the words, hoping he could read my lips.

Cope's chest rose with an inhale, and his mouth opened. "The first thing Teddy Jackson said to me was that if I was going to be a hotshot hockey player, I needed better style."

The crowd broke into laughter, and Cope's mouth curved slightly, but he still didn't take his eyes off me. "We were sixteen and spending the summer at camp in the Middle-of-Nowhere, Minnesota. It was an hour and a half away from any sort of civilization, but Teddy somehow managed to throw a party in the woods, complete with a DJ and booze. And that was the first time Teddy got me grounded."

Cope went on to share funny and heartwarming stories, ones that painted a picture of exactly who Teddy was. His fingers tightened on the podium as he finally forced his gaze to Teddy's parents in the front row. Cope swallowed hard and began speaking one more time.

"You raised an incredible son. One who brought fun and laughter to everyone he was around. But so much more. He was the kind of man who always had his friends' backs. The kind who always took the time to check on me when he knew I was struggling. The kind who gave so much more than he ever took. And I promise you, I am a better man because I knew your son."

Teddy's mom broke then, her tears coming fast and free. Cope strode from the podium straight to her as she stood and hugged the woman hard. He fought his own tears, those dark-blue eyes shining under the church's lights.

When he released her, the minister asked everyone to stand. I didn't hear her closing words, only snatches of things that promised Teddy lived on in each of us and the lives he touched. I only had eyes for Cope as he moved toward me.

He slipped into the pew, his arm sliding around me, and his face pressing to my neck as he breathed deeply. "Thank you, Warrior."

"I didn't do anything."

Cope pulled back, his eyes shining. "You lent me your strength."

CHAPTER TWENTY-TWO

Cope

MY HAND FOUND SUTTON'S AGAIN AS WE FILED OUT OF THE pew. I couldn't stop touching her. It was as if she grounded me somehow. Gave me a flicker of peace during the riot currently living inside me. The moment my fingers touched her skin, the accusatory voices muted, muffled by something uniquely Sutton.

I kept hold of her hand as I stepped into the aisle, coming face-to-face with Marcus, whose green eyes were more than a little thunderous. A new wave of guilt crashed over me. He might've thrown the first punch this time, but I'd goaded him into it. I'd fix it, just like Teddy wanted me to, but not today.

I let Marcus step ahead, two other teammates sticking close, likely because they didn't trust us not to get into a fistfight in the middle of the sanctuary. I didn't blame them. People spoke in soft tones as we moved down the aisle.

When we reached the doors, I heard security order some photographers back. "Hell," I muttered.

Sutton glanced up at me, her eyes flaring wide. "What is it?"

"Vultures trying to snap a picture to sell to magazines or a sports blog," I ground out.

Sutton's face paled as she fumbled in her purse.

"Are you okay? Your face just went white."

She nodded but the motion was jerky. "I can't believe they're at the church."

I could. They were bottom-feeders. People whose only sustenance was others' misery. "They won't be able to get close, don't worry."

Sutton's hand trembled as she pulled out a huge pair of sunglasses. "I know."

When she slipped them on, they took up half her face. I wasn't up on what was fashionable, so maybe this was the look.

"Cope," a soft voice said.

I turned to see Angie standing near the doors. She did her best to hide the hurt in her eyes, but I saw it. And I was the asshole who still couldn't let go of Sutton's hand, even when Angie's gaze dipped to it. "Lincoln has a car waiting for you around the side of the church to take you to the airport."

"Thanks, Ang. I appreciate it." It was all I could give her. And maybe that was for the best. She'd think Sutton being here with me was more than the simple kindness it was. But as I thought those words, I knew one thing: I wanted it to be more.

The moment Sutton and I landed in Sparrow Falls, it was as if reality set in. After helping her into my SUV that I'd left at the airport, I forced myself *not* to take her hand as I drove. Instead, I kept both hands on the wheel and navigated the two-lane roads back to my house.

"Who stayed with Luca?" I asked, slowing at the gate to my property.

Sutton's mouth curved. "Arden. He was very excited because she said she would take him on a trail ride."

Good. That was good. Luca deserved all the adventures and fun he could pack into his days.

"She loves introducing people to her babies. I swear those horses are better trained than any I've ever known. They come when called like dogs. Do tricks like pups, too."

Sutton looked out the window at the darkening sky. "I like watching them, petting them, even. But I can't seem to imagine getting on one."

My lips twitched. "Why not?"

"That saddle is *very* far from the ground."

I chuckled as I navigated my SUV down the aspen-lined lane. "Fair enough. But you might get the bug if you watch Luca and Arden ride. It's pretty damn fun."

Sutton arched a brow in my direction. "I'm surprised your team lets you ride. There aren't any restrictions on the kinds of activities you can do?"

"Oh, there are. But what they don't know can't hurt them. I'm surprised you knew that since sports puck isn't really your thing."

Something flashed so quickly over Sutton's expression, I couldn't quite pin it down. Her mouth curved, but the action looked strained. "I think I read an article about pro athletes and their rules somewhere."

I forced my gaze back to the road as we hit the bridge that crossed the creek. I could just start to make out the lights from within the house—a place that felt a hell of a lot more like home, knowing Luca was there. That Sutton soon would be, too. It wasn't an empty, cavernous space anymore. It felt alive.

I pulled to a stop in front of the steps but didn't shut off the engine. Instead, I turned to Sutton, really taking her in. Her blond hair hung in soft waves around her shoulders. Her turquoise eyes looked even lighter thanks to a navy color accenting the corners of her lids. She was the kind of stunning men fought wars over. But it was so much more than that.

"You flew to Seattle to be there for me." My words were coated in a grittiness I couldn't shake because she'd come. Spent money to do it when I knew she was desperately trying to save. Left Luca when they were usually joined at the hip. For me.

Sutton's expression softened. "I should've ridden with you from the beginning. I'm sorry—"

I shook my head, cutting her off. "You were there when I needed you." I couldn't resist touching her. My hand slid along her jaw and into her silky strands. "Thank you. I don't know what I would've done without you today."

Sutton's lips parted, and whatever she wore on them made them shimmer in the lessening light. "I wanted to give you a little of what you've given me. It's not enough, but it's something."

Fuck. She would destroy me.

My thumb stroked across her jaw, dangerously close to those beautiful lips. Her scent filled the SUV, wrapping around me in a stranglehold. Cinnamon and sugar with just a hint of vanilla. Maybe it was all the hours she spent in the bakery. Those scents were branded into her skin.

They teased and tugged, pulling me closer. Because I wanted to know if her skin tasted as good as it smelled.

"Cope!"

Luca's voice cut through my lust-induced haze and had us both jerking back. I couldn't help the curse that slipped free.

A small laugh escaped Sutton. "Little ones always have impeccable timing."

I grinned back at her. "He's lucky he's fucking cute."

We slid out of the SUV, but Luca was already running down the steps and rounding the vehicle. He threw himself at me, hugging me hard. "Are you okay? Mom said you needed to say goodbye to Teddy."

Fuck. It wasn't just Sutton who would destroy me. Luca would, too.

I hugged him back. "I'm all right."

Luca looked up at me, turquoise eyes shining. "Was it sad? Saying goodbye?"

"It was everything," I told him honestly. "Sad but also funny and happy. We told lots of stories about Teddy."

Luca worried his bottom lip. "Think you could tell me some of those stories one day?"

My chest constricted as I forced the lump in my throat down. "I'd like that."

"Good," Luca said, then grinned up at me. "I set up a movie marathon for us. All three *Mighty Ducks,* plus popcorn and brownies and lots of other snacks. Arden helped me after we rode horses. *The Mighty Ducks* always make me feel better when I'm sad. The snacks, too."

I chuckled. "How can I say no to that?" I glanced up at the doorway where Arden waited. "Thanks for hanging with Speedy."

She just shook her head. "Luca's good people. I'll hang with him anytime."

Luca grinned even wider. "Arden's going to teach me how to gallop!"

Sutton's face paled. "Gallop?" she squeaked.

Luca nodded so fast his head was a blur. "Yup! And maybe I can do barrel racing one day."

Sutton pressed a hand to her chest. "You can't love golf?"

His face scrunched up. "Sweater vests, Mom. Ew."

I laughed as I moved to wrap an arm around Sutton. "Give it up, Mama. Your kid is way too cool for golf."

She sighed, slumping against me. "It was worth a try."

My phone buzzed in my pocket, and I released Sutton to pull it out.

Angie: This just got sent to me. I thought you might want a heads-up.

An article from a huge sports site was linked. *Copeland Colson Uses Friend's Funeral to Show Off New Girlfriend.* I scanned the article, my temper spiking hotter with each sentence. Accusations that called into question whether I cared about Teddy's memory at all.

Fucking hell.

Then the page reloaded with an update.

This just in. We're hearing Cope decked teammate Marcus Warner, son of the late, great Weston Warner. When will the Sparks have enough and finally trade this risk to their organization? We're hearing it might be sooner rather than later.

CHAPTER TWENTY-THREE

Sutton

D O YOU THINK COPE IS OKAY?" LUCA ASKED AS I SET THE BOOK we were reading on the nightstand.

My tenderhearted boy. He might be a mini adrenaline junkie, but that didn't mean he didn't have a softer side. I loved the balance that continued to grow within him, and I wanted to nurture those empathetic pieces, even if it meant he had to live with worry. Because if there was one thing I could dream for my boy, it was for him to be kind. And kindness meant feeling things deeply.

I brushed those light-brown locks away from his face, exposing eyes that were almost identical to mine. "I think he's hurting, but he'll be okay."

Luca's lips pursed. "I wish I could make it better."

"Me, too, baby. But I know you helped tonight."

His brows rose. "I did?"

"Are you kidding me? A *Mighty Ducks* marathon with all the snacks in the world? What could be better than that?"

Luca let out a soft giggle. "It's the best movie ever."

I grinned at my kid. I'd memorized every word of the film over the past couple of years. It was a miracle we hadn't worn out the DVD with as much playtime as it got.

I leaned down and brushed my lips across Luca's temple. "So proud of you."

Pink hit his cheeks. "Moooom."

"I am. Nothing makes me prouder than seeing how you care for other people, how kind you are."

"I get it from you," Luca said softly. "You take care of everybody. Even the bees."

My heart squeezed. "I love you, Luca. More than bees love honey."

"More than bees love honey," Luca echoed, his voice sleepy.

"Get some sleep. You need your rest to be a hockey superstar."

"I do…"

His words trailed off, and I switched off the light as I stood, taking a moment to watch him sleep. I'd only been gone twelve hours, yet he somehow looked bigger. Sometimes, I blinked and could swear he'd grown.

An ache took root in my chest. I wanted to freeze each of these moments in my mind forever.

I finally forced myself to move. My slipper-clad feet padded silently across the floor as I stepped out into the hall, softly shutting the door behind me.

I couldn't help taking a few steps past my door, toward the opposite end of the hallway—to Cope's room. The door was shut, and I saw no light beneath it.

It made sense. It was already after nine. Luca had stayed up past his bedtime, thanks to all the sugar. And Cope had been through hell these past few days. He probably hadn't gotten much sleep and needed to catch up. But still, disappointment flared.

I wasn't sure what I'd have done if that light had been on. Walk down the hall and open the door? I didn't know if I was ready for that. For a million different reasons.

But standing in that hallway, I could still feel Cope's hand in mine. The feeling of his rough fingers holding mine tightly. The warmth that bled into me from his touch. It was a heat I hadn't felt in far too long.

A sound moved through the air, light at first, almost like the whine of an animal in protest. I frowned, not quite sure where it was coming from. Then the noise grew louder, more pained.

It was coming from the direction I was currently staring in. My feet were moving before I could consider the wisdom of the action. A shout sounded behind Cope's door, and I picked up to a jog.

I didn't hesitate for a single moment, just closed my hand around the doorknob and jerked the door open, hurrying to close it behind me so Luca wouldn't wake up. Cope's bedroom was massive, a study in gray tones as the moonlight streamed in through the large windows, unhindered by any curtains.

There was no time to take in the beauty of the photographs on the walls or any other design choices. My focus was on the man thrashing around on the bed that looked larger than a king. The sheets and blankets were twisted around his waist, exposing his bare chest.

At any other time, I might've been distracted by all that muscled skin on display, but not now. Not when Cope's beautiful face was contorted in pain. I recognized instantly that he was having a nightmare—a brutal one. But it was so intense I wasn't sure what to do.

I remembered reading that waking a person from a night terror could be dangerous for them and you, especially if you woke them with a physical touch. But I couldn't let him suffer either.

Moving to the side of the bed, I was close enough to speak in a whisper but outside of striking range. "Cope," I said softly, remembering the article's instructions to talk in calm, soothing tones.

Cope showed no signs of recognition or waking. His arm flailed to the side. "Dad!"

The shout had me jerking back, pain lancing my chest. It made sense that Teddy's death had brought back memories of Cope losing his dad and brother. But knowing how deeply he was suffering hurt worse than anything I could remember in a long time.

"Cope, you're safe. I'm right here." I did my best to keep my tone calm but raised my volume slightly, praying I could break through.

Cope flung his arms out like he was reaching for someone, trying to break free.

"I'm not going anywhere. Come back, Cope. Come back to me."

Cope's body jerked, then his eyes started to flutter. "Sutton?" he croaked.

His voice sounded as if he'd been screaming for hours, but relief flooded me. I moved then to sit on the bed, my hand instantly going to his. I needed the point of contact, something to assure me he was okay.

"Just a nightmare," I whispered. "You're okay."

Cope's hand spasmed around mine. "How did you know?"

"I heard you cry out after I put Luca down. I, uh, just wanted to make sure you were okay. I'm sorry I barged in—I—"

Cope gripped my hand harder. "Thank you."

A new sort of relief swept through me. I hadn't considered that I was invading Cope's privacy until just now. The fact that he wasn't bothered by it eased something in me I didn't want to look at too closely.

I studied Cope for a long moment. His light-brown hair clung to his forehead in spots so I brushed it back with my free hand, something I had done countless times to Luca. But this felt nothing like that. "Do you want to talk about it?"

A guardedness swept across Cope's dark-blue eyes. "Not especially."

I tried not to let that hurt. I wasn't especially good with secrets, not with everything I'd gone through with Roman. But I breathed through the sting, reminding myself I didn't have the right to all Cope's wounds, the things he buried deep. And it wasn't as if I'd given him all of mine. Sometimes, every single thing about me felt like a half truth.

"What can I do?" I finally asked. That was the only question that really mattered, wasn't it?

Cope stared at me for a long moment, his hand never releasing mine. "Stay."

CHAPTER TWENTY-FOUR

Cope

I WOKE TO FLAMES, THE SORT OF HEAT THAT COULD BURN A MAN alive but was so enticing you'd happily be reduced to ashes. It was everywhere, pulling me in deeper until I was lost.

The form in front of me arched, letting out a soft moan. My eyes flew open, finally taking in the source of the heat. Sutton's blond hair lay in wild waves around her. Only pieces of her features broke through it all: long lashes that fluttered with each exhale, her adorable nose, her plump lips, slightly parted, in the perfect shade of pink.

My dick stiffened where it had made itself at home against her ass. *Shit. Shit. Shit.* But I didn't move. Didn't release my hold on her. I couldn't.

Sutton had woven some sort of spell around me. One that held me captive. The only thing was, I didn't want to escape.

She let out another of those little moans, and my balls responded with an ache that would likely require a very cold shower later. She shifted and then froze, suddenly becoming aware of her surroundings. But I still didn't let go. I knew I should. Knew I was the last thing Sutton needed, but I couldn't make myself release her.

"Morning," I rasped, my lips teasing her ear.

"You're awake," she squeaked.

"Not sleep-talking."

"You, uh—I should move."

My mouth curved. "Should you?"

"You, um, have..." Her words trailed off.

"I'm hard, Sutton. Because it's morning, and I'm pretty sure I've been holding you all night. Plus, your ass is perfect."

She let out a choked laugh. "Thank you?"

"Really, I should be pissed as hell. This is torture to wake up to."

Sutton shifted then, pulling away and making me groan. She rolled over to face me, the early morning light casting her in a pink glow. Those damn bumblebee sweats made her look even more adorable. "Are you okay?"

"You mean other than having a hard-on from hell?" I asked.

She pinned me with an exasperated look. "Cope."

I chuckled and then took a mental survey. I felt far better than I had any right to. "I'm good. Thank you for waking me. And for staying."

Sutton's expression softened, and her fingers found mine beneath the covers, linking us. "Of course. How do you feel now? Were you able to sleep?"

I stared back at the woman opposite me. "Slept better than I have in over a decade."

Those turquoise eyes flared. "A decade?"

I shifted slightly, not releasing Sutton's fingers. "I haven't slept well since we lost my dad and Jacob."

"Nightmares?" she whispered.

I nodded. "Haven't been able to share a bed with anyone since because, well, you saw."

Sutton's mouth opened into an adorable O shape. "But last night—you—I—"

"You're different." That's what some part of me had recognized in my half-asleep state last night. Maybe because I'd felt her calming effect at the funeral. Maybe because I'd just fucking *needed* her.

Confusion swam in Sutton's eyes, but she didn't speak it. "I'm glad it helped. Having me here. If you need to talk about—"

I shook my head quickly. That wasn't a place I could go. Not ever. If I really dove into the memories, the loss, the guilt, I wouldn't come up for air again. It would drown me.

Sutton worried her bottom lip. "Okay."

I heard the pain in that single word. *Fuck.* She was the last person I wanted to hurt. "It's not you. I just—I can't, Warrior. Can't go there with anyone. It's too hard."

The pain transformed into empathy. "It's not healthy to keep it all stored up. You don't have to talk to me, but you should talk to *someone.*"

My gut churned. "I'll think about it," I lied.

Sutton was quiet for a moment and then reached to lay a palm on my cheek. "I know what it's like to have memories that haunt you. I'm here if you're ever ready."

The feeling in my gut shifted and changed, a different sort of fear taking root. "Sutton—"

My phone's alarm went off. I cursed as I broke contact with her and moved to shut it off. By the time I fumbled with the damn device, Sutton had already gotten out of bed and was moving to the door.

"I need to shower and get Luca up. Are you okay with taking him to hockey today?"

Nothing in Sutton's words was cold, but I felt the wall she'd put up between us. One that kept me from knowing what she'd been through and what ghosts she was hiding. Fear's icy claws dug in deep.

"Of course."

"Thank you," she said quickly before ducking out of the room.

I collapsed back onto the pillows, playing different moments over and over in my head. Ones that hinted at Sutton having been through more than she was letting on. My fingers itched to type out a text to Anson and ask him to have his hacker look into Sutton in addition to his dirt-finding mission on her landlord.

I fisted my hand, resisting the urge. I knew Sutton would see it as a betrayal, and I had a feeling the only way to get her to open up would be to share my scars.

My phone dinged, breaking me away from my swirling thoughts. I grabbed the device and swiped my finger across the screen. The sibling text chain popped up. Today's group name was *Flounder's Fan Club*. Flounder was the fish we'd had growing up that our mom finally confessed was actually half a dozen fish. She'd replace them when they died.

Fallon: Cope, did you make it back okay?

I wasn't surprised that she was the one checking in first. I also knew she'd already likely gotten all the info she could get from Arden.

Me: I'm back. All good. Getting back into the hockey coach life today.

Kye: Hope you don't break one of the kid's noses if they look at you wrong.

I glowered at the screen.

Rhodes: Not helping, tattoo man.

Kye: What? You guys want to know what happened, and your tiptoeing around will take way too fucking long. I haven't had coffee yet.

Fallon: Careful drinking that from now on because I'm going to mix some ex-lax with your creamer.

Shep: You know you've stuck your foot in it when Fal is threatening you, dude.

Fucking great. It was clear my siblings had a side chat going where they were all worrying I was cracking.

> **Me:** I'm okay, really. Marcus is a douchebag who deserves a broken nose. But I only bruised his ribs. And I'm reining it in. No more punching in churches.
>
> **Kye:** Notice he didn't promise not to punch elsewhere.
>
> **Fallon:** You punched him in the CHURCH? I thought it was in the parking lot or something.
>
> **Shep:** Fal has a point. You could get smited for that or something.
>
> **Me:** You guys are giving me a migraine.
>
> **Rhodes:** Seriously, Cope. Are you okay? We're worried.

That just had more guilt digging in. My siblings didn't need more stress right now, especially after everything Rhodes and Shep went through in the past few months. But I knew the only way to ease their concern was to give them something. A piece of the truth but not all of it.

> **Me:** I'm not okay. Losing Teddy hurt like hell. And it messed with my head. But I'm pulling it together. Sutton helped.

There were no responses for a moment, and I worried I might've screwed up. With my family, admitting you weren't okay could lead to eight people showing up on your doorstep.

> **Fallon:** I like her.

Kye: Careful, dude. "I like her" is Fal code for her planning your wedding.

I couldn't help a low chuckle at that. Fallon was the most hopeless romantic of us all, and nothing could quash that.

Fallon: Kyler Blackheart, I mean Blackwood, I am going to glitter bomb your office.

Fal followed up her text with half a dozen glitter explosion GIFs.

Trace: My advice? Don't ignore her. Remember my truck?

This time, I didn't chuckle, I outright laughed.

Rhodes: She's tiny but vicious, and she's got a harsh vengeful streak.

Fallon: He told Mom I was sneaking out to meet Cooper at the river. He deserved way worse than a truck full of magenta glitter!

Trace: I tried for months to get that shit out. Nothing worked. I finally had to sell the damn thing. And it wasn't even me. It was Kye!

Kye: Dude, you did not just throw me under the bus.

Fallon: Blackheart, you're going down. Prepare for glitter Armageddon.

More glitter GIFs, emojis, and even a video were sent.

Arden: It's six in the morning. Why are there 82 million glitter explosions on my phone?

Rhodes: Fal is planning epic retribution.

Arden: Makes sense.

I flipped the chat to silent and dropped the phone onto the mattress as I slid out of bed. My siblings might be interfering as all hell, but I was so damn lucky to have them. A pang lit along my sternum as Jacob's face flashed in my mind. Who would he have been in this chat? A shit-stirrer like Kye and me? Law and order like Trace? Or something uniquely him?

We'd never know. And I'd have to carry the weight of that for the rest of my days.

CHAPTER TWENTY-FIVE

Sutton

SOFT STRAINS OF OLD-SCHOOL GARTH BROOKS FILTERED through the speakers as I gently squeezed the piping bag. It was a delicate balance I'd learned over the years. Not so hard that the frosting exploded in a mess onto the cupcakes, but with enough pressure to get the exact flow I needed for each design.

Today's project was a combination of unicorns and rainbows for an eight-year-old girl's birthday. I'd gone all out with the rainbows, using blue frosting for the base and decorating them with fluffy, white clouds that anchored a gummy rainbow candy. I knew the little girl's mom would be thrilled with the end result.

I moved on to the next set of clouds, trying to focus on the music. Because if I didn't think about the music, my mind filled with thoughts of Cope. How it had felt to wake in his arms the other morning. The firm pressure of him pressed against my ass. How I'd wanted to arch into him and—

"Sutton?" Thea cut into my thirsty space out.

I pressed too hard on the piping bag and sent a glob of frosting flying.

Thea's eyes went wide, and her hand covered her mouth. "I'm so sorry. I thought you heard me come in."

I shook my head, grabbing a towel to clean up the mess. At least I hadn't ruined the cupcake itself. "Not your fault. I was in la-la land apparently." A la-la land where all I could think about was Cope's hands and—*nope, nope, nope.* I could not go there.

Thea rounded the worktable so she faced me head-on. "Are you okay?"

"Sure," I said, trying to refocus on my decorating. "Why wouldn't I be?"

"Oh, I don't know, maybe because you moved in with a bossy hockey player a few weeks ago and haven't shared one tidbit of info with me. Your *best* friend. And then he loses *his* friend, and you run off to Seattle to go to the funeral with him, and *still* no info for your bestest friend. And finally, I had to see all over sports and gossip blogs alike that you two looked *extremely* cozy leaving the church. And still, you haven't said a word."

I didn't shoot frosting across the table this time. I dropped the bag altogether, the blood draining from my face. "There are pictures of us?"

I knew the photographers had been there, but I'd hoped they were taking shots of the players and that I would simply be in the background.

Thea's brow furrowed as she pulled out her phone. "Lots of speculation on the two of you."

My hand shook as I took the device from her. *Copeland Colson Gets Cozy with Mystery Woman.* There we were, front and center on the gossip blog. The text below touched on the fight between Marcus and Cope, even going so far as to question if it was about me.

"Why are these people so awful?" I muttered.

"Trust me, I'm not a fan of the paps or the vicious sites they feed. But I didn't read anything too bad."

Thea would understand better than most. She had a history

with a famous actor who'd been far from golden. One who had almost ruined her life.

She moved around the table until she was at my side. "What's going on?"

My throat burned. I couldn't lie to her, not after everything she'd shared with me. But I couldn't get myself to give her the whole truth either. "I just—I don't want my photo getting out there. There are a few people I'd rather not know where I am."

Thea stiffened beside me. "Luca's dad?"

I nodded. "He's one of them."

"Did he hurt you? I swear to God, I will castrate him with a rusty spork if he—"

"A spork, huh?" I asked, trying to inject some levity back into our conversation. But Thea didn't take the bait.

"Sutton."

"He didn't hurt me. Not in the way you think."

Thea didn't look appeased. "I know there is more than one way to inflict pain."

Unease settled in my gut. "He wasn't abusive in any way. He's an addict. Got hooked after an injury, and that disease ripped our whole world apart. He got mixed up with some bad people, and I needed to get Luca and me far away."

There. I'd said it. It was the most I'd opened up in years.

Memories pressed against all the walls I'd carefully constructed in my mind. The blow to my ribs and the blinding pain that followed. The burn when my lip split. The worry that the men would do so much worse.

"Sutton," Thea whispered, her hand covering mine.

"I'm okay," I croaked. "I just don't like going back there. Remembering. Luca and I got a fresh start when we came here, and I want to keep it that way."

Thea's fingers curled around my hand, squeezing. "Okay. Just tell me, does Cope know?"

I shook my head. "Why would he?"

"Maybe because you two have been attached at the hip for almost a month now, and he looks at you like you're the sun, moon, and stars all wrapped into one."

My heart hammered against my ribs. "He does not."

Thea sent me a droll look. "Girl, you know I love you, but I am not going to play idiot so you can pretend you two haven't gotten thick as thieves."

Thieves was probably the most accurate term Thea could've picked. Because Cope was a damn thief. Without me realizing it and without my permission, he'd stolen my heart.

"Sutton. I know he has his demons, but he's a good man."

"The best," I choked out, trying to fight back tears.

"Hey, hey." Thea pulled me into a hug. "What are the tears about?"

"I'm scared," I admitted.

She pulled back. "Of Cope?"

I shook my head quickly. "Well, kind of. I'm not sure he's in a place to be more than what we are."

"Which is?"

"Friends?" I mumbled. "Best friends?"

"How dare he?" Thea said, lips twitching. "Trying to steal my best-friend status..."

I tried to smile, but my lips couldn't quite get there. "I don't know how to explain it. We lean on each other. Share things I don't think either of us has let anyone else in on. But at the same time, we never tell each other the whole story."

Thea frowned as she mulled over my words. "I get that. Shep and I had some of those moments."

"That's different," I argued. "Shep was clear about his interest in you from day one. He was a man possessed."

"If you don't think Cope looks at you the same way, we may need to take you to get your eyesight checked."

I shook my head. "He's never even kissed me."

Thea's mouth flattened into a firm line. "Maybe he's waiting for you to show him you're ready."

"I don't think so. I know he's attracted to me, but I'm not sure he'll ever take that leap. And maybe that's for the best."

Thea released her hold on me. "You know what we need?"

"Margaritas and a two-week Caribbean vacation?"

She chuckled. "Let's look into that. But in the meantime, we need a girls' night out."

I opened my mouth to argue, but a new voice cut me off.

"Did someone say girls' night?" Lolli singsonged. "I have been *waiting* for this. I just got some new cowboy boots that need to see a dance floor."

Thea's mouth stretched into a wide smile. "The country bar?"

Lolli did some sort of line-dancing move that ended in a twirl. "The cowboys are calling my name."

"I've got a cowboy hat," Walter called from behind the counter. "And I could come up with some creative things to do with that rope."

I choked on a laugh, and my cheeks flamed.

"I'm not a woman to be tied down, Walter. I need to fly free," Lolli said, her hands going to her hips and sending her endless stream of bracelets jangling.

He just grinned at her, making the lines in his face more pronounced. "I might not succeed, but we'll have the time of our lives trying."

Thea covered her laugh with a cough. "Throw the man a bone, Lolli. He's been trying to win you over for years."

Lolli lifted her chin in defiance. "I'm too wild for him."

"I'll show you wild," Walter said with a little growl in his voice. *Oh, boy.*

"Excuse me," a male voice said, cutting through our ridiculous conversation.

Walter turned to face the middle-aged man at the counter. "Welcome to The Mix Up. What can I get for you?"

The poor man probably wished for one of those *Men in Black* mind eraser things after what he'd likely overheard.

"Is the owner or manager in?" he asked.

His voice had a professionalism that had me shifting into business-owner mode. I did a quick appraisal. He was likely in his forties, wearing khakis and a polo shirt, and holding a clipboard. I moved toward the counter. "Hello, I'm Sutton Holland. I own the bakery. How can I help you?"

The man gave me a curt nod, not cold in any way but efficient. "I'm Craig Leonard. I work for the Oregon Health Authority. There was an anonymous complaint about your establishment. I'm here to do a spot check."

And with that, my world dropped out from under me. I was a stickler for cleanliness in my bakery, being one of those people who was over the top in my dislike of germs. But you never knew what an inspector might find that wasn't exactly as the code required.

And if he fined me or paused me being able to serve? I'd never recover.

CHAPTER TWENTY-SIX

Sutton

THE LAST THING I WANTED TO DO TONIGHT WAS GO OUT TO A bar—not even one that had a country band playing. Not after the day I'd had.

The inspector from the Health Authority hadn't found anything that would affect my license to serve food and beverages, but when I'd asked what the report had been about, he'd gotten cagey. Thea had swooped in to get more information, telling him we wanted to fix anything a customer perceived as not being up to our excellent standards.

That had seemed to set the inspector at ease, and he shared that someone had reported we weren't washing the dishes properly. I knew that was complete bull. We had a three-step process *before* putting them in an industrial washer.

It had to be Rick trying to mess with my business. I knew he was annoyed that he couldn't up my rent, but I never thought he'd take it so far as to shut me down. The thought had my stomach churning. If I got booted from my current spot, I didn't have enough reserves to set up elsewhere. And I needed every cent I was saving on rent now to get settled in a new apartment.

My phone dinged on the bathroom counter, and I forced my thoughts away from all those depressing possibilities.

> **Thea:** We're five minutes away. If you're in pajamas, I'll make you come anyway.

One corner of my mouth kicked up as I picked up my phone and quickly typed out a reply.

> **Me:** It's not you who scares me. It's Lolli. So, I'm almost ready.

> **Thea:** Wait until you see her outfit…

I grinned down at the device. Lolli never disappointed.

I set my phone down and picked up my makeup brush. If we were doing a girls' night, I was going all out. I dabbed a smoky color on the outside corners of my eyes, sweeping it across the lids. Then I swapped the color for something lighter with a glittery accent that made the turquoise of my eyes really pop. I followed it with eyeliner and lip gloss and figured I was ready.

Stepping back, I surveyed myself. It wasn't half-bad. It had been so long since I'd had a reason to really dress up. Not that my outfit was fancy, but having a reason to put a little more effort in was nice. I wore a floaty dress in a dark blue that hit me right at mid-thigh. The spaghetti straps and lacy bodice did great things for my boobs, and the skirt's gauzy material gave it a flouncy, fun air.

I was thankful I'd grabbed a pair of cowboy boots at the thrift store a couple of months ago. The only thing I didn't have was a hat. But that would've ruined the hour I'd spent taming my hair into loose curls.

Taking a deep breath, I grabbed my clutch and headed out. As I moved into the hallway, I heard voices below. It wasn't just Luca and Cope; I heard Arden's mixed in there, too. It sounded like they were playing a game.

Luca hooted. "Four spots, baybeeeee."

As I descended the stairs and turned toward the living room, my mouth was already curving. Luca stood on the couch, shaking his booty in a ridiculous dance that had both Arden and Cope fighting laughter. "Is he dominating Candyland again?"

Their heads turned toward me, and Arden shot me an amused smile. "I've never met anyone with such good luck. You should take him to Vegas."

"Mom," Luca said almost reverently. "You look *so* pretty."

I fought a blush, partially at the attention and partly because it was embarrassing that my kid was this shocked over my appearance. But I couldn't respond because I was too distracted by heat. I could feel Cope's gaze sweeping over me, settling on all sorts of different places. My legs. My chest. My face.

"He's right," Cope said, grit coating his words. "You look stunning."

I bit my bottom lip. "Thank you," I whispered, tripping over the simple statement. "Arden, are you coming with us?"

Her lips twitched, those gray-violet eyes twinkling as though she knew exactly what I was doing. "Do I look like I'm going?"

I did a quick sweep of Cope's sister. She wore what looked like a workout outfit: leggings and a tee that slid off one shoulder, exposing a sports bra. "Looks like you're ready to dance."

Arden scoffed. "Not really my scene."

"Not really mine either," I admitted.

"You don't have to go," Cope said quickly. "You could stay and hang with us. We're going to play Monopoly Junior after this. Party of the century."

Arden smacked Cope's stomach with the back of her hand. "Sutton deserves a night out with friends. Let her live."

Cope scowled at his sister. "This is living, too," he grumbled.

Arden rolled her eyes before shaking her head. "*Go.* Have fun. And don't come home before midnight, at least." She waggled her eyebrows. "Or don't come home at all."

The glare Cope sent his sister would've had me swallowing my tongue, but Arden didn't seem fazed in the slightest. But before he could say another word, the front door swung open, and Thea and Rhodes filled the entryway.

"Let's go shake our asses with some cowboys!" Rhodes shouted.

"She has more game than all of us put together," Rhodes mumbled as she sipped her margarita on the rocks.

Thea chuckled. "I would never want to compete for a man with her. I'd lose every time."

I took a sip of my own margarita, the tequila warming me from the inside as I studied Lolli on the dance floor. She had come to play. She wore black boots, black jeans, and a black button-down. They were all decorated in a western-wear pattern, but the design itself was made up of tiny jewels with pot leaves at the center. She'd currently charmed three cowboys into dancing with her, and I wouldn't be surprised if another two joined soon.

"She's a true legend," I said, laughter coating my words.

"Soooooo," Rhodes began, the light in her hazel eyes dancing. "My brother certainly had his eyes on you when we left tonight."

My face flamed. "He's probably just worried I'll end up kidnapped because I wasn't aware of my surroundings or something."

"Kye's that way. It's a miracle if I get anything past him," Fallon mumbled, taking a sip of a pink drink.

That had me fighting a smile. Kyler's protective streak when it came to Fallon was legendary. "Well, we made it out with no babysitters."

"Dang straight," Fallon said, lifting her glass in cheers. We clinked, and then she stood. "Come on. Since we're free, we should dance."

I slid off my stool as the band shifted into an upbeat song I recognized from the radio station I always had playing at the bakery. "I like the way you think."

Lifting the glass to my lips, I downed the rest of my drink in one slug.

"Uh-oh," Thea said, humor lacing her words. "Lolli isn't the only one who came to play."

I shot her a grin. "As Shania Twain says, 'Let's go, girls.'"

Rhodes let out a hoot, downing her drink. And then we all headed to the dance floor as the band sang about cold beers and tight jeans that fit just right. We danced and jumped and laughed our asses off.

Thea was right. I'd needed this. A reminder of why I fought so hard. So I could truly *live*. I hadn't been doing enough of that.

The music slowed, and a figure in a cowboy hat moved into my space, holding out his hand. "Can I have this dance?"

The man was tall and more than a little good-looking, but I couldn't help comparing him to Cope in my mind. His shoulders weren't quite as broad. There was no scar on his lip that somehow made him more gorgeous. No adorable crook in his nose.

I'm an idiot.

Cope wasn't here. He hadn't made any sort of moves that let me know he was interested in any more than a flirty friendship, and nothing in those few *almost* moments showed he was serious about us being *more*. But here was a handsome man asking me to dance, being clear about his intentions.

I took the proffered palm. "I'd love to."

The man swung me into his arms with ease. It was clear he knew what he was doing on the dance floor, and I let him sweep me away as the band slipped into a ballad. But the man's hold wasn't comfortable and heated the way Cope's was. It didn't have me fighting the urge to lean in closer.

He swung me into a spin and then back, and I knew I should be enjoying the dance more than I was. The man pulled me a bit closer, his face not far from mine. And then a hand landed on his shoulder.

"I'm afraid I'm going to have to ask to cut in."

That voice. The smoky heat and grit had my body responding instantly. I sucked in a breath as my gaze locked with dark-blue eyes. But I could only get out his name.

"Cope."

CHAPTER TWENTY-SEVEN

Cope

I WANTED TO KILL HIM. AND I DIDN'T WANT TO MAKE IT AN EASY death either. The urge to rip his limbs from his body was so strong it stole the damn air from my lungs.

But murder was wrong. And I didn't especially want to do twenty to life for beating a man to death with his own arms. But when I'd seen his hand dip lower on Sutton's back, I thought it might be worth it.

She blinked up at me, shock evident in those hypnotic, turquoise eyes—eyes I could lose myself in for eternity and never get bored. "W-what are you doing here?" she stammered.

The man who still had his damn hands on her looked between us. "You know him?"

Sutton nodded quickly. "He's my, um, friend."

Jesus. Her friend? Sutton saying it out loud made me realize just how wrong that was. I wanted to be so much more than that. Tonight, all the reasons I'd been holding myself back seemed to evaporate in a single breath. Sutton had been slowly chipping away at my defenses, but seeing her in this dress? It had sent my remaining walls crumbling to dust.

"You want to talk to him?" the man asked.

My temper flared, but it was mixed with a grudging respect for his ensuring Sutton was comfortable. The dude had no idea who I was with my ballcap hiding half my face. And even if he had, checking with her was the right thing to do.

She nodded quickly. "I'm good. Thank you for the, um, dance."

The man tipped his cowboy hat to her. "Thank *you*. Enjoy your night, ma'am."

"Ma'am?" I scoffed the second he was out of earshot.

Sutton's confused expression morphed into one of anger. "It was polite. Which is saying something since you rudely interrupted."

Heat crept up my neck. "You wanted to keep dancing with him?" I hated the jealousy that flared hot and bright, making my pulse thrum in my neck.

"It was nice," Sutton bit out.

"Nice?" I growled, pulling her into my arms as the band shifted into another song. It wasn't fast or slow, somewhere in the middle.

"Yes," she clipped. "And this was supposed to be a girls' night. No boys allowed."

"Good thing I'm not a boy, then." I moved her closer to me, my thigh shifting to between her legs. Sutton's eyes sparked with blue heat, the kind that scalded. But I'd wear her burn scars with pride.

"You know what I mean." Sutton's words had a breathy quality that had my dick stiffening in my goddamned jeans.

"We thought you might need a ride home." It was a complete lie. When I texted Shep, he'd told me that he and Anson had already planned to ride out to pick up the girls and their vehicle, but not until closer to midnight. I'd changed that real quick. And it was a damn good thing I had.

Anger flashed through me, that green-eyed monster jealousy curling in my gut. I didn't want Sutton dancing with some strange asshole. I wanted to be the only one who held her. And that was fucked. Because I didn't deserve her. Not even close.

I didn't deserve to touch her silky skin, tangle my fingers in those soft locks, or take that mouth like a man possessed. She deserved so much better than me, but it didn't change the fact that I wanted her anyway. And would do anything to have her, whatever she'd give.

The shade of Sutton's eyes shifted, turning a darker teal like the Caribbean Sea before a storm. "Cope…"

"I don't deserve you," I rasped.

Her eyes widened, shock filling them.

"You should have everything. Someone who isn't broken or fucked up, whose head isn't a nightmare on a good day. You need someone good. Someone who will do everything to take care of you and Luca. Someone so much better than me."

Sutton ripped herself out of my arms and gave my chest a shove. "Don't you think *I* should have a say in what and who I deserve? What I *need*?"

"Sutton—"

"No," she snapped, cutting me off. "I've worked so damn hard to stand on my own two feet. I'm in charge of my life, Cope. And if you would've stopped long enough to ask me what I wanted, you might've found out it was you."

Before I could say a word, she stalked off.

Fuck.

My legs were already moving. I should've trusted my body more than my brain, anyway. My mind always twisted things, changing how the world looked. And not being able to trust what you saw was a hell of a thing.

I moved through the crowd, trying to catch up with Sutton, but she was tinier, slipping easily around people as she darted for the back hallway. It was less crowded there. A handful of folks waited for the restrooms, but Sutton kept moving past them.

The red *Exit* sign loomed at the end of the hall, and I knew where she was headed. I picked up to a jog, reaching her just before she got to the door.

"Cope—"

I cut her off by grabbing her hand and tugging her toward the office. Relief swept through me when the knob turned. I'd have to thank Rob for keeping it unlocked tonight.

"What are you doing?" Sutton demanded, her temper still hot. "You can't just break into someone's office."

"It's not breaking in if the door's unlocked. And I know the owner," I clipped, locking the door behind me. I wasn't about to let an interruption derail this conversation.

Sutton crossed her arms under her breasts. I knew she'd done it out of irritation, but it only thrust those swells higher, short-circuiting my brain.

"What?" she demanded. "What is *so* important that you had to interrupt a perfectly nice evening just to tell me how much you don't want me? You don't think we should be together? *Fine*. Now, can we be done with whatever this is?"

I prowled toward her, eating up the distance in long strides. "I never *once* said I didn't want you. Fuck, Warrior. I think about you with every other breath. I dream about you. And when I wake up, I swear I can still taste you on my tongue."

Sutton's eyes went wide. "You dream about me?"

"Haven't had dreams like these since I was thirteen and going through puberty," I growled. "But it's so much worse. Because your smell is everywhere. That cinnamon, sugar, and a hint of vanilla. I swear it's burned into the walls. I haven't changed my sheets since you slept in my bed because I don't want to smell anything else. It's hell. But I'll gladly go down in those flames."

"Cope," she whispered.

"It's torture. Being so close to you and not having everything. All of you. Knowing what your skin feels like and wanting to know what it feels like *everywhere*. Wondering if you taste as good as you smell."

"Cope."

"And the way you say my goddamned name. I want to know how your tongue curves around it when I sink into you. When you're pulsing around my cock and sucking me deep."

Sutton shifted, adjusting her stance, and my gaze dropped to her legs.

"Killing me. The way you press those pretty little thighs together… But it's a death I'll take every time."

Sutton's mouth dropped open, forming a perfect little O.

"Tell me what you need, Warrior. You want to be in charge? Take it."

Sparks flashed in those turquoise eyes, lighting them from within. "I want you, Cope. I want you to take me. I want to know what it's like to lose myself in you and forget my own name. I want it all."

"About fucking time," I muttered. And then I was on her.

CHAPTER TWENTY-EIGHT

Sutton

COPE DIDN'T HESITATE. THERE WAS NONE OF THE UNCERTAINTY from the dance floor. None of the determination to protect me from himself. It was as if my words had broken some self-imposed dam, leaving only need.

Cope ate up the final space between us in two long strides. His hands sank into my hair, and he pulled me toward him. There was no gentle easing into things. Cope gave me exactly what I'd asked for. He took.

His fingers tightened in my hair, tipping my head back and giving him better access. His tongue dove in, demanding. As his taste flooded me, that minty bite with something uniquely him, my knees nearly buckled.

But Cope didn't let me fall. One hand slipped to my waist, holding me to him. That's when I felt it—his hard length pressing against his jeans. My core seized, grasping nothing but how badly I wanted to feel Cope inside me. To know what it was like to have him powering into me with all the force he was capable of.

Cope tore his mouth from mine. "Fuck, Warrior. You taste even better than in my dreams."

My core fluttered this time as if he were speaking straight to my very center. "Cope," I breathed.

Those dark-blue eyes hooded, and Cope backed me up until I hit the desk. He lifted me in one easy move, sitting my ass on the edge and sending a pencil holder flying, its contents spilling onto the wooden surface. My legs encircled him on instinct, not wanting to lose the feel of him, even through our clothes. He growled as I pulled him tighter to me.

"Demanding little thing, aren't you?" he asked, one corner of his mouth kicking up.

My lips curved in answer as I knocked his ballcap free. "That's how you get what you want."

"Damn straight." Cope's fingers trailed down my neck to my collarbone. He traced it with featherlight fingertips until he reached the strap of my dress.

My nipples pebbled in response to the touch, the promise, *him*. He twisted the fabric, pulling it down in a painfully slow move. My breasts came free with the final shift, and Cope's pupils dilated.

"No bra?" he snarled.

I pressed my lips together to stop a giggle from escaping. "Can't really wear one with this dress."

"Fucking hell, Warrior. So goddamned beautiful." Those clever fingers traced the underside of my breast, and I sucked in a breath, my palms bracing me on the desk. "So perfect." Those fingertips rose, a single digit tracing the outskirts of my nipple.

The peaks twisted tighter in response, almost painfully, as if every nerve ending in my body was waking up after years of nothing but numbness. Cope's head dropped, and he took one bud into his mouth, pulling it deep.

I nearly bowed off the desk as I arched into him. A moan slipped from my lips as I lifted one hand to his beautiful hair, my fingers tangled in the strands, gripping him tightly.

Cope let out a growl, sending vibrations through my skin and a rush of wetness between my legs.

"Cope." His name was a moan, but I couldn't find it in me to care. Just like I couldn't care that we were in someone's office at a bar. It only heightened every touch and sensation.

Teeth grazed my nipple, and I pulled Cope's hair harder, my legs gripping him tighter at the same time. "Killing me," Cope snarled, pulling free.

He moved before I could say anything, sinking to his knees with a force that made my legs unhook from his waist. Cope's hands slid up my calves toward my thighs. "I've dreamed of what this skin would feel like, of having my hands between these pretty little thighs. Tell me you'll give that to me."

My breath came in quick pants as I nodded.

Cope squeezed my legs. "Need your words, Warrior."

"Yes," I whispered.

That was all Cope needed. He spread me wide and leaned in, running his nose along the fabric of my lacy thong. "You smell even better than in my dreams, too."

My legs tried to squeeze closed, but Cope kept them forced wide. There was no escape. I couldn't help the whimper that slipped from my lips as his finger stroked me over the fabric.

"Memorizing this image. Know it's only going to get better. But I'm not going to miss a goddamned thing."

My whole body shuddered as wetness gathered between my thighs. My heart thudded against my ribs as Cope reached for something on the desk. A second later, cool metal slid against my skin. The juxtaposition between that and the heat coursing through me sent a delicious shiver through me. My gaze snapped down, searching out the source.

A pair of scissors.

I gaped as Cope twisted the band of my thong on one hip and snipped the fabric clean through. The cool metal slid across my lower belly, making me suck in a breath. But before I could get out another word, Cope snipped the other side.

"You did not," I said, staring down at him.

A wolfish grin spread across Cope's face as he tugged the fabric free. "Saving these." He reached behind his back and slid the scrap of lace into his pocket.

The sight had more heat and wetness gathering at my core. Cope set the scissors on the desk, and then his hands were back, sliding up my thighs and pushing them wider. Every part of me was on display. For him. And he looked at me the way an artist stared reverently at the ceiling of the Sistine Chapel.

I squirmed on the desk, and Cope's hands tightened on my thighs, his gaze lifting to my face. "Don't hide from me." One hand slid higher, his finger stroking my seam. "I want all of you. My dreams come to life."

It was more than heat now. It was the buildup of all my feelings breaking free. Cope was a damn thief, sneaking in and stealing what I didn't think I'd ever be able to give again. My eyes burned, but that was stolen, too, as his deft fingers teased my opening.

"Cope," I breathed.

"Love the sound of my name on your lips. But I love your pretty little moans more." His head moved as he slid two fingers inside me. His tongue lashed across that sensitive flesh in a move that had my ass lifting right off the desk as Cope lifted my legs over his shoulders.

His tongue circled my clit, teasing, toying, and bringing it to attention. My legs gripped him tighter as a sound that was more animal than human left my lips. I should've been embarrassed. Should've tried to rein myself in. But I couldn't.

Or maybe it was that I didn't want to. Cope made me feel reckless for the first time in years. He made me want to reach for a freedom I thought was lost to me forever.

So, I did.

My back arched as I gripped the edge of the desk behind me. Cope's fingers drove deeper and circled in a twist that had my inner walls trembling.

"Don't come," he ordered, speaking against that bundle of nerves. The vibrations only sent my body higher.

"I don't really control that," I said between breaths that came out in short pants.

"My girl can hold it back. Fight it off. For me." Cope's fingers swirled again, and I let out a whimper. "So beautiful. My warrior."

His fingers pumped in and out, his tongue flicking out and teasing my clit in a pattern I couldn't predict. The tempo would be the death of me. I'd have a stroke trying to keep from shattering.

The edge of the desk bit into my palms, and the pressure helped me to fight off the orgasm, but as Cope's fingers dragged in an arc against my walls, I cried out.

"Please."

"Didn't think she could get any more gorgeous. And then she begs."

Cope's voice was coated in sandpaper and need. And that only added to his potency. The heels of my boots dug into his back as if I were trying to give him a little of the pain I was experiencing. The discomfort of trying to hold off the tidal wave of sensation.

He let out a growl against my clit. "Want to feel those boots digging into my ass as I take you."

Fucking hell. This man would kill me. "Then do it," I snapped, a mixture of desperate need and frustration coursing through me.

Cope read my tone and moved in a flash. "Tell me you're on birth control."

The ordered plea only sent more wetness between my legs, my core pulsing as it missed Cope's fingers. "The pill. I've been checked."

"I get physicals on the regular. Tell me I can take you bare."

More of that rough plea. It had my nipples tightening to the point of pain. I wanted that. Wanted to feel every part of him, moving in me, releasing. I wanted it all.

"Yes," I breathed.

Cope's hands were on the button of his jeans then, his fingers deftly undoing them and sliding them down his thighs. His cock stood at attention, long and thick, and I couldn't help but swallow.

"Cope..."

His hand encircled his dick, stroking once, twice. "For the love of God, tell me you aren't having second thoughts."

"You have a big dick." The words were out before I could stop them.

His lips twitched. "Thanks for noticing, baby."

"I, um, uh—"

Cope moved between my legs, one hand sliding into my hair and taking hold. "You're ready for me. Don't worry, Warrior. It'll fit."

I shuddered as his tip bumped my entrance, but my nerves slid away because, God, I wanted him inside me. Cope's lips skimmed the column of my neck. "Tell me you're ready."

There was only one answer. "Yes."

Cope's hand tightened in my hair, arching me back as he slid inside in one long, powerful thrust. My mouth fell open in a silent O as he filled me. The sensation fluttered along that line of pleasure and pain, the kind that only drove every feeling higher.

Cope slid out and then back in, deeper this time. "Fucking heaven."

My legs encircled him, my boots digging into his ass, driving him deeper. It was all he needed. Cope powered into me with a force that had my eyes watering and my muscles quaking.

"Cope," I whispered.

His fingers tightened in my hair. "Hold on. Need more of you. More of this perfect heat."

He took me. Over and over. My whole body moved with his, attuned to his every shift.

"Warrior," he snarled.

I knew he was ready. And that nickname, roughly sworn, tipped me over the edge. I clamped down on Cope, my inner walls convulsing as my heels dug in harder. But he didn't stop. Every wave of my orgasm only drew him deeper.

With a rough curse, Cope came. The feel of him releasing inside me pulled another wave from my body, and I couldn't hold back the cry that escaped my lips. Cope rode each tremor, dragging them out until I collapsed back onto the desk.

He ran a hand down my neck, between my breasts, and over my now-bunched dress to circle my navel. "I've never seen anything more beautiful than this sight. Need to burn it into my memory."

My chest heaved as I tried to catch my breath. Cope came into focus in snapshots. His hair wild now. His dark-blue eyes lighter. Color in his cheeks. He was more alive than I'd ever seen him. I never wanted to forget this moment either. "You're beautiful."

His mouth quirked. "I've got nothing on you."

Slowly, Cope slid out of me, and I couldn't help the slight wince. His hands were instantly there, gently lifting me, concern all over his face. "Was it too much?"

My hands went to his cheeks, the scruff tickling my palms and reminding me what it had felt like against my thighs. "It was perfect."

His concern melted into a softness that had the contents of my chest rearranging. Cope leaned over, his lips brushing mine. "Was it worth me breaking the girls' night rule?"

A laugh bubbled out of me. "Definitely worth it."

His eyes searched mine. "Stay with me tonight?"

My heart thudded against my chest. This was different. I wasn't soothing him from a nightmare. It was more. *We* were more. But I still found one reckless word breaking free. "Yes."

CHAPTER TWENTY-NINE

Cope

COACH KENNER BLEW HIS WHISTLE, AND THE TINY MONSTERS flew into action on the ice rink. Some of them had real skill, but others were a comedy of errors. All in all, they were having the time of their lives, and that's what mattered.

Kenner shot a glance in my direction. "They're getting better."

"They are," I agreed but winced as one of the kids took a header into the boards.

Kenner chuckled. "Sometimes." He was quiet for a moment as the scrimmage continued. "I heard Sutton and Luca are staying with you."

Something about the statement had me stiffening. It shouldn't have surprised me, given how gossip moved in Sparrow Falls, but I didn't want people whispering about Sutton.

"Yeah. They are." I wasn't giving him more than that. If he wanted to know something, he could grow some balls and ask.

Kenner studied me for a moment before turning back to the ice. "That's nice of you. I know she's good friends with your sister."

Annoyance flickered through me. I knew the play he was making.

"I don't love my sister that much," I muttered. That was a lie. I'd do anything for Rhodes or any of my siblings, but Kenner was pissing me off.

His focus snapped back to me, and I didn't miss the flare of heat in his dark gaze. "There something between you two?"

I felt that telltale flutter in the muscle along my jaw. Sutton and I hadn't exactly had a chance to discuss what was going on between us. We'd gotten home to Arden last night and then crashed. Hard. And Sutton was up before the sun this morning. She and I would have words later about her leaving without a goodbye.

I knew she was probably processing everything and what it could mean, but I wasn't about to give second thoughts a chance to set in. Just like I wasn't about to let Kenner fuck this up.

Turning to face him, I kept my arms crossed over my chest. "Yeah. There is."

I expected my fellow coach to bluster or make some alpha statement. Instead, he sighed and shook his head. "Damn you. I knew I should've asked her out when I had the chance."

A chuckle escaped me. "I gotta say, I'm not sorry you didn't."

"At least I know you're a halfway decent guy," Kenner muttered.

"Careful, those sweet nothings could go to my head."

Kenner laughed. "I think your ego is big enough."

"You've got a point there." I caught movement out of the corner of my eye. Anson and Shep were crossing the building's foyer and heading for the rink. My stomach dropped, worry setting in. "Be right back," I muttered, but I was already moving before Kenner could answer.

I crossed the space in a matter of seconds. "What's wrong? Is Sutton okay? Is—?"

Shep clamped a hand on my shoulder. "She's fine."

Relief swept through me, but my pulse still thrummed in my neck. "Maybe don't show without warning, man. That's a dick move. Worse than a *can we talk* text."

"Told you," Anson said.

Shep sent him a scowl. "He would've told me not to come."

"Hey, you two bickering lovebirds want to tell me what's going on?" I snapped.

All hints of amusement on Anson's face slipped away. "Dex found the mother lode on Sutton's landlord."

My blood turned to ice. "That's your hacker friend?"

Anson jerked his head in a nod. "Rick Anderson is a sleazeball of epic proportions. Dex found that he has been systematically raising rents across all his properties, falsifying repair records that he charges tenants for, and even shutting off water when people can't pay."

"That's illegal. Why has no one reported him?" I asked, my temper stewing.

"He's preying on those less knowledgeable about their rights," Shep said, a muscle in his jaw tensing.

"There's more," Anson added. "He's got some shady investment stuff. Dex sent me the records. He's cost a lot of people their life savings with bullshit building renos."

My anger shifted to fury. This asshole likely planned to take Sutton for all she had. But I wasn't about to let that happen. "Get a file together," I ground out. "I'm going to the bastard today, and he's going to sell me everything he has."

Shep shifted in place. "I had a feeling you were going to say that."

"Like you'd do anything differently if this was Thea," I snapped.

Shep's brows flew up. "Is that what this is?"

Hell.

The last thing I wanted was my family involved in my relationship with Sutton, but after last night, I knew my days of them staying out of my business were limited. "I care about her."

That wasn't even remotely close enough to the truth. It was so much more than care. But saying that out loud was ridiculous. I'd only known the woman for a month. Yet she was turning my world upside down in the best ways imaginable. And I'd do whatever it took to protect her.

Anson held out a hand to Shep. "I'll take that twenty now."

I looked between the two of them. "Did you *bet* on me?"

Shep gripped the back of his neck. "Just a friendly wager on whether you were sunk or not."

I glared at my brother. "You know, I covered for you when you came home wasted from that field party your junior year. How do you think Mom would feel if she knew the reason her fiddle leaf fig bit the dust was because you used the pot as a urinal?"

Shep's eyes narrowed on me. "You wouldn't."

I arched a brow. "Wouldn't I?"

Anson chuckled. "Sometimes, I love your family."

"Jesus," Shep muttered. "It still weirds me out when you smile like that."

Anson grinned like some creepy clown, making me shudder.

"Get me the file," I clipped.

"Cope," Shep began. "I think we should take this to Trace. Dex can send it to him as an anonymous tip."

I met my brother's stare. "Is it enough to fry Rick's ass? I'm talking jail time and him forced to turn over the buildings."

Shep and Anson shared a look.

"I'm taking that as a no. So, this is what we're going to do. We'll get him to sell, and then Dex can drop the files to Trace. But he needs to sell *first*. Because I'm not risking Sutton's livelihood." She'd worked too hard and put everything she had into that bakery.

"This could come back to bite you. You'll basically be blackmailing him," Shep warned. "Do you really think it's worth it when you're already on thin ice with your team?"

"Yes," I snarled. Because Sutton would always be worth it. No matter the risk.

CHAPTER THIRTY

Sutton

NERVES BUBBLED IN MY BELLY AS I WALKED UP THE FRONT STEPS to Cope's house. The anxiety had been my ever-present companion throughout the day, just like the hum beneath my skin. It was as if my body was reliving the feeling of Cope's hands on me, his mouth, his—*nope, nope, nope.*

I needed to get ahold of myself. This was ridiculous. Cope was just a man. *A man who gave you the best orgasms of your life.* I shoved that thought down as I punched in the lock code on the front door.

Steeling myself, I opened it and stepped inside. I didn't hear anything at first, and then there was a shriek. Not one of terror but one of joy. I moved through the house and toward the sounds of laughter coming from the backyard.

As the rear windows came into view, all my nerves melted away. I wasn't worried about whether sleeping with Cope was a horrible mistake or if he would break my heart far worse than Roman ever had. All I could think about was how happy my kid looked.

Luca let out a peal of laughter as Cope threw him into the air. He hit the water with a massive splash, and Cope grinned. I slid open the back door just as Luca's head broke the water's surface. He shook out his hair like a dog would shake water out of its fur.

"That was…AWESOME!" Luca shouted.

Cope turned at the sound of the door closing behind me, his glistening golden skin on display. "She's home. Finally."

"Yeah, we've been waiting *forever*," Luca complained.

A hint of guilt stabbed at me. I had stayed later than usual today, and I wasn't finished.

A cake still needed frosting, so I'd have to go back after dinner to finish it. Or maybe after I put Luca down.

"What's with the frown, Warrior?" Cope asked.

I shook my head as I toed off my sneakers and sank my feet into the lush grass near the pool. "Just a long day. And I have to go back after dinner to finish up a cake."

"Aw, man," Luca complained.

"Sorry, kiddo," I said, guilt digging in deeper.

"That just means you and I get a boys' night." Cope grinned at Luca.

"Thea said she could babysit," I said quickly. "You don't have to—"

Cope shot me a look that had me snapping my mouth closed. As Luca chattered on about what a boys' night included, Cope climbed the pool steps and walked toward me. His swim trunks hung low on his hips, revealing too many abs to count and a trail of hair that disappeared into his shorts. I nearly swallowed my tongue.

He moved into my space, his hand dipping under my hair. "I really want to kiss that worried look off your face right now."

"Cope…"

His eyes searched mine as his fingers squeezed the back of my neck. "I know you're probably not ready for that. Not in front of Luca. But know I want it."

A burn lit behind my eyes, and I suddenly recognized the true fear behind my anxiety. I'd been afraid Cope wouldn't want more than one night. That he'd stolen my heart but hadn't given me his in return. "Okay," I whispered.

Cope moved in a flash, scooping me into his arms bridal-style.

"Now, I think it's time for a little afternoon swim."

"Copeland Colson, don't you dare!" I shrieked.

But it was too late. Cope was already running toward the pool's edge. He jumped with me in his arms, sending us both crashing into the water. I spluttered and coughed as we broke the surface. Cope laughed as Luca hooted.

"You're both grounded!" I shouted.

They just laughed harder. But the truth was, it was exactly what I needed. We swam and played until my energy wore out, and I moved to the edge of the pool, hoisting myself out and hoping my shorts and tee would dry a bit before I headed inside.

Cope moved to the edge with me, pushing out of the water with ease. We sat there, watching Luca demonstrate his dives and cannon-balls, and Cope laid his hand over mine. He didn't link our fingers but still gave us that point of contact.

The move made my chest ache. It respected my wishes but still gave me a taste of affection. I turned to look at him and took in all that sun-kissed beauty. "I hope you guys wore sunscreen."

Cope's lips twitched, his scar looking more pronounced. "My mom taught me well. I used the spray kind and made Luca rotate like a rotisserie chicken."

The mental image had me fighting a grin. "Thanks for giving him a great day."

Luca yelled, "Cannonball!" and hit the water with a splash as if to punctuate the statement. My stomach churned, a million worries setting in. Luca was getting used to this life. To Cope. And none of it was permanent.

"Where's Luca's dad?" Cope asked softly.

I stiffened, the urge to bite Cope's head off strong. But the truth was, it was a miracle this was the first time Cope had asked about it. My throat worked as I swallowed. "Probably back in Baltimore. He's not in the picture anymore."

Cope was quiet, but I felt his eyes on me, his gaze probing. "Can't imagine being willing to give up a relationship with that kid."

The burn behind my eyes was back, and there was pressure along with it now. Wasn't this always what I'd wanted? What I'd wished for? Someone who saw Luca for the amazing tiny human he was? So, why did it feel so terrifying?

"He doesn't talk about him. His dad," Cope pressed.

"No." Because he didn't. After I'd healed from my so-called *car accident* and we left Baltimore, the only thing Luca had said was, "*Dad's not coming, right?*" God, that had shattered my heart. Because even though Roman had never hurt Luca or me, he'd disappointed us over and over again. He'd broken promise after promise. Had stolen from us both.

"Did he hurt you?" Cope's voice was a low growl now, so contrary to Luca's cheerful shouts in the background.

"No," I whispered. "Not like that. But he's not healthy enough to be in Luca's life. The courts agreed."

I felt a little of the tension bleed out of Cope. "Losing the two of you should've been a wake-up call to get healthy."

It should've. But it never was. And some tiny part of me would always wonder if it was because I wasn't enough.

Cope grabbed my hand, tugging me toward him as I headed for the front door. I hit his chest with an *oomph*, sending him a chastising look. "I have to go. And Luca will riot if you aren't down to watch that game in about sixty seconds."

Cope gave me a full-on pout. "You work too hard."

I couldn't help the way my muscles stiffened. "I'm building a business."

"Yes, and you were there by four this morning. Working this late on top of it isn't healthy. You're pushing too hard."

I shoved away from Cope's chest. "I'm working this hard because standing on my own two feet is important to me." And after the pieces of my past I'd shared with him today, Cope should understand that.

He scrubbed a hand over his face. "Okay. I get it. I just…I worry about you. These are long hours, and I don't want you getting sick."

I softened at the genuine worry in his tone and moved back into his space. "I just have the frosting left. It should only take me an hour or two tops. Then, I'll be home and—"

"Coming to bed with me," Cope said, a growl lacing his tone.

I couldn't help the smile that stretched across my face. "That depends. Do you promise not to throw me into the pool again?" My hair was still damp from my after-swim shower.

His wolfish grin was back. "That's a promise I can't make. You look too good in a wet T-shirt."

I smacked Cope's chest. "You're hopeless."

"I'm honest," Cope said, pulling me against him. "Text me when you get there and when you leave?"

He'd taken to requesting these check-ins, even in the early morning hours. Said he liked waking to the knowledge I was safe. Something about that grabbed the organ in my chest and wouldn't let go. "You could implant a homing beacon in my arm."

Cope smiled against my mouth. "Don't tempt me."

I gave him a lazy kiss, one that easily could've turned into more, but I pulled back, cutting it short. "I need to go."

Cope didn't release me.

"The sooner I leave, the sooner I'll be back."

Cope let go then. "I might be motivated to dole out rewards if it's less than two hours."

I chuckled. "Bribery?"

"I never said I was noble."

No, he hadn't. "You're way better than noble, Cope. You're the best man I've ever known."

A look of surprise morphed into something that resembled pain, but Cope quickly masked it. "Text me when you get there."

I frowned but nodded. "Okay."

I headed out the front door and down the steps toward my SUV, but I felt Cope's eyes on me as I went. His stare felt different than any other I'd experienced. There was a warm strength to it. A sensation that somehow managed to ground and heat all at once.

As I beeped the locks and slid behind the wheel, I glanced up at the entryway to Cope's house. There he stood, hands in the pockets of a pair of joggers that hugged his hips perfectly. But there was something in his dark-blue eyes in that moment. I swore it was sadness. It could've been a memory of Teddy surfacing perhaps. But something told me it wasn't.

I stared back for a long moment before forcing myself to start the engine and head into town. Darkness was just starting to coat the landscape in a breathtaking deep purple. I didn't mind the drive, not when I got to take in this sort of beauty. But I did miss popping downstairs to the bakery to frost in my pajamas. Or hopping up to the roof to tend to my bees in just a bathrobe.

That thought reminded me that it was time to harvest honeycombs from another one of the hives. Cope had said he wanted to learn how. I added it to my mental to-do list as I pulled into a spot behind the bakery. As far as I could tell, Rick hadn't had much luck renting the apartment upstairs. I couldn't help the tiny flicker of satisfaction I felt at that. Sometimes, karma came through.

I grabbed my keys and purse and headed for the back door. It only took me a matter of seconds to get inside and lock up behind myself. I shot off a quick text to Cope, letting him know I'd made it, and flicked on the lights. I moved to the stereo system, and waves of country music filled the air.

As I moved into the kitchen, I refastened my hair in a tighter bun. It was a compulsion when I was baking or decorating. I couldn't stand hair falling in my face and impacting my vision. The only problem was that I constantly lost my hair ties. So, when I couldn't find one, I got creative, using butter knives, piping bags, or anything else that could tie my hair back.

Thankfully, I had a silk scrunchie in my possession tonight, so no cooking utensils were needed. I crossed to the sink and thoroughly washed my hands, drying them on a fresh towel. Then I turned toward the cake.

It was one of my largest. Four tiers. A belated graduation party for a local boy. I didn't know him or his family, but I had a list of his interests, and his mom had given me free rein. Her only instruction had been, *"Make it fun."*

That, I could do. The rising college freshman was into dirt bike racing, so my plan was to create a track all around the cake while his other hobbies served as landmarks along the way. At the top, I'd have him on his dirt bike.

Grinning, I reached for the frosting and dove in. One of the things I loved most about baking was how I could lose myself in the process. Five minutes or five hours could pass, and it wouldn't matter because it transported me to another world. Everything disappeared but the music and the art I was making. It forced me to stay in the present, like an active meditation.

It was that altered state and the music that kept me from hearing what I should've, the squeak of a shoe against the tile floor that had me stilling and then whirling. What I saw came in snapshots. A tall, broad figure. A man. All in black. Wearing some sort of ski mask that hid any distinguishing features other than the fact that he was white.

The seconds it took my brain to register what I was seeing were seconds too long. The man lunged. I tried to dodge and escape his grasp but wasn't fast enough. He caught me by the hair, yanking me to him so my back was to his front. Cold metal pressed against my jaw.

"Empty the register," he snarled. But it wasn't a normal voice. It was distorted somehow. Robotic, like a computer's tone. Or affected in some way.

My heart hammered against my ribs, and blood roared in my ears. The man shook me by the hair, and I couldn't help the cry of pain that left my lips.

"Open the fucking register." He pushed me forward toward the counter, the gun jabbing into my jaw.

A million thoughts ran through my mind: the pepper spray at the bottom of my purse, the self-defense move that meant sending an elbow to the man's ribs. But none of that helped when a gun was pressed to my head.

My hand shook as I punched in the code, and the drawer shot open. There wasn't much in there, just enough to get us started tomorrow. I'd taken everything else to the bank on my way home. Just like I'd done every day since moving in with Cope.

"Put it in a bag. Nice and slow."

My trembling didn't let up as I reached for one of our to-go bags under the counter. Luca's face flashed in my mind. "Please don't hurt me. I have a son—"

The man's hand tightened in my hair, and he shook me with a ferocity that stole my breath. "I don't wanna hear it, bitch."

A strangled noise left my throat, but I swallowed any words that wanted to escape. I grabbed for the bills in the register and stuffed them into the paper bag. I'd worked so hard on the design. The adorable little emblem that went with the words *The Mix Up*. It was quirky and a little off-kilter, so in opposition to a violent crime.

"Where's the rest of it? I know you've gotta have more on hand with your fancy-ass hockey fuck buddy."

I stiffened, my muscles locking as if cement had been poured into the sinew. "Th-this is all I have."

The man's grip changed, moving from my hair to my throat, his fingers constricting my airway. "You'd better be fucking with me. Because if there's no more cash here, I'll take my payment in flesh."

I shook violently as I struggled to suck in air. "I take it to the bank every day," I croaked.

The man's grip on my throat tightened, and he whirled me around, shoving me against the counter so hard that white-hot pain flashed through me. "I'll find it my goddamned self."

In the kitchen lights, I saw a glint of metal behind the man, and then it was colliding with my face. The pain was all-consuming, taking over every inch of me before I felt the world falling away and descended into blessed nothingness.

CHAPTER THIRTY-ONE

Cope

THE PHONE RANG FOR THE DOZENTH TIME AS I PRESSED THE cell harder to my ear, as if I held it tightly enough, it would make Sutton answer. Her voice came over the line, but it was the recording telling me I'd reached a number I knew was hers. Her voice was so bright and cheery—the opposite of the worry currently coursing through me.

I glanced at my watch as I hung up. She should've been home almost an hour ago. Luca was already fast asleep upstairs.

My gut churned as I hit another number on my cell. Arden answered on the third ring, her metal music cutting off quickly. "This'd better be good because I was right in the middle of a nice flow."

I heard the bite in my sister's words but didn't take it to heart. I knew just how much she loved me by how she'd answered at all when evenings were her prime creation time. "I need you to come to the house."

"What's wrong?" Arden asked, but I could already hear her moving, snapping her fingers for her massive dog, Brutus, to follow her.

"Sutton was supposed to be home from the bakery an hour

ago and she's not picking up her phone." I heard the strain bleeding through my words and knew Arden had to pick up on it, too.

She paused for a moment, the sound of feet crunching on gravel coming across the line as she made her way from the workshop to my house. "She probably just got caught up. It's easy to do when you're in the zone."

God, I hoped that's what it was. I'd seen Sutton in her element while working on some baked-good creation. The rest of the world ceased to exist. "Yeah. That's probably it."

But I could hear the doubt in my words. She always let me know if she was running late. All I could think about were the dark roads from town to my place, and the lack of streetlights. And how it had taken a lot less for Teddy to find his end.

I grabbed my car keys from the dish in the kitchen and headed for the front door. As I opened it, I caught movement. Arden came into view at the side of the house, a flashlight in hand, her dark hair piled in a messy bun on her head, and her clothes splattered in paint and who knew what other artistic substances. Brutus stayed tight to her side, the cane corso's height reaching past her waist.

"Where's my guy?" Arden asked.

"He's asleep upstairs."

Arden lifted her chin in a nod. "I'll get a snack with Brutus. You got any leftovers?"

I knew what she was doing—trying to keep things light and easy as if there was nothing to be concerned about. "Spaghetti and meatballs in the fridge."

She shot me a grin. "Just the kind of payment I like. I'm starved."

"Have you eaten anything today?" I asked, my eyes narrowing on my sister. She was notorious for forgetting anything and everything in the quest for her art.

Arden winced. "I might've missed breakfast."

"Eat," I demanded. "I'll be back in an hour tops."

"Text me when you get eyes on Sutton, okay?" Arden requested. The fact that she was even asking meant she was worried, too.

And that set me on edge. I jerked my head in a nod and headed for the garage. I was off my property in a matter of minutes and made the drive into town in a third of the time it should've taken. If the cops tried to pull me over, they'd have to wait until I got to the bakery to write me a ticket.

My headlights swung across Sutton's SUV parked at the back of the building. I caught sight of the back door as I pulled into a parking spot. It stood slightly ajar as if someone hadn't bothered to close it all the way.

I grabbed my phone and shut off the engine. My fingers fumbled for Trace's contact as I slid out of the SUV. He answered on the second ring. "Hey, Cope—"

"I'm at the back of the bakery. Sutton was late getting home and wasn't answering her phone. The back door's ajar—"

"Stay in your vehicle," Trace commanded. "I'm sending units and am on the way."

"You know I can't do that." I was already halfway to the door, and nothing would stop me from going inside.

"Damn it, Cope. You don't know what's on the other side of that door."

I didn't give a flying fuck. All I knew was that Sutton was in there. A million different possibilities flooded my mind as I stepped inside—none of them good.

About a third of the lights were on in the bakery, giving it a shadowy look that made it almost unrecognizable. The country ballad playing over the speakers was so at odds with the scene that it grated on my ears. I crept down the hallway, scanning the space, Trace's voice from the phone demanding to know what was happening.

My gaze swept the café, not seeing a single sign of life. Then I turned toward the counter. There, just behind it, cabinets had been torn open, their contents thrown about. My heart jerked in my chest, and I picked up my pace, rounding the case that was normally full of desserts.

I froze the moment I got to the other side. My blood went

ice-cold as I saw Sutton crumpled on the floor. Her skin was unnaturally pale, none of her typically golden glow present. The only color at all was a dark red substance at her temple.

The color jolted me into movement, and I shouted for Trace to send EMTs as I ran toward Sutton, my phone clattering to the floor. I sank to the hardwood, my knees cracking against the surface as I reached for her neck. I held my breath and pressed two fingers to her flesh, praying I felt something. Anything.

At the faint throb of her pulse, my breath left my lungs in a painful whoosh. It was as if the air were barbed. "Sutton," I croaked.

There was no response. It was then that I saw the red marks on her throat—marks that looked a hell of a lot like the outline of fingers. Fiery rage swept through me in a wave of flames, but I kept my touch featherlight as I brushed the hair away from her face. "Sutton, baby, come on. You gotta open your eyes for me."

Pain pulsed through me at the lack of color in her face and that trickle of blood at her hairline. I didn't have the first clue what to do. If Trace or Shep were here, they would know. They both had extensive first-aid training, but I was just the idiot who'd gone on to play hockey.

Sirens sounded. That was good. Help was coming. Sutton just had to hold on until then.

My thumb swept across her cheek. "Come on, Warrior. Fight. For me. For us."

There was a little movement behind Sutton's eyelids as if she were trying to open her eyes.

"That's it, Warrior. Show me those ice-blue eyes. The turquoise depths I could drown in."

They fluttered in earnest now, the motion matching the beat of my heart against my ribs. Then, they opened. Sutton quickly squinted against the light and let out a little moan.

"It's okay. You're okay," I told myself as much as her.

"Cope?" she rasped.

"I'm right here. I've got you. Help's coming."

"What happened?" Sutton croaked.

I couldn't give her that answer, but I *would* find whoever was responsible. And I would make them pay.

CHAPTER THIRTY-TWO

Sutton

EVERYTHING HURT. IT WAS LIKE THE TIME I'D GONE BODY surfing in Maryland and ended up tumbling against the rocks. But this time, I had the migraine of a lifetime on top of it. I should've been grateful they'd at least turned the lights down in the ER bay. But that was only after Cope had barked so ferociously that the nurse had almost wet himself.

I had a feeling it was also Cope's presence that had landed us in a closed room instead of one of those curtained-off areas like most people got. But I couldn't be sorry for it. Not when it meant less noise and light.

Cope's thumb stroked the back of my hand, the pattern resembling a figure eight. "The doctor should've been back by now. MRI results don't take that long." He released his hold on me and shoved to his feet. "I'm going to go find him and—"

"Cope." My voice was a touch raspy thanks to the strangling I'd received, but that had nothing on the new stitches I sported on my forehead.

He turned back to me, a mixture of agony and fury in his eyes. "They need to get you meds."

"They're moving as fast as they can. There may be people here who need their attention more than I do."

Apparently, that was the wrong thing to say because a muscle in his cheek began to flutter wildly. "Then they should hire more staff," he spat between gritted teeth.

As if he'd conjured the doctor with his annoyance alone, the door swung open, and a man in a white lab coat with an unnaturally orange tan stepped inside. "How's my patient?"

The over-the-top smile Dr. Bentley sent my way had Cope full-on growling in his direction. The doctor's grin faltered.

"Where are her pain meds?" Cope snarled.

Dr. Bentley patted his pocket, his blinding smile returning. "Right here. We got the results from the MRI and X-ray. There are no signs of fracture, bleeding in the brain, or traumatic brain injury."

That muscle in Cope's cheek began to flutter wildly again. "So, give her the damn drugs and help her pain."

"Cope," I chastised gently.

He cut his gaze to me. "You've been lying here in agony for hours while they walk around with their thumbs up their asses."

I heard it in his voice then: the strain and how desperately he was trying to stay in control. I didn't blame him. He might be acting like a grouchy bear currently, but it was because he was freaked. I couldn't say I would've been much different if I'd found *him* unconscious and bleeding from the head.

Dr. Bentley bristled. "I am the head of this ER. I don't have my thumb stuck anywhere. Patients beg for me to treat them. I am known far beyond this county—"

"Doc," Cope snarled. "Give her the meds."

"He meant to add *please* onto that," I cut in.

The doctor turned to me and let out a huff. "I know professional athletes have tempers, but this is ridiculous."

I sent Cope a look to keep him in check. Whatever I'd managed despite the throbbing in my head seemed to work.

Dr. Bentley donned gloves and then removed a syringe from

his pocket. He uncapped it and slid the needle into the IV tubing. "This will start you out with a stronger dose of pain medication. Are you nauseous at all?"

"A little," I admitted.

He pulled out another syringe. "I'm going to give you some Zofran for that. I'll write you a prescription for that and oxycodone that you can take home with you."

A wave of something that felt a lot like fear swept through me. "I don't need the oxy."

Dr. Bentley's brows rose. "Are there addiction issues I need to be aware of?"

"No. But I don't like taking that stuff." I wasn't about to let that poison get a foothold.

"Sutton," Cope said softly, crossing to the bed and taking my hand. "You need pain meds while you recover. You have a concussion and stitches. Both will take time to heal."

"I can take Tylenol." Whatever the doctor had put in my IV was already easing my pain and making me feel a bit floaty. I couldn't help but wonder if this was the feeling Roman was always chasing.

Dr. Bentley cleared his throat. "I'll have the prescription filled. If you don't need it, that's great. But if you do, it'll be there."

"I don't—"

"Warrior," Cope said, cutting me off. "We're taking the prescription home."

I snapped my mouth closed, the action making pain flicker in my head.

Cope turned to the doctor. "Can she go home tonight, or does she need to stay in the hospital?"

Dr. Bentley's gaze swept over me, assessing. "I want to keep her for another hour to make sure there's no vomiting after the meds. If not, she can go home. But someone needs to be with her."

"I will be," Cope ground out.

"All right. You have to wake her every three hours. Ask simple questions like her name or what year it is."

"That's no problem," Cope assured him.

"Good," the doctor clipped. "I'll ready the discharge paperwork."

As Dr. Bentley slipped out of the room, Cope lowered himself to a chair next to my bed. I sent him a pointed look. "You weren't very nice to him."

"Guy's a pompous prick."

I shrugged. "Maybe you need a little of that to deal with holding people's lives in your hands on a regular basis."

Cope sighed and scrubbed a hand over his stubbled jaw. "I'm sorry. I just hate seeing you in pain."

"The medicine's helping already." I wanted to reassure him, but I couldn't help feeling on edge about having an intense painkiller coursing through my system.

"Sutton—"

Cope's words were cut off by the room's door opening again. But it wasn't a doctor or nurse this time; it was a familiar face. Trace's gaze swept over me, assessing every mark and injury. His expression remained carefully neutral, but I didn't miss the flicker of anger in his green eyes.

"How are you doing, Sutton?" he asked, crossing the room in three long strides.

"Feeling better now."

"Did you find anything?" Cope demanded.

Trace gave his head a small shake. "Crime scene techs are still combing the scene." He glanced back at me. "Your wallet was gone from your purse. Thea got us the card numbers from the emergency file you gave her, and we got those canceled. Your bank is issuing new cards as we speak."

My stomach churned, acid swirling there. "Were there charges?"

"A few, but your bank already reversed them. You won't be responsible for any of it," Trace assured me.

"Thank you," I whispered. I suddenly felt small. And more than that, dirty. All I wanted to do was scrub the places that man had touched and remove all evidence of his hold and the pain he'd inflicted.

Cope seemed to sense the shift and took my hand again, weaving his fingers through mine. Trace didn't miss the move, but I couldn't read his reaction to it.

"Everyone but Arden's out in the waiting room. She said Luca's still fast asleep. I know everyone will want an update. What did the doctor say?" Trace asked.

"They shouldn't have come out in the middle of the night," I muttered.

Trace's mouth curved the barest amount. "If you haven't realized it yet, you're an honorary Colson. If anything happens, good or bad, we show up en masse."

Something about that hurt worse than the head injury I was currently nursing. Because I wanted it to be true so badly. Needed to belong to a family as wonderful as the Colsons. But it somehow seemed out of reach.

Cope leaned in, his lips brushing my unmarred temple. "They care about you. Let them."

My eyes burned, and my throat tightened. When was the last time someone had shown up for me like this? Probably when I got an awful case of the flu in college. My gran had driven five hours to come take care of me in my dorm room.

But I hadn't had that unwavering support since then. Not really. Roman had thrown money at problems, but looking back on it, he'd never solved anything with only his presence and energy.

Pleasure and pain warred within me, but I did everything I could to hold on to the good. "Will you thank them for me? And tell them I'm okay. They're going to let me go home in an hour."

Trace nodded. "Of course. I need to get a statement from you. But you get to decide whether that's tonight or tomorrow."

"Tomorrow," Cope growled. "She's been through enough."

I squeezed his hand. "No. I want to get it over with so I can leave it all behind." Because I knew I needed to share everything with Trace, and it was time for Cope to hear it, too. Even if it was the last thing I wanted him to know.

"I get that," Trace said, softening his voice. "Would you prefer a female officer to take your statement? I can have Beth do it—"

"No," I said quickly. "I'd rather it be you." At least I knew Trace, trusted him. It would be better than a stranger.

Trace nodded, pulling his phone out of his pocket and tapping on the screen. "I'm going to record this so, hopefully, we don't have to go back over anything. Are you okay with that?"

"It's fine," I lied. I didn't want this on record. Didn't want strangers listening to what an idiot I'd been. Didn't want them hearing all the ways I'd been hurt. Because it all made me feel like a victim again.

Trace laid his phone on the gurney and lowered himself into a chair on my opposite side. "Let's start from the beginning. Is it common for you to work this late?"

I took a long breath and let it out slowly as Cope kept a hold of my hand. I tried to focus on that source of warmth and strength. "Not common, exactly. Maybe once a week or so when a special project comes in."

"And what was the project this time?"

"A graduation cake." Just saying it reminded me that the family would be picking it up tomorrow at noon. "I need to call my client. She's expecting—"

"Thea said she'd finish the cake first thing in the morning. She's got it all under control," Trace assured me.

The air left my lungs with a whoosh. *Good. That was good.*

Trace looked down at his notepad. "What time did you arrive at the bakery tonight?"

"It was around 7:45, I think. A little before 8:00."

"Was anyone else around?"

I shook my head, instantly regretting the action as my vision swam.

"Easy, Warrior," Cope said, his thumb tracing delicate designs on the back of my hand.

I kept my eyes closed for a minute, then opened them. "I didn't see any other people or cars. I let myself in and locked the door be-hind me. No one should've been able to get in."

Trace sent me a look of sympathy. "The intruder jimmied the lock. You didn't do anything wrong."

I bit the corner of my lip but gave him a small nod, one that wouldn't send my brain reeling.

"Walk me through what happened once you were inside."

I swallowed, trying to clear the lump of fear in my throat. "I turned on the radio and started working on the cake. I always lose myself in the process. Hours pass in what feels like seconds. I didn't hear him come in. Not until his shoe squeaked on the floor."

I gripped Cope's hand tighter, my fingers digging into his flesh and holding on as if he were my lifeline. And maybe he was. "It took me a second because what I was seeing didn't make sense—a man in all black, wearing one of those ski mask things."

"A balaclava?" Trace clarified.

"Yes. Before I knew what was happening, he grabbed me and told me to empty the register."

"Was there anything familiar about his voice?" Trace asked.

I shivered, and Cope pulled my blanket up with his free hand. My mouth felt dry as I remembered the creepy tone. "It was like his voice was computer generated or something. It sounded like that horror movie. You know, the *Scream* ones?"

Trace and Cope shared a look, but it was Trace who spoke. "Those sorts of distorters are pretty easy to come by. You can get them for twenty bucks on the internet. He probably had it inside the mask."

So, it could've been anyone. Somehow, that was more terrifying. I swallowed the knowledge and forced myself to keep going. "I emp-tied what we had in the register, but he wasn't happy because there wasn't a lot. He said he'd find it himself and hit me with the butt of the gun. At least, I think that's what it was."

The ugly words he'd said about Cope and me flashed in my mind, but I couldn't give voice to them, not when I knew Cope would blame himself for me becoming a target. And what did it matter anyway? Anyone could've seen those tabloid articles or heard gossip around town.

"You need to bring Rick Anderson in for questioning," Cope ordered.

"I'll pay him a visit right after I leave here," Trace assured me.

I straightened on the gurney. "Do you honestly think my landlord would do this? He's a jerk for sure, but this is extreme."

Cope gripped my hand harder. "He's mixed up in some shady dealings. I wouldn't put it past him to try to scare you out of your lease."

It didn't surprise me that Rick was shady. I already had a feeling he was behind my visit from the health department, but violence was something else entirely.

Trace studied me, his gaze somehow managing to be both gentle and probing. "Is there someone else you think it could be?"

My tongue stuck to the roof of my mouth as if I'd just eaten a spoonful of peanut butter. I wasn't ready. Not for any of the Colsons to see me differently, but especially not Cope. His hold on my hand stiffened as though his muscles had become full of lead. "Who do you think did this?"

My eyes burned, but I forced myself to keep staring down at my lap, not at Trace. And definitely not at Cope. I had to get it out. The quicker, the better. "Luca's dad and my ex-husband. He was a professional football player. Roman Boyer."

"Wide receiver out of Baltimore, right?" Trace asked.

I nodded, not looking away from the cheap hospital blanket and its fraying threads from being washed so many times. "He got injured several years ago. Torn ACL. The surgery had complications, and they prescribed him oxycodone." Cope's hand spasmed around mine. "He got hooked."

It was a truth they already knew was coming, but I went on anyway, needing to get it out of me, purge it like the violent poison it was. "I didn't realize until it was too late. He got booted from the team, which only made him get into the harder stuff. He emptied our bank

accounts, would disappear for weeks on end. And when he did manage to come home, he was erratic at best. I didn't have any choice."

"You divorced him," Trace supplied.

"Yes," I croaked. "I filed the day our house was foreclosed on.
I moved Luca and me into the best apartment I could afford on my
waitress's salary. But it wasn't in the best neighborhood."

I felt the shudder go through Cope, but I still couldn't look at
him. Heat bloomed in my cheeks, and I struggled to beat it back.
"Roman came back around about six months later. Said he'd cleaned
up his act and was going to meetings. He seemed…better. But I wasn't
about to trust him with Luca. So, I let him come to my apartment,
but only when I was there. To help Luca with his homework or for
dinner. I didn't want Luca to lose his dad."

"There's nothing wrong with that, Sutton. You were doing your
best," Trace said quietly.

It felt like acid burned the backs of my eyes, but I forced myself
to keep going and get it all out, once and for all. "Roman came over
one afternoon and didn't stay long. He seemed distracted. I stepped
out to take a call from my boss and was gone for five minutes tops.
When I came back, everything seemed fine, but Roman made an excuse about having to leave. He stole Luca's tablet, the necklace my
grandmother gave me, and some other jewelry—anything he thought
he could hock quickly."

"Bastard," Cope ground out.

"Everything else was just stuff. But that necklace was all I had
left of my gran. It was one my grandfather had given to her. It had
a bumblebee on it because she always used to say, 'I love you more
than bees love—'"

"Honey." Cope finished the phrase for me, having heard me say
it to Luca countless times, but the single word was pained. "I'm so
damn sorry, Warrior."

But I wasn't done. And if I didn't get it all out now, I worried I
never would. "There was a knock on the door that night. I thought it
was my friend from down the hall, but it wasn't. It was two enforcers

from a Russian organized crime family. They said Roman owed them and that I had to be a warning. They beat me. Broke my ribs and collarbone, split my lip. Doctors had to remove my spleen. And all of that while my little boy slept just feet away."

That was the thing that finally broke me: the memory of just how easily they could've gotten to Luca. It was a miracle that Marilee found me and called the ambulance and that my boy had slept through it all with no harm coming to him.

Tears streamed down my face, dripping from my chin and sliding down my neck. Cope didn't wait. He moved in one swift motion, slipping into the bed beside me and gently holding me to him. "You're safe, Warrior. You're both safe."

But I could feel the fury pulsing through him in blasts of brutal rage and knew Trace felt the same when he spoke. "Tell me the Baltimore PD got them."

"They got the enforcers. They're doing fifteen years and had to pay a small settlement. But their boss, Petrov? He didn't get a thing because they didn't turn on him."

"Fucking hell," Cope swore as he dropped his face to my head, nuzzling me as if he needed to make sure I was still there.

"I knew I had to get away from there." I hated the tremor in my voice, but there wasn't a damn thing I could do about it. "Out of Petrov's and Roman's reach. I already had sole physical and legal custody of Luca. Roman didn't even show up for the hearing."

"I remember reading about this somewhere."

Trace's words finally had me looking up, only to find fury written all over his face.

I swallowed hard, reminding myself that the fury wasn't directed at me. "Roman wasn't a player who got a lot of press. He was good but not a superstar. Though when everything happened, it hit the media."

Cope stiffened, pulling back. "That's why you didn't want to go to the funeral. Because you didn't want to be recognized. Didn't want him or the garbage he got mixed up with to know where you were."

I forced myself to look at Cope. Just twisting in the bed had fresh pain surging to the surface, but I did my best to ignore it. "I'm sorry. It was stupid. I should've been there for you from the beginning. I—"

"Bullshit. You should've stayed right here. I'm the selfish bastard who forced you into something you weren't comfortable with. Put you at risk. How can you even stand to look at me?"

CHAPTER THIRTY-THREE

Cope

I STARED INTO THE STARRY NIGHT AND TOOK A DEEP BREATH OF the air that always seemed to help me find peace, but I was reaching for it harder now as if it was just out of my grasp. Gripping my phone tighter, I walked farther into the grass surrounding my pool. "Were you able to start today?"

"Cope." Shep used my name as a chastisement, like putting a toddler in his place. "We just finished the plans. We still need the supplies to be delivered and—"

"But you said the demo might be able to start soon," I pressed. I needed this. Needed to be doing *something* when the past two weeks had been nothing but powerlessness. Sutton was healing and had even returned to work, but Trace had nothing. Not a damn thing that might lead us to whoever had hurt her.

Between Trace's and Anson's contacts at the bureau, we had a damn good picture of Petrov and his operation. And all of it turned my fucking stomach. But that knowledge had nothing on the photos I'd found of Sutton's bruised and battered face. Pictures that had become public record during the trial of the two men who had assaulted her.

Those images flashed in my head, haunting me like they had every single day since I'd seen them. Sutton. My warrior. Broken. For no other reason than she'd fallen for a weak man. Some part of me knew it wasn't weakness; it was an illness, but I couldn't connect with that part of me when I knew Roman Boyer had gotten Sutton mixed up with the men who'd caused her untold pain.

"Cope," Shep snapped.

"Sorry. I'm listening."

He let out a long sigh. "We'll get the apartment renovated. It'll look amazing, but all that takes time."

I nodded, even though he couldn't see me. "Okay."

This had been the only thing I could focus on since getting that bastard, Rick, to sell his buildings to me on the cheap. He'd blustered and babbled, saying it was all lies, but he'd caved and sold me everything at a steal when I dropped the file of proof on his desk.

I was working with Trace to get some of the discounted funds back to the people who'd been robbed in the first place. And since Dex had slipped his findings to Trace via a completely untraceable and anonymous email address, Rick had also found himself in hot legal water. He had an alibi for the night of Sutton's attack, but for all we knew, he'd paid for it with some of his shady earnings. I just hoped like hell that wasn't the case, because if it was, I had yet another thing to blame myself for.

My hold on the phone tightened. I might not be able to send Rick to prison or do a damn thing about the Russian mob yet, but I *could* do something about Sutton not having a home. I could give her a beautiful apartment that would always be a safe harbor for her.

Just thinking about her leaving my house had a feeling of panic racing through me. Even if I knew her independence was the right thing for her, it sure as hell wasn't for me. But our time was limited. There were only weeks left before I had to go back to Seattle—to hockey and my empty life there.

"Cope. Are you okay?" There was genuine concern in my brother's voice, worry that had more guilt slipping in.

"No," I admitted.

"Want me to come over? We can have a few beers and talk it out."

I appreciated the offer more than he'd ever know, but it wouldn't fix anything. This wasn't fixable. I'd be there for Sutton and Luca in every way I could, but they were better off without me in their day-to-day lives. Because the attention that swirled around me put them at risk.

"Maybe another night," I said, gripping my neck and squeezing hard. "But I appreciate it."

Shep was silent for a long moment. "I'm worried about you."

Fuck.

"Don't be." I forced my tone to be lighter. "You know I always land on my feet."

My brother got quiet again, then sighed. "I'm here whenever you're ready to *really* talk."

"Good night, Shep." It was all I could say because I wasn't remotely ready for that sort of conversation.

"Night, Cope. I love you."

My throat burned like it always did when one of my family members said those words. Because I didn't feel like I deserved their love. But still, I gave him the words back, not wanting to be the cause of more pain. "Love you, too."

I hit *end* on the call before Shep could wreck me any further. Then I turned and stalked toward the house. I slipped inside, locking the door behind me and rearming the alarm. A friend of Anson's would be coming out to do a security analysis of my property and the bakery.

Holt Hartley was a now-silent partner in a security firm, but he was riding out here as a favor to Anson. He was supposed to be the best of the best—exactly what Sutton and Luca deserved.

I jogged up the stairs to the second floor, pausing at a giggle coming from down the hall. That innocent sound made my chest ache. Luca didn't have a clue what was circling his mom and him. He thought Sutton had tripped at the bakery and hit her head. But now that the stitches were out, and the only remnant of Sutton's injury was a faint bruise, he'd forgotten all about it.

The soft strains of Sutton's voice came then, hitting me center mass. They wrapped around me and dug in as she read her son a story. That was all she should have to worry about, what book to read, and whether or not she could do all the voices.

I ripped myself away from the sound I wanted to drown in and forced my feet to take me into my bedroom. I headed straight for my closet, quickly changing into workout shorts and a tee, then donning sneakers.

I needed a run. And more than just an easy jog. I needed the feeling of my lungs on fire and my muscles quaking. I needed the sort of run that burned everything to ash.

Hurrying down two flights of stairs, I headed straight for the treadmill. Outside would've been better, but I wasn't about to leave Sutton and Luca alone, even with the alarm set. I grabbed the remote to the stereo and selected some rock that Arden would *almost* approve of, but it still wasn't quite enough to make your ears bleed.

Starting in a warm-up jog, I let my muscles loosen. Those images of Sutton still played in my head, a revolving slideshow that would've had me puking if my stomach wasn't empty. I picked up my pace, tipping into a run. Those images interchanged with others: memories of twisted metal and sounds of agony, pictures of the wreckage splashed across our local paper...

I ripped off my tee and tossed it onto the floor as sweat gathered between my pecs and down my spine. I bumped up the speed when a new song started, and the burn began. My lungs started to smolder as my muscles heated up with the barest hint of strain.

Pressing harder, I fought with the treadmill, my feet slamming into the belt with such force that it was a miracle the thing didn't snap in two. I let the run eat at me. I let the pain take root and welcomed it. Because I deserved it all. Every last ounce of it.

The music cut off, and I nearly tripped. A misstep at this pace would've been catastrophic, but I caught myself just in time, quickly lowering the speed until I was back at a jog, just enough to keep warm.

Sutton stalked toward the treadmill, wearing a look that said she was supremely pissed off.

"What's wrong?" I hit *stop* on the machine and jumped off.

"What's wrong?" she parroted. "What's wrong is I want to know why the hell you're trying to kill yourself!"

My eyes flared. "I was just going for a run."

"*That* was not a run. *That* was trying to escape the hounds of hell."

She had no idea how close to the truth that statement was. No idea how the nightmares had come back with a vengeance when I suggested she stay in her bed while she was healing.

Pain streaked across Sutton's face. "Talk to me, Cope. Don't shut me out."

Agony swirled anew, a fiery burn taking root for a reason besides running. "I'm fine."

"You're not." Sutton's voice got quiet. "Please, don't lie to my face. If you want us to leave, I get it. You probably look at me differently—"

"What the hell are you talking about?" I snapped.

Sutton's hands curled into fists, her fingernails digging into her palms. "You've barely touched me since the hospital. You watch me like a hawk but haven't even hugged me."

Fucking hell.

"It's not you," I ground out.

She let out a soft scoff. "Let me guess. 'It's not you, it's me?'"

"You didn't do a damn thing wrong. What happened is no one's fault but Roman's and those other animals. You didn't deserve any of this. Not a damn thing. You fought for Luca, for yourself. You were smart and got free. Worked hard to build a good life for you and your boy."

Sutton's beautiful eyes glittered with unshed tears. "Then why have you been putting up all these walls?"

"I don't deserve you," I croaked. "I'm not good for you or Luca. I put you at risk."

Her whole face transformed then, empathy filling her expression as she closed the distance between us. "I thought we'd been through this. *I* decide what I deserve and what's good for me."

"You don't understand." My throat felt like it was on fire. "You don't know."

Those turquoise eyes searched mine. "Then tell me."

I saw it then. This was the only way. The truth would send her running. So, I spoke the thing I'd buried for seventeen years. "I killed my dad and brother."

CHAPTER THIRTY-FOUR

Sutton

COPE'S WORDS ECHOED AROUND THE ROOM LIKE A CANNON shot, reverberating off the walls and bleeding into me. I stared up at the man I knew I was falling for. There was only one word to describe his face: ravaged.

"What?" I whispered, not wanting to add to the weight of his statement.

"I. Killed. Them." The words sounded torn from his throat. As if someone had ripped them free and left a bloody trail in their wake.

"It was an accident—"

"Was it?" He cut me off.

"Cope." His name was barely audible, but it was all I could get out.

"We were coming home from *my* game. They wouldn't have been there if it wasn't for me."

"That's not—"

"Stop," he bit out. My mouth snapped closed, and Cope went on, almost as if in a trance. "It was winter. Got dark early. It was only 7:30 at night, but it was pitch-black. We were driving home on one of those two-lane roads, Dad and Jacob in the front, and Fallon and me in the back."

Cope wasn't seeing me now; he was somewhere else entirely. Back there, on that day. "We'd lost, and I was in a shitty mood. Took it out on Fal, needling her about something stupid. She snapped back at me, and we started fighting in earnest. Yelling about who would get Jacob's room when he moved out that summer to go to college. It was so stupid."

My rib cage tightened around my lungs. I could feel his pain like a living, breathing monster between us. But the invisible kind. The kind you couldn't see to fight off but left bloodied wreckage in its wake.

"Dad turned for a split second. Just long enough to tell us to quit it. But that was all it took. Jacob shouted. There was a damn deer in the middle of the road. Dad tried to swerve, but it was icy. We went over an embankment and hit a tree. I came to, and all I could hear was pain."

I wanted to touch Cope so badly, to soothe him somehow. But I knew if my skin grazed his, this story would stop, and something told me Cope needed to get this off his chest more than anything.

"I listened as my dad and brother died, but I couldn't get to them. Couldn't help. They needed me, and I wasn't fucking there. Pinned in the back seat next to my unconscious sister, not knowing if she was dead or alive, just knowing it was all my fault."

Tears streamed down Cope's cheeks and dripped off his jaw and chin, forming darker spots on the floor around us. "I killed them. Fal doesn't remember because she had a head injury. That whole night is just gone for her. But I remember it. I live with it every single day— the knowledge that I tore my family apart."

I moved then, unable to hold back any longer. It didn't matter that Cope was covered in sweat from his run or that he didn't think he deserved this. I wrapped my arms around his waist, pressed my face to his chest, and held on with everything I had.

"How can you bear to touch me?" he croaked.

"Cope," I rasped. "You are a good man."

"I'm not."

"You're a good man, and it wasn't your fault."

"It's on *me*," he growled.

I pulled back, my hands lifting to grab his face. "You were a thirteen-year-old kid who was bickering with his sister. If you think that condemns you to a lifetime of misery, then every single human with a sibling would suffer that fate."

The remnants of tears swirled in his shadowy blues. "They died because of me. And I've never told a single soul."

"They didn't. There is no reason for their deaths. That's why it's called an accident. Because no one is at fault. Certainly not *you*."

It killed a piece of my soul that Cope had been carrying this around for the past seventeen years. That he'd held this kind of pain and guilt without telling *anyone*. It made so many things make sense, though.

Why he held himself apart from his family yet would do anything for them. Why he didn't typically spend much time in Sparrow Falls, as if he could hide from the memories. Why he went after anyone who hurt one of his teammates on the ice as if he could protect them the way he hadn't with his brother and father. And why he was holding himself back from me now as if that would keep him from being hurt again.

Fear and atonement.

It was a lethal mixture. One that could destroy Cope's life. It was more toxic than even the drugs that had pulled Roman under.

Cope's chest rose and fell with his ragged pants as he recovered from his punishing run and letting loose that story. I kept a hold of his face. "It wasn't your fault."

"Sutton," he croaked.

"It wasn't your fault." I'd say the words over and over until he had no choice but to hear me.

"You don't know—"

"I do," I said, cutting him off. "You think I haven't gotten to know your family over this past year? That I don't know how they'd react to knowing you've been shouldering this burden for seventeen years? They'd be heartbroken. Not because they think you're responsible but because you've been carrying all this weight without letting them help."

I knew that with every piece of my soul. Because that's who the Colsons were. They met you wherever you were and surrounded you with love and acceptance. It killed me that Cope thought he'd get anything different.

Cope stared down at me, his chest still rising and falling with those rough breaths. His eyes searched mine, but I couldn't pin down what he was looking for. "I'm reckless. And it wasn't just that night. I snapped on the ice and got Teddy injured. Snapped at practice and nearly got suspended. Could've really hurt a teammate who, while an ass, wouldn't have deserved it. And all of it came around to bring Teddy here. Because he was checking in on my mess of a self. If he hadn't, he'd still be alive."

That was a knife to the chest. "Cope."

"But even worse, I guilted you into going to a funeral that exposed you to people you're hiding from because they broke your goddamned body and left you for dead." His chest heaved with his labored breaths that had nothing to do with recovering from his run.

But I kept a hold of his face and didn't let go. "First, you're human. You went after a player who messed with one of your friends. From what I've learned about hockey, that's pretty typical."

"Sutton—"

"I'm talking," I clipped, anger pressing to the surface, not at Cope but at the game of torture his mind was playing on him.

Cope snapped his mouth closed.

"From what I understand, Teddy got hurt after that incident because another player cheated. The only person that's on is the other player."

Cope's jaw worked back and forth, but he didn't try to interrupt again.

"And Marcus?" I asked. "That guy is a pompous, jealous jerk-face."

There was the barest flutter in Cope's lips. "Jerk-face?"

"Am I wrong?"

"Not wrong, Warrior. But he probably didn't deserve the punch."

I let out a long breath. "No, he probably didn't. At least not one to the face."

I got a full lip twitch this time but knew it wouldn't last because I had to say the next part and knew it would hurt. I gripped Cope's face tighter. "Teddy died. And it happened on the way home from visiting you."

Cope tried to pull back. "Sutton—"

"He died on the way home from visiting someone he loved. From sharing the sport he adored with new athletes. If you're blaming yourself for that, are you going to blame the kids, too? Are you going to blame Luca?"

"Of course, not."

"Good." I stretched up onto my tiptoes to press my forehead to his. "Because it was no one's fault. And I know it must have stirred up all kinds of demons, but you can't let them win."

Cope's arms slid around me then, and he breathed me in. "Okay."

I pulled back, surprise making my eyes flare. "Okay?"

He nodded. "I'm sorry I let the demons win for a minute."

All the air left my lungs in a whoosh. "I'm sorry, too. Because you need to know, you're the best for me. You jumped in to help with Luca. You gave us a place to stay. You make us dinner every night. You're giving Luca everything he's ever dreamed of. We might not have forever, but that doesn't mean we shouldn't soak up everything we can right now."

I said the last piece for myself as much as for him, an audible reminder that there was a time limit on this. Because Cope would return to Seattle while Luca's and my lives were here in Sparrow Falls. But I wouldn't hold myself back from Cope. I planned to soak up every ounce of him I could get because the memories would have to get me through when he left. Just like I wanted his memories of me to remind him what a good man he is.

Cope's eyes flashed a brighter blue, defiance making a home there. "Soak up everything we can because this has an expiration date, huh?" His hand slid to my waist, scorching me through the thin cotton of my tank top.

"It's the truth. You'll go back to Seattle, and I'll be in Sparrow Falls."

That hand dipped beneath the fabric of my shirt and circled my belly. "Ever hear of a long-distance relationship?"

"Cope…" That wasn't practical—for a million different reasons.

"You wanna do this, then we *do* it. No half measures. And no throwing up walls after you break down mine."

The accusation had my blood heating. "Says the man who's been avoiding me for the past two weeks."

Cope's rough palm pressed into my belly, pushing me back one step, then two, three, until my back hit a solid surface, but not one that caused any pain. The movement and how it felt told me it was a punching bag.

"Because you scare the hell out of me, Warrior. Because you make me feel more than I ever thought I could."

The air seized in my lungs, pulling in muscle and sinew with a violent contraction. It was my fear that hit me then. The idea of falling for a man with the potential to crush me. "Cope."

"So, tell me, are you ready to go there with me?"

That hand on my belly was all I could feel. The heat of it, my need for more contact, more of *him*. Cope's fingers twisted in the hem of my tank and then jerked it up and over my head.

The cool air of the gym instantly had my skin pebbling and my nipples tightening. But there was nothing but liquid fire in Cope's eyes. "Do you want me to touch you, Warrior?"

"Yes," I breathed.

He didn't hesitate. He lifted my hands above my head in a flash. "Grip the chains."

The words were roughly ordered, sending a pleasant shiver down my spine. Instantly obeying him, my fingers curled around the heavy bag's thick chains. Annoyance flickered that my body seemed so eager to please, but that annoyance quickly melted into shock as Cope used my tank top to tie my hands above my head and fasten them to the chains.

"Cope," I gritted out.

He just grinned at me, the kind of sharkish smile that should've had unease sliding through me. There was none of that. Heat flared between my legs at the promise of that smile, and wetness quickly followed.

"I asked if you wanted *me* to touch *you*, not the other way around." Cope stepped back, his thumb grazing his lower lip as he took me in. "So fucking beautiful. Back arched, pretty little nipples on display."

My breaths came quicker. Something about him watching me and being at his mercy had more wetness gathering at the apex of my thighs. "Cope."

Those dark-blue eyes twinkled with mischief. "Is there something you need, Sutton?"

My eyes narrowed. "Stop playing games."

One corner of his mouth kicked up. "You going to be in this with me?"

My mouth dropped open. "This is sexual blackmail."

Cope chuckled, the sound low and throaty. "Love that little O your mouth makes when you're shocked. Makes me think about it taking my cock."

Holy hell.

Now that was all I could think about. Me on my knees as I took Cope.

"You like the idea of that."

It wasn't a question. My gaze snapped back to Cope's face. "Untie my hands, and maybe you'll find out."

"My warrior likes to play." He grinned. "Not today. I have other plans for you."

Cope moved toward me, prowling like a predator stalking its prey. "Plans to make you beg. And if you're good, maybe I'll reward you. Make you come so hard you see stars."

My breaths came in quick pants now, my hands gripping the chains so hard I knew they would leave indentations behind.

Cope's hands lifted. One palmed my breast while he circled my nipple with the thumb of the other. "Look at you responding to my touch, your breasts reaching out for more. Your body's with me. But I'm greedy. I want all of you. Your mind, heart, *and* your fucking soul."

I gripped the chains even harder, making them rattle. "Cope."

"Are you ready for that?" he rasped.

I wasn't. Not yet. The idea terrified me. Because the last time I'd truly let someone in, my whole world was decimated.

Cope's thumb circled closer to the peak, making the bud tighten to an almost painful state. "Not there yet. But you will be." Cope lowered his head and took the bud into his mouth, sucking deeply.

I let out a nonsensical sound as my back arched. It was both too much and not enough. But the fact that I was pressing myself harder against Cope's face told me I only wanted more.

Cope's hand moved between my thighs, cupping me through my light sweatpants. I pushed against him, seeking friction and more contact. His hand was gone in a flash, and his mouth left my breast. He tsked. "You're not in control. Not today."

I made a sound that resembled a growl.

Cope only grinned at me. "I love it when you beg."

"You won't love it when I return the favor."

Cope chuckled. "Probably not. But it'll be worth it."

Then he dropped to his knees. I sucked in a sharp breath at the sight of him. His light-brown hair just a little wild, and his dark-blue eyes alight with fire. He reached up, his fingers tucking into the band of my sweats and boy shorts. Slowly, he began tugging them down.

His leisurely pace was the sort of thing that could make you combust. Cope's knuckles grazed my hips and ran down my thighs, but his gaze never left mine. Finally, my sweats dropped to the floor, and Cope gripped one leg gently. "Lift," he ordered.

What was it about those rough commands? My body instantly obeyed, my right foot lifting.

Cope slid the fabric off my leg. "Again," he ordered.

My left foot was up before he could finish the word.

Cope tossed my sweats and underwear to the side and then leaned back on his heels. He took me in like he was studying some work of art in a museum. Something about the look in his eyes made me feel powerful beyond measure.

"Could stare at you forever," he whispered, but there was a roughness to Cope's barely audible tone. Much like the man himself.

My heart hammered against my ribs as it tried to break free. I did everything I could to keep it in place.

"You in this with me?" Cope asked. "Wherever the road takes us?"

"Cope," I croaked.

"Still not there. Let's see if I can change that." He pushed to his knees, his hand skimming from my calf to my thigh. "Like golden silk."

I shuddered from his words and his touch, determined not to break. It was then that I realized I'd been determined not to let him in fully. I'd let him into the friendship, and I'd let him into my body, but I hadn't let myself hope for more. Because it was that *more* that would leave me in shambles when he left.

Cope's knuckles grazed the apex of my thighs. "Heaven. Been dreaming of your taste since that night at the bar."

My face flamed, and my skin heated at the memory. The feeling of Cope moving inside me, of how reckless we'd been. Because Cope made me want to take chances. To truly *live* again.

Cope's fingers parted me, and I gasped at the feel of him. He wasn't even inside me, and I was ready to beg for mercy. My hands pulled harder against the chains. The rattling sound was just more proof of how weak I was for Cope.

"Are you with me?" Cope asked, his voice low and coated in grit.

"Cope," I begged.

His thumb circled my clit. "Come on, Warrior. Shatter with me. Let go."

But I knew it was so much more than letting go with my body. Cope had said he wanted everything.

Two fingers slid inside me as Cope kept circling that bundle of nerves with his thumb. I couldn't hold back the moan that left my lips as I arched into the intrusion.

"Fuck, Warrior. Want to drown in those moans. Want to hear nothing else for the rest of my days."

And I wanted to give that to him. Even if I knew it was beyond reckless. I wanted us to drown in those moans together. To lose myself in Cope and never come up for air.

He added a third finger and made an arc as he dragged them down my inner walls. I couldn't hold in my cry and thanked the building gods that the basement was soundproof.

"Not yet, Warrior. Not until you give me everything."

My inner walls trembled as I battled with myself.

Cope leaned in, his tongue replacing his thumb on my clit. He teased the hood, coaxing that bundle of nerves free. My knees nearly gave out.

"Cope, please," I begged.

He pulled back a fraction and looked up at me. "All I'm asking is that we try. No half measures. All in. It may not work, but if we're going to play with fire, let's not settle for matches. We deserve fireworks and infernos."

I stared down at him, realizing just how safe I'd played it since Roman. Just how careful I'd been. Some of it had been necessary. But other pieces? They'd been selfish self-protection. Me living a life in fear. How was it fair for me to ask Cope to give me everything when I was still holding so much back?

"Okay," I whispered. The word was out of my mouth before I could stop it. But once it was free, I found I didn't want to snatch it back.

Cope's eyes flashed a brighter blue—the color of hope and pleasure. "Okay?"

"Okay," I echoed.

Cope didn't wait. He'd been taking me in a teasing rhythm, but now he took me in a way that would brand me forever. Those fingers inside me twisted and curled. Cope's lips closed around my clit, and he sucked hard.

I cried out, pulling harder on the chains. That bite of pain drove me higher as the tip of Cope's tongue teased that most sensitive place. My legs trembled as Cope's fingers pressed that spot inside me, the one that had little black dots dancing across my vision.

I wasn't sure if I was even breathing anymore, but I didn't care. I'd given myself over to Cope. There was trust there. Something I hadn't given in so long. Trust that gave me back the freedom I hadn't known I needed.

Pressing myself harder against Cope's face, I let every sensation wash over me. I took everything he had to give. Those fingers moved faster as Cope flicked his tongue against my clit. I shuddered, black dots filling my vision again.

I reached for them, everything in me pulling taut like a bowstring. Then Cope fired the arrow. His lips closed around that bundle of nerves, and he sucked deep as his tongue pressed down.

I didn't just break. I shattered.

The pieces rained around us as I finally let down the last walls I'd built all those years ago, the ones that had kept me safe but also kept me alone. Cope rode the wave with me, coaxing it to last longer than I'd ever dreamed possible. Until my legs gave out altogether.

He caught me with his free arm, my hands on the chains steadying me, then held me up as he pulled the last of every feeling from my body.

The world was fuzzy as Cope's fingers and mouth left me, as he held me up while freeing my hands. He scooped me into his arms. "Thanks for letting me in."

I looked up at the slightly hazy vision of him. "Thief," I muttered.

His mouth curved. "Never afraid to play dirty when it comes to you."

CHAPTER THIRTY-FIVE

Cope

I KNEW SUTTON WAS STILL WORRIED ABOUT ME WHEN SHE DIDN'T take the sunrise shift at the bakery. Instead, she helped me make breakfast for the three of us but watched me with hawk eyes.

"Mom, are you *sure* it's okay for you to help?" Luca asked from his spot on the banquette along the kitchen wall.

Sutton sent him a slightly exasperated look. "I'm not going to ruin breakfast."

Luca didn't look convinced. "Your baked stuff is amazing, but your scramble game isn't the best."

Sutton turned accusing eyes toward me. "You're spoiling my kid."

I chuckled, holding up both hands in surrender. "I solemnly apologize for being the most kickass chef to ever walk the Earth."

Sutton scowled. "With an ego to match, Hotshot."

Luca giggled. "He is pretty awesome."

"Do you have all your gear ready to go?" she asked him, artfully changing the subject.

Luca's face scrunched in thought. "I'd better double-check."

He was off the bench seat and running for the mudroom before we could say another word.

"You gotta give it to the kid," I said. "He's dedicated to hockey."

Sutton sighed, a wistful look in her eyes. "I'd really hoped for golf."

I laughed, leaning over to press a kiss to her temple. "Sorry, baby. He's got hockey in his bones. It's a done deal."

Sutton's eyes found mine. There was a warmth in the turquoise that was different than before. Things had changed last night, and even though parts of that transformation scared the hell out of me, I wouldn't let fear destroy what was brewing between us.

She set the knife down where she'd been chopping green peppers and moved into me. Stretching up onto her tiptoes, she pressed a kiss to the underside of my jaw. "How are you feeling today?"

Another artful transition to the topic I knew she'd wanted to broach since we woke up in my bed this morning. I wrapped my arms around her fully. "I feel good."

It wasn't a lie. I felt lighter—the gift of telling someone about the ugly stew of memories and emotions that'd always lived inside me. And the gift of Sutton not running for the hills in response. She didn't realize just how much that meant.

Sutton tipped her head back. "Good." She worried the corner of her lip.

I lifted a hand to tug it free. "Tell me what's going on in that beautiful head of yours."

"I think you should talk to your mom." The words came out quickly. "Tell her what happened. What you've been carrying. I think it'll help."

I released my hold on Sutton, turning back to the egg mixture I was concocting. "I don't need to. I told you. That's enough."

"Cope—"

"I don't want to open old wounds. She still misses them so damn much. This would be like throwing acid on that wound."

Sutton leaned a hip against the counter and faced me. "Of course, she misses them. She loves them. But she also loves *you*."

I shook my head roughly. "It's not worth the pain it would cause." But some part of me knew that was a lie. What I really feared was that my mom would look at me differently—that my whole family would. And that wasn't a risk I could take.

Luca had been quiet as he helped Coach Kenner and me clean up the gear from camp. I was used to him going over every event from the day's camp, but not today. I was about to head to the skate rental station to ask him if he was okay when movement caught my attention.

Evelyn Engel gestured wildly from where she'd clearly stopped Kenner in his tracks. He held a mesh bag full of cones and some balls for a game we'd played at the end of camp and looked at her with a panicked, deer-in-the-headlights expression.

Evelyn just kept right on gesturing, a woman on a mission. Kenner lifted a hand placatingly, but the woman just yelled something I couldn't make out in his face before storming off. Kenner stared after her before turning slowly and heading back in my direction.

"What was that about?" I asked, pitching my voice low so Luca couldn't overhear.

Kenner glanced in Luca's direction. When he saw that he was engrossed in helping Hayden put the rental skates back in their cubbies, he turned back to me. I didn't miss his wince. "I guess Evelyn saw the news coverage of you getting in an altercation with that teammate of yours, Marcus Warner. She was stating her case that you weren't a good role model for the kids and should be fired."

I stiffened but forced my voice to stay light. "Does she know this is a volunteer gig? I'm not sure I *can* get fired."

Kenner chuckled. "She might've missed that. She also accused you of playing favorites with Luca and not giving Daniel enough attention."

"Jesus. She can't have it both ways. Fired or pay her kid more attention?"

Kenner scrubbed his hand over his face and sighed. "You'll learn you can't win with some of these parents. They want you to act like their kid is the second coming. Destined for greatness and never make any mistakes."

"Poor Daniel," I muttered.

"You're not wrong there. That kid has enough pressure on his shoulders to give him an ulcer. He's *seven*."

God, there was so much wrong with that. Even as I started to rise and joined more competitive leagues, my dad never let me forget that, at the end of the day, hockey was supposed to be fun. I'd forgotten that until recently. But coaching these kids had brought it back.

"I'll make sure I spend some one-on-one time with him tomorrow. Not for her but for Daniel."

Kenner's brows lifted, respect filling his gaze. He clapped me on the shoulder. "You're a good man, Colson."

His words sent an ache deep into my chest cavity, but I didn't find them quite as unbelievable as I usually would've. And that was all thanks to Sutton.

I sent Kenner a grin. "Go get yourself a beer. I'd say you've more than earned it."

Kenner chuckled. "Truth."

I headed for the skate rental station, grinning at Hayden. "How's the wrist shot coming?"

She gave me an answering smile, her amber eyes lighting. "I don't have it 100 percent of the time, but when I do, it's freaking awesome."

I chuckled but had to admit that her joy for the game was infectious. And the teen had skills. If she kept at it, she could easily land a college scholarship. I planned to ask Linc if he had any scouts he could get to come in and take a look at Hayden this fall.

"No better feeling than when it's all working."

Hayden nodded, but before she could answer, a little girl

appeared at the booth. She was a mirror image of Hayden with dark hair and amber eyes. "Hay Hay, I'm hungry."

Hayden instantly rounded the counter and hoisted the little girl into her arms. "Then let's get you a snack." She tickled her belly, and the little girl giggled. "Gracie, can you say hello to Mr. Colson?"

The little girl's gaze dropped shyly, but she waved. "Hi, Mr. Colson."

I remembered what Arnie had said about Hayden taking care of her two younger sisters a lot. That had my gut churning, but I forced a smile. "It's very nice to meet you, Miss Gracie."

"I'd better get her something to eat before she gets hangry on us," Hayden said with a grin.

"Never want to unleash the hangry monster," I said with a chuckle.

Hayden gave me a wave and carried Gracie toward the snack stand. I didn't miss how expertly she moved with the little girl as if she'd done it too many times to count. Arnie might not be willing to talk to Fallon about her, but I would.

I turned to Luca, who was sliding the final pair of skates into their cubby. "You ready to go?"

He nodded but didn't say a word. That tweaked my radar, but I didn't push. There were too many people milling around the rink.

I grabbed Luca's and my gear bags and headed toward the exit. Once I'd stashed the bags in the rear of my SUV, I helped Luca into the booster seat and checked the latch after he'd buckled himself in. He still didn't speak.

My jaw worked back and forth as I closed Luca in and climbed behind the wheel. But I didn't turn on the engine. Instead, I twisted in my seat so I faced Luca. "Wanna tell me what's going on?"

"Nothing," Luca muttered softly.

"Well, it's not nothing. You're too quiet for it to be nothing. You don't have to tell me, but I hate the idea of you being sad. If we talk it through, maybe I can help." It was the best approach I could think of, but I couldn't help but wonder if Sutton would've done it better.

Luca was silent, staring down at his shoes. It went on for so long that I almost gave up and started the engine, thinking I'd drive him to the bakery so he could talk to his mom. But then he spoke so softly it was almost inaudible. "It's stupid."

"It's not stupid if it makes you sad. Sometimes, little things make me sad, too."

Luca's turquoise eyes lifted to mine. "Really?"

I nodded. "Like losing a preseason game or when someone says something not nice about me on the internet."

Luca's face scrunched. "People are mean sometimes."

That had an invisible fist grinding into my gut. "Was someone mean to you?"

Luca shook his head quickly. "No. Daniel got a dog."

My brows pulled together. "Daniel got a dog…" I repeated Luca's words as if that would help me understand.

"I want a dog," Luca whispered.

I remembered him telling me he wasn't allowed pets in the apartment above the bakery. The only animals he and Sutton had were the bees on the building's roof, and those weren't exactly cuddly.

"You're jealous," I surmised.

Luca nodded, his gaze dropping again. "I know it's wrong, but it's not fair. I've wanted a dog forever, and Daniel just decided he wanted one last week. And now, he's got one."

"Hey, now," I said gently. "I know it might not be fair, but let's not take something away from Daniel just because he hasn't wanted it for as long as you. I get the sense that he has a lot of pressure on him. Maybe he could use a furry friend."

Luca's eyes lifted at that, and he tugged on the corner of his lip with his teeth. "His mom is always yelling at him to practice stuff more. And his room always has to be like *perfect*."

"That sounds like it would be pretty hard. Your mom doesn't do that to you, does she?"

Luca kicked his feet against the seat. "She tells me to clean my room sometimes, but only when it's really messy."

I chuckled. "My mom did that, too."

"I'm pretty lucky. Mom always lets me have treats, and Daniel never gets any."

"Sounds pretty lucky to me."

Luca sighed; the sound was so beyond his years. "Maybe Daniel does need the puppy."

"Yeah, he might." But staring at Luca's disappointed face, I couldn't take it. "You know, I've been thinking about getting a dog."

Luca's brows flew up. "Really?"

I nodded. It wasn't a complete lie. My apartment in Seattle was too damn lonely. "Maybe you could help me pick one out and help me train it. It would be good practice for whenever you get your own."

Luca jolted upright. "I'd be the best picker! I'll choose the awesomest dog ever and help you teach it all the things. I'll even pick up its poop!"

I couldn't help but laugh. "I really wasn't looking forward to the poop."

Luca grinned. "I've got you covered."

"Come on, let's go find me a dog."

CHAPTER THIRTY-SIX

Sutton

"HOW ARE YOU FEELING?" THEA ASKED, THAT NOW-EVER-present worry line creasing her brow. "Today was a lot."

She wasn't wrong about that. We'd been slammed from the moment I got here until about thirty minutes ago when the lunch rush finally eased. The time we closed between 2:00 and 4:00 in the afternoon was always the quietest, especially during the summer. Once school started back up, we'd have some people stopping in after classes or parents treating their young kids. But it was mostly when we scheduled custom-order pickups.

"I'm good," I assured Thea. "The doctor cleared me, remember?"

Her lips pursed. "I just wanted to make sure."

I pulled her into a quick hug. "I know. And I appreciate it. Just like I appreciate that you haven't let me be here alone even once. But I'm good."

I wasn't about to let some asshole ruin what I'd worked so hard to build. I wouldn't let him steal my happy place. Trace and Anson had stopped by Cope's a few days after my attack to share that there was no evidence that anyone in Petrov's organization had traveled to Oregon recently. Apparently, the FBI was keeping close tabs on them.

What no one could determine was where Roman was. He'd completely dropped off any law enforcement radar and hadn't shown at any of the shelters he normally stayed at. The fact that I hadn't received any more texts had me uneasy—not for me, but for him.

Because I could see that attack as a simple crime of opportunity now. Some local who'd seen Cope frequenting my bakery, saw our closeness, and assumed my establishment would always be flush with cash.

"I just want to make sure you aren't pushing too hard," Thea said, cutting into my thoughts.

"I'm not. I promise. I actually feel really good." That wasn't a lie. After last night, I felt great. On more than one level. Because Cope and I were giving this thing a real go. And as much as it scared me, it also gave me hope.

Thea studied me for a long moment, and then her mouth popped open in a silent O. "You got laid," she whisper-hissed.

"Shhh!" I said, grabbing her arm. "I really don't need Walter or our patrons knowing the details of my sex life."

Thea grinned in a way that made her look slightly deranged. "*Sex life* means more than once."

My cheeks heated.

"At the country bar?" she pressed.

"Maybe," I whispered.

"I knew it! I told Shep you two looked way too rumpled to have only been *talking* back there."

I worried the corner of my lip. "Tell me I'm not being the stupidest person on the planet."

All amusement fled Thea's face. "You're not. I've seen how Cope looks at you. And the night of your attack, he was beside himself. I thought he was going to set that hospital on fire if you weren't given the best care possible."

"I'm scared," I admitted.

"Of course, you are. You're human, and you've been hurt before. But if we don't risk our hearts, then we miss out on life's true beauty. There's no reward without risk. Trust me, I've been there."

She had been. Thea knew better than most how to build walls to keep people out, and only after Shep demolished every last one did I see her truly happy and living life to its fullest.

I pulled her into another quick hug. "Love you, Thee Thee."

She grinned as I released her. "Love you. And love seeing you with that light in your eyes and color in your cheeks."

I knew exactly what had put it there.

"Oh," Thea said, turning and grabbing a stack of mail. "I forgot. I grabbed this for you on the way in."

"Thanks." I took it from her and pawed through it. Mostly junk, though there were a few bills and catalogs I wanted to keep. Then my gaze caught on a local return label that said *Monarch Property Management*.

Plenty of businesses used the Monarch Mountains or Castle Rock in their names, but I wasn't familiar with this one. Though it was possible I'd simply ended up on a mailing list after my apartment search. I ripped open the seal and tugged the letter free. As I scanned the text, I gaped.

"What is it?" Thea asked, moving to my side.

"My building has a new owner. They're cutting my rent and renovating the apartment upstairs. They'll let me rent it back for less than what I was paying before. Am I being punked?"

Thea tugged the letter from my grasp. "This is legit. They do a lot of work with Shep. I wonder if he'll be on the reno."

"It doesn't make sense. Rick was so determined to buy up half of Sparrow Falls. Why would he sell?"

She shrugged. "Maybe because he couldn't rent that apartment for his ridiculous prices. He was probably losing money daily."

That was a good point, but he didn't seem like someone who gave up that easily.

The bell over the door jingled, and I forced thoughts of Rick and rent cuts down as I looked up. "Evelyn, hi."

My smile was a little strained around the edges as I tried to brush some flour off myself. She looked perfect, as usual, in a collared blouse and khaki shorts with pearls in her ears. Not a strand of auburn hair was out of place. I was pretty sure a tiny frosting knife was currently holding my hair in its bun.

Evelyn returned my smile, but hers was more than a little strained. "Hello, Sutton."

Daniel ran around her to the bakery case. "No way! You have skateboard cupcakes? These are freaking awesome!"

That had a more authentic grin stretching across my face. "I've got one with your name on—"

"That isn't necessary," Evelyn clipped.

I straightened from where I'd crouched to grab Daniel a cupcake. I guessed this wasn't a friendly visit.

"Mom," Daniel pleaded.

She sent him a look that would've had me cowering. "We have homemade desserts back at the house."

"With no sugar," he muttered under his breath.

I couldn't help my wince, but I followed it with another forced smile. "What can I help you with today?"

Thea had slipped back into the kitchen—the traitor—but I could feel her eyes on me, likely watching the show with rapt attention.

Evelyn's lips pursed as if she'd been sucking on a lemon. "We need to discuss Copeland."

"Why?" The word was out before I could stop it. My back went up the moment she used his formal name. Not to mention that talking about Cope behind his back felt all sorts of wrong.

Evelyn bristled, her shoulders squaring as she stared down at me. "*Because* he is a horrible example for the children attending the camp. He curses multiple times a day, he gets into fights—"

"Has he gotten in a fight at camp?" I asked, mock confusion filling my voice.

A muscle in her jaw fluttered. "No, but children can access the internet."

"Sounds to me like a parental guidance issue."

Evelyn ground her back molars. "You may be all right with exposing your son to an animal like Copeland Colson, but I am *not*."

Anger flared, deep and fierce. "That's your prerogative. Remove Daniel from camp if you feel so strongly. But let me tell you, you'll be keeping him from learning from the best. And I'm not just talking about hockey. I'm talking about how to be the best man."

I sucked in a breath, struggling to keep my voice even. "How to be generous, kind, and gentle. How to put others before yourself. How to give back in every way. But if you want your son to miss out on all of that, be my guest."

"*Mom*," Daniel pleaded. "Stop talking mean about Coach. He's the best and way nicer than you are."

Evelyn turned to her son, gaping. "Daniel—"

"No! You talk mean about everyone behind their back. And I know that's not right. I know *you're* not right."

Evelyn flushed, her head jerking toward me. "Do you see what you've done?"

I met her stare, not looking away. "I'm pretty sure this one is all on you."

I pulled up in front of Cope's house, taking a minute to soak in the beauty of it. It wasn't just in its majesty but in the thought he'd put behind it. How he'd considered his family and the setting when designing every nook and cranny.

Twisting my head to the side, I popped my neck. I *might* have overdone it today. And Evelyn's little visit didn't help. My heart ached for Daniel, and I felt more than a little guilty for having it out with his mom in front of him, even if I had held back on what I wanted to say.

I shut off the engine, grabbed my purse, and slid out of my SUV. All I wanted was a long soak in Cope's tub, gallons of whatever pasta dish he'd concocted, and to sleep for a week. As I reached the front door, I heard shrieks and giggles from inside.

Those sounds had warmth spreading through me—joy that my kid got this every afternoon I couldn't be with him. I punched in the code to the door and opened it. The volume intensified, and a bundle of blue-gray fur streaked toward me.

I quickly shut the door behind me and sank to my knees to greet the little guy or girl. They looked to be mostly pit bull, with soulful dark eyes and a tongue lolling out of their mouth.

"Hi," I greeted, scratching behind their ears. They looked to be a few months old at least, but definitely less than six.

Luca bounded toward me, much like the dog had. "Mom! Cope got me a puppy!" My heart plummeted to my stomach. "Well, it's his puppy, but I got to name it and I picked Gretzky and I get to cuddle him all the time!"

My gaze lifted to the man behind my son. "Did you now?"

Cope sent me a lopsided grin and shoved his hands into his pockets. "I've wanted a dog for a while now."

"I just bet," I muttered. I knew my kid could tug on those heartstrings when he wanted something, but as I stared down at the adorable pup, I knew I would've been helpless, too. "Gretzky, huh?"

The puppy barked and then took off running down the hallway to the living room, Luca fast on his heels. I sucked in a breath as I pushed to my feet, listening to the giggling coming from the living room.

"On a scale of one to ten, how pissed are you?" Cope asked.

I sighed, taking him in. His light-brown hair was rumpled right along with his tee and joggers. I knew it was likely from rolling around on the ground while playing with the new dog and Luca. "Cope, what happens when we move out, and Luca has to leave the puppy behind? Or if you and I don't work out? He's getting used to all of this. To you. And I don't want to think about how much it'll hurt if he loses it."

Cope crossed the distance between us in three long strides. His hand slid along my jaw and into my hair, gently forcing the strands back. "Thought you were with me and giving this a real go."

"I am, but that doesn't mean I shouldn't consider how this impacts Luca. How it would hurt him if you just disappeared from his life." Just saying the words out loud had fear thrumming through me.

Cope's fingers tightened in my hair. "Warrior, don't like you assuming we won't work out. But *if* we don't, I'll never bail on Luca. I'll have his back for the rest of his life, and nothing will ever change that."

My heart thudded against my ribs. He couldn't have given me a better answer. It was a promise that stole another piece of my heart. "Thief," I whispered.

Cope grinned down at me. "Whatever it takes."

"Mom?" Luca called. His tone had changed, and that slight difference had my mom senses on alert.

Cope released me just in time for us to see Luca walking down the hall a little drunkenly, a hand on his stomach. "I don't feel good."

He barely got the words out before puking all over Cope's entryway.

CHAPTER THIRTY-SEVEN

Sutton

THE THERMOMETER BEEPED, AND I PULLED IT AWAY FROM LUCA'S forehead. 101.7 degrees. I winced. I needed to get some Tylenol in him, but that would be difficult when he'd already thrown up three times in a row.

Cope hovered behind me, peering over my shoulder. "Shit. Should we take him to the emergency room? That's high."

His concern had everything in me warming. And, God, it was nice to have someone with me. Someone who could make a run to the store or the pharmacy. For the first time in too long, I didn't feel quite so alone.

"He'll be okay. I just need to get some Tylenol in him, but we need his nausea to get better first," I said.

"I might be able to help." Arden's voice came from the doorway. She'd come over to take charge of Gretzky, her massive dog, Brutus, very unsure how he felt about his new cousin. She lifted a glass jar with what almost looked like tiny pieces of bark. "Sassafras tea. My mom always made it for me when I was throwing up. It helps nausea better than any medicine."

It was the first time I'd heard Arden mention her mother—or family of any sort, for that matter. I didn't know much about her history, family or otherwise, just that she'd come to live with the Colsons when she was twelve.

I pushed up from the bed and crossed to her. "I've heard about this and meant to try it."

She sent me a gentle smile, but her gaze quickly moved to Luca in the bed, worry filling her eyes. "If this doesn't help, we can call Dr. Avery. He'll make a house call."

"Maybe we should call him now," Cope cut in.

"Let's try this first," I said. "I don't want to make him come all the way out here for a simple stomach flu."

Luca twisted in the sheets, waking fitfully. "Mommy?"

God, it had been so long since he'd used that term, and it was like a knife to the gut. I hurried over to the bed, sinking back onto the mattress. "I'm right here, baby." I set the jar on the nightstand and picked up the washcloth from the bowl of ice water. Wringing it out, I pressed it to his forehead.

"Hurts," he croaked.

"Where?" I asked, a little more worry niggling at me.

"Everywhere."

Cope snagged the tea from the nightstand. "I'll get this stupid bark tea brewed, but if it doesn't work, I'm calling Dr. Avery." With that, he stormed out of the room.

"Don't take it personally," Arden said as she moved toward the bed. "Cope doesn't do well when the people he loves are hurting."

That word—*loves*—had my heart beating a little faster as I moved the washcloth to Luca's cheek. "I get it. I hate when Luca's sick."

"I hate it, too," Luca mumbled and then drifted back into that restless sleep.

"I don't know how you do it," Arden whispered. "It's like your heart is walking around outside your body."

I put the washcloth back into the ice water. "There have been more than a few days where it's been heart attack inducing."

Arden's gaze moved from Luca to me. "He's lucky to have you."

"I'm not doing anything."

"You are." Steel bled into Arden's voice. "Not everyone puts their kid before themselves. You do." With that, she turned on her heel and left.

I couldn't help but wonder about Arden's story.

A hand gently landed on my shoulder, and my eyes jerked open. "Wha—?"

"It's just me," Cope said.

I blinked against the dim light in Luca's room. The small clock on his nightstand read 3:15 in the morning. I stood from the over-stuffed chair and crossed to the bed to grab the thermometer. Luca's cheeks were still pink but not that angry red color anymore. I hoped that meant the fever had gone down.

After one more puking session, we managed to get some Tylenol in him. The thermometer beeped. 100.5 degrees. Better.

"That's good, right?" Cope asked, the concern still clear in his voice.

I nodded, my eyes burning. "It's good. We just have to stay on top of the meds now. He can take more in two hours."

"Then you can get a little sleep." Cope took my hand to lead me out of the room, but I shook my head.

"No. I want to stay here."

"Sutton." Cope pinned me with an I-mean-business stare. "You won't be any use to Luca if you're wrecked. You're still recovering from your injuries."

"I'm not. I—"

"You may feel better, but your body's not 100 percent," Cope argued.

I had to admit that I felt a little loopy. Between the long day at the bakery, the run-in with Evelyn, the dog, and Luca's tour du barfing, I was exhausted. "All right," I muttered, turning back to Cope. "But I need to set an alarm to give Luca his next dose."

Cope frowned at me, his eyes zeroing in on my face. "Give me that thermometer."

"Why?"

He snatched it from my hand, pointed it at my forehead, and pressed the button.

"Cope, I'm fine."

"You're flushed," he clipped. A second later, the thermometer beeped. "One hundred and one. Into bed with you."

"It has to be wrong. I—" I turned to grab the thermometer back, and a wave of dizziness hit me. Fast on its heels was the overwhelming nausea. "Uh-oh." I bolted for the bathroom.

CHAPTER THIRTY-EIGHT

Cope

LUCA GIGGLED AS I STEPPED THROUGH THE OPEN DOOR. "WHAT are you wearing?"

He was still a little flushed and sleeping more than usual, but he'd certainly turned a corner. He'd spent most of the day playing video games and asking when Gretzky could come back from Arden's.

I made a show of snapping my long rubber glove and adjusting the doctor's mask and ski goggles on my face. "There's only one person who hasn't fallen, and I'm doing whatever it takes to stay barf-free."

Luca sent a baleful look at the bowl next to him on the bed. "You're smart. Getting the pukes is the *worst*."

He was right there. And I was throwing that bowl in the trash as soon as Luca was out of the woods. Hell, I was having this whole house decontaminated. "Did you finish your soup?"

Luca nodded. "And the bread and ginger ale. Think I can have real food next?"

I chuckled but didn't miss the feeling of relief running through me. Luca was so small. Seeing him that sick had scared the hell out of me. But more than that, it made me realize just how much he meant to me. "My mom says mashed potatoes are the next step after soup and dry toast."

Mom and Lolli had shown up that morning with a massive container of chicken noodle soup. Lolli had tried to make a case for the fact that cannabis was used to treat pediatric cancer patients' nausea so she could make a little something for Luca. Mom had just gaped at her. I told Lolli that I really didn't feel like getting murdered when Sutton came out of her flu state and realized I'd given her kid drugs.

"Mashed potatoes are fire. I'm ready," Luca said with a grin.

"Well, let's hope they aren't *on* fire. I'll bring you some in an hour or two after I check on your mom."

Luca's nose wrinkled. "Does she still have the pukes?"

"It's mostly a fever now," I told him. Sutton had barfed in spectacular form for hours last night, but once we got some sassafras tea in her, that had calmed. But despite a few rounds of Tylenol, she was still struggling.

"She'll be okay, right?"

I hated the tiny bit of fear I heard in Luca's voice. "Of course. She's just sleeping for a while. Like a bear in hibernation. I hope she doesn't snack on either of us when she wakes up."

Luca giggled. "Make sure you've got snacks waiting."

"I will." I glanced at the TV. "You've got *Mighty Ducks*?"

Luca bobbed his head in a nod. "I'm going to watch all three in a row."

I didn't know how he didn't have them memorized by now, but if they made him happy, he could watch them a dozen times in a row. "Nothing like a good brain rot to cure what ails you."

Luca grinned, a new tooth just starting to peek out from his gums in that incisor spot. "Best medicine ever!"

I chuckled and pointed at his nightstand. "Use the walkie-talkie if you need anything." I'd asked my mom to bring over the ones my siblings and I used to play with, and it had come in handy with how big the house was.

"Code name Speedy reporting for duty," Luca shot back.

I gave him a salute and headed toward the hall. I made it to the next room and slowly opened the door. Sutton was sprawled like a starfish in the middle of the bed, her hair in messy disarray. I slowly crossed to the side of the bed to take in her face. Her cheeks were a little less red, and I hoped that meant we were past the worst of the fever.

As I leaned over her, Sutton's eyelids fluttered. When they finally opened, she let out a startled shriek. "What in the—?" she croaked. "What are you wearing?"

Her voice was a little raspy, but she sounded way more like herself than the two other times I'd woken her for a dose of meds. I took a step back, gesturing at myself. "You don't go into battle unarmed."

Sutton's lips twitched as she pushed up against the pillows. "Are those ski goggles?"

"Shocker, but I didn't have any science ones left over from high school chemistry."

As she blinked sleep away from her eyes, she stiffened. "Luca—"

"Is fine. No fever. Kept down soup and bread. We're moving on to mashed potatoes soon."

Sutton's hand moved to her belly. "Don't talk about food. It's too soon."

Another wave of worry sliced through me. "How do you feel?"

"Gross," she muttered. "I think my fever broke because I'm all sweaty."

I picked up the thermometer on the bedside table and pointed it at her forehead. A second later, it beeped. "Ninety-eight point five."

"Thank goodness," Sutton said, collapsing back onto the pillows. "I feel like I just ran a marathon."

"Why don't I run you a bath and then heat up some broth for you? We can see how that goes down. My mom brought over her homemade chicken noodle soup, and it cures everything."

Sutton blinked up at me, her eyes filling with tears.

I quickly ripped off my goggles and mask, moving closer to the bed. "Hey, what's this about?"

"You could get sick. You should stay back."

I tugged off the rubber gloves, tossed them to the floor, and slid onto the bed next to her. "Not even those nasty germs will keep me away if you're upset." Sutton burrowed her face into my chest. "Tell me what this is all about."

"You took care of us," she croaked.

"Okay…"

"No one's taken care of me since my grandma. Not really. My parents weren't in the picture. Roman was never any help. And when Luca's sick, I have to do it alone."

Pain lit in my chest, and I held Sutton tighter to me. "I'll always take care of you. Always."

Sutton just cried harder. "Don't promise me that."

"Why not?" I asked, my voice dropping low.

"Because if I lose that promise, I'll break."

"Fuck," I muttered. I cradled her against my chest. "I'm afraid it's too late."

"Too late?" she croaked.

My fingers sifted through Sutton's hair, tangling in the strands. "I'm already in love with you."

CHAPTER THIRTY-NINE

Sutton

I COMBED OUT MY DAMP HAIR AND THEN RAN MY FINGERS through it in a half-hearted attempt to air-dry the strands. I might not have the energy to blow-dry it, but at least my hair was clean. I'd also been vomit-free for over twenty-four hours, which meant I felt like a new woman.

The feeling of Cope holding my hair back and rubbing a hand down my back flashed through me. Just like his words from the day before still echoed in my mind. *"I'm already in love with you."*

I'd played them over and over, with alarming frequency. It wasn't fair. Not when I hadn't given them back. Cope saying them at all had startled me senseless, but he didn't wait for my response. He simply carried me into the bathroom and ran me the perfect bath, not leaving my side for a second.

Staring into the mirror, I studied my face. My skin had regained most of its color, and my eyes had lost the dullness they had while I was sick. With a few good meals, I'd be back to normal and could hopefully return to work.

Strains of laughter came from downstairs, making my mouth

curve. I needed to go relieve Cope *and* Arden, who'd gone above and beyond while taking care of Luca. I slid my feet into comfy slippers and headed for the stairs.

I might've been out of breath by the time I reached the bottom, but none of that mattered when I caught sight of the vision in front of me. Luca raced in a circle around the living room. It was impossible to tell whether he was chasing the massive cane corso and adorable yet bumbling puppy, or if they were chasing him.

"Throw it to me!" Luca shouted.

"Incoming," Cope called, launching a tennis ball toward my son.

I couldn't help but stop and stare. Cope had on a pair of black joggers that fell loosely around his hips. The gray tee that read *Seattle Sparks* clung to his defined chest as he released the ball, his biceps flexing. But it wasn't his body that had my heart halting. It was the light in Cope's dark-blue eyes as he looked at my son. The joy in his expression at the chaos that reigned in his living room.

Warmth spread through me, but fear followed fast on its heels. Because as much as this all felt like a dream, it also felt tenuous at best. As if the safe harbor Cope had given us could be broken at any moment. Shattered beyond recognition.

Luca caught the ball with a shout, and I worried Arden's large dog might take him out. He easily could've, given he probably weighed twice as much as Luca. But the dog just barked in what could only be sheer joy. Gretzky tried to leap at Luca but fell into a sort of tumbling roll instead, then bounded off to the other side of the room.

"Arden, did you see that?" Luca shouted. "That catch was sick!"

Arden grinned from where she sat cross-legged on the floor. "Maybe baseball is in your future, too."

Luca just shook his head. "Naw, I just want to do hockey and jiu-jitsu, like you."

I couldn't help the groan that left my lips. All three heads turned to me. "Hockey wasn't bad enough?" I asked, my lips twitching. "Now, you actually want to fight people?"

Luca grinned widely, exposing the tooth that was growing in. "Fighting is the best part of hockey, so yeah."

I turned to Cope. "I blame you for this."

He held up his hands in mock surrender. "I'm not the one who let Luca watch me spar with Kye."

"And it was freaking AWESOME!" Luca yelled.

Arden simply shrugged. "I couldn't miss a workout, and Kye's gym has a class for kids."

"It starts this fall," Luca said, bouncing on the balls of his feet. "Kye said I'll just be old enough. Do you think I can take it? Do you?"

My stomach lurched, and I knew it wasn't from the twenty-four-hour bug I'd had. Cope crossed to me, wrapping an arm around my shoulders. "Let's give your mom a break. She just got puke-free. We don't need the thought of her kid battling in a fight circle making her nauseous."

Luca's chin took on a stubborn angle. "I'm not gonna forget about it."

Cope chuckled. "Trust me, I have learned that your stubbornness is legendary."

That only made Luca smile huge again. "That means I get what I'm after."

Cope leaned in closer to me, speaking in a stage whisper. "Sometimes, he scares me."

Luca giggled. "Kye showed me his tattoo gun, too. I definitely want ink when I turn eighteen. But if you give me permission, I can get it before then."

I stepped out of Cope's hold, looking between him and Arden. "Anything else I should know about from the twenty-four hours I was out? Were there piercings? Tequila shots with a rock band?"

Luca just laughed harder, but at my movement closer to my

son, Brutus stepped between me and him, taking on a defensive stance and letting out a low growl.

"*Ruhig*," Arden clipped. "*Komm.*"

In an instant, the dog eased and trotted over to Arden. He plunked his big, furry butt down, and Arden scratched his head. "Sorry. He's become partial to Luca."

"What was that?" I asked, staring at Brutus.

Arden's hand slid down to Brutus's chest. "He's a trained guard dog. Personal protection. He's bonded to me, but those instincts take over with Luca because he loves him."

"Aw," Luca said, jogging over to the dog and throwing his arms around his neck. "I love you, too, big guy." Brutus licked his cheek in answer.

Cope moved in closer to me. "He's trustworthy. Promise. Trace had him trained at one of the best facilities in the country. He's been with our family since Arden was seventeen."

I looked between the dog and Arden, yet again wondering what her story was. But before I could ask any careful questions, a ball of blue-gray fur tore across the living room with something in its mouth.

"Gretzky!" Luca yelled, launching to his feet to chase after the dog.

"That's my slipper," Cope shouted, moving in the direction that Luca and the dog had gone.

Brutus took off after them, thinking it was some new game.

Arden pushed to her feet, shaking her head. "You shouldn't chase him. It only reinforces that it's a game."

"Tell that to my slipper," Cope shot back, making a dash for the shoe but missing as Gretzky ran back in my direction.

"Someone had better find the other one," I warned. "That's liable to get holes in it, too."

"I've got it," Arden said, heading for the far hall as the boys raced after Gretzky.

I lowered myself into the overstuffed chair. This was too much excitement for my first venture out of bed in a day and a half.

"I found the other one," Arden called. "But I don't think you're going to want to use it again, Cope."

Cope strode back into the living room with Luca, Gretzky, and Brutus on his heels, just as Arden appeared holding a shoe out in front of her, as far away as possible, a big ole dog poo right in the slipper.

Cope's jaw dropped. "There is no way all that shit came out of that tiny, adorable creature."

Gretzky let out a yipping bark, dropping the slipper.

Cope turned to the puppy. "Tell me you didn't expel that from your tiny body. It was Brutus, wasn't it?"

Arden scoffed. "If it was Brutus, I wouldn't be able to lift the slipper."

Cope scrunched his nose. "For the love of God, take that thing outside. The puppy, too."

"It's okay, Gretzky," Luca said, patting the puppy.

Cope sent them both a mock glare. "Tell that to my poor slipper."

My phone dinged in my pocket, and I reached for it. I hoped like hell Thea wasn't drowning at the bakery without me. But as I opened my text thread, I felt the blood drain from my face.

There was a screenshot of some sports blog featuring a photo of Cope and me coming out of the church after Teddy's funeral. My head was tipped down, and my sunglasses covered much of my face. No one should've known it was me. But someone did.

> **Unknown Number:** You think I don't recognize your sweet little body, Blue Eyes?

My phone dinged again and again.

> **Unknown Number:** Or that fucking necklace around your throat.

My fingers lifted to my neck. It was a little silver star adorned with gemstones. I wore it often and had since college. I'd only managed to hang on to the necklace because Roman knew the silver and gems were fake.

Unknown Number: Should've hocked that instead of that stupid, goddamned locket. Only got fifty bucks. And I'd say you owe me a hell of a lot more than that.

Unknown Number: I gave you everything. Clothes, cars, the house of your dreams. And you and that kid just took and took and took. It's time you paid me back. Now I know where you are. Know you've got cash from your hockey player. I knew you could whore yourself to get what I needed.

Unknown Number: Pay up Blue Eyes or I'm coming for you and that kid.

CHAPTER FORTY

Cope

I WATCHED THE BLOOD DRAIN FROM SUTTON'S FACE AS SHE STARED at the phone. Ding after ding. She just kept staring.

"Arden, take Luca and Gretzky outside," I clipped.

Arden's gaze flicked back and forth between Sutton and me. "Cope—"

"Please." My voice dipped lower as I let a pleading note bleed into my tone.

Arden's jaw hardened, her telltale defiance beginning to show. But then she jerked her head in a nod. "Come on, Luca. Help me dispose of this shoe."

"Mom, are you okay?" Luca asked.

I'd learned that he was an empath through and through. He made sure all the other kids at camp always felt included. He gave pep talks and cheered for everyone. But he was most attuned to his mom. It spoke of how deep their bond was.

Sutton blinked a few times, then forced a smile. "Sorry, Superstar. Just some bakery math doing my head in."

He frowned but nodded.

"Come on," Arden encouraged. "Before this whole house stinks like Gretzky's butt forever."

That had Luca giggling and following after Arden. The moment the two of them and the dogs disappeared outside, I took the phone from Sutton.

"Cope, I—"

"What the fuck is this?" Each text was more vile than the one before.

"Roman," she whispered.

My gaze flew from the screen to her. When I saw tears gathering in her eyes, I wanted to fucking kill someone. "You're sure?"

She swallowed hard, trying to battle back her emotions. "He's the only one who calls me Blue Eyes."

My back molars ground together, but I gently pulled Sutton into my arms. I lifted a hand, my fingers skimming the delicate skin beneath one of her hypnotizing orbs. "Warrior, your eyes are so much more than blue. They're like a sea in the tropics. They change shades and tones with your emotions. They'll dip into a storm with your fierceness or spark with light when I take you. And they turn this soft teal when you look at Luca."

Sutton's breath hitched on a hiccupped sob. "Cope."

"You aren't anything he said you are. You're so much more."

She pressed her face into my chest, burrowing into me. "I don't even recognize him anymore. He used to be funny. Caring. It used to matter to him that we were taken care of. He doesn't even use Luca's name."

A pang lit in my chest, agony for all Sutton had endured. I rested my chin on her head and held her to me. "Sometimes, that kind of poison changes you. Morphs your mind."

"Or maybe I never knew him at all," Sutton whispered.

I wanted to fix it. Erase every ounce of pain she'd experienced at this asshole's hands, or because of his choices—choices that had put the people he should've loved most at risk. But I couldn't do anything to change the past. All I could do was make sure Sutton and Luca were safe now.

"We need to call Trace."

Sutton pulled back, shame mixing with the torment in her eyes. "Do we have to?"

I nodded. "I'm sorry. He needs to know. We have to do everything possible to keep you and Luca safe."

She tugged her bottom lip between her teeth. "Do it. Just get it over with."

The defeat in her voice had rage surging to the surface again. I was going to find Roman Boyer. And when I did, there wouldn't be a chance that he'd contact Sutton ever again.

If one thing could be said about my family, it was that we were good in a crisis. Overbearing? Yes. Slightly unhinged? Quite possibly. But we showed up. Always. As they did for me now.

When I told Trace that we didn't want Luca to be freaked, he said he had it covered. Apparently, *having it covered* meant as many of the Colson crew as possible descending on my house all at once.

I heard strains of sound from my mom and Rhodes in the kitchen, cooking up a storm. Trace had brought Keely with him, and she was currently having a diving-for-rings contest with Luca in the pool. Kye was apparently in charge of tossing the rings, which he did from his lounge chair, dressed entirely in black with motorcycle boots and shades in place.

Fallon sat in the chaise next to him, critiquing his form in true needling fashion. Shep and Thea tossed the ball for Gretzky on the lawn while Lolli seemed to be showing Arden some new work of art.

I could just make out snatches of conversations through the open doors, but even with Anson and Trace sitting opposite us, Sutton didn't take her eyes off Luca. She held her breath with every dive until his head popped out of the water. Each time he hurried around the side of the pool, she tracked his every step.

"Sutton," Trace said softly.

She jerked slightly. "Sorry. What did you say?"

I moved in closer to her on the couch, weaving my fingers through hers and simply assuring her that I was there and wasn't going anywhere.

"When's the last time you heard from Roman? Before this," Trace asked. He was careful to pitch his voice at just the right volume. Years on the job had taught him how because his gruff tone could intimidate people if he wasn't careful.

Sutton's fingers tightened around mine in a vicious hold, and she swallowed hard. "I hear from him every now and then. I used to change phone numbers, but he always found my new ones, so I just gave up. When I block him, he only texts from a new number."

Anson and I shared a look at that. None of that was a good sign. A guy in the throes of addiction shouldn't have the wherewithal to find the phone number of a woman who'd moved across the country.

"But it's been a little bit. I think the last time was..." Sutton's voice trailed off, and then she turned to me. "That family dinner a month or so ago. When you came out to talk to me by the pasture."

This time, it was *my* hand that tightened around Sutton's. "You looked sad. And a little scared."

Fucking hell. If I'd known what was happening and what she'd been through, I would've moved her and Luca in with me right then.

"So, you didn't hear from him around the time of your attack?" Trace pressed.

"No, I—" Sutton's eyes widened. "Do you think it was him? Do you think he's in Sparrow Falls?"

"We don't have any reason to believe he's currently here," Trace said quickly, his voice taking on that soothing tone again. "But the Baltimore Police Department hasn't been able to locate him at any of his last-known residences. His usual dealers haven't seen him either."

Sutton's knee started bobbing up and down nervously. "I don't see how that's even possible. His family cut ties with him after what happened to me. They were never the warmest, but I don't blame them for needing to close that door. And he burned every friendship to the ground. Borrowed so much money from people that they just stopped taking his calls."

A ringtone cut through the air, and Anson shifted, pulling his cell out of his pocket. He silenced the call but stood. "I need to take this."

Trace's gaze shifted. "You got something?"

"Not sure yet." Anson moved deeper into the house to take the call.

It was a minor miracle to see those two working together like this. Trace had not been a fan of the broody ex-profiler when he took up with our sister, Rhodes. But Anson had won him over by how hard he'd fought for her and everything he'd done to keep her safe.

"Do you know if Roman might've borrowed money from any other people who might take more drastic measures to get it back?" Trace asked.

Sutton's bouncing intensified, and I reached over and put my hand on her knee to still it. "You're safe, remember? Luca's safe. I've got you. Holt Hartley's team is arriving to install the new security system here and at the bakery tomorrow."

She stiffened at that. "The bakery. I forgot, there's a new owner. They may not want—"

I squeezed Sutton's knee. "I let the property management company know. They said it was all right."

Trace arched a brow at me. He knew I'd bought the building. He also knew that Sutton would have my head when she found out I was lying to her. But this wasn't the time to share that piece of news. We had bigger fish to fry.

"Okay," she breathed, then turned back to Trace. "I honestly have no idea. He hid everything from me. I didn't know until he was getting let go from the team. And even then, he played it off as a one-time screwup. I didn't realize he had addiction issues. It wasn't until he started disappearing for days and acting erratically that I knew I had to leave. I was so naïve. Stupid."

"Hey," I cut her off gently. "Don't talk about my girl like that."

Sutton's turquoise gaze swung to me. "I should've seen it."

"Sometimes, the people closest to us know the best ways to hide things," Trace said quietly.

My gut churned at his words. I knew he'd been through more than his share of secrets and lies. Trust would never come easily to Trace. Yet he always showed up for the people he cared about and his community.

"I just wish I could go back. Leave so much earlier," Sutton said.

My fingers tightened around hers in a gentle squeeze. "You were doing the best you could with the information you had. You couldn't have known things would get as bad as they did."

"Maybe," Sutton muttered.

Anson's footsteps sounded on the hardwood. "Dex found something."

Something about Anson's tone had my skin prickling. There was a tightness to it that told me he was trying to keep his anger contained. And when I took in his gray-blue eyes, I knew the rage had a choke hold on him.

"What?" Trace clipped.

Anson shoved his phone into his pocket. "Dex might've found a way into Petrov's computer system."

Trace pinched the bridge of his nose. "I didn't hear that." There was nothing worse for my rule-following brother than coloring outside the lines.

"Then you definitely won't want to hear that Dex found out why Roman hasn't popped up on any radar recently."

Trace's head jerked up, his eyes narrowing. "Why?"

"Roman is working off his debt. In the organization," Anson said, his voice cooling. "The only problem is, the longer he works there, the more debt he racks up."

Sutton's fingers dug into the back of my hand. "They're still supplying him?"

Anson nodded, a grim look on his face. "It's how they keep him chained. He deals, he uses. Rinse, repeat. But the word in interoffice communications is that they've started using him as an enforcer. Apparently, he has a taste for it."

Color drained from Sutton's face, and I glared at Anson. "Was that really necessary?"

Sutton shook her head. "I needed to know." She looked up at Anson. "And if they know I'm with Cope now. That he has money..."

That fury was back in Anson's face. "They could come for you and Luca both."

CHAPTER FORTY-ONE

Sutton

WALTER SET A DISH ON THE STACK OF CLEAN ONES, AND I nearly jumped out of my skin. He stilled, the lines around his eyes deepening with concern. "Are you all right?"

I did my best to force a smile but knew my performance was less than Oscar-worthy. "My sleep schedule is all off thanks to those couple of sick days. I didn't get enough last night."

That wasn't exactly a lie. My sleep had been fitful at best. Every time I found it, it was punctuated by nightmares of Roman grabbing Luca or hurting Cope. Finally, I'd given up altogether.

But when Cope found me in the kitchen, nursing a cup of tea, he'd taken me back to bed and distracted me in all sorts of ways. I hadn't minded that as much.

Walter's mouth thinned into a hard line. "You don't have to tell me exactly what's going on, but I know it's more than just a break-in. Those guys puttin' in the new security system look like ex-military. So, you just tell me what I need to keep an eye out for."

I sighed. I couldn't outright lie about this to Walter. It wasn't fair. Pulling out my phone, I scrolled to the mugshot Trace had texted

Cope and me this morning. It was the most recent photo of Roman he could find.

The man looking back at me from the image was a stranger. He'd lost a good forty pounds, his eyes were sunken in, and there was an almost gray cast to his skin. Still, I forced myself to show it to Walter. "If you see this guy, or if anyone comes in here with a Russian accent, call Trace."

Walter glared down at the photo. "Who is he? Russian mob?"

"He used to be my husband," I whispered.

Walter's eyes flared. "Seriously?"

I nodded. "And now he's bad news."

Walter's jaw hardened, and anger flickered in his eyes. "He's not going to hurt you here. I've got a frying pan and know how to use it."

Warmth flooded my chest, and I couldn't stop myself from throwing my arms around the older man. "I love you."

He patted my back. "Love you like you were my own. And you deserve so much better than whatever he gave you."

"It was worth every ounce of pain because he gave me Luca." I would've taken that beating and heartbreak over and over if I got my son.

Walter pulled back, the anger in his eyes melting into pain—for me. "That boy is so lucky to have you as his mama."

"Walter, I do not need to cry on top of everything else today."

He chuckled. "Fair enough. But I want you to tell me if you need anything."

"I will. I promise. But I think Cope and his family have it pretty well covered."

Walter shot a grin in my direction. "Good to see that boy doesn't need any more common sense knocked into him. But I'm still gonna warn him to treat you right."

"Walter..."

"It's my duty as your honorary grandpa."

The threat of tears was back, but I swallowed them down. "All right. He can take it."

"Ms. Holland," a deep voice cut in from the entryway to the kitchen.

I turned to take in Anson's friend, Holt Hartley. Apparently, he no longer worked for the security firm he was still a partner in, but he'd come all the way from Cedar Ridge to do his friend a favor. That told me everything I needed to know about the man.

"I told you. Sutton, please."

He nodded at me with a smile. "Sorry. Old habit now that I'm back in the field."

"Fair enough. What can I help you with?"

"We're done putting in the system. If you'd like me to walk you and your staff through how to use it, I can."

"Holy testosterone," Lolli called as she bustled in behind Holt, a package tucked under her arm and copious necklaces jangling. "I don't think my hormones can handle all this hotness."

"I'll give your hormones something to handle," Walter shot back, a slight growl to his words.

Lolli waved him off. "Oh, hush, you old codger. You're interrupting my view." She took a step back and did a head-to-toe sweep of Holt. "You certainly know how to hire help, Sutton."

Holt's cheeks flushed as he leaned down to whisper in my ear. "Are those pot leaves on her cowboy boots?"

Lolli groaned. "Don't tell me you're one of those law-and-order types like my grandson. No fun at all." She drummed her fingers against the parcel under her arm, eyes twinkling. "Though it might be fun to get you to break the rules."

"Should I be scared?" Holt asked.

"Very," I muttered.

"Aw, come on now," Lolli shot at me. "You might be taken now, but you're not dead."

I grinned at her. "I might be alive, but I also don't want to make anyone feel uncomfortable."

Disappointment slid through Lolli's features. "Oh, all right. Here. Open this." She handed me the package wrapped in brown butcher paper. "It's for you. I wanted to do something to brighten your day. I thought it would be perfect as bakery décor."

Wariness slid through me as I took the present, which was obviously some kind of artwork. Given what she'd gifted many of the people in the Colson family, the work of *art* could be anything. But the fact that Lolli had taken the time to do something for me, just because she knew I was going through a hard time, had a feeling of belonging settling into me. That wasn't something I'd felt in a long time. And, God, it was nice.

My fingers slipped under the seam of the wrapping paper, and I tore it from the framed artwork. Letting the paper fall to the floor, I took in the piece. It was a diamond art still life comprised of countless glittering gemstones that formed a tower of baked goods. Everything from pies to cakes, scones to croissants. And at the top of the pile were three donuts. Two round ones and one of those butterscotch bars. The shape they formed was somewhat familiar.

"Is that a...donut dick?" Holt muttered.

Lolli beamed at him. "I knew I liked you. Art is all about the hidden message."

"And that message is bakery penises?" I squeaked.

"Don't be a prude, Sutton," Lolli admonished. "Sex and the human body are things to be celebrated."

Holt pulled out his phone. "I gotta take a picture of this. My brother Nash is going to want one of these. His two favorite things are donuts and being inappropriate."

"Well, inappropriate diamond art is Lolli's specialty," I said.

"Tell him I take custom orders," Lolli commanded.

"Sutton."

I turned at the new voice, one I knew so well now. But the second I took in Cope's face, I knew something was wrong. I handed the diamond painting to Holt without thinking, crossing to Cope. "What is it?"

His throat worked as he swallowed. "There's a story in the press about us. They have your identity and photos from your attack in Baltimore."

CHAPTER FORTY-TWO

Cope

FURY WASHED THROUGH ME AS I SETTLED SUTTON IN HER TINY office in the back hallway. There was just enough room for a small desk and two chairs opposite it. As she sat in one, I scooted the second closer, my hands looping around her thighs. "Talk to me."

Sutton stared straight at me, but her gaze was unfocused as if she were somewhere else entirely. "I knew it would happen eventually, that someone would put two and two together. I just thought I'd have more time."

A fresh wave of anger slid through me. These gossipmongers never thought about how their actions affected the people they wrote about. It only made me more furious because Sutton hadn't asked to be in the public eye; I was the one who'd forced her into it.

And there was more I had to tell her.

My fingers tightened on Sutton's thighs, trying to bring her focus to me. "Roman gave an interview."

Sutton jerked as if she'd been shot. "What?"

"With one of the worst gossip sites. Probably because they pay cash for those kinds of things. He played the aggrieved ex and said he had a problem but was better now. That you left him when he needed you the most." As if it wasn't bad enough that several sites had picked up the story, sharing those photos of Sutton's brutalized face. One just had to take it to the next level by giving her ex a platform for his lies.

I expected hurt, maybe even tears. Instead, Sutton shoved to her feet and stalked across the tiny space. "When he needed *me* the most? How about when *I* needed *him*? When his *associates* beat me so badly, I didn't think I would survive. When I was lying in the hospital, and it hurt to even breathe. When I had to beg a friend to stay with Luca so he didn't go into the system while I recovered."

Each statement was worse than any blow I'd taken on or off the ice. The reality of what Sutton had endured was more than I could take.

She stilled her pacing halfway across the room and took in my face. She let loose a creative curse and crossed to me, dropping into my lap. "I'm sorry."

I held her to me, trying to assure myself she was okay. Safe. "I should be the one comforting you."

"I know it's hard to hear," Sutton said, her voice dropping.

"It is. But it was a hell of a lot harder to go through." My hand slid along her jaw as my thumb traced the faint scar bisecting her lip, the one so similar to mine. "I hate that they hurt you. Would do anything to take away the pain, the memories."

"Cope," Sutton whispered. "I'm okay. I got out. I survived. And now I know I have the ability to stand on my own two feet. To take care of myself and Luca. That's a gift. But it also means it was that much sweeter when you came along just when I needed you most."

Her fingers lifted to my face, tracing my mirroring scar. "You gave us a safe place to land. A harbor in the storm."

"Warrior," I croaked.

"I—"

The door opened, cutting off Sutton's words. "Are things getting frisky back here?" Lolli asked. "I was just bringing Sutton some tea, but it looks like that might not be necessary."

Sutton flushed. "All clothes are firmly in place, Lolli."

"Could still be getting up to some dry humping. I'm kinda partial to that myself."

"Lolli!" I clipped.

She just glared at me. "I thought I could count on you not to be a stick in the mud."

I pinched the bridge of my nose. "Someone save me from this nightmare."

Sutton giggled softly, and the sound wrapped around me, bringing relief. She was okay. We'd make it through whatever came our way.

Sutton pushed off my lap. "I need to get back to work."

"You will do no such thing," Lolli snapped. "I am going to help Walter finish up. We'll have Hottie Holt teach us the security system, and he said he'd send a video tutorial to your phone, as well. Cope is going to take you home."

Sutton's brows lifted. "Who knew Lolli could be bossy about more than the medicinal effects of pot?"

"Damn straight, my darling." Lolli crossed to Sutton and wrapped her in a tight hug. "You matter, and I'll do whatever I need to do to make sure you're taking care of yourself."

Sutton's gaze connected with mine over Lolli's shoulder, her eyes filling. But I knew it wasn't sadness spurring the tears; it was the force of Lolli's love. I knew Sutton had been closest with her grandmother and that she'd lost her right after college. I could kiss Lolli for stepping in to fill a little of that void.

As Lolli released her, I stood. "Come on. We can pick up Luca on the way home. Kenner's keeping a close eye on him. Arnie, too."

Sutton nodded, turning to Lolli and taking her hand to give it a squeeze. "I wish you could know how much that meant. Thank you."

It was Lolli's turn to get a little misty. "Don't you dare make me cry, young lady. I won't have Walter thinking he has a chance to swoop in and *comfort* me."

Sutton chuckled. "Throw that man a bone."

Lolli simply huffed. "He hasn't earned me yet." And with that, she flounced out of the office.

Sutton turned to me, a smile playing on her lips. "I admire the hell out of her."

I wrapped an arm around Sutton's shoulders. "Just don't tell Lolli that."

The ride to the rink was mostly quiet, and I didn't push Sutton for more. I knew there were countless things she needed to think through, and I could give her all the time in the world for that. But just as I pulled into a parking spot, she spoke.

"Have other outlets picked up the interview with Roman? Ones outside that gossip site?"

I winced. I'd hoped we wouldn't have to go there, but there was no getting around it now. "They have. It's not huge, but there are more than a few."

The original interview had been posted last night. More mainstream media had picked it up early this morning. And even more by this afternoon. I would've been oblivious if I hadn't gotten a text from Angie letting me know. I just hoped like hell the photographers and reporters didn't make their way to Sparrow Falls.

Sutton let out a long breath, slumping against the seat. "We'll deal. Right?"

Turning off the engine, I took her hand and pressed her knuckles to my lips. "It's you and me, remember? We're in this together."

She worried the corner of her lip. "I'm sorry you have to deal with it because of me."

I gripped her fingers tighter. "Don't even think like that. I'd walk through fire for you any day of the week."

"But you shouldn't have to," Sutton whispered.

"Life isn't perfect. It's not always sunshine and rainbows. It's about finding people who will weather the storm with you. Who will find ways to dance in the rain."

One corner of her mouth kicked up. "You want to dance in the rain with me?"

I leaned across the console, taking her mouth in a long, slow kiss. "Always. Now, let's go get our boy."

"Okay," she murmured.

I released Sutton only long enough for us to get out of the SUV, then I held her hand again. By the time we made it into the rink, there was a crush of parents and kids getting ready to leave. I didn't miss the dirty look Evelyn sent our way as she took in our joined hands or the huffy one that figure skater gave me before turning her sights on a more age-appropriate kid. But I didn't have time to worry about their bullshit today.

Kenner waved us over. "Luca has his stuff all packed up."

"Thanks for helping out," Sutton said.

Kenner's gaze softened on her. "Anytime. Luca had his best sprint time yet this afternoon."

"That's awesome, Speedy," I said.

Luca barely glanced up. "I'm ready to go."

Sutton and I shared a look. Something was off. I bent to grab Luca's gear bag and hoisted it over my shoulder. "See you tomorrow, Kenner."

"See ya, Colson," he shot back, turning as a parent called his name.

Luca was quiet as we loaded into my SUV and completely silent on the way home. The longer he went without speaking, the more worry I saw settling into Sutton's features. The moment I pulled up to the house, Luca unbuckled himself from the booster seat and jumped out of the vehicle.

"Luca," Sutton admonished, quickly climbing down from the SUV. "You know you have to wait until I say it's okay to get out."

"Whatever," he muttered.

"Not whatever. That's a rule to keep you safe," she said.

I grabbed Luca's bag and mine from the back, eyeing him and Sutton.

"I'm not a baby!" Luca shouted. "I know what's safe."

"Hey," I said quietly. "Don't yell at your mom."

He glared at me. "Why do you care?"

That had me reeling back. "Because I love her and you. That means I always want people to treat her and you with respect and kindness. And I'm always going to step in when they don't."

Luca's lower lip began to tremble, and tears filled his eyes. His gaze shot back to Sutton. "Did Dad hurt you?"

Oh, hell.

CHAPTER FORTY-THREE

Sutton

THE WORLD FELL AWAY AT LUCA'S WORDS. ALL THAT EXISTED was his question and the pain in his eyes. *"Did Dad hurt you?"*

I could handle the media if it only impacted me, but if it hurt my son? I'd burn every blog, newspaper, and entertainment show to the ground.

I forced myself to breathe. In and out. Slow and steady.

I'd always known this day would come, where I'd have to explain everything to Luca. But I'd thought I'd have longer to prepare.

Because as it was, Luca didn't have questions about his dad. He didn't ask to see him or talk to him. He didn't ask where he was.

"Let's go inside." My voice was remarkably calm, so different from every emotion rioting inside me.

"Don't lie." Luca's words were pleading, as if he didn't want me to have time to cover.

I moved then, lifting him into my arms. It wouldn't be long before he was too heavy for me to do this, but I could still manage. I trailed a hand up and down his back as Cope unlocked the front door. "I won't, baby. You can ask me whatever you want."

I'd watch my words, but I wouldn't lie. Because once broken, that was the kind of trust you'd never get back.

Cope held the door open for me, and I carried Luca inside. I didn't stop in the entryway; I went straight back to the living room and sat us on the couch. I half-expected Cope to bail, but I shouldn't have been surprised when he sat right next to me, helping me settle Luca between us.

I brushed the hair away from Luca's eyes. "Want to tell me what happened?"

Luca nibbled on his bottom lip. "Daniel asked if my dad was a bad guy. He said he heard his mom talking on the phone this morning. Saying my dad was a bad guy. That he was trash, and he hurt you."

Hell. I was going to kill Evelyn. I didn't love that she was gossiping about me to begin with, but she could've at least made sure her kid wasn't within earshot.

"It wasn't a car accident, was it? He hurt you," Luca pushed.

I pulled in a deep breath, my gaze colliding with Cope's dark-blue one. And with that breath, I pulled in all the strength he lent to me in that moment, then turned back to Luca. "Do you remember when we talked about how there are a lot of ways to hurt someone?"

Luca nodded. "How it's not just hitting. You can hurt someone with your words or by leaving them out."

"That's right. Your dad never hit me. But he is sick. And the illness he has makes him hurt the people around him."

Luca's face scrunched up. "Then why doesn't he go to the doctor? The doctor makes you better. Even if you have to have a shot, it'd be worth it."

My chest ached, and with that pain came a heaviness. "His illness makes it so he doesn't want to go to the doctor. At least, not yet. Maybe he will one day, but right now, he can't make himself."

"Because he doesn't love us enough," Luca whispered, tears beginning to fall. "It's why he never calls or sends me a birthday card."

"Oh, baby." I pulled him against me, wrapping my arms around him. "He will always love you, even when he can't show it."

"Not enough!" Luca wailed. "I don't want him to be my dad! I want Cope to be my dad!"

I stilled, pain and panic searing through me. My gaze collided with Cope's, and I saw agony and longing in his eyes. Cope leaned in, rubbing Luca's back.

"It would be the biggest honor of my life if I got to be a dad to someone who's as amazing as you are," Cope croaked.

Luca twisted in my arms, turning to face Cope. "I want you to be. I don't want a bad-guy dad."

Cope squeezed Luca's knee. "Family is so much more than blood."

Luca's face scrunched again, as though he didn't believe Cope. "What do you mean?"

"Look at my family. Only me, Fallon, Mom, and Lolli are related by blood."

Luca's brows rose. "Really?"

Cope nodded. "Shep was adopted as a baby. Arden and Trace came to live with us when they were twelve. Rhodes, when she was thirteen. Kye, not until he was sixteen."

"But you guys are so close. Like a real family," Luca whispered.

I squeezed Luca in a hug. "Because they are a real family."

"Family isn't defined by blood," Cope said. "It's defined by how we care about one another. How we show up in good times and bad. How we love one another."

A fresh wave of tears spilled down Luca's cheeks. "I want that."

God, I'd never felt like more of a failure. I hadn't given Luca that. Hadn't given him what he needed.

"Speedy, you have it," Cope whispered. "You belong with us now. You're part of the Colson crew whether you like it or not."

Luca's lower lip trembled. "I don't have your same last name."

"Neither does Arden, Rhodes, or Kye. It doesn't make them any less a part of our family."

"Really?" Luca asked.

"Really," Cope echoed. "You're with us. A part of our family. And you always will be."

Luca threw himself at Cope, and Cope caught him easily. Luca cried in earnest now. They were tears of relief and of letting go. "I love you," Luca hiccupped.

"I love you, too," Cope whispered. "More than you'll ever know."

Every piece of myself that I'd been holding back lost itself to Cope in that moment. Every wall I'd been desperately clinging to crumbled. And I knew, without a shadow of a doubt, I was in love with Cope. And that would never change.

CHAPTER FORTY-FOUR

Cope

SLOWLY, LUCA'S SOBS LESSENED, AND HIS BREATHING EVENED out. His complete weight slackened against me. So small and vulnerable. It killed me that he felt like he didn't belong, and I would've given anything to change that.

"He's asleep," Sutton whispered.

I knew that already, but I still couldn't find it in me to speak. A million questions swam through my mind. Ones that asked if I'd handled this right, if I'd overstepped, if Luca would be okay.

I shifted his weight, bracing to stand. "Why don't I carry him up to bed? He probably needs some rest."

Sutton nodded. "Are you sure you've got him?"

One corner of my mouth kicked up, even if it was half-hearted. "If I can't carry a seven-year-old up to bed, I've got problems."

Sutton returned my smile, but hers wasn't full-on either. How could it be? Her boy had been hurt. And it made me want to burn every news media outlet who'd carried the story to the ground.

Since I couldn't do that, I pushed to my feet, holding Luca to me. His breathing was heavy in my ear, but it was reassuring, the quiet promise that he was all right—or at least he would be with time. I vowed to give him all the family belonging I could. I would call my mom tomorrow and bring her up to speed. If there was one thing Nora Colson was good at, it was bringing lost sheep into the fold.

I took the steps one at a time, knowing I had precious cargo. It didn't take me long to reach Luca's room, one it was beyond time to truly make *his*. I'd get on that immediately. Just like I would think of any way imaginable to make Sutton feel at home here, too.

Because I didn't want them moving back to that apartment over the bakery, no matter how amazing Shep and his crew made it. I wanted Sutton and Luca here with me. Forever.

Sutton rounded me and hurried to pull back the blankets on Luca's bed. I laid him down, and we each went to work on a sneaker. I glanced at her. "Is he okay sleeping in these clothes?"

The workout pants and T-shirt that read *Hockey is Life* looked comfortable enough, but I didn't know the rules.

Sutton's expression softened, and she nodded. "He'll be okay in these. I'll have him change when I wake him up for dinner. I still want him to be able to sleep tonight."

"Okay." I carefully pulled the covers over Luca's small body, tucking him in. But I didn't move for a moment afterward. I just stared down at him, thinking about everything Roman was missing out on and all the damage he'd done.

Finally, I forced myself to turn to Sutton. I wrapped my arms around her, holding her to me. "Are you okay?"

She didn't answer right away, but eventually, she pulled back, her eyes searching mine. "I love you."

My whole body went wired. I'd tried not to get in my head about the fact that Sutton hadn't returned my sentiments when I gave her those three words the other day. Tried not to overthink what it could mean. I knew she had trust issues, and that it wouldn't be easy for her to give her heart to anyone.

"Say it again," I rasped.

Sutton's mouth curved. "I love you."

"Fuck. You don't know how good those words are to hear."

"I'm sorry it took me a little while to give them to you."

I shook my head. "You needed to go on your own timetable."

Sutton's eyes glistened. "What you just gave Luca, it made me realize that you've given us both the gift of belonging. A family."

"Warrior," I growled. "Tell me this means you'll stay. Here, with me. Tell me we'll find a way to make this work."

"Yes," she breathed.

I moved then, hauling her into my arms and striding out of the room. Sutton's legs hooked around my waist as her mouth met mine. If I hadn't memorized the hall's path long ago, I likely would've been bumping into walls and sending artwork crashing to the floor.

This woman's taste. *Hell.* I could drown in it forever. She tasted like she smelled: cinnamon and sugar with a hint of vanilla. The scents of the bakery imbued into her very being. I didn't know, and I didn't care. All I knew was that I never wanted it to end.

The moment we crossed the threshold to my room, I shut the door, locking it quickly behind us. "Say it again," I commanded.

"I love you." Sutton whispered the words across my lips so I could not only hear them but also feel them.

"Gonna be greedy for those words for a while, Warrior."

I slowly lowered her to the floor, the feeling of her body sliding against mine making my dick harden. I'd never had a woman affect me like this. It was so much more than simple attraction. It was as if she held my soul hostage. But I didn't give a damn. I'd be her willing prisoner for the rest of my days.

My hand slid along Sutton's jaw, tangling in her hair. "So fucking beautiful."

One corner of her mouth kicked up. "I'm probably covered in flour."

Sutton did come home with smears of flour in all sorts of interesting places. "I like finding out where it's all gotten to."

Sutton's breaths came a touch faster now. I loved watching how the movement changed, the way her body responded to my words, my touch. My fingers tightened in her hair, tipping her head back.

The pupils in those haunting turquoise eyes dilated as her lips parted. I took her mouth then. My tongue slid inside, demanded more—demanded *everything*.

Sutton moaned into my mouth, and the sound went straight to my dick. The tone, the vibration. I swore she could make me come in my goddamned pants from her sounds alone.

"Cope." She breathed my name like a prayer, the single syllable playing over my lips.

I tore my mouth from hers. I needed to see her, touch her, bury myself so deep in her body that she'd never forget the feel of me.

My fingers gripped the hem of her tee that read *The Mix Up*. I pulled it free in one tug and sucked in a breath. Pale-pink lace lay beneath. The kind of bra that let me see the darker pink of Sutton's nipples peeking through.

"You trying to kill me, Warrior?"

A little line of confusion appeared in her brow.

My thumb ghosted over her nipple, then circled. "Knowing you've been wearing this all day. Walking around like temptation incarnate just covered by cotton."

My head bent, and I pulled her nipple into my mouth through the lace. Sutton's back arched as she gave herself over to me. "Cope."

I released the bud, my fingers going to the button of her jeans. "Shoes off," I commanded, my voice getting rougher, the need demanding to break free.

Sutton kicked off the slip-ons she favored for work as my fingers hooked in her jeans. I tugged the denim down until it pooled on the floor. I sucked in a breath as I took in the pale-pink scrap of lace. The thong looked so delicate I could rip it from her body without even trying.

"Step. Out," I ordered.

A shiver raced through Sutton, and her breaths came quicker. One foot lifted, and then the other. I threw the jeans to the side. I didn't want anything getting in the way of my view. Nothing that would keep me from memorizing every inch of this woman.

"Never going to forget this moment. So perfect, bound in lace." I lifted a hand, my knuckles grazing over her center. "Already wet. Tell me, Warrior, are you aching?"

Those eyes sparked with blue heat, the hottest type of blaze. "Yes."

"Let's see what we can do about that." My fingers moved, twisting in the band of Sutton's thong. And with one swift jerk, I snapped it free.

CHAPTER FORTY-FIVE

Sutton

I GAPED AT COPE. "YOU DID NOT JUST DO THAT...AGAIN."

He grinned up at me with mischief, heating my blood. The lace fluttered to the floor a second later. "Are you really going to complain about one more ruined pair of underwear when it lets me do this?"

Cope moved so fast that I didn't have time to prepare. His fingers parted me, and I gasped, gripping his shoulders as two slid inside. My hips thrust forward, moving on instinct to greet him, a moan slipping from my lips.

"Fucking heaven," Cope gritted out. "Do you know how good you feel? Soft silk, gripping my fingers like you're going to grip my cock."

The combination of his words and touch was almost more than I could take. I clutched his shoulders harder, my nails digging in. "Cope." His name was a plea.

"Not yet." Those devilish fingers slid in and out, twisting. Then, the curl.

My hands twisted in his tee. "Please."

Cope's dark-blue eyes flashed. "You want to come with me inside you, taking you, reminding you of everything you've given me?"

"Yes," I breathed.

"Always going to give you what you want, Warrior. What you need."

And then his hands were gone. The loss of them was almost painful. My need for him to fill me, take me...nearly feral.

Then I was in motion. Cope hauled me into his arms and carried me to the bed. He laid me down with such gentleness despite that need coursing through us both. As he stepped back, Cope didn't take his eyes off me.

With one hand, he ripped his tee free. I didn't look away. I let my eyes feast on the wall of muscle, his body honed to be the perfect weapon. The defined pecs were dusted with hair, dipping down into so many abs I lost count. But I traced each and every one with my gaze.

Cope kicked off his shoes as his fingers locked in the band of his joggers. In one swift move, his pants and boxer briefs were gone, and he stood before me completely bare. Nothing obstructed him from view.

Cope's fingers curled around his cock, and he stroked once, twice, a third time. My core tightened, closing around nothing but the promise of him.

"Back against the pillows, Warrior. Spread your legs. I want to see you. All of you," Cope demanded.

A shiver raced through me as wetness gathered between my thighs. I did exactly what he commanded, shoving myself against the pillows and sliding my bare feet over the soft duvet. The cool air ghosted over my skin, making my nipples pebble.

I'd never felt more vulnerable, but I'd also never felt stronger, bolder, or more empowered. And as Cope stared at me, I'd never felt more beautiful.

Those dark-blue eyes became hooded as he stalked toward the bed. "Do you know how perfect you look? Legs spread, glistening. Nipples pressed against that lace, just dying to break free."

My fingers fisted in the duvet, holding on as I stared at the man I'd fallen so deeply in love with. "Take me, Cope. Make me *yours*."

It wasn't ownership that I was looking for; it was belonging. And Cope understood that. Understood that he was mine as much as I was his. That we belonged to each other. That we gave one another a home when we'd been missing exactly that.

Cope didn't make me wait. He was on me in a flash. He slid between my thighs, and my legs hooked around his waist. His gaze locked with mine. I saw fire there, but so much more. "Tell me again."

"I love you."

"I want to feel it," he growled.

And with that, he slid into me. My back arched, my hips rising to meet him. The stretch was almost painful but stopped just shy of it as if my body were made to take his. As if this had all been written in the stars.

My lips parted as Cope thrust deeper, my eyes watering, and my heels digging into his hips. Cope didn't move for a second. "Feel that love, Warrior. The way you're gripping me says you won't let go."

My eyes watered for a whole different reason now. "I won't."

"Promise me," Cope rasped.

"I promise."

That was all he needed. Cope retreated and thrust back in deeper this time. My body welcomed him, cried out for more. My hips rose, meeting him there, in the places that were now only ours.

It was as if our bodies could speak without words. But I wanted to give him those words, too. I gripped Cope's shoulders as my walls trembled around him. Each time he slammed into me, it nearly took me over the edge.

"Hold on," Cope growled. "I need more of you. More of this. Don't ever want it to end."

My fingernails dug into his shoulders, so deep and hard I knew they'd draw blood. "Cope," I pleaded.

He arched into me, sending little explosions of light dancing across my vision. And I knew I couldn't hold on for much longer. I forced my eyes open, moving my attention to him.

Cope met me there, our gazes locking. I didn't look away as I gave him the words again. "I love you."

And with those three little words, I came, clamping down so hard around Cope that he let loose a snarl. But he didn't stop. He took me over and over, riding out my orgasm until he came, emptying into me. And I took it all. I wanted every last piece of him.

Cope's forehead dropped to mine, our breaths mingling as we struggled to get enough air. "I love you. With everything in me. All I am is yours. Brokenness and all."

My fingers tangled with Cope's as he drove through Sparrow Falls. My head was on a swivel, looking for any signs of them—the media that had descended on our tiny town. The place that had become my safe harbor.

"I'm sorry." Cope's voice wasn't loud, but it wasn't a whisper either.

I shifted in my seat, turning to face him. "It's not your fault."

A muscle in Cope's cheek began to flutter. "They're here because of me. Because of my stupid career."

I squeezed his hand as hard as I could. "They're here because they're vultures."

Trace had called last night, letting us know he'd gotten word from a few hotels and motels in town that news vans were gathered there. Cope's new security cameras—courtesy of Holt Hartley—had told him a handful of reporters were already outside his gates.

"I hate that I'm putting you through this."

"You're not." My voice cracked like a whip. "If you take this on, it's really going to piss me off. And you do *not* want to piss me off, Copeland Colson."

His lips twitched. "If she's pulling out the formal name, I'd better be careful."

"Damn straight."

Cope slowed as one of the three stoplights in town shifted to red. He turned to me. "I love you."

God, those words were the most beautiful music I'd ever heard. And the fear I'd felt because of them in the past was no longer there. Getting through what we had with Luca had taught me something: We were stronger together. And we could make it through whatever came our way.

I leaned across the console, brushing my lips against Cope's and then staying close so he could feel what I was about to say. "I love you, too. We'll get through this together."

His fingers sifted through my hair, and he held me there, right against him. "Together."

A horn sounded behind us, and Cope scowled into the rearview mirror but eased off the brake. "Everyone's always in a hurry."

A laugh bubbled out of me. "Can't be holding up traffic for a make-out session."

"Baby, you start really kissing me, and I'm not gonna stop at making out."

I bit my bottom lip. "That would certainly give the reporters a show."

Cope chuckled and turned onto a side street. "Pretty sure Linc would fire me if I showed the world my ass."

"When do they get here?" I asked.

Cope glanced my way as he headed toward the bakery. "Tomorrow. I think it's a good idea. Linc's right. It'll shift the focus of the story."

The owner of Cope's team had called last night with an idea. He was going to bring the Sparks to Sparrow Falls for a week-long kids' hockey clinic, one held in honor of Teddy. Since the media was already here, having the entire team present would send them into a frenzy. And hopefully, they'd forget all about little ole me.

"I think I'm just a little nervous to meet all of them," I admitted. Sure, I'd seen them at the funeral, but there hadn't been a lot of proper introductions, given all the drama with Marcus. And since my personal life had just been tossed around in the media, I wasn't sure what they'd think of me.

Cope pulled into a parking spot in the back alley behind The Mix Up and turned to me. "Sutton. You are the most incredible woman I've ever met. So strong…getting yourself out of the unimaginable. So damn smart, building a business from nothing. So dedicated to being the best mom imaginable. And one of the best people I've ever known."

A burn lit behind my eyes. "Have I told you lately that I love you?"

One corner of his mouth kicked up. "Never get tired of hearing it."

I leaned across the console and whispered the words against his lips. "I. Love. You."

Heat lit in those dark-blue eyes. "Warrior, now I need to fuck you. And that is real damn inconvenient."

I started to laugh, but the sound got cut off by shouts. I turned to see reporters running toward the SUV, cameras of all kinds at the ready, questions already hurling. Was Cope being traded thanks to the dustup with Marcus? When did Roman find out I was involved with another athlete? Was I hiding from the Russian mob?

Cope cursed, but I grabbed his hand and squeezed. "We're in this together."

Those dark-blue depths searched mine. "Together."

We headed into the mayhem.

CHAPTER FORTY-SIX

Cope

LUCA BOUNCED UP AND DOWN ON THE BALLS OF HIS FEET. "I can't believe I get to meet *all* of them. Every single one. Randal the Ravager. Frankie the Finisher. And Marcus freaking Warner."

Gretzky yipped as if agreeing with him, and then the puppy tumbled as he tried to attack his leash. I tried not to scowl at that final name. If Marcus was mean to Luca just because he despised me, I wasn't sure I'd be able to stop myself from decking him in front of dozens of little kids. At least most of them weren't here yet.

Arden's lips twitched from where she stood behind Luca. "Yeah, Marcus is my favorite player on the Sparks, too."

There was no helping my scowl this time. "Traitor," I shot at her.

Arden laughed, picking up Gretzky. But I didn't miss the unease in her gaze as it traveled over the vast space. She wasn't one for large groups, always wondering if there was a chance someone from her past life would show up and recognize her. So, it meant even more that she was here.

"Don't worry, Cope. You're still my number-one favorite of all time," Luca assured me.

I chuckled and held out my knuckles for a fist bump. "Good to know you've still got my back."

"Always," Luca vowed.

In the way only a kid could, he'd bounced back from finding out pieces of the truth about his father and had taken the media attention in stride. We'd had Arden and Kye or Anson and Rhodes take him to and from hockey to avoid his photo ending up in any media coverage. But Luca had turned it into a game, pretending to be a superhero escaping all the villains—the reporters being the bad guys. And he wasn't wrong there.

But Sutton and I still kept a close eye. She'd asked him a couple of times if he had any more questions, but Luca said no. And my family had swooped in to surround him with all the love. Hence why all of them had homemade jerseys with *Holland* on the back, along with Luca's number.

But something about seeing *Holland* had something lighting deep inside me: the need to see that name changed to *Colson* on the jerseys. Because I wanted Sutton and Luca to have my last name. To feel every bit a part of my family as possible.

"Oooooh, I see hottie hockey players," Lolli called, doing a shimmy. She'd blinged out her jersey so it sparkled in the rink lights. "Do you think I could get one of them to throw me against the boards?"

"Lolli," my mom hissed. "Children will be present at this event. Please, rein it in."

Lolli just waved her off. "It's good for them to see healthy sexuality."

Fallon pinned her with a stare. "I'm not sure asking one of these poor, unprepared players to throw you against the boards is healthy sexuality."

Lolli let out a huff. "Always ruining all my fun."

Kye wrapped an arm around her shoulders. "Come hang out with me. We can cheer on the violence and bloodshed."

Lolli grinned up at him. "Well, that is my second favorite thing to do."

Thea looked up from the table where she and Sutton had spread out an array of baked goods for everyone to snack on while we got set up and waited for the kids to arrive. "I thought special brownies were your second favorite."

"That's just a way of life, dear," Lolli assured her.

Sutton laughed, light catching in her eyes. God, she was beautiful. I could stare at her forever.

"You've got a little drool," Arden muttered, wiping at the corner of her mouth with a smirk.

The urge to elbow my sister in the gut was strong. "Shut up." I looked back at Sutton and mouthed, "*You okay?*"

She nodded, but I didn't miss how she pulled her lip between her teeth. Before I could make my way across the room to her, the doors to the rink opened, and players and staff poured in. My family greeted them, having met most over the past several years.

Luca wasn't bouncing up and down now; he was full-on jumping. "Frankie the Finisher!"

Frankie's lips twitched. "You must be Luca. I've heard a lot about you."

Luca stilled. "You have?"

Frankie shot me a look. "Reaper goes on and on about you. Said you fly across the ice."

Luca's eyes widened as his head snapped toward me and then back to Frankie. "I'm trying to get faster." His voice dropped. "Teddy was teaching me, too."

A shadow passed over Frankie's features, but he crouched down. "You know, Teddy taught me a lot over the years. Maybe I can keep helping you where he left off."

"Really?" Luca asked.

"Really." Frankie held out his knuckles for a fist bump.

Luca returned the gesture, grinning. "You better fuel up. My mom brought all her best stuff from the bakery, but the cupcakes are my favorite!"

Frankie straightened and patted his stomach. "I never say no to baked goods."

As Frankie headed for the bakery table, my gaze connected with Marcus's. There was no warmth there. "Figures we'd have to swoop in to save your ass."

A muscle in my cheek started to flutter, but before I could say a word, Arden stepped forward just as Gretzky let out a little growl from her arms. "Just consider it returning the favor for that time he saved *your* ass when you lost the puck in the game against Phoenix."

Marcus's green eyes flashed in annoyance and something else. Surprise, maybe?

Luca giggled at my side, not reading the underlying tension in the exchange. "He did save you."

Marcus's gaze flicked to Luca, and I braced. I had a feeling both Arden and I would take him down if he was unkind to Luca. But Marcus shot him a grin and crouched so he was on the boy's level. "I bet you would've done a better job of getting me out of that jam. Would've stolen that puck a heck of a lot faster, too."

I clapped a hand on Luca's shoulder. "There's no doubt about that."

Luca grinned up at me. "I can't wait to make it to the pros."

"Oh, my fucking cupcake gods," Frankie mumble-yelled around a mouthful of cupcake. "This is heaven in baked form. There are Oreos in this." He held up a non-half-eaten one. "And look at the little hockey dude on top."

Everyone turned toward him, a few teammates picking up treats and taking bites.

Frankie turned to Sutton as he swallowed. "Please, tell me you'll move to Seattle and open a bakery. Hell, move to Seattle and marry me."

One of the enforcers choked on a laugh. "Uh, Frankie, you may wanna reconsider those words. Reaper looks like he's about to straight-up murder your ass."

Frankie shoved another bite of cupcake into his mouth. "Don't care. It would be worth it."

Sutton blushed and shot me a look, shaking her head.

A flash of red hair caught my attention, and I winced. I should've guessed that Linc would want Angie here, but I hadn't thought about Angie and Sutton being in the same space for a prolonged period.

She crossed to me, a warm smile in place. Even in her sharp business suit with a pencil skirt and high heels, she still had to stretch up onto her toes to kiss my cheek.

Fuck.

I instantly stepped back, but Angie didn't read the move. She just beamed up at me. "How are you, Cope?"

"Good, Ang. You?" I asked, but my gaze flicked to Sutton.

Sutton busied herself at the bakery table, but I didn't miss how her expression had gone impassive. Not mad or hurt, just... nothingness.

A hand landed on my forearm. "Cope, are you listening at all?"

"Sorry." I moved out of Angie's range again. "What?"

"I thought it might be good for you to give the reporters outside a few minutes. I'll be with you the whole time."

I couldn't help the scowl that rose to my mouth. "Don't you think that completely contradicts the whole point of this? We're supposed to be getting eyes *off* me and on the rest of the team. Have a couple of the other guys do it. Marcus and Frankie. They're good in front of the camera."

And maybe between that and Luca's charm, Marcus would chill the hell out for a while.

Angie's lips pursed. "They want to talk to *you*. I'm not sure they'll be happy with Marcus and Frankie. I can guide the conversation away from your friendship with Ms. Holland."

"My relationship," I said, dropping my voice a fraction until I had eyes on Luca. We hadn't talked about what Sutton and I were with him yet, and I wouldn't do that without Sutton's okay. But Luca had run off to where Lolli was feeling up one of the enforcer's arms as he flexed for her.

I turned back to Angie. "Sutton is my partner. I love her, and

I'll do whatever it takes to get these vultures to leave her alone. Right now, that means staying out of the limelight."

Angie's eyes were wide, and her face had gone pale. "You... love her?"

"Yes," I said, dropping my voice again. I didn't want to hurt Angie, but she needed to know.

"But you—you said you weren't cut out for that sort of thing. For more."

Fuck.

"I didn't think I was. But sometimes it just takes the right person to change everything."

Pain lashed across Angie's face. "And that person wasn't me."

"I wasn't the one for you. But you'll find him one day. I know you will."

Angie shook her head. "I had him. It's just too bad he never gave me a chance."

Guilt churned in my gut as Angie turned on her heel and strode away, heels clacking on the floor. But that guilt only intensified when a turquoise gaze met mine from across the room—with a look that held nothing but hurt.

CHAPTER FORTY-SEVEN

Sutton

I TRIED TO FOCUS ON REARRANGING CUPCAKES AND THE OTHER baked goods Thea and I had brought. As if making the perfect display would erase the images in my mind. But I couldn't. I just kept seeing that woman's lips on Cope's cheek, her hand on his arm.

My stomach churned, nausea settling in. It wasn't that I thought Cope had done anything wrong; it was that he hadn't told me he worked with an ex. It might not have been a lie exactly, but it was one hell of an omission.

"Sutton."

Cope's voice skated over my skin in that familiar sandpaper way. My body reacted instantly, the traitor. I looked up and forced a smile. "What do you need?"

Cope's mouth pressed into a hard line as he rounded the table and gently took my arm, tugging me off to the side.

"I need to help. I—"

"Warrior," he cut me off. "There's nothing between Angie and me, not anymore."

My mouth snapped closed, my back teeth grinding together. "But there was."

It wasn't a question, but he answered anyway. "We dated for a couple of months. It wasn't serious."

"Looked like it was serious to her."

I knew what it felt like to look at Cope and wish for something you couldn't have. But Cope had come along and given me a dream I hadn't thought was possible. Today was just a reminder of what I could lose.

Cope scrubbed a hand over his face as guilt splashed across his features. "I didn't realize she felt that way until today."

I tugged the corner of my lip between my teeth. "You should've told me. I know you have a past, but you should've given me a heads-up that I was about to meet that past."

"I didn't know she would be here—"

"Cope." I cut him off with that single word.

"I should've assumed."

"And you should've told me that you work with someone you were involved with. That's respect. You want this to be more, but you have to treat it like that, too. I don't want to be in another relationship where someone lies to me. By omission or otherwise."

A muscle fluttered in Cope's jaw. He opened his mouth to speak, but Frankie cut him off. "Reaper, stop flirting. We gotta suit up."

Cope's gaze swept over my face. "Later."

I gave him a quick nod, but unease settled in my belly. I didn't like being at odds with Cope. Didn't like having something hanging that felt unfinished. But more than that, I hated the sting of doubt making its home in my chest right now.

The Sparks moved across the ice with an ease I'd never truly seen before, and this was only an exhibition scrimmage. There was a beauty to it I hadn't expected. And Cope was one of the best out there. At least, as far as I could tell.

He dodged and weaved, escaping one player and then another, sending the puck flying into the net. The kids leapt to their feet in the bleachers, cheering their heads off. I spotted Luca jumping up and down, going absolutely wild.

"Thank you for feeding my team," a deep voice said to my right.

My head swiveled to take in Lincoln Pierce. He wasn't wearing a suit like I expected. He was dressed casually in jeans, worn boots, and a button-down. But something told me each item of clothing had cost more than I pulled in during an entire day at the bakery. And I didn't miss the glint of gold at his wrist where a watch peeked out.

"It's the least I could do. Thank you for making these kids the happiest I've ever seen." Having the Sparks here for a whole week would be something they'd never forget.

Linc watched the players skate back across the ice. "It's good for my team, too. To remind them what it's all about. Might be something we need to do every year."

"That would be incredible. I know the community would love it."

Frankie shot the puck and just made it into the net. As the kids cheered, he did some kind of dance across the ice. I couldn't help but laugh.

"This really is a whole other world," I mumbled.

I felt Linc's eyes move to me. "You'll get used to it. The attention on the guys can feel like a lot, but you won't even notice it before long."

I tried my best not to shift at Linc's ability to read my thoughts. Because I wasn't sure I'd ever handle this kind of scrutiny well. "I'm not great with it. The attention. For obvious reasons."

There was no point in pretending Linc hadn't seen the articles or the news coverage. He was here for a reason. And that was to change the narrative. That meant he, like countless others, had seen the photos of me at my most vulnerable. Bruised and broken.

"I'm so sorry that happened to you. Any man who lays hands on a woman—on anyone more vulnerable—is no man at all."

There was a ferocity to Linc's tone that had me searching his face. His hazel eyes sparked with a gold fire that spoke of rage, something he shouldn't have felt for a woman he barely knew. I felt the bizarre urge to comfort him. "I'm okay now. I got out. Got free."

Linc gave me a clipped nod. "You did. Which tells me you're strong as hell."

One corner of my mouth kicked up. "I try my best."

"You've been good for Cope, too."

That had me shifting from one foot to the other. "I like to think we've been good for each other."

Just saying the words aloud reminded me. Reminded me of the belonging we'd given to one another, the home. How Cope loved my boy and me. It didn't matter how many exes were waiting in the shadows or how many eyes were on Cope. Whatever lay in our path, we'd figure it out.

Linc smiled, and his whole face changed. It was then that I realized the man didn't do it often. I'd seen him grin, caught his lips twitch, but not a full-out smile. Until now. And when he did, it was devastating.

"That's how it should be. Give and take, each person making the other stronger," Linc said.

"What about you?" I asked. "Do you have a partner who gives you that?"

The smile dropped, and the light went out of those hazel depths. "No. Hasn't been in the cards for me yet."

I hated that I'd made the light in his eyes dim. Because it was a shame when the shadowy coolness slipped back in. "You'll find them. I have no doubt. And sometimes, they come around when you least expect it."

Linc's lips twitched. "Maybe I just need to move to Sparrow Falls. Seems like something's in the water over here."

Movement on the ice caught my attention. Cope was battling for the puck with another player. The other player turned, revealing his jersey. Warner.

Crap.

They shoved at each other, but Marcus slammed into Cope, sending him flying back a few paces as he stole the puck. Marcus wasn't quite as artful as Cope, but he managed to dodge the few players between him and the goal and slapped the puck in.

Linc shook his head. "I really hope those two don't kill each other one day."

I winced. "The whole violence piece of this sport isn't really my favorite."

Linc glanced down at me for a moment and then burst out laughing. "Sutton, I needed that."

I fought a grin. "Are you saying I'd better get used to it?"

"That or buy a blindfold for the games. It's up to you."

I sighed. "Blood and gore, yay."

Linc just grinned. "I can see why you're so good for Cope. Keep at it. If there's one person who deserves light in his life, it's him."

With that, Linc turned and strode off. But something told me Linc also needed light in his life.

CHAPTER FORTY-EIGHT

Cope

DUDE, WHERE IS YOUR HEAD AT?" FRANKIE MUTTERED AS HE ran a towel over his short hair.

I grabbed my tee from the locker and pulled it on, annoyance flickering through me. "It was a scrimmage. For kids."

But I knew he was right. I'd played like shit, getting bested by people who normally didn't have a shot.

"Just do us a favor and get your head on straight before the season starts," Marcus clipped, grabbing deodorant from his locker.

"Worry about your own game," I shot back.

Marcus grinned, but it had a sharkish quality to it. "I don't have to. I'm too busy stealing yours."

I flipped him off as I lifted my gear bag over my shoulder and headed out of the locker room. I only made it two steps before nearly running into Sutton. She looked so unsure, nibbling her bottom lip and twisting her fingers together as if she were wringing water out of a towel.

Fuck this.

I grabbed her hand and pulled her into an office with *Manager* on the door. It was a miracle it was open, given it was the weekend, and Arnie usually gave his management the time off. Flicking the light on, I closed the door behind us.

"I'm sorry," Sutton blurted.

I moved into her space, my hand sliding along her jaw and into her hair. "I'm the one who's sorry, Warrior. I should've told you about Angie. But I don't even think about her anymore. Maybe that makes me a bastard, but it's the truth."

Sutton's lips twitched. "Maybe just a little bit of a bastard."

I chuckled. "There's only one person who has ever slept in my bed, and that's you." Sutton's eyes softened as my mouth ghosted over hers, and I dropped my bag to the floor. "Only you. Because you're the only one I've truly let in. The only one who soothes my demons."

"Cope," Sutton breathed against my mouth.

"I don't want you to ever doubt how much you mean to me. How much I love you."

Those turquoise eyes searched mine. "Your world...it's a lot. I might've had a mini freak out that I wasn't ready."

My fingers tightened in Sutton's hair, a flicker of panic igniting. "Warrior," I growled. "Tell me you're not bailing."

"I'm not," Sutton said quickly. "I think I was just scared." Her eyes glistened with unshed tears. "You've given me so much that the idea of losing it, losing you...it's like I can't breathe."

"I'm not going anywhere. It's you and me. Whatever comes our way, we'll handle it together." Because I knew exactly how Sutton felt. Just thinking about life without her had cinder blocks pressing on my chest and panic setting in.

Sutton stretched up onto her tiptoes. "I love you."

I felt the words against my mouth—the vibrations, the heat. It was my favorite way to hear those words, as if they were bleeding into every part of me. "Fuck, Warrior."

She pressed her body against mine, my dick hardening at the mere hint of her heat. "I love you."

"Again," I commanded, my fingers trailing up her bare thigh, diving beneath the cotton of her sundress.

"I love you," Sutton whispered.

My fingers stroked her through the lace covering her core. "Nothing makes me harder than those words. They wrap around my cock just like your pretty little fingers. Like the promise of your lips. Your heat."

Sutton's hips flexed into my hand, seeking more.

"Is my girl greedy?"

"Yes," she breathed. "Never get enough of you."

Fuck.

I needed her. Needed to lose myself in her body, knowing she'd claimed my soul. Needed to feel the certainty of forever with her.

My fingers trailed over her skin, and I couldn't resist cupping that perfect ass. Sutton moaned into my mouth as I squeezed the globes. God, those sweet sounds. I wanted to drown in them forever.

I forced my hand away from Sutton's ass, my fingers twisting in the band of delicate lace at her hip. Sutton's head pulled back, heat filling her eyes. "Don't you dare, Cope. Not *again*. I will not walk about this arena underwearless."

I grinned, leaning down so my lips hovered just against hers. "But that's just how I want you. So whenever you feel a breeze, you'll feel me, remember me moving inside you, remember what's ours."

Sutton whimpered against my mouth.

The sound was too much for me. I twisted the fabric, snapping the delicate fibers and sending the lace fluttering to the floor. Then my fingers were sliding home into that wet heat. My dick stiffened to the point of pain. It wanted all of her, just like the rest of me.

"You like the idea of that? Walking through the rink still feeling me inside you. Knowing I've marked you."

The blue of her eyes danced and transformed with blistering heat as Sutton's fingers gripped my hair, pulling my head back. "Only if I can mark you right back."

"Baby," I growled. "I'm carrying your nail marks on my back. I'd have Kye tattoo them on me, but you're burned into my goddamned soul. I carry you with me every second of every day."

Those fingers tightened in my hair, pain flickering across my scalp. "Cope?"

"Warrior."

"Fuck me."

I lifted her, and her legs encircled my waist. "My goddamned pleasure."

I strode to the desk, lowering her to the floor and then flipping her around so she faced the piece of furniture I wasn't sure was sturdy enough for us. But if we broke it, I'd buy the dude another one.

"Grab the desk." My voice had deepened, taking on a desperate edge.

Sutton drew in a breath but didn't hesitate, simply bent over and grabbed the wooden edge. Her perfect ass curved in front of me, the cotton of her sundress caressing it the way I wanted to do with my hands, my tongue.

I trailed a hand down Sutton's spine, and she shivered at the touch. The heat of her skin bled into my palm as I reached her ass. My fingers fisted in the fabric, and I flipped up the skirt.

"Fuck," I growled. "Do you know how perfect you are?"

My fingers slid through her wetness, trailing it to her clit. Sutton let out a moan.

"I could stare at you forever. Play with you until that wetness trails down your thighs."

Sutton's chest rose and fell in quick pants. "Don't tease me."

My girl didn't want to wait, and who was I to keep her from what she wanted? My hand left her heat, and I missed it instantly. The feel of her curving around me, her need pulsing into me. But I'd have it again. I'd have it all.

I shucked my shoes and pants, not even bothering with my damn shirt. It would take too long. My fingers slid through Sutton's hair, wrapping it around my fist, giving her something to pull against, that bite of pain to increase the pleasure.

My tip bumped against her entrance, and my cock wept. Just the promise of her could bring me to my knees.

"Cope," she breathed.

"Tell me what you want," I gritted out, barely able to hold myself back.

"Fuck me. Make me feel you for days."

I'd always give Sutton what she needed, but she gave the same right back to me. And right now, we needed to remember we belonged to each other. I gripped her hair and slid inside with one forceful thrust.

The sound I let loose had an animalistic edge, but I didn't give a damn. All I could think about was the heaven of sliding home. To Sutton.

I took her again, each thrust deeper than the one before. Sutton pushed against me, seeking more, wanting me so deep I'd never leave. I powered into her, giving her everything I had.

Those perfect walls fluttered against my dick, telling me she was almost there. Everything in me tightened as I struggled to hold myself back.

"Finger on your clit, Warrior. Find it. Find it with me."

Sutton let out a whimper, and one hand left the desk and slid between her thighs. There was no whimper when her finger met that bundle of nerves. There was a cry. "Cope."

Her walls clamped down around me like a vise grip. It took all my strength to power through her hold. I rode each wave as she convulsed around me until my control shattered. Her name left my lips on a shout as I emptied into her. Everything I had, just like she wanted.

We rode the waves, easing as one. That was the thing about coming together. It didn't matter if it was rough or tender; it always ended with us feeling like we were one. A team.

I released my hold on Sutton's hair, brushing it off her neck and dropping a kiss where her spine began. And then I whispered against her skin, "I love you. Now. Tomorrow. Twenty years from now. Fifty. It's never going to end."

"Cope." The word was barely audible as I slid from her body. She turned, her hand cupping my face. "Love you. Thank you for reminding me of what's ours."

I kissed her, my tongue stroking hers, coming home. "Always," I whispered against her mouth.

Breaking away, I quickly pulled up my pants and slipped on my shoes as Sutton giggled.

"What is it about us and desks?" she muttered.

I chuckled and grabbed a fresh tee from my bag, kneeling at her feet. "Think I could find a reason to put a desk in every room at the house?"

Sutton's lips twitched as I slid the shirt between her thighs as gently as possible, her hands landing on my shoulders. "I don't know. I think I'm partial to punching bags, too."

My dick gave a painful twitch. "Hell. Please don't turn me on again. I might die of a stroke."

Sutton laughed. "Sorry. Can't have you keeling over on me."

I shoved the shirt into my bag, hauling the duffel over my shoulder and Sutton into my arms. "Hate to tell you this, but you're stuck with me."

She brushed her lips across mine. "Nowhere I'd rather be."

Taking Sutton's hand, I led us into the hallway. We headed toward the rink and found Frankie and Marcus along the way.

Frankie shook his head and grinned. "Sounds like you two made up."

Sutton let out a squeak, shoving her face into my chest as I glared at my teammate. "Don't make me deck you, asshole."

"And here I thought I was the only one Reap liked to punch," Marcus said with a smirk.

"I can make sure you get yours, too. Don't worry," I shot back.

"Geez," Frankie muttered. "You'd think getting some would have put you in a better mood."

I flipped them both off as I guided Sutton past.

"I'm never going to be able to look them in the eye again," she said into my chest.

I just chuckled. "Trust me, they've done way worse."

Sutton stole a look up at me, her cheeks pink. "Not in front of me, they haven't."

I kissed the tip of her nose. "You're cute when you're embarrassed."

"This isn't funny, Copeland!"

I just grinned wider. "Warrior, never going to mind that people know we can't keep our hands off each other."

She let out a little huff of air.

"What?" I asked.

"Why do you have to be sweet when I'm annoyed?"

My grin widened. "I could always fuck you again to help with that."

Sutton shoved at my chest. "Men!"

I laughed as she went in search of Luca, and God, that felt good. The release of the stress I'd been carrying around for the last few hours. But more than that, knowing we could hit bumps in the road and make it through every damn time.

CHAPTER FORTY-NINE

Sutton

THE WEEK OF THE SPARKS' CAMP FLEW BY IN A MIX OF PRACTICES and mock games, ending with a scrimmage today where professionals and kids mixed to form two teams. The kids had the time of their lives playing like they were in the professional league themselves, and thankfully, Marcus and Cope hadn't gotten into any more scuffles.

All in all, it was a huge win for the team, the kids, and my little family. Because with no new drama coming to the surface, all but a couple of reporters had vanished from Sparrow Falls. So, we planned to celebrate it all with a barbeque to end all barbeques. The Sparks, the kids and their families, and, of course, the whole Colson crew.

But something was off with Cope. He'd been edgy since we left the rink, tapping his foot and drumming his fingers on the steering wheel. As we came to a stop in front of his house with two large catering vans parked to the side of us, he didn't turn off the engine right away.

I twisted slightly to face him. "Okay, what the heck is going on with you?"

His gaze flicked to the rearview mirror, checking on Luca, who was currently engrossed in a game on his tablet. A fresh wave of nerves slid through me, and I pitched my voice even lower. "Cope. Are you okay?"

He muttered a curse under his breath. "I wanted it all to be a surprise, but now I'm realizing I should've asked first."

I reached over, pulling his hand from the wheel and linking our fingers together. "Hey, together, remember?"

One corner of Cope's mouth pulled up. "Together." His fingers squeezed mine. "Are you ready to tell Speedy about us? That you guys are staying?"

That wave of nerves turned into a tsunami, but I knew it was time. Luca would be overjoyed. And he deserved to know that this was more than a friendship between Cope and me. "I'm ready."

"What are you guys whispering about?" Luca asked from the back seat, lowering his tablet. His eyes narrowed on us as Gretzky panted in the seat next to him.

Cope chuckled. "Can't sneak anything past this one."

I twisted in my seat to face my son. "Cope and I have something we want to tell you."

That got Luca to set his tablet on the seat next to him. "What?" There was suspicion and a little bit of hope in his tone.

Butterfly wings beat against the walls of my belly. "Well, Cope and I... We, um, we're more than just friends. We're dating. A couple."

Luca stared at me for a long moment. "I know."

My jaw went slack. "You know?"

Luca let out a little huff of air, a sound far beyond his years. "I'm not a dum-dum. You guys hold hands and stuff. Cope's always touching you. And me and Gretzky saw you kissing in the kitchen the other night."

Heat flooded my cheeks, but Cope just burst out laughing, making the pup bark.

"What?" Luca demanded.

Cope grinned at my son. "You are too smart."

Luca straightened at that, pride sliding across his expression. "You better not forget it."

Cope held up both hands. "Never."

I just shook my head. "Do you have any questions about us, um, dating?"

Luca's little brows pulled together. "Are you gonna be all mushy-gushy? Like *a lot*?"

"I'm hoping so," Cope said, humor lacing his tone.

"Gross," Luca muttered.

"Does that mean you don't like us dating?" I asked, a niggle of worry making a home in my belly.

"I think you guys should just get married so we can stay here forever. But no mushy-gushy stuff."

A giggle slipped free before I could stop it. "So, cool with the dating, not with the mushy-gushy."

"Yup," Luca said, popping the P.

"Since you're okay with the dating, how would you feel about staying here with Cope? Not finding a new apartment."

Luca froze, his gaze jumping back and forth between me and Cope. "Seriously?"

Cope's grin widened. "Nothing would make me happier."

"Yes! Yes! Yes! Times a million billion! I get to keep my room and swim in the pool and play in the creek and ride horses with Arden and—"

"Take a breath," I told Luca, laughter in my voice.

Luca's gasping inhale was audible from the back seat. "This is gonna be freaking awesome! Cope, does the pond freeze in the winter? Can we skate on it?"

"You know, it does. My brothers and sisters and I play a game on it every Christmas," Cope said.

Luca's eyes went huge. "And I'll get to play?"

"Speedy, you know I can't win without you. And I *really* don't like to lose."

A pang lit along my sternum. Cope wasn't just giving me a sense of belonging and a home. He was giving it to Luca, too. Giving us all a family.

I squeezed Cope's fingers. "I love you."

Cope's dark-blue eyes heated. "Warrior..."

I leaned over the console and brushed my lips across his.

"Gross," Luca moaned from the back seat. "You guys *are* going to be all mushy-gushy all the time, aren't you?"

I laughed against Cope's mouth. "You'd better believe it."

"I guess the pool is worth it," Luca mumbled, scratching Gretzky behind the ear.

Cope chuckled and shut off the engine. "Well, I've got a few other surprises. Maybe that'll make it *more* worth it."

Luca's eyes lit. "I love surprises!"

He was out of the SUV before I had the chance to chastise him, Gretzky bounding after him. I had no choice but to follow. Cope punched in the door code and led us inside. I heard a commotion from the kitchen, where I knew a catering company was preparing for the team barbeque here this afternoon, but Cope pointed to the stairs. "This way."

Luca ran up them two at a time, Gretzky charging ahead of him before they both stopped on the landing to wait for us. "Where now?"

Cope's lips twitched. "Let's check out your room."

Luca took off running down the hall. Before I could ask Cope anything, I heard Luca's squeal of delight and then, "No freaking way!"

I glanced up at Cope in question. He just wrapped an arm around my shoulders and pulled me against him. "It was time he really had his own room."

We paused in the doorway, and I gaped. The room had been transformed into a little boy paradise. Against the far wall were bunk beds with bedding covered in hockey icons. There was a desk with bookshelves in the corner. The shelves were full of Luca's favorite books.

The wall closest to the door had what almost looked like a mural of hockey players braced for the start of play, but I realized they were stickers, one on either side of an even larger TV. In front of it were beanbag chairs and a massive gaming setup below it.

Luca ran to Cope, hurling himself at him. Cope caught him easily, and Luca flung his arms around Cope's neck. "This is the best thing ever! Thank you!"

"I had way too much fun picking it all out," Cope said, hugging him back. "We're gonna get you some signed jerseys for that wall, too."

Luca wiggled free, racing around the room to check everything out in detail, Gretzky sniffing alongside him. I turned to Cope, my eyes burning. "Thank you," I whispered.

"I'm not done yet, Warrior."

"I'm not sure I can handle anything else," I murmured.

Cope slid his fingers through mine. "My girl can handle anything."

He tugged me into the hallway and back to the landing at the top of the stairs. He guided me toward the huge picture window that overlooked the backyard, pond, and wilderness area.

"Look right over there." He pointed to a grove of aspen trees. In the middle was an array of six beehives. "I know you love tending those bees of yours. Having fresh honey to bake with. So, I wanted you to have some hives here, too."

My eyes started to water, the tears sliding down my cheeks. "You got me bees?"

Cope pulled me against him. "You know I'd do anything to make you happy. I want this to be your home. We can decide if we want a place in Seattle, too, or if I'll commute on my time off. Linc already said he'd loan me his plane if we want Sparrow Falls to still be our home during the season."

"Cope," I choked out.

"There's one more thing."

"I can't take one more thing."

Cope brushed his lips across mine. "Yes, you can." He reached down, grabbing what looked like some rolled-up papers. "I had

Shep draw up some plans for a commercial kitchen right here on the property."

I sucked in a breath. It was too much. All of it. My body felt like it might explode from happiness, from all the care Cope was pouring out over me and Luca.

He unrolled the papers. "We can tweak them however you want. It'll go on the other side of the garage. That way, you don't have to drive so early in the morning or late at night. You can prepare everything you want here and transport it in the van I ordered."

"Cope."

His gaze moved to my face. "Too much?" I flung myself at him much like my son had done, and he caught me with an *oomph*. "Not too much?"

"I love you."

"Warrior, you know what that does to me."

I grinned against his mouth. "Think there's time before everyone gets here?"

"I'll make time," Cope growled against my mouth.

And he certainly did.

CHAPTER FIFTY

Sutton

MUSIC DRIFTED OUT OF COPE'S METICULOUSLY HIDDEN speakers and into the party. I couldn't help but grin as I heard the strains of an old-school Tim McGraw song. As if I didn't have enough proof that Cope loved me, his letting me play my country proved it, even though it was his least favorite kind of music.

Thea bumped my hip with hers. "Now, that is the smile of a happy woman."

My cheeks heated. "It feels like it would be impossible to be any happier."

Thea's eyes glistened in the sunlight. "No one deserves that more than you."

I pulled her into a tight hug. "Please, don't make me cry. If Cope sees me crying, he's going to get very cranky."

That had Thea laughing as she released me. "Fair enough."

As I stepped back, I took inventory of the dessert table. Linc had paid for caterers to kit out the barbeque, and while he'd returned to Seattle after the first day of camp, he'd gone all out for the party, even though he wouldn't be here to enjoy it. But I'd asked if I could handle the desserts, and he'd grudgingly agreed.

Thankfully, Thea and I had gone all out, too. There were cookies in the shapes of pucks, sticks, and little hockey players, complete with the Seattle Sparks logo. But the cupcakes were the real showstoppers. We'd done the hockey player Oreo ones Frankie was so fond of, strawberry-lemonade ones with little, pure-sugar lightning bolts coming out the top, and triple-chocolate ones with all the different players' numbers on them.

And it was a good thing we'd made a lot because they were going fast. As we stepped up to the table, Frankie turned around, his face full of cupcake. "What'll it take to get you to dump Reaper and marry me?"

Marcus chuckled and picked up a cookie from the table. "It really would be the smarter play."

I shook my head. "Stop stirring up trouble, or I'll ban you from the dessert table."

Marcus shoved the cookie into his mouth, holding up both hands as he walked away. "I didn't say a word," he mumbled around the cookie.

"Smart man," Frankie called back. "Cause this shit is fire!"

"Watch your language," Evelyn hissed, walking up as if she had radar for someone breaking her rules.

Frankie's brows rose. "What's wrong with fire?"

Evelyn's jaw clenched. "Not that word, the other one."

Frankie just looked confused.

"The s-one," she spat.

"Lady, that's not even a curse."

Evelyn glared at me. "This is what you would have our children exposed to? And all this"—she gestured wildly around—"*sugar*?"

I stared back at her for a long moment. "Evelyn, look around you. Everyone's having a good time...except you. Maybe you just need to relax for a second and try to have some fun."

Frankie slung an arm over her shoulders and lifted a cupcake for her to take. "One bite. It'll change your world."

Evelyn clamped her lips closed and shook her head, making some sort of noise in the negative.

"Come on, now. A little triple-chocolate never hurt no one," Frankie cajoled.

"I said—" Evelyn opened her mouth to put him off, but Frankie was faster. He was trying to give her a bite but ended up all but shoving the entire cupcake in her face.

Everyone froze.

Then Thea let out a strangled laugh. I couldn't help it and joined in. Frankie winced, slowly letting go of Evelyn's shoulders as chocolate dropped onto her perfect white shirt. "I'm sorry, I—"

"Oh, my God," she mumbled around the cupcake. "This is the best thing I've ever tasted."

My eyes went wide, and my gaze snapped to Thea in shock. Thea only laughed harder. "We tried to tell you, and I wouldn't steer a sister wrong."

"It's incredible. What the hell was I thinking? Carob is *not* the same thing."

A huge grin spread across Frankie's face. "She said the h-word."

"I know," Thea whisper-hissed.

Frankie threw an arm around Evelyn's shoulders again, guiding her away from the table. "This is just the beginning. We're hitting up the trampoline next."

Evelyn looked up at him with wide eyes and chocolate all over her face. "We are?"

"Damn straight."

As they disappeared, Thea collapsed into me. "Who would've thought all it took to melt the ice queen was Frankie's charm and one of your triple-chocolate creations?"

I shook my head, watching as Frankie hoisted Evelyn onto the trampoline, and she started...jumping. "Maybe this is the breakthrough she's been needing."

"God, I hope so. Otherwise, I worry for her kid."

I did, too.

"Mooooom!" Luca yelled, running toward me with a water gun. "We're playing water tag hide-and-seek. You gotta play with us!"

"It's the best, Miss Sutton," Keely called, firing a shot in another kid's direction.

I should've said no. I needed to watch the table. I was in a sundress and sandals. But I threw all that out the window. Because my kid wouldn't ask me to play with him and his friends for that much longer. So, I grinned at Luca. "Where's my weapon?"

He giggled and handed me a ridiculously over-the-top water pistol. "We have to the count of a hundred to hide, and then everyone's fair game. Tag as many as you can. Ready, set, go!"

I didn't wait. I took off running across the field and toward the trees. I could use them to hide. I wasn't about to embarrass my kid and get knocked out in the first five seconds. I slipped into some forest cover, trying to see where everyone was headed.

Two went by the trampoline, and another three headed into the party, weaving between players, parents, and Coach Kenner. But Luca, my smart boy, went for the hives because he knew most kids would be too scared of the bees to venture there, and he could sneak back around to surprise them all.

A laugh bubbled out of me as I watched him pump a fist in the air. But the laugh caught in my throat as someone grabbed me by the hair and yanked me backward, clamping a hand over my mouth. "Did you miss me, Blue Eyes?"

CHAPTER FIFTY-ONE

Cope

I LIFTED THE BOTTLE TO MY LIPS AND TOOK A SWIG OF LOCAL ALE, the hops playing on my tongue. It wasn't as good as the taste of Sutton, but it was good enough. I could still see her after our stolen moments earlier this afternoon.

Her head tipped back, the sun catching on her blond locks as she laughed full-out as Lolli caught us coming downstairs afterward. That was something I'd noticed lately. Sutton laughed harder—and more often—these days. There were fewer shadows in her eyes.

"I don't think I've ever seen you this happy."

I jolted slightly at the sound of my mom's voice. I glanced down, seeing her eyes shine with tightly held emotion. "Mom."

She wrapped an arm around my waist and squeezed me tight. "Ever since the accident, you've had shadows. It made sense, but knowing how much you were hurting killed me."

My ribs tightened around my lungs, making it hard to take a full breath.

"I wanted more than anything for you to heal. To let someone

into your life who could lighten your load. Sutton's that. A true partner," Mom whispered.

"She is," I croaked. "She made me start to see some hard truths."

My mom looked up at me, questions swimming in her eyes.

Hell. I didn't want to go there. Not today. Not with so many good
things swirling around us. But some part of me knew that if I didn't
say the words now, I never would.

"It was my fault. Or I thought it was," I began, my voice sounding foreign to my ears.

Mom's green eyes flared. "Copeland—"

I shook my head, cutting her off. "Let me say this, or I never will."

Her mouth snapped closed as pain swept across her face.

"It was my game. Jacob and Fallon didn't even want to go, but
Dad talked them into it like he always did. Bribing Fal with candy and
Jacob with a weekend off ranch duties."

I took a deep breath before continuing, trying to steady myself.
I wished Sutton were here, that her hand was in mine. But just as I
wished it, I could feel her. That buzz of energy that swirled through
me, a steady acceptance. It didn't matter if she was across the yard or
a million miles away. She was always with me.

I held on to her as I spoke. "We were late getting on the road—I
was messing around with friends in the locker room. And when we
were driving, Fal and I got into it. I started it. Needling her. Telling
her I was going to get Jacob's room when he left for school."

In reality, no one would. None of us wanted to touch it after he
was gone. "Dad told us to quit it. He glanced back for just a second
to give us the dad stare. But it was a second too long. Jacob tried to
warn him about the deer. He swerved. But it was all just too late."

Mom's grip on my waist fell away, and for a second, I thought
she'd leave, that all my fears were founded. But then she threw her
arms around me. "My beautiful boy. You've been carrying so much
pain." She hugged me tighter. "It wasn't your fault. It was an accident.
Something no one could've prevented."

"I distracted him," I croaked.

"You were a kid bickering with his sister. How many fights have I broken up over the years?"

"Too many to count," I mumbled into her shoulder.

Mom released me but kept a hold of my arms. "That's right. Because that's life. Fighting and making up. Loving the people around you and wanting to wring their necks at the same time. That doesn't make you a monster. It makes you human."

She shook her head, her eyes glistening. "I hate that you've been carrying this alone."

"I'm not carrying it alone anymore," I whispered.

A single tear spilled down my mom's cheek. "I'm going to hug the hell out of that Sutton."

I chuckled. "She'll like that."

"Are you going to ask her to marry you?" Mom asked, a different sort of gleam in her eyes now.

"*Mom,*" I chastised.

She laughed, letting me go. "It's my job to stick my nose where it doesn't belong."

"I'm going to marry her." There was no doubt in my words, no uncertainty. I knew what I wanted my future to be. And that was Sutton and Luca. To make them feel safe and loved. To give them the family they deserved.

A laugh bubbled out of my mom. "No asking?"

I grinned at her. "I know it's meant to be. That *we* are. Just like I know we're all going to give Sutton and Luca the family they always should've had. We're going to show them the acceptance you're so good at giving all of us. We're going to give them a love that never ends, no matter what."

"Cope," Mom said, her voice breaking on my name.

I brushed a tear away from her cheek. "I love you. Thank you for loving me even when I'm not perfect."

She threw her arms around me again. "You're always perfect to me. Well, maybe not that time you and Kye puked in my lilac bushes after sneaking out to go to a field party."

I barked out a laugh as I released her. "I didn't think you knew about that."

Mom's nose wrinkled. "I know *everything*."

Movement caught my eye. Luca raced across the back lawn toward us, dodging kids and adults alike. "Have you seen Mom? I can't find her."

I glanced around, searching for those familiar turquoise eyes. I saw Thea manning the dessert table, and Arden throwing the ball for Brutus and Gretzky, but I didn't see Sutton anywhere. "I'm sure she's around here somewhere."

My phone buzzed in my pocket. I slid it out and saw Sutton's name flash across the screen in a text alert. Relief swept through me as I swiped my finger across the screen. "It's your mom. She probably needs to run to the bakery because these monsters have eaten all her cupcakes."

Luca giggled. "It's definitely Frankie's fault."

"Definitely." But as I took in the text, everything stopped. Filling the screen was a photo. Sutton, wide-eyed, with tape over her mouth, hands cuffed in zip ties. The message was from her phone but not from *her*.

> **Sutton:** I'm watching. Let anyone know something's wrong, and I'll put a bullet in her brain. Say you need to get something inside. Come to the barn instead. Bring your phone. And your bank login.

Money. Someone was doing this for money? It had to be Roman. Blood roared in my ears as panic grabbed hold.

> **Me:** Don't hurt her.

> **Sutton:** That depends entirely on you. Step away from the old lady and the boy. Start walking.

I should've known. Life had been too good. Too happy. And I knew too well that all that goodness could be taken away in a flash.

CHAPTER FIFTY-TWO

Sutton

THE ZIP TIES DUG INTO MY WRISTS AS I STARED AT THE MAN I used to know. Someone I once thought I loved. A man who had given me Luca.

Now, he was nothing but a stranger dressed in a caterer's uniform. Far too skinny for his six-foot-two-inch frame and paler than I'd ever seen him. He looked nothing like the photo I'd shown Walter the other day. But it was more than his appearance. It was his actions.

Roman had hurt me and Luca countless times by lying, cheating, and stealing. Not showing up when we needed him the most. But this? This was a choice. An active decision to hurt me, the mother of his child.

Roman's eyes narrowed on me, a color I'd once thought of as amber but could now see was just mud brown. He adjusted his grip on a gun, shoved one phone into his pocket, and picked up another. Mine. "You even *think* about screaming, and I'll put a bullet in your brain faster than you can blink. Then I'll go for that little brat next."

I pressed myself harder against the barn wall as if it would somehow save me. It didn't.

Roman stepped forward, grabbing the edge of the tape and tearing it free in one swift tug. I wanted to curse or cry out but wasn't about to give him the satisfaction. And I wouldn't scream either. Not until I knew Luca was safe.

For all I knew, Roman had Petrov's men with him. How many could infiltrate a small-town catering company? I hadn't heard any Russian accents, but that didn't mean they weren't there.

For now, I would be quiet. Smart. I'd watch and listen. Wait for the perfect moment.

And then I would fight.

Because I had too much to live for. My son. Cope. The family we were building.

A sob pressed against my vocal cords, trying to break free. But I shoved it down. Not now.

Roman's upper lip curled in disgust like some over-the-top Bond villain. "What's the matter, Blue Eyes? Cat got your tongue? Usually, you won't shut up. Always nagging me about something."

Who was this? It was more than a transformation. It was as if I'd never known him at all.

"What do you want me to say, Roman?"

He winced when I said his name. As if I'd reached out and slapped him. So maybe he could still feel something.

"I want you to say you're fucking sorry," he snarled.

I reeled back. "Sorry?"

"Yeah, bitch. You took everything from me. My money. My house. My goddamned kid."

I gaped at him, shock sweeping through me in nonstop waves. "Your addiction did that. Your choices."

Roman's hand snaked out so fast, I didn't have a prayer of blocking it. His palm cracked across my cheek so hard I tasted blood. The coppery tang filled my mouth as I doubled over, trying to breathe through the pain.

"Ever think I needed the drugs just to be able to live with *you*?"

I focused on my breathing—in through my nose, out through

Broken HARBOR   331

my mouth. I spat blood onto the stone floor of the barn, strands of hay scattered across it. All I could see was how Luca's face lit up as Arden led him around the ring on one of her horse's backs. The way Cope curved his arm around me as we watched, our boy so happy. And that's what he was.

Ours.

He wasn't Roman's. Not anymore. Roman didn't have that right.

I forced myself to straighten, even as my head swam. I met the stranger's dark-brown eyes. "You never deserved us. Me or Luca."

Roman grinned then, revealing yellowed teeth clearly in need of a dentist. "Oh, and your precious hockey player does?"

I squared my shoulders. I wouldn't cower. Never again. Not to the men Roman worked with and certainly not to him. "Yes. Cope is more of a man than you will ever be. He's been more of a father to Luca than you ever were."

Roman's grip on the gun tightened, and his breathing grew ragged. "We'll see about that. See if you still love the prick after I drain his fucking bank account."

I stilled. Was that what this was? Still all about money and nothing more. "That's all you'll ever care about, isn't it? How to get that next fix?"

"I care about what's mine," he snapped. "You bled me dry, and now I'm going to do the same to your pimp here."

"How?" It was a simple question and should've been easy enough to answer, but I had a sinking feeling it wouldn't be.

Roman's jaw worked back and forth, annoyance flaring there. "He's gonna wire it. Twenty mil. His bank to the one I set up in Mexico. That's what you're here for. A little motivation." He held up the phone, showing me the text he'd sent to Cope from my device.

My stomach cramped. Was Roman really this far gone? So past living in reality that he didn't remember that banks put limits on those sorts of things? He might get a couple hundred thousand, but millions? It wasn't even possible.

But worse, Cope was on his way. Headed straight here because

I was in danger, and that's what he did. Ran in with no thought to his safety, only caring about mine.

"I see it's all coming together for the little blue-eyed bitch. But not all of it." Roman lifted the gun, pointing it directly at my head. "Because the moment that transfer goes through, I'm giving you both what you deserve. A bullet in the brain. Maybe I'll even grab the kid on the way out just for shits and giggles."

And there'd be nothing I could do to stop him. Not if I didn't run right now.

CHAPTER FIFTY-THREE

Cope

EVERYTHING IN ME HAD GONE NUMB. EXCEPT FOR MY HEART. Panic and fear were currently shredding it to dust, pulverizing it because someone had Sutton. They'd taped her mouth, zip-tied her hands, and God knew what else.

I swallowed the panic rising in my throat as I turned to my mom. "Hey, can you get Luca a sandwich while I go help Sutton with something?"

Mom gave me a puzzled look. "Are you sure? I—"

"I'm sure," I cut her off.

Something in my expression must've said I was desperate because she nodded, wrapping an arm around Luca's shoulders. "Come on, let's go get you some food; otherwise, you're likely to turn into frosting."

Luca giggled. "The frosting's the best part, so I'm okay with that."

Mom chuckled. "Of course, you are."

"Tell Mom she broke the rules by hiding in the house, so I'm the water gun tag hide-and-seek king!" Luca yelled over his shoulder as he let Mom guide him away.

Every word was like a knife to the gut. It was all I could do to keep it together and start walking. Just like the text had said. But it was the other thing the person had said that had my head on a swivel.

I'm watching.

I didn't see anything out of place: kids and my teammates playing, parents chatting, caterers moving throughout the party.

My gut twisted. There was no way to know who could be watching. Or if they were using tech to do it. Because if they'd snuck past security, who had a list of attendees, and grabbed Sutton, they were good.

So, I did the only thing I could. I started walking.

It was stupid as hell, but I didn't really have a choice. I'd do anything to keep Sutton safe. Even trade my life for hers.

But I wasn't going in without backup, either. I walked toward the house, then turned onto the road that led toward Arden's place and the barn, just like instructed. I still had no way of knowing who was watching. But at least I knew there was no one around to hear me.

I pressed the button on the side of my phone and held it down. "Text Trace."

I couldn't risk a call, not if someone was watching the party and me. If they saw my lips moving and Trace picked up his phone, that could be it. I'd have to hope he saw the text and would do what was necessary. That he would get Sutton out, even if I couldn't.

A muted robotic voice sounded. "What would you like to say to Trace?"

Wasn't that the million-dollar question?

I swallowed hard and picked up my pace. "Someone has Sutton. They told me to come to the barn and bring my bank details. They have eyes on me. Proved it. I don't know if it's one person or multiple, but I need backup. I need my brother. Trusting you to come quietly and get help here. Get Luca and Mom inside. I'm already on my way to Sutton."

I hit the button on the side of my phone again, and the device read my message back in that same robotic voice. It had gotten a couple of things wrong, but Trace would get the message.

"Ready to send it?" my phone asked.

"Yes." Then I picked up my pace, walking as fast as I could without running as I clicked my phone to silent. I couldn't risk Trace texting back. Or worse, calling.

The barn came into view in the distance, the structure I'd built for my sister so she could have peace. But there wasn't peace there now. It was anything but.

Images of Sutton filled my mind. They came in flashes, paired opposites of our best and worst moments. The smudge of grease across her cheek that first day we'd met in the parking lot. Her ashen face and blood at her temple after her attack. The fire in those turquoise eyes as I took her against the desk at the cowboy bar. That photo of her beaten face after her attack in Baltimore. The way that face went soft in Luca's bedroom the first time she whispered the words I needed the most.

I love you.

I couldn't lose her. She was everything. And not just to me. To Luca, too. I wouldn't let her be stolen from us both.

Desperation swirled, making me pick up my pace as the sun beat down. Sweat dotted my brow, my muscles battling between pushing and restraint. But as I rounded the bend, I saw it.

A flash of movement. Blond hair. Someone running.

It was just a glimpse of those turquoise eyes, a flicker of hope.

"Run!"

Her single word caught on the air, but it wasn't enough. Because before she made it two steps out of the barn. Someone grabbed her from behind, and all I could hear then was her scream.

CHAPTER FIFTY-FOUR

Sutton

MY SCREAM LODGED IN MY THROAT AS A BLOW HIT MY SIDE, stealing all the air from my lungs. "I warned you, bitch!"

Roman yanked me by the hair, hauling me back against him and pressing the gun to my temple. "You move now, and you're dead. But I'll make it hurt."

A whimper left my lips before I could swallow it down. So close to freedom but not close enough.

Footsteps pounded against the gravel. Someone running. I knew it was Cope.

I wanted it to be anyone but him, but he wouldn't be the man I'd fallen in love with, someone who would give everything for me, if he hadn't shown up now.

"Don't," I rasped, my voice raw from pain and trying to run.

Roman dragged me back into the shadow of the barn, jamming the gun harder against my head. "You had a choice. But you made your bed the second you ditched me, the minute you stole my kid from me."

A child he didn't even care about. One he'd never asked the courts to see. One I would do anything to keep safe.

"Don't hurt her. I'll do whatever you want. Just don't hurt her."

Cope's voice was unlike I'd ever heard it before. Raw. Ravaged. And full of more fury than should be possible.

Roman scoffed, yanking me in front of him like a human shield. "Always the fucking hero. Heard you liked to play that card."

"I'm not playing anything," Cope said, the words trembling with the force of his anger. "I just want you to tell me what you want so I can give it to you and get my girl out of here."

"Don't. He's just going to ki—"

My words cut off as Roman shook me like a rag doll, shoving the gun under my chin. "You wanna try that again, Blue Eyes?"

Cope's jaw ticked at the nickname, confirmation of who this man was and all he'd already stolen from me. "You want money. I've got money."

Roman's grip on my hair tightened. "Hot shit hockey star just drowning in cash. We'll see how you like it when you're struggling along with the rest of us. Twenty mil, or your whore gets it."

Cope's eyes flashed, and I hoped like hell Roman thought it was anger and not surprise. I was sure there was anger in the mix, rage, even, but Cope likely wondered how Roman thought he could magically get him that kind of money. He opened his mouth to say something, but I gave my head the smallest shake in warning.

Cope halted, reconsidering his play. "You want me to wire it?"

"No, I want you to write a check," Roman said drolly. "Of course, I want you to wire it." Slowly, he released his grip on my hair. "Don't even think of moving. I can shoot with one hand, no problem."

I swallowed hard, my heart hammering against my ribs. This was my chance. Not right away because Roman would be braced for that, but soon, the moment he was the slightest bit distracted.

Cope's eyes collided with mine, and I saw so much panic and pain there. But love shone beneath it all, and I hoped that would see us through.

"*Trust me,*" I mouthed.

Cope didn't say anything, but I felt it. That trust. The understanding. Love.

Roman grabbed his phone from a tack box just inside the barn, keeping the gun pointed at my head. The moment the device was in his hand, he was back to using me as cover. But that was just fine with me. In fact, I needed it that way.

"I'm texting you the wire info. You do anything stupid, call 9-1-1 or your brother, this one pays the price." Roman shoved the gun against my chin as if to punctuate the point.

"They wouldn't get here in time, so it wouldn't matter if I tried to call, would it?" Cope ground out.

"That's right, asshole." Roman's fingers moved across the keyboard, awkwardly trying to copy and paste from his notes app.

I knew this was it. My moment.

But I couldn't help but steal one more look at Cope. "*Love you,*" I mouthed. And then I whirled as fast as I could. My knee came up, connecting hard with Roman's balls. He howled in pain, a sound far more animal than human and satisfying as hell. As he doubled over, I brought my bound hands up in a clasp-fisted punch.

I missed his nose since I couldn't see, but I got his temple. There was no sound this time. It was as if Roman were a puppet, and someone had cut all his strings. He simply crumpled to the ground, out cold.

Cope rushed forward, catching me as I stumbled backward. "Are you okay? Are you hurt?"

"I-I'm okay. Luca?" Panic zipped through me.

Cope held me tighter, breathing me in. "He's fine. We're all fine."

"Are you sure about that, *Reap*?"

Everything in me stilled at the voice. It was familiar but different. There was so much hatred dripping from it now.

"I guess if you want something done right, you have to do it yourself."

I stared at the man I'd watched all week. One I'd known had a chip on his shoulder, but nothing that suggested a darkness like this. "Marcus?" I croaked.

"Sorry about this, Sutton. It's nothing personal." And then he leveled his gun and squeezed the trigger.

CHAPTER FIFTY-FIVE

Cope

T HE POP WASN'T NEARLY AS LOUD AS I'D THOUGHT A BULLET would be, but it still did damage. Roman's body jerked as if it had been electrocuted. But instead, there was a single bullet hole in the center of his forehead.

Sutton let out a strangled sound, pressing her face against my back at the horror of it. It wouldn't matter to her that the man whose life was bleeding out on the barn floor had wished her harm, even death. She never would have wished the same on him.

Marcus strode forward, annoyance twisting his pretty-boy face. He kicked Roman's foot before bending to pick up his weapon. "You know, Sutton, you really have shit taste in men. First an addict, then one who's going to get you killed."

My blood turned to ice. "You're not going to hurt her."

The annoyance in Marcus's expression morphed into amusement. "I'm not? Because it looks to me like I'm the one who's going to be the hero for once. I'm the one who's going to get the glory. Not fucking you."

"You planned this," Sutton whispered.

Marcus chuckled, but there was no warmth in it. "Yes, I planned this. After I realized who you were, I had to fly to Baltimore and hunt down your disgusting ex, who was living in filth, by the way. I had to stoke his rage and tell him how my teammate, who has everyone believing what an *incredible* guy he is, was fucking his wife."

"I'm not his wife," Sutton bit out as I reached behind me to squeeze her side.

Marcus grinned. "He still thought of you as his. And he *hated* you for leaving him. I just had to fan those flames. Tell him how much money Cope had. Money that could be his. That *should* be his. And all he had to do was take it."

Blood roared in my ears. "You set him up."

"Poor Roman was never going to make it out alive. But every story needs a bad guy. A villain and a hero. What's everyone going to think when I find him killing you both in the barn? I was just seconds too late to save you, but I managed to shoot your murderer. Think about how the press will eat that shit up."

"I wouldn't be so sure about that." Trace's voice cut through the air like the cold steel of the sharpest blade. "Marcus Warner, this is the Mercer County Sheriff's Department. Lower your weapon."

It all happened so fast. One second, Marcus's eyes were rounding in shock, and the next, he was yanking me in front of him like a shield. Like Roman had done with Sutton, two monsters pulling from the same playbook.

But at least I knew he didn't have her. Sutton would make it out. Trace wouldn't let it play out any other way.

Marcus pressed the gun against my temple. "You take another step, and I'll make sure my finger slips."

Trace stilled, but I saw the cold rage swirling in his dark-green eyes. But I couldn't let it register. Not now. I only had time to make sure of one thing.

My gaze collided with Sutton's, horror overtaking her expression. "Go," I rasped.

She instantly began shaking her head.

"Sutton, go!" I put as much force as I could into the single word.

Tears streamed down her face. "I can't leave you."

"You can, and you will. You're going back to that beautiful boy who's pissed as hell that you cheated in water gun tag hide-and-seek. And you're going to tell him that you love him and that I do, too."

"Cope." Her voice cracked on my name, more tears spilling over.

"Do it for me."

"For fuck's sake," Marcus snarled. "I'll kill you both just so I don't have to listen to this."

His gun moved from me to Sutton for just a split second. Panic surged, and I knocked into Marcus, throwing him off-kilter just long enough for me to shout, "Go!"

Sutton skittered back out of the barn, and that's when I saw him. Just a brief flash, but I recognized Anson's scowl as he grabbed Sutton and got her out of the line of fire. That meant there was help. More than Trace. I just had to keep Marcus talking until they found their opening.

The gun smashed into the side of my face, making my vision blur. Marcus grabbed my shirt tighter. "You'll pay for that."

"Lower your weapon, Marcus," Trace ordered again. To any outsider, it would've sounded like my brother didn't give a damn about me. But I knew what it meant. He'd gone to that other place, the one where he turned everything off.

Marcus let out a derisive scoff. "Sorry, Trace. You know that's not going to happen. And it's nothing against you. I actually like you. It's your piece-of-shit brother who needs a lesson."

With each word, his grip on my shirt tightened. I could feel the rage pulsing through him in waves. I just didn't understand why. But maybe the reason would keep him talking and give us the time we needed.

"What the hell did I ever do to you?" I growled.

Trace's eyes flashed in warning, and I read the underlying message: *Don't poke the bear.*

"What did you do to me?" Marcus pulled my shirt so tight the collar strangled me. "You stole *everything* from me."

My brows pulled together, confusion sweeping through me. I knew Marcus and I were compared often. We'd come up in the ranks together, so it made sense. And the fact that he'd grown up only a few hours away meant we'd played together as kids quite a bit, too.

But in my mind, we'd always been fairly evenly matched. One of those situations where he had the edge one year and I did the next. We were drafted into the pros the same year, and I was picked one round before him. Still, we were both prize catches for the Sparks.

I dropped my voice. "What did I steal?"

"It *all* should've been mine," Marcus snarled. "From the beginning. The Pacific Northwest Youth League MVP. You know they only gave you that because your dad and brother died."

My muscles stiffened to stone. The award had come six months after the accident. I'd thrown myself into hockey as soon as I healed enough to get back on the ice. It was my only escape. I trained for hours before and after practice, losing myself in the physical toll it took on my body.

I could see now that it had been punishment. The escape I'd found on the ice wasn't escape at all. And it had taken finding Sutton and Luca to show me that. But it was more. Experiencing hockey through Luca's eyes had helped me find the joy in it again. Helped me remember the bond I'd shared with my dad. They'd brought him back to life for me in so many ways.

Marcus pulled back the gun and then jammed it under my chin so hard my skin tore, and my teeth clacked together. "Do you know what *my* dad did to me after that awards banquet? Took a belt to me so hard I couldn't sit for weeks. Couldn't lie on my back. But he forced me right back on the ice the next day. Telling me I needed to be more—like—*you*."

My mind reeled as I tried to pull the threads together. I was still coming up empty. Because none of this sounded like the man I'd known growing up. Weston Warner had always been one of the first parents to greet me with a back slap and an attaboy when I scored a goal. He'd even pulled me aside for pointers on shots here and there, sharing his expertise from his years in the pros.

But it was more than just the sports piece. Weston served on the board of charities, fundraised for youth hockey programs across the country, and often sponsored gear for kids on our teams who couldn't afford it.

"What?" Marcus sneered. "Don't believe dear ole dad was such a monster? He put on a good show. Just. Like. You."

Marcus punctuated each word by shoving the barrel of the gun against the underside of my chin. "Smiling for the cameras, then beating me behind closed doors. Telling you what an *incredible* job you did, then telling me I was his worst disappointment."

My gut roiled at the sheer pain in Marcus's voice because it told me he wasn't lying.

"Do you know what he said to me on his deathbed?" Marcus asked, his voice dipping low.

I didn't answer right away. Couldn't.

"DO YOU KNOW?" Marcus screamed, shaking me and making Trace lift his gun higher, looking for a shot.

"I don't," I croaked.

"He said he wished he could've lived just one day thinking you were his son instead of me."

Jesus. Marcus's father had used me to torture his son. He may have been the monster, but I was the weapon he reached for most often.

"I'm sorry." I struggled to get the words out with the gun jammed under my chin. But they weren't a lie. No kid deserved what had happened to Marcus.

Marcus hauled back and slammed the butt of the gun into my jaw. "You're *sorry*? You're just like him."

My vision swam from the force of the blow as I tried to get my bearings. "Like him?"

"Everyone thought he was so smart, so kind, generous. Threw his money around to get everyone on his side. But they didn't know how ugly he truly was. How twisted. That's you. Everyone thinks you're this golden boy. Volunteering at a kids' camp, donating to youth hockey, so dedicated to the sport. But you're just out for yourself. You don't give a damn about your team or anyone else."

Marcus sucked in a breath and gripped my shirt tighter. "I tried to show them. Tipped off those reporters to the truth. Leaked the footage of you punching me to show them how you treat your *team*."

"You goaded me into that." The realization hit me like a physical blow.

"I showed them who you really are," Marcus snarled. "But the rest of the world needs to know, too. It was never enough. Not the anonymous report of steroid use. Not even when I frayed the brake lines on Teddy's car. They should've known it was all your fault. All your fault that he drove out to bumfuck because poor Cope was struggling. Just had to go check on him. But no, they just *loved* your eulogy like the pathetic sycophants they are."

He gripped my shirt harder, pulling it so tight the neckline cut into my airway. "Do you know how much time I wasted following him down here? Paying a hacker to loop your security footage so I could sneak onto your property and mess with his brakes?"

"You killed Teddy." My ears rang with the words.

"*You* killed Teddy. He wouldn't have died if it wasn't for you. Just like your brother and dad wouldn't have."

Rage ignited, fast and fierce. Marcus had stolen Teddy from us. Not some freak accident and slick roads. Someone we'd considered a teammate, a brother.

"And now I'm going to kill you," Marcus snarled.

I didn't wait, knew there wasn't time to try to keep him talking and hope Trace or Anson would find a shot. I had to move. Now.

Rearing my head forward, I threw it back as hard as I could and connected with Marcus's nose with a vicious crack. He howled in pain, the gun dropping away for the briefest moment.

I didn't waste a second. I tried to pull the few sparring lessons I'd gotten from Kye into my mind and prayed my muscles would remember. I grabbed the arm Marcus held the weapon with and brought up my knee. I was aiming for his goddamned balls like Sutton had with Roman, but missed, catching his inner thigh instead.

"You don't get to win!" Marcus howled.

He shoved the gun harder in my direction. I fought with all my might, remembering just what it was I was battling for. Luca. Sutton. The family we were building together.

Marcus let out a cry of fury, and a pop sounded right before fiery pain exploded through my ribs. My eyes went wide, and I struggled for breath. Shouts sounded all around me, but it was like they were coming from far away.

It felt like flames engulfing my entire torso as I dropped to the ground. My vision tunneled, and as everything went black, I swore I heard Sutton yell my name.

CHAPTER FIFTY-SIX

Sutton

I 'D HEARD A BULLET LEAVE A GUN TWICE NOW, BUT IT STILL didn't sound like I'd thought a gunshot would. It didn't crack through the air like in the movies. It was more of a *pop*. Something that I wouldn't have even associated with a bullet if it weren't for the way the blood drained from Cope's face as I raced around the corner of the barn.

Everything happened in snapshots that alternated between slow motion and super speed—as if we were in a comic book or superhero movie.

Only, we weren't.

This was life. Mine and Cope's. And as he crumpled to the ground, blood blossoming on his white tee, I knew his was in danger of fading. Of seeping into the stone floor, never to be found again.

Shouts sounded as Trace tackled Marcus to the ground. Marcus's rage-filled ramblings didn't reach the part of my brain that could register what they meant because every part of me was focused on Cope.

I hadn't realized I was running until I was almost to him. I dropped to the ground, my knees connecting with the rock floor so hard my jaw clacked together and my spine jarred. But none of that truly computed.

All I saw was blood. Seeping out and blooming over the left side of Cope's chest, far too close to where I guessed his heart would be.

"Pressure," Trace ordered as he struggled to get Marcus into cuffs. "Pressure on the wound."

No part of me hesitated. I leaned over Cope, placing my palms over his wound and pressing all my weight against him. His eyelids fluttered, and I knew it was likely because I was causing him pain.

The tears came then, falling fast and furiously down my cheeks and mixing with the blood that seeped through my fingertips. "I'm so sorry. The last thing I want to do is hurt you. But I have to. I have to hurt you so you stay. You can't leave, Cope. Not when we're just beginning. Luca needs you. *I* need you."

Sirens sounded in the distance, getting closer with each passing second. Anson dropped down next to me, his fingers going to Cope's throat. "I've got a pulse. It's weak, but it's there."

The tears came faster, but I didn't make a sound. I just kept pressing on Cope's chest as if I could keep the life force inside him with my strength. As if I could hold him together the way he had done for me so many times.

New voices called over the ringing in my ears. Sheriff's department officers flooded the barn. Someone called for the EMTs.

Hands closed around my shoulders. "You can let go now. The medics are here."

Some part of me recognized Trace's voice, but I couldn't look up to confirm it, couldn't look away from Cope, too afraid he'd disappear on me. "I can't," I whispered. "I'm holding him here. I can't let go."

Trace's fingers squeezed my shoulders this time. "You'll still be holding him. You're with him always. But the EMTs need to do their work."

One was already at Cope's other side, inserting a needle into his vein. The other found a spot at Cope's head, putting some sort of mask in place. But I couldn't move. It was as if my body had become set in stone. "I-I can't. I'm not going to leave him. He never left me. Even when he should've."

I felt Anson shift at my side, some foreign energy moved behind me, and then I was lifted into the air. The sound that left my lips was animalistic, nothing human in its notes. It was a cry for Cope and Cope alone.

"I have to save him!" I wailed the words, barely coherent against Trace's chest as he held me tight.

"You did, Sutton. You saved him. But the EMTs need to help now so we can get him to the hospital."

A shout sounded behind me, someone calling for a defibrillator. I twisted in Trace's hold, needing to see Cope. I watched in horror as a paramedic cut Cope's T-shirt down the middle. The other placed pads on his chest.

"Clear," one barked.

Cope's body jolted in the most unnatural way, and then the world went silent around us.

A symphony of sounds played around me: the hum of the overhead lights, the ticking of the clock on the wall, the punctuating beep of the heart monitor. I held tightly to that last sound, letting it reassure me with each little blip.

It was a promise. It told me over and over that the paramedics had gotten Cope's heart beating again. The doctors had repaired the hole in Cope's lung and got it to reinflate.

Now, we simply had to wait.

There was no way to know how those minutes without oxygen had affected Cope until he woke up. No way to tell if there would be other complications. If he would ever play hockey again.

My fingers threaded through Cope's, and I wasn't letting go. I couldn't help but stare at the stains on my fingertips. The way the blood still lived in those little lines and whirls. I turned my free hand over, studying how Cope's life force had settled into the lines on my palm. Those life and heart lines someone had once pointed out to me, grooves that were supposed to tell the story of your existence.

It was fitting that Cope had marked them. Because he'd marked me. I'd never be the same, thanks to him, and that was exactly how I wanted it.

A fresh wave of tears filled my eyes, falling into those lines, but it didn't wash the now-pink stains away.

I dropped my head to the bed, my lips ghosting over the back of Cope's hand. "We're in it together, remember? And you always keep your promises." The tears kept coming. "You gave us a family, a place to belong, a home. And none of it is whole without you."

There was a flutter beneath my lips, fingers twitching. I jerked upright, my gaze flying to Cope's face. Those beautiful, long lashes fluttered, his lids trying to open.

And then I saw them. Those hypnotizing dark-blue depths I wanted to come home to for the rest of my days.

Cope's mouth opened in a barely audible rasp. "Warrior."

CHAPTER FIFTY-SEVEN

Cope

THREE WEEKS LATER

A KNOCK SOUNDED ON MY DOOR, AND I SCOWLED AT THE WOOD plank. "Come in."

It swung open, a familiar figure filling the opening. "You'd think a guy who got a second chance at life would sound a little happier. Joyful, even."

The scowl pointed in Linc's direction only deepened. "You try being stuck in bed for almost a month and having every member of your family hovering over your every waking move."

Linc's lips twitched as he crossed to the chair positioned near my bed. "Well, you did rip a hole right through your chest. It makes sense they're worried about you. Because, for some reason, they love your surly ass."

He had a point, and I grumbled as much under my breath.

Linc chuckled as he sat. "Plane's fueled and ready to take you guys to Seattle. I also conveniently left dossiers on five different locations for The Mix Up's Seattle location."

God, I was lucky to have him as a boss and a friend. "You know you didn't have to do that."

Linc arched a brow. "I'm not an idiot. I know a good business opportunity when I see one. And I've tasted Sutton's baked goods. I'll take her nationwide if she wants."

I had no doubt. Linc's business mind was unparalleled, but I only cared about Sutton and Luca being *happy*. They were making a big sacrifice, spending most of the year in Seattle with me so I could try to get back on the ice.

Sutton and I had gone around and around about whether it was a good idea or not. But I finally realized that I didn't want things to end like this. I wanted a chance to finish what I'd started, which was reclaiming hockey as something that brought me joy.

"I might not be able to get it back," I said quietly, finally voicing the fear that was swimming inside me.

Linc leaned forward, his gold watch glinting at his wrist, so incongruous with his hiking boots, jeans, and worn tee. "All we can do is give it our best shot. I've got the top rehab team in the Pacific Northwest ready to see you on Monday."

I nodded, my back teeth grinding together. "I'm ready to *really* move. And I don't mean these stupid walks down the driveway and back."

"I bet," Linc said. "Kye might've sent some colorful texts about having to help you to the bathroom those first few days at home."

My scowl was back. "I'm going to kill him."

Linc chuckled. "No better motivation than kicking a sibling's ass."

"Truer words have never been spoken." I shifted on the pillows, still feeling a slight stab of pain as I did. "What are you doing here anyway? You didn't have to escort us back to Seattle."

Linc leaned back in his chair. "I actually got in yesterday. Came to look at some properties and meet with Shep."

My brows rose in surprise. "You're thinking about building here?"

"There's something about the landscape. Those gold rock formations and imposing peaks. Felt like it might be somewhere good to have a spot."

I guessed I shouldn't have been all that surprised. Linc might be drowning in billions, but he was also a nature lover at heart, opting for an estate outside the city instead of some high-rise penthouse.

"You know you can stay here if you want," I offered. "It'd be a hell of a lot better than finding a rental while you're getting started on construction."

"I might take you up on that," Linc said.

"I just need to give Arden a heads-up since she looks out for things while I'm gone."

He winced. "Heads-up might be a good idea since she almost killed me at our last little run-in."

"She wha—?" My words were cut off by Sutton entering the room with a tray in hand.

"Time for lunch and meds before we head out."

God, she was beautiful. Those turquoise eyes never dimmed their shine, no matter how surly I got over my recovery. She and Luca had stuck by my side every second of the process. And I'd lost count of the number of times I'd seen *Mighty Ducks*.

Linc pushed to his feet. "I'll leave you to it, but I'll be downstairs if you guys need any help with the bags."

Sutton set the tray on the bed and moved to Linc, kissing his cheek. "Thank you for everything."

"Always here for whatever you need," he assured her, heading out.

Sutton turned back to me. "How's the pain level?"

"Tylenol status," I said, even though it was probably slightly out of that range.

She pinned me with a stare. "We're going to be moving around a lot more than normal today. Even with Nora helping out, you'll be pushing it."

When the doctor had prescribed me opioids as a part of my

recovery, I'd seen the fear in Sutton's eyes. And I didn't blame her. Those drugs had sent her last partner down a spiraling road that had nearly cost Sutton her life. So, I'd put her in charge of the medication and told the doctor as much.

"I want to avoid it as much as possible leading up to rehab. They're going to kick my ass, and I know I'll need the heavier stuff then."

Sutton mulled that over for a moment. "How about we start with Tylenol? If you need the prescription at any point today, just say the word."

"Deal. Now, come here."

The moment Sutton was within grabbing distance, I tugged her down to the bed and took her mouth with mine. She moaned, and my dick twitched. *Hell.* I missed this. Missed *her.* If there was any motivation for getting back in shape, it was that.

The sound of a throat clearing made Sutton pull back and flush. Anson grinned from the doorway. "Sorry to interrupt."

"Like hell you are," I grumbled.

He laughed, still a bizarre sound to hear from the broody bastard. "I had some news I wanted to deliver in person."

Sutton grabbed for my hand and held it tightly. "Petrov?"

"Yes," Anson said, his expression hardening. "I heard from my contact at CID an hour ago. There was a multi-agency bust on Petrov's entire organization this morning. Three enforcers turned state's evidence. They've closed on multiple drug operations as well as a forced prostitution ring. All of them are going away for a long time, including Petrov."

Tears glittered in Sutton's eyes. "It's for sure? They won't be able to hurt Luca?"

Anson's expression gentled. "Luca's safe. And so are you."

God, it felt good to finally hear that. I knew we'd gotten most of the way there with Marcus behind bars. The Washington State Police had found two decades' worth of journals detailing his fixation on me. How his mind had grabbed hold of me as the reason for all his pain.

He'd been the one who leaked all the stories about me to the press. The one who'd dropped the anonymous accusation about The Mix Up to the health department. And also the one who hired someone to break into Sutton's bakery to assault her, hoping she'd blame me for making her a target. Or better yet, I'd blame myself. But that guy would also be doing at least fifteen years for his role in it all.

Marcus had wanted to cause me pain in every way possible. And in many ways, he'd succeeded. But his actions had brought me back to Sparrow Falls, which gave me Sutton and Luca. I would never be sorry about that. I just wished Teddy hadn't had to pay the ultimate price.

Sutton's hand gripped mine tighter as she looked at Anson. "Thank you. I can't imagine a better gift to get today."

He shifted uncomfortably, not a fan of praise. "I'm just glad they got them."

"Free cupcakes for life," Sutton vowed.

Anson chuckled. "That, I'll take."

"Thanks, man," I said, meeting his gaze so he knew how deeply I meant the words. "I owe you."

"You don't. This is family. We take care of each other."

A different sort of pain slid through me. The good kind. The type that told me I belonged—that we all did. We might not be perfect, but we were always there for each other when we needed one another.

"Damn straight."

"Nora said some bags need loading," Anson said, sliding away from the emotion of the moment. "I'm gonna get to that before she threatens to withhold the lunch she just made."

I chuckled. "Probably smart."

He disappeared down the hallway, and Sutton turned to me. "We're free."

I brushed the hair out of her face. "We're free."

"I love you," she whispered.

"You know those words make me want to fuck you."

Sutton laughed and patted the uninjured side of my chest. "A couple more weeks, Hotshot."

I grinned at her. "Oh, don't worry, I've got it marked on the calendar."

"I'm sure you do."

I pushed up higher against the pillows. "I know you said Anson's news was the best present you could get today, but I've got a little something for you, too."

Sutton's brow quirked. "How do you have a present for me? You haven't left the house."

"I have my ways. Open the drawer on my nightstand. Papers first."

Those sea glass eyes twinkled as she reached for the drawer. She stared down into the space. "Cope, there are three things in here."

Just like I knew there would be.

"Papers first."

Sutton tugged the corner of her lip between her teeth before reaching delicate fingers into the drawer. She pulled out some papers rolled together and tied with a turquoise ribbon, the closest color to her eyes Thea could find for me.

Sutton pulled on one end of the ribbon, letting it flutter to her lap. As the papers unrolled, she scanned their text. "The bakery building. You bought it? I own it?"

"Just like it always should've been. You've fought for this dream tooth and nail. You should own it all." And now that that shyster Rick was about to go on trial for defrauding dozens, she wouldn't see any blowback from that direction either.

The smile that stretched across her face hit me right in the chest. It was the most beautiful sort of pain. "Cope," she whispered.

"The bigger box next."

Sutton laughed. "So bossy. Isn't an entire building enough?"

"Not even close," I rasped.

Her expression gentled, and she took a breath before lifting the next present out of the drawer. This one was about the size of a deck of cards, only slightly thicker. She unwrapped the shimmery paper, revealing a jewelry box. Her throat worked as she swallowed. When the lid opened, she gasped.

"Cope." My name was barely audible as tears gathered in Sutton's eyes. Her fingers trembled as she lifted the gold piece from the box and opened the locket. "How? It's my grandmother's. Even the picture is the same."

"I got a PI referral from Anson. He searched every pawn shop Roman was known to frequent. Finally found the one he sold it to and bribed the owner for the address of the woman who'd bought it. Then, he offered her triple what she'd paid. But when she heard the story, she gave it to him for free. Wanted you to have it back."

Tears streamed down Sutton's face. "I can't—I—this is too much."

"Stick with me, Warrior. There's one more. Last box."

She let out a shuddering breath before reaching into the drawer one last time. She knew when she saw it. Dark-blue velvet. A ring box. Her gaze flew to mine.

"Open it," I whispered.

Sutton flipped the lid but did so with her eyes on me, not losing my gaze for a single second. When she finally looked down, the tears came faster. The ring nestled in the box was an oval diamond surrounded by turquoise sapphires that reminded me of Sutton's eyes.

I lifted the box out of her hands. "Marry me. Make us a family. You, me, and Luca. Give us forever."

She was already nodding. "Yes. You didn't ask, but yes."

I chuckled as I slid the ring onto her finger, leaning up so my mouth could meet hers. "I love you."

"Forever," Sutton whispered against my lips.

"Now, can you be my dad?" a little voice cut in.

Sutton pulled back, her face wet. She glanced back at me, giving me the ultimate gift, the chance to give this to the kid who'd stolen my heart right along with her. And after everything he'd been through, being his dad would be that much more precious a role.

"Never going to have a better job than being your dad," I told Luca.

He flew at us. Running and jumping onto the bed. I didn't give a damn about the flare of pain because I had what I'd always wanted, what I'd always needed, and that would never change.

EPILOGUE

Sutton

TWO YEARS LATER

THE CROWD WAS DEAFENING AS WE WALKED INTO THE ARENA. I'd never get used to that feeling, the way the chants and cheers vibrated your whole body and not just your ears. Luca *lived* for it. He didn't miss a single home game if he could help it.

We'd found our balance over the past two years. The Mix Up had firmly established a home in both Seattle and Sparrow Falls. And thanks to an incredible managerial staff, I was thinking of adding a third bakery in Portland. As for the three of us, we spent school years in Seattle and summers and as many vacations as possible back home in Sparrow Falls. Because that's what it would always be. *Home.*

In the house Cope had built with his family in mind, but the one he had made ours. As my hand drifted to my still-flat belly, I couldn't help but wonder which room we'd put the little one in. Just thinking about it sent a fresh wave of nerves swimming through me.

But the timing couldn't have been better. Because win or lose in this last game of the finals, Cope was retiring. He'd done exactly what he'd vowed to do. He'd made hockey his. He'd rediscovered the love of the game. And through that, he was playing the best he ever had.

Some of his teammates jokingly called him Gramps, but I also knew they were sad to be losing their team captain, the one who'd brought them back after the revelations about Marcus had almost ripped them apart. While Marcus was serving life in prison without the possibility of parole, the Sparks had begun to rebuild. And now, they were tighter than ever.

I glanced up at the box where half the Colson crew was positioned. Fallon waved wildly, doing a dance in the window that made me laugh. I spotted Kye behind her, keeping a close eye—like always. Keely was near the window, too, taking in all the action, and I knew Trace had to be close by. Just like I knew Arden and Linc were in there somewhere, along with the others.

Linc had given Cope the hard sell, wanting him to come coach for the Sparks. But Cope had other plans in mind. He'd bought the rink in Roxbury from Arnie and planned to be the coach of Luca's team and others right at home. There would be no more crazy travel or endless interviews.

It would just be...us. As it was always meant to be.

"Wooooo, doggy," Lolli hollered as the rink came into view. "I'm ready to see my guys demolish the Lions."

Luca laughed. "Bloodthirsty, Supergran. I like it."

He'd taken on Keely's nickname for her great-grandmother, just like he called Nora Grams. It brought them both great joy, but nothing compared to how Cope's eyes lit up when Luca called him Dad.

Nora's hand slid into mine. "You've got the poster?"

I held it up in its rolled form, more nerves settling in. "Is this a horrible idea? Maybe I should tell him at home."

"No way," Thea said, cutting in behind me. "Win or lose, this is going to be the best prize of the night."

"Win, Thorn," Shep corrected her. "They're going to win."

Thea rolled her eyes. "I'm pretty sure Shep has gotten more superstitious than the entire team."

"For the love of God, please tell me you're washing your drawers," Anson muttered.

Shep flipped him off. "Yes, I am. But I sure as hell made sure I had my lucky hat for tonight."

I glanced over at his Sparks hat with Cope's number in bold font.

"I prefer the one Kye made me," Rhodes chimed in, adjusting the brim of her ballcap that read, *I KNEW REAPER WHEN HE WAS TERRIFIED ET WAS GOING TO KIDNAP HIM.*

I chuckled as I slid into the first row of seats. "It's good to make sure his ego is in check."

"You sure you're good down here?" Anson asked.

I appreciated his concern. The crowd was definitely rowdier tonight, but there was only one place I wanted to watch Cope play, and that was from as close as possible.

"Mom can hang, Uncle Anson, don't worry," Luca assured him.

Anson waited for my nod of assurance. After everything that had happened with the Petrovs and Marcus, all the Colson crew had become protective of me and Luca. Anson especially. His gruff care meant the world.

"I'm good," I told him. "Ready to watch Cope win."

"Dang straight," Lolli called from down the row. "I promised the team some of my special brownies if they win."

"Please, do not get the entire team suspended because they failed their drug tests," Shep chastised.

"You sound like Trace," Lolli harumphed.

I just shook my head. There was no family like this one. And no other I'd want as mine.

The overhead lights dimmed, and music erupted, along with a light show. Luca grabbed my hand, something he didn't do as often these days, and tugged me down to his level. "Dad knows we love him no matter what, right?"

My heart squeezed. "He knows, baby. We tell him every single game, and I think we told him triple this time."

Luca bobbed his head in a nod. "More than bees love honey?"

"More than bees love honey," I echoed, fingering the locket at my neck, the one I rarely took off.

His eyes reddened. "He's the best dad I could've hoped for."

My eyes filled. *Damn these hormones.* "I know."

The clock counted down in a threatening staccato beat. Eight seconds. Seven. Six.

Cope slid between two players, slipping the puck between the legs of one of them. He caught it on the other side, and I held my breath. My ears rang as deafening screams sounded around me. But there was only Cope, the puck, and the ice.

He faked left, then skated right. No one remained between him and the goalie.

Five seconds. Four.

Cope was only feet away.

Three seconds. Two.

Cope shifted his weight, his stick moving in a combination of movements I could now identify as a wrist shot. The goalie didn't have a prayer. It hit the top left corner of the net, and the siren sounded. The crowd lost it. Screaming, jumping, hugging.

The Sparks poured onto the ice, collapsing around Cope in one giant pile-on hug. Tears streamed down my face as I felt their joy, the culmination of all their hard work, of Cope's dream coming true.

It only took a minute or two for Cope to extricate himself from the team. He instantly skated toward us.

"Mom! The poster!" Luca shouted.

I grabbed it from where it rested at my feet and unrolled it. Luca helped me press it to the glass. We'd drawn it together—with Arden's help since she was the true artist. Big bubble letters read, *HOW ABOUT ADDING ONE MORE JERSEY TO THE TEAM,*

DADDY COLSON? And we'd drawn a jersey for Cope, me, Luca, and a tiny one for Baby Colson.

I watched as Cope slowed, taking in the poster. His jaw dropped, his gaze instantly cutting to me. *"You're sure?"*

The words weren't audible, but I read them clear as day. We'd been trying for the past year with no luck. Even had an appointment scheduled with a specialist for next week. But then, a few days ago, I'd realized I was late. More than two months late. After a quick trip to the doctor, I knew for certain. But I'd wanted to save the reveal for this moment.

"I'm sure," I mouthed back.

Cope shot forward as I lowered the poster. He tugged his gloves free and dropped them to the ice, then pressed his hands against the glass. I mirrored one, while Luca mirrored the other, just like we always did.

"I love you," he yelled as loudly as he could.

I grinned through the tears. My whole life was in this arena. And we'd all gotten to watch Cope get two dreams, the Cup and a baby. There'd never been anything sweeter.

For an exclusive bonus scene, scan the code below and join Catherine's newsletter. The scene will be delivered to your inbox instantly. Happy Reading!

https://geni.us/BrknHrbrBnsScene

ACKNOWLEDGMENTS

An author's journey, at least mine, is full of ups and downs, mountaintop moments, and those that linger in a valley. As I was sitting down to write this, I was reminded just how important it is to have people in your life who will show up for both. The happy, fun times, and the sobbing-so-hard-you-can't-breathe, panicked phone calls. I am incredibly lucky to have a whole bunch of people who will do that for me. And I'd like to take a minute to thank them and all the ways they helped during this book.

One person has to be thanked first: the friend, author, and sports puck queen who made me dare to think I could write a book that is *kind of* a sports romance. Rebecca Jenshak, thank you for answering endless questions, reading this whole book, and then answering more questions. You're the best, and I really hope you don't hate me after enduring this process with me.

Sam, my forever alpha reader, sounding board, and...let's be honest, keeper of my sanity most days. I can't thank you enough for always listening and sharing the gift of your incredible empathy. Forever grateful for your friendship.

Elsie, I feel confident you received at least a dozen panicked voice memos during the creation of this book. I can think of three off the top of my head right now. Whoops! Thank you for always being a voice of reason and a safe place to land, for celebrating new milestones, and for helping me find my way when I'm struggling. Immunity necklaces forever.

Laura, thank you for sprinting with me for five hours straight to finish the edits on this one, for holding my hand through crises and celebrations alike, for always answering the phone when I need you, and, of course, for playing me the *Rocky* theme song whenever I need it. This world is a better place because you're in it.

Willow, my sweet, tenderhearted friend. Thank you for listening, cheering, and supporting me as if my ups and downs were yours. I'm so grateful I know you, and am even more thankful that I tricked you into being my friend because you're stuck with me now!

Amy, thank you for sprinting, cheering, reading countless blurbs, and generally being one of this community's most positive forces. So thankful to have you in my life.

Kandi, thank you for the endless encouragement, the kind inclusion, and always being that moment of authentic support every single release day. Your spirit is infectious, and you make us all better humans.

The Lance Bass Fan Club—Ana, Elsie, and Lauren—you make this job so much more fun. Thank you for your endless support, hilarious videos, and, of course, manifesting the NSYNC reunion tour with me.

Jess, thank you for talking this book through until you were blue in the face and cheering me on through the drafting, edits, and everything else that goes along with it.

Paige B, thank you for the epic pep talks, hilarious videos, and always being the best damn glam squad a girl could hope for (even when you're thousands of miles away).

To all my incredible friends who have cheered me on and supported me throughout the making of this book, you know who you are. Romance books have given me a lot of things, but at the top of that list are the incredible friends I am so lucky to have in my life. Thank you for walking this path with me.

And to the most amazing hype squad ever, my STS soul sisters: Hollis, Jael, and Paige, thank you for the gift of true friendship and sisterhood. Thanks to you, I always feel the most supported and celebrated.

To my fearless beta readers: Glav, Jess, Kelly, Kristie, and Trisha, thank you for reading this book in its roughest form and helping me to make it the best it could possibly be!

The crew that helps bring my words to life and gets them out into the world is pretty darn epic. Thank you to Devyn, Jess, Tori, Rae, Margo, Chelle, Jaime, Julie, Hang, Stacey, Katie, and my team at Lyric, Kimberly, Joy, and my team at Brower Literary. Your hard work is so appreciated!

To all the reviewers and content creators who have taken a chance on my words…THANK YOU! Your championing of my stories means more than I can say. And to my launch and influencer teams, thank you for your kindness, support, and for sharing my books with the world.

Ladies of Catherine Cowles Reader Group, you're my favorite place to hang out on the internet! Thank you for your support, encouragement, and willingness to always dish about your latest book boyfriends. You're the freaking best!

Lastly, thank YOU! Yes, YOU. I'm so grateful you're reading this book and making my author dreams come true. I love you for that. A whole lot!

ABOUT THE AUTHOR
CATHERINE COWLES

Writer of words. Drinker of Diet Cokes. Lover of all things cute and furry. *USA Today* bestselling author, Catherine Cowles, has had her nose in a book since the time she could read and finally decided to write down some of her own stories. When she's not writing, she can be found exploring her home state of Oregon, listening to true crime podcasts, or searching for her next book boyfriend.

STAY CONNECTED

You can find Catherine in all the usual bookish places...

Website: catherinecowles.com
Facebook: catherinecowlesauthor
Facebook Reader Group: CatherineCowlesReaderGroup
Instagram: catherinecowlesauthor
Goodreads: catherinecowlesauthor
BookBub: catherine-cowles
Pinterest: catherinecowlesauthor
TikTok: catherinecowlesauthor